PAX OF WILDLY WOMEN

by

V. C. BESTOR

Fanged Wilds & Women Publishing

Fanged Wilds & Women Publishing

Disclaimer

"Any resemblance between the characters in this book and any persons, living or dead, is a miracle." All characters in fiction are fictitious, allowing for satire herein of public figures and celebrities: if you resemble a character in this novel, you may be famous or anthropomorphized and not to be confused with a real person.

Reprint Permission Requests

Director@FangedWilds.org

Ordering Information via FangedWilds.org
ISBN: 978-0615688626
EAN: 0615688624
Cover Illustration by V.C. Bestor

First Print Edition 2013
Manufactured in the United States of America

"Terror is glamour."

~ Salman Rushdie

"I think of few heroic actions,

which cannot be traced to the artistical impulse.

[S]he who does great deeds, does them from [her] innate
sensitiveness to moral beauty."

~ Walt Whitman

"I sing the carnivorous body electric."

~ Farraga D., Founder,

Fanged Wilds and Women Program

Table of Contents

8

CHAPTER FORTY-ONE

....

259

CHAPTER FORTY-TWO

....

267

CHAPTER FORTY-THREE

....

272

CHAPTER ONE

MANHATTAN, NEW YORK, U.S.A.

A shark swam nearby, unseen. Diana, a young office manager, hurried, late to work. Near the deli famous for chopped liver, she flagged down a gondola. Stepping into the craft, she tried to keep her balance as men on the neighborhood garbage barge wolf-whistled at her. She grabbed the rusted rail with her free hand. The roughness of the boat's peeling black varnish ensured her footing, yet she regretted wearing high heels.

McCARTHY, OREGON, U.S.A.

Alone in the bathroom, a handsome college professor studied his girlfriend's eco-fashion catalog. The slim models looked better than his busty girlfriend, Farraga, who, even now, wore hemp-and-bamboo lingerie as she sat in the living room, talking to her laptop. She'd missed an appointment with her stylist, the professor remembered, after he finished his business, emerged and saw that the back of her head looked like a feral yak.

FLAKSIN, MICHIGAN, U.S.A.

Political campaigns in the States had an unspoken rule to depict national candidates as All-American. The foremost proof was to showcase their enthusiasm for hunting. He invited the press to his ranch, a perfect setting for Rocker and Republican Presidential Nominee Ted Nugat to demonstrate his prowess as a hunter. Camo-uniformed Nugat was already known for bagging trophy animals (including the stunning seventeen-year-old Hawaiian Piele Maska, whom, due to age, he couldn't marry; Nugat became her legal guardian.) Today's photo opportunity involved the brazen Republican nominee besting all previous politicians by hunting not with a gun but with a crossbow and – in a crocodile-skin quiver on his back – titanium arrows. He pointed to some glossy photos tacked to hay bales and showed off his aim by skewering the pages of playfully posed women from the "Fanged Wilds and Women Program" calendar.

"Lesbo-Nazis," he jeered at the pierced targets.

The white lion which Nugat would bag had been released from its transportation crate into the fenced facility the night before, making the ranch into a stage for a theatrical convoy of reporters, photographers, videographers, and other entourage in six slow-moving Jeeps. The soft breeze of the mild Spring day belied the bloodbath ahead.

The caravan tailed the Presidential-hopeful as he swaggered. "The outdoors is a natural high, gentlemen," he called back to the mixed crowd. "Contribute ten thousand bucks to my Political Action Committee and you can walk in my footsteps, to shoot a bison or boar." He yodeled a Tarzan yell. His voice echoed off a stand of trees. He chortled, "Of course, *me*, I need to bring down nothing less than the King of Beasts."

Nugat turned with a flourish. Always on foot, he followed the paw prints. Their tips were dragged in the dirt. The candidate crouched occasionally to confirm the marks or tweak a strand of white fur from a twig; then the aging man sprang back up like a matador. After walking for twenty minutes, finally Nugat tracked down the feline to where it cowered in the underbrush, still woozy with sedatives. Shaking its white mane at the approach of the Jeeps and the hunter, the lion stood. Nugat pulled out an arrow, positioned and aimed it. Many cameras followed suit, clicking in the tense silence.

The lion roared, stepping forward, its jungle cry ending with a sneeze or cough that diminished its primal aura. So Nugat came closer, to try to inspire the animal to further feral display that would be sure to make the nightly news. The medicated lion lay back down in the grass beside the bushes, coughing again. Nugat shouted,

"Kill it and grill it," trying to rescue the PR disaster with humor. His campaign manager started to say something but Nugat waved him back, bellowing, "Are you ready to rumble?" He walked closer and closer to the ailing critter till the lion rose to its feet, lunged forward in desperation, ignored the arrow piercing its neck and grabbed Nugat's shoulder from the man's ear to his atherosclerotic heart.

At Nugat's funeral, the new Republican nominee Alice Coopher eulogized him as "Fearless to the end, Ted was a lion of a man."

RATHIE, SCOTLAND

Thatched roofs covered a cluster of tidy, raised hutches, cozy beside a towering pine in the dim dawn. An aroma of smoke issued from chimney beyond. Yellow daffodils nodded. Sheep bleated on the far side of a stone wall. Through the quaintness of the scene hurtled an almost-human scream, causing the wooden hutches to shake with the thumping feet of startled inhabitants, their ears up, whiskers twitching. Near the Scots pine, in a shelter of drying racks, two diminutive gentlewomen butchered a rabbit. They snagged the rear hocks of the floppy corpse onto a hook to allow the neck to bleed. An already drained rabbit they deftly skinned in one piece, then dropped the pelt in a bucket of ice water.

"Have dominion over every living thing," said Abby, the younger, on her way to fetch the next live victim.

"Ha, ha. Ah-*men*." Her friend Martha finished the gutting. Martha was careful with hygiene, wary of airborne tularemia: the disease, carried by ticks, spread easily as a bio-terrorism agent.

The ladies had established, literally, a cottage industry of fur coats. The apparel wasn't intended to flaunt fashion or flout animal rights. The coats were charity to warm the flocks of climate refugees who fled desertification elsewhere: the weather in Scotland had become irresistible.

Martha stretched tanned skins on racks. As their morning's chores neared completion, Abby patted Martha on the back and asked, "Care for another cup of iced tea, dearie?"

"Is it too early for a spot of haggis? I *am* peckish." In the distance sounded a hunting bugle. Martha indicated the hunt party with her chin as she rinsed off her hands. "They do rattle the sheep." The bugle tattooed the air.

NANIRAUÁ, BRAZIL

The rain on the leaves sounded like a fusillade... but a *happy* sort of fusillade, as if bullets were gumdrops. Past candy-colored bromeliads, an endangered toucan, like a Fruit-Loops box come to life, hopped on a towering tree. More toucans called to him: "Fruit! *Real* fruit!"

This paradise's Bird of Schnoz cocked his head and took to flight, swooping through a forest even bigger than the Mall of America. The Amazon was more vast even than India. The spread of jungle seemed like a living encyclopedia of biodiversity: an anaconda snaked around a branch tangled with Disney-like vines that crept with "It's a Small World" of bugs.

And, clinging to one draped liana, dressed in gaudy colors, a frog waited – as if a jalopy at a drive-up – for his car-hop delivery of winged green milkshake; to him, insect legs tasted like French fries. The liana drooped with the weight of the snake, slithering toward the frog. The frog was oblivious. Could it be that he was in hot water, and didn't even know it? Was he in a suburban sort of stupor, the proverbial "boiled frog"?

This frog had a reprieve. As fast food, the anaconda turned and seized in its jaws a little *monkey*. The monkey's shrieks echoed sharply among the wet leaves. Its cries were so heart-wrenching, thank heavens it was not the primate reading this.

Caw, caw! "Monkey? Serpent?!" A flock of parrots discussed the implications as urgently as if they were a Dixie school board with science teachers who present Darwinism as more than just a whimsy of nihilists.

Silence! That monkey was *raw food!* This is no joke!

The agitated birds rustled the trees and plunged. The gumdrop-barraged air weighed and buffeted their wings. The parrots' exodus followed the path of the river that stretched below, the mighty Amazon. The open water's flow was only perceptible where vegetative overhang frilled its edges. The repetitive rain on the river's ripples obscured deeper movement. But it had a direction, and the river's progress could be impeded only with geologic upheaval or industrial-strength effort. Don't rivers lend a sense of proper momentum and, thus, hope: isn't one thing still inarguable in the world: flow?

Soothingly, the rain dissipated to steamy mist. The hiss subsided even as the bird calls, more distant, carried further. Vapors hovered over the hushed, silty green water.

Along the bank, the intrusion of civilization – a beached motor boat – could disappoint an eco-tourist immersed in the biome. But stylishly printed on the boat's side was something to bolster a nature-lover's hope: "Fanged Wilds and Women Anti-Poaching Patrol."

Four tribal women were loading provisions into the motor boat. Per tribal custom, their straight black hair was bowl-cut. Their faces were dyed red like a raccoon's mask around the eyes. With less honor to their heritage, less political correctness – had anyone notified the local NAACP? – they wore crisp, institution-green ranger shirts.

Oh no! This wasn't politically correct at all! One woman had a gun! The holster hung against her shirttails. With help from another woman, the armed native poured something from a metal can into the motor. One may only pray that it was ecologically sustainable bio-fuel from organic, non-food crops.

As they pushed the boat away from underbrush, toward the green water, the women revealed bare legs. Their tanned, naked flesh might be titillating if witnessed by your average male. "Could these females be persuaded with trinkets?" he might wonder. "Brazilian wax job: ancient indigenous tradition?" The women, living so close to nature, exuded primitive animality. The hypothetical outsider might even be motivated to discover the tribe's mode of romantic greeting, be it kissing, or nose-rubbing, or other form of friction or gentle contact. (Remember: *gentle* contact, *gentle*! She has a gun.)

The average male might be further stimulated by the uniforms (with impressive "Fanged Wilds and Women Anti-Poaching Patrol" insignia) and the methodical labor, implying, as they did, a purpose and competence. Who isn't more attracted to a person who applies herself to an unusual goal that appears, at least to her, challenging and meaningful? Don't you at least want to ask, "Whatchya up to?"

The ladies (if they were not really very simple and uneducated) might have responded indignantly, "Poachers here in the Amazon Basin kill the *boto*, the pink river dolphin, for his penis. It's a powerful fetish to enhance virility!"

Speak of the devil: along a jungle path, men from the tribe stalked toward the women. The boat was not quite launched onto the river. Behind the men lagged apprehensive crones, bare babies inert in their arms. Black-haired children darted past to see what would transpire. Toy bows and arrows dangled in the boys' hands.

One of the men wore a ragged old T-shirt from a Sting concert. He might have been some sort of chief, because, in Nheengatu dialect, he shouted in a commanding voice: "We men need that boat for fishing!"

Another by-indigenous-standards robust man, Frank Mata, erected himself to his full five feet to pitch in, "And for hunting!"

Alya, the Ribeirinho woman packing the holster, fixed the men with a weary, respectful, but determined stare. Then Alya turned back to finish pushing the boat. Over her shoulder, she delivered a statement that downplayed yet justified her defiance. "This is our job. We will be able to pay for the children's school."

The first, most assertive man wasn't stymied. He hesitated only a moment before firing, "*We* will pay for the children." His black eyes solicited the other men to confirm this moral stance. Frank Mata's expression corroborated, as if to say, "Well, of course! How could you ever think otherwise? Naturally we will devote all resources to the children's schooling."

One of the uniformed women – the loudest man's wife – scoffed to another. "He'll pay for whores and liquor."

Her friend nodded. "Or gamble it."

The bossy man's wife sighed, giving in to her constant daydream: if only she'd married the boy whose kisses were like honeysuckle nectar, who left to become a logger. That boy had never returned. The unhappy wife fingered the tin crucifix at her neck, feeling the jaguar fur wired to its blades.

The first, most dominant woman, Alya, wavered. But she agreed with her companions: a few hours away was a logger's cantinha where men from the tribe had spent a recent night. The men eyed her gun. Alya introduced another consideration: "You'll probably hunt the animals we promised to protect. You use dolphin meat for catfish bait."

The first Ribeirinho man, Malicio Rego, reached the boat. He grabbed the side proprietorially, with a triumphant laugh. For his buddies' sake, he joked, "We'll *need* some boto penis if you keep this boat from us."

As if on cue, as shocking as nudity can be, two pink dolphins leaped in the river beyond. The slick mammals splashed in the now glimmering water. Unexpected sun illuminated the rain forest in all its glory.

CHAPTER TWO

MANHATTAN, NEW YORK, U.S.A.

The Statue of Liberty had water up to her fungal-blotched skirts. Erected on her head, a wind turban kept spinning, giving the impression of a lady considering all her options.

At her ankles, marine traffic looked shabby. A few sails were jury-rigged even on big vessels. The city itself was swamped. Sloops and other boats made their way between buttressed skyscrapers, many of whose windows near water level were boarded up. At one dilapidated, mossy office tower, a gondola taxi arrived at a window adapted as an entrance: chained to its ledge creaked a small dock bobbing on old truck tires. Above the window was a new shingle inscribed: "Fanged Wilds and Women Program, International Non-Profit Organization."

While the passenger of the teetering gondola stood up and searched her purse for the fare, her cell phone rang, its tone the classic Brazilian "Manha de Carnaval."

"Yes, good morning, *bom dia?*" The young lady's jacket suggested egalitarian idealism, its fabric patterned with monochromatic, international flags. Diana's English accent suggested Old-World courtesy. And her tone on the phone conveyed an eagerness to please, intensified perhaps by her guilt at being late for work. That morning, she'd dawdled in her studio apartment, writing in her blog about whether British class consciousness caused a herd mentality: resisting her secret elitism, she tried to honor everyone irrespective of their station in life.

Yet, despite Diana's noble inclinations, the gondolier was preoccupied with her physical attributes. He ogled her up and down, undistracted even when a cormorant dove into the water nearby. The bird reappeared with a wriggling fish and chugged its wet veil of tail past the silver head.

Still on the phone, Diana prepared to hand money – with a significant tip – to the man. "The Ribeirinho women in Naniraua want a second boat?" The non-profit's finances were already stretched, she knew. She betrayed a moment's irritation, crossed her eyes and said, "I'll notify management." Then she took a misstep, her stylish pumps slipping on the damp wood of the floating dock.

The gondolier was at the ready, steadying her with a quick hand to her buttock. There, on Diana's slim black pants, was cross-stitched a Death's-head wolf, briefly obscured by the man's rough, reddened fingers. "Nice pants," the man leered.

"Thank you," she said, magnanimous. She didn't want to seem like a snob.

The gondolier couldn't take his eyes off the region of his previous hand-hold. Panting, he said lasciviously, "Good panting is *hard* to *come* by."

In the wake of another vessel, his boat rocked further away. From the wobbling pier, Diana practically had to throw him the fare. With the motion, she accidentally dropped her phone into the water. She gasped: as she watched, the silver phone drifted down, gently spinning underwater, its blue glow dimming in the depths. A dense shadow moved smoothly and closed in on the last glint: a shark swallowed her phone.

"Tough break, missy," the gondolier snorted, pushing away from the dock with his oar. Hardship came to a female who was too good for him: his face showed pleasure.

Schadenfreude, Diana thought, looking away from him and rolling her eyes to the brilliant sun. Another muggy day. She was a linguist, and, seeking philosophical equanimity, she wondered: What would be the German word for finding joy in shade? Not *Schändenfreude*. That's joy in sin. Stiff upper lip, she reminded herself, turning away from the gondolier's smug sneer. Remnants of a dead fish floated near the building, and, looking at it, she sighed: Keep Calm and Carrion.

CHHARATPUR, INDIA

Quite close to Kharujaho spread the white-hot jumble of Chharatpur. Limed mud
bricks and chalk-painted walls opened into the heart of a village, where the
desultory bustling of multicolored saris surrounded a water pump. Female
foreheads were marked with a red dot. Traditionally it was placed right where your
head would hit if you bowed down the ground. Could it represent submission to
others, or to the gods? Certainly the *bindi* symbolized that a woman was married or
chaste. The group here looked appropriately industrious. All with families to care
for, some women rinsed copper pots, while some waited with containers to fill;
others scrubbed laundry that would soon be soiled again. Many wells had dried in
the decades of drought, so some of the housewives had full metal urns on their
heads to carry to homes several miles away. Their head scarves helped pad the
weight, hiding how thin were the necks on which balanced the slopping burdens.
Though men had stronger necks, they never carried water: they would be laughed
at. What could be worse than that?

But laughter need not be caustic. Around the women's skirts, ragged girls giggled as
they tickled or clasped one another; boys played, bouncing a ball, or chasing a dog;
a group of ragamuffins, all skinny and dusty, sometimes grinned when least
expected, teeth surprisingly even, brown cheeks like parentheses. Several ganged
up to tease one child. As the children shouted, the women's voices rose in a chatter
of chastisement, syncopated with the clang of water cans and the creak of the pump.

One lovely young villager, Ganika, rinsed her face, preparing for a fresh *bindi*.
Beneath black brows, her eyes were as big as crown jewels in her small face.
Drying off with the end of her muslin sari, she avoided the stare of a prostitute.
Instead she gave the carefree children a pent-up glance and parted from the crowd.
Her sandaled steps had a catch, crossing the road. The hitch was more emotional
than physical. Did the return to her home in fact launch a departure? She stepped
over the gutter onto the stoop.

Inside her hovel, the reason for her ambivalence became clear. Radiant with anticipation, Ganika took her new "Fanged Wilds and Women" ranger shirt gingerly from a rough hook on the wall. Her twigs of fingers gently brushed road dust from the neatly tailored garment. May it transform her like a magic cloak! She put it on over her simple *choli* shirt, then checked in a tiny hand mirror, trying to see herself, as it were, reincarnated. Her downy mustache set off her shining smile.

Her aunt who lived nearby babysat Ganika's young siblings. The aunt too was in the "Fanged Wilds" micro-finance collective, repaying her loan by working as a seamstress. The older relative now came in from the street, biting a loose thread from culottes that she'd sewn for Ganika. Aunt, too, treated the uniform with reverence. She held up the pants. "Wash the clothes tonight, when you're done."

Ganika couldn't imagine that night would ever come. Would she ever have completed her first day as leader of the anti-poacher squad? To conceal her awe, she asked a question to which she already knew the answer. "And the children's dinner?" Other women in the collective were charged with cooking enough dal and chapatis for all the active participants and their offspring. Ganika's orphaned siblings qualified as dependents.

"The women will feed the children." Her aunt folded Ganika's sari for her, looking around. "Have you the hat?"

From behind mosquito netting, Ganika produced a flimsy box. She finished pinning up her hair. Then she carefully opened the box: a light pith helmet completed her outfit. A mirrored strip hung from its back, to help distract animals from attacking; she held the strip aside and put the hat on. Her aunt fastened the chinstrap for her. Ganika turned. At the back of the helmet was printed a large photo of Hillary Clitown. Clitown's eyes were emphasized, as if they were outlined with kohl for a festival, or as if she were an untouchable gypsy dancer.

Ganika's aunt was ravished. She didn't want to cause Ganika conceit, so she lavished all her admiration on Hillary Clitown. "Oh! Isn't she beautiful!"

Applying her protective *bindi* of red sandalwood paste, Ganika didn't nod, but she agreed. She had heard that Mrs. Clitown somehow prevailed even after her husband shamed their family with public philandering. Ganika's own husband was killed in a religious conflict while he'd been patronizing a seedy neighborhood; rumor said her husband had been visiting a brothel. So, to Ganika, Hillary Clitown's strength held special meaning for her personally. "Her eyes will keep tigers from creeping up behind me," the young widow said reassuringly to her aunt. Her parents' and husband's deaths had already marked Ganika as unlucky, sensitizing her relatives to the risk of obligations her existence imposed on them. Ganika knew her aunt was concerned about the children becoming completely dependent if Ganika died.

So Hillary Clitown was an antidote to the past, and a talisman for the future. Ganika's aunt said, "She is like a goddess, protecting you."

Ganika mumbled a reminder to herself: "The trainers said we must not rely on goddesses, but must use our gun instead." She belted on her macramé holster. Then she removed her anklet and put on the orange and black canvas boots. When she was dressed, Ganika went to her doorway, glancing back at her aunt for moral support. Her aunt pursed her lips.

People outside immediately noticed Ganika's uniform. For the first time in her life, she had to endure being the center of attention. Fortunately three other village women in "Fanged Wilds and Women Program" uniform were already outside, on their way to fill canteens at the water pump. Other women, even strangers, stepped aside for the *van rakshak sahayaks* – forest protectors – even though the F.W.W.P. squad's holsters were all empty. The aunt shut the door and followed Ganika protectively.

The other *van rakshak sahayaks'* pith helmets were imprinted with photos of Golda Meir, Indira Gandhi, and Cher. Rattling her bracelets nervously, Ganika's aunt expressed ambivalence: "May their eyes see and protect you. If only their ears could hear what is being said behind your backs."

The women retrieved their gun from its safe haven at the local magistrate's. Then they set out. Diverging from the road along a trail, the group headed for the periphery of the jungle. At first quiet on their way, they raised their voices to help a farmer who was scaring monkeys off his vegetable plots. They hailed again, further along, as they passed other farmers: "Giving Voice" was part of their training. Song synchronized team spirit. For a while, they wailed a Bollywood marching ballad. Soon they reached the periphery of the national park, where their patrol protected tigers from conflicts of interest. In many of India's reserves, guards were armed with little more than sticks. In Maharashtra, poachers could be shot on sight. The "Fanged Wilds and Women Program" offered a middle route.

Deep in the jungle, unmolested for the moment, a tiger dined.

CHAPTER THREE

DROUGHTERBERG PLATEAU, NAMIBIA, AFRICA

Deafening, a calf dangled and spasmed in a cheetah's clenched jaws. Thickening the din clanked a noisemaker clutched in the shaking fingers of a lanky Namibian. Her "Fanged Wilds and Women Program" uniform fit her twenty-something figure sleekly. The woman rattled her tin again. The cheetah, also sleek, looked unperturbed. He was hungry.

The calf-crunching cheetah was also unimpressed by the sticks and spears of scrawny herdsmen who ran to the scene. These rural Africans were as upset about their calf as you'd be if, say, someone re-programmed your I-Pod: like imposing someone else's musical tastes on your own earbuds, the calf's pitiful mooing was an abomination to the men.

The young patroller, Lydia, shouted into a tiny walkie-talkie. "Sirleaf! Sirleaf!" Her unit's call code was a tribute to Ellen Johnson Sirleaf, historic female president of nearby Liberia. Lydia's little brother was sold to a rancher to herd cattle holistically; her parents died from AIDS; the twenty-one year war of independence from South Africa had lasting fallout; dusty drought was the norm. But Lydia herself had a promising future. She might even be president of Namibia someday. Her campaign slogan might be, "A guard dog in every kraal." She threw a noise-maker tin-can at the cheetah.

The cheetah froze. The calf shuddered and finally went limp. The herdsmen halted to hurl their spears and sticks. Then Lydia yelled, with halting conviction, as if she were Captain Kirk on Star Trek, "Money! Stop! We will pay you for your cattle!"

Her countrymen hesitated. Staring at them, Lydia pointed her gun at the cheetah, to render their spears redundant. "Stop!" Dexterously her left hand ripped another noisemaker from her belt and threw it toward the cheetah, her eyes still on the farmers. (Females can multitask.) "Stop! Money for you, if you spare the cheetah!"

The cheetah yowled rudely, mouth full. Cheetahs rarely attacked humans; the farmers were bold and would ignore Lydia's intervention, if not for her vivid uniform. Just then, with clattering noisemakers, blowing hunting horns, several other young women approached at a run. Similarly attired, they exuded supreme heroism despite – or perhaps enhanced by – the gleaming whites of their eyes. The resolute gaze of Somali Doctor Hawa Abdi was printed on the back of the dusky damsels' safari hats. The Namibian herdsmen's eyes, in turn, widened to see the stampede of brave, colorful women lacking traditional headcloths.

The cheetah, its eyes like a tragic clown, slinked back into forest, abandoning its mortally injured meal. Cheetahs preferred wild prey, but this one had been edged into human territory by the local lions' pride. Those lions were so stuck up.

MANHATTAN, NEW YORK, U.S.A.

Facing her own Pyrrhic victory, Diana confronted the vast emptiness of her hand-me-down desk. She was homesick for England, even though it had a freezing snap there so right now everyone had to dress like tea cozies. But things in America simply were too big, even since the climate-and-economy Crash. What had merely been big when America was a super-power, now was immense and often...

...evacuated.

Diana's heart felt empty, too. She was getting the hang of her new job, only to discover the boredom inherent in working a low-budget, one-man office, with a thermos of tea as her only sensual luxury. She aimlessly rearranged the international-crafts items in front of her. They were souvenirs, gifts from grateful recipients of the micro-finance credit, for instance: African-gazelle salad forks. Also adorning the office were prototypes of products that program participants could potentially manufacture in their rudimentary industries, in Asia or wherever.

Sewing, gluing, and weaving seemed to be international favorites, as far as ladies' ambitions were concerned. Shelves on one wall displayed a Nicaraguan pine-needle trivet, Rwandan note cards, Cambodian pill boxes, Haitian lavender sachets, and a multitude of shopping bags, belts and scarves that micro-financed women had sent, all items decorative, as if women all over the world couldn't imagine other needs beyond gift-shopping and accessorizing.

Other walls were covered with maps, various locations on them marked with colored pins. Diana shook dust off a Namibian place mat she put under her laptop. Apparently place mats were an inexhaustible need of the human race; a strain in her solitary life, Diana tried to imagine a plethora of huge families at long tables of sloppy eaters. Other women's charities had capitalized on such weavings, along with the market for folk-art jewelry and trendy handbags made of recycled sandals.

She contemplated a tribal mask, then set it down and put it to use by sticking cheap bamboo-twig pens in its mouth. Diana could picture the larger, more popular philanthropic organizations whose engines, at it were, consisted of the creation and sale of cottage-industry knick-knacks, tea-cloths and doilies that lent moral authority to Ladies Who Lunch. And here she was, all alone, manning the central headquarters of a non-profit that teamed Mother Nature with soccer moms; real grizzlies with mama grizzlies; feral felines with fearless females....

Diana ran out of silly alliterations. What now? Ambition might alleviate her boredom. Maybe she could impress her boss by developing an edgy advertising campaign. "Think Wolves are a Bitch? Women are a Bear? Ladies need Tofu, not Guns? Get a load of Carnivores, Colt cartridges and Cooch..." Clearly, it was hard to be clever purely in English. Back in school, her idea of a good joke combined the various languages she was studying. Books of macaroni verse were her *joie de livre*. Maybe that was when she got used to being a loner.

Life could be worse. Her salary was peanuts, but at least she didn't have dependents yet. Even in Britain, government social programs were largely abolished in austerity measures, and if she had kids, the law of the jungle would rule her life.

Mouths to feed would devour the idealism she currently entertained so lavishly. (Lavish, in a manner of speaking: she could find a job that was somewhat more lucrative, surely?) She started to surf online for baby names. Global warming had started a trend of names like (Boy) Hurricane, Drought, Flood... (Girl) Sahara, Famine, Cyclone, Refugee... (trans) A/C...

She was no super-hero: she'd need a more mercenary job if she had offspring. Unlike a politician's, her kids wouldn't serve to parade around to prove her family values. How did some women manage to keep their kids as a sort of career fashion accessory? The irony was that one of the current U.S. administration's Promise-Keeper, dominion-theology mottos (Government Aid to Families is the Crutch that Cripples) mirrored a premise of Fanged Wilds: danger breeds *esprit de corps*.

She personally found danger distasteful. Her mom raised her to think of Americans as gun-waving barbarians, so, for Diana, just coming to New York had been a huge adventure. But her true ambition was for civility. The more desperate the world got, the more manners could be perceived as weakness. Sensitivity was effeminate. In religions, worship of power transmuted into misogyny. In America, ladies' tendency was toward Steel Magnolias packin' to battle at "every man for himself."

She herself just wasn't that sort. Not only was she not a Mama Grizzly, she wasn't even dating. She occasionally went dancing with other expatriates but spent most evenings alone at her studio apartment. When a teen, she'd been diagnosed with "Social Anxiety Disorder" and prescribed a medication that gave her nausea and then seizures; another pharmaceutical had the side-effect of reducing sex drive, incurring her mother's worry that she'd not find a partner because she'd stop looking. Indeed, briefly taking The Pill to regulate her period, she'd been drawn to effeminate men: the hormones tricked her body as if she were already pregnant and safely nesting. Now, free from all meds, her menses were regular but scant. She seemed deficient in natural urges. Her maternal instinct was mainly to stop extinction of species, including human.

Having a child would give her a way to bond with strangers. But solitude wasn't so bad. Alone, Diana could daydream, ignore the absence of romance or companionship, and study her latest language goal: Portuguese.

Sadly, one word in particular, *saudade*, popped up insistently in all her exposure to literature and songs in Portuguese. *Saudade*, longing. It was a sentiment that seemed truly foreign in America, the way its yearning implied an emptiness, a loss that could never be redeemed, an un-American submission to fate. Like extinction. Couldn't replacements be manufactured, newer and better?

Saudade. Foreign words were like French kisses. Each sound could be a sensual new exploration of her tongue, and palate, and teeth. Words had personality. Romance languages' words for beautiful – *belle, beau, bellissimo* – joined her lips into an ignition; other words positively exploded, with vowels looping between consonants like detonation cords. *Occupy!* Some words hushed and soothed like a breeze extinguishing a flame. *Saudade*.

She sang a *fado* to herself and was idly testing the soil moisture in a safari-theme potted palm-tree when her desk phone rang with a Namibian tune. She thought quickly. "Yes, hello? You speak English?" Deciphering the speaker, Diana searched under the place mat and other folk-art to find her note pad. Holding the note pad, she reached for and knocked over the thatch of pens that she'd placed in the tribal mask. The pens skittered over the desk and onto the linoleum floor as if the mask had regurgitated a plague of mantises. "You need three hundred American dollars for a small cattle? Holy cow." Flustered, she typed one-handed on her laptop. But there had been a misunderstanding. "Yes! No! One WHOLE cow, yes."

Thuds outside the window indicated someone had arrived at the little entrance pier. Diana balked at this new obstacle to communications with Namibia. To make matters worse, it was the cute delivery guy on whom she'd developed a humiliating, fluttering crush. Handsome and boyish, he bobbed, head and shoulders, standing beside the mast of his unseen boat. Seeing her see him, Derek smiled and waved before he jumped onto the dock.

As he stuck his tousled head in the window, to her relief, he gave a reverent nod to acknowledge the sacrosanctity of her business. Gingerly he set some cardboard packages inside the room, adjacent to her "Outgoing" area. With some embarrassment, he struggled with the weight of the boxes she had set out for him to mail. He grunted, heaved, and climbed in and out of the room. In the process, the content of her conversation overcame his discretion: Diana was confirming, "If a cheetah or lion is involved, but unharmed, we will replace any cattle killed." Silently, Derek mimicked a bull, holding his fingers like horns on his forehead, flaring his nostrils, and rolling his eyes.

Diana had to giggle. She turned away from him, blushing, and unscrewed the lid of her thermos of tea to pour herself a cup. She glanced back at his bull impression, charmed, then grabbed her notepad, trying to look even busier. Derek bent to pick up the pens from the floor and handed them to her. She whispered, "Thanks, Darryl. I mean, Derek," as she snatched and set them down, then picked one up and fumbled with it. True to form, she dropped the pen. Then, when she ducked into the darkness under her desk, her chair rolled from under her thighs, so she sprawled forward, down into blessed privacy. "The cheetah got away? Good for her. Yes, excellent. Till later, then." Concluding the phone call, she decided to stay hidden till Derek was gone. "Cherio," she said, pretending to still converse till the young man was gone.

She listened to confirm his departure. She startled with a squeak as a hand appeared over the edge of the desk. Looking up, she stared into Derek's face; he mouthed, "The invoice." With her phone as a tiny shield, Diana cringed and took the envelope. He modestly averted his eyes from her embarrassment. With a showy flourish of efficiency, Derek tapped an update on the tracking program on his i-Pad. When he looked back at her, Diana, moving her lips to convey gratitude, wished she could disappear back into the little cave that happenstance had too briefly made her sanctuary... from love. Derek offered her his free hand, but instead she tried to lift herself via the edge of her chair. Its wheels denied any assistance, her imbalanced duck-walk pulling the chair forward so she fell back under the desk, banging her skull. Undefeated, Diana reached up and pulled on a drawer handle.

Sliding out, it provided no leverage. She reached higher. In her effort to get a good grip above her head, she accidentally pulled the place-mat with her thermos on top. Her short skirt was disheveled so Derek had chivalrously looked away again and was thus unable to stop the thermos from falling and soaking her chair and half the papers on the desk.

Little did she know, the hot water also shorted the operation of a tiny microphone glued under the open drawer.

CHAPTER FOUR

McCARTHY, OREGON, U.S.A.

Farraga tried to make Professor Vimvole's house a home. Her boyfriend had arranged enough upscale Western décor – galloping-horse art, leather couch – to make the building appear inhabited. But Farraga considered her F.W.W.P. cushions to be what transformed the masculine setting into a genuine "living" room: fluffy lime and purple tiger stripes combined with trims of Middle-Eastern camel tassels, creating a sort of pillow oasis in what otherwise might be an encampment, his own private Idaho.

An ordinary bottle can hold a genie: Farraga was an elixir in an unlikely container. Wrinkled but spry, sporting jaguar-print rayon pajamas with furry silk fringe in pink – inappropriate for her age – she looked like a buxom teenager, curled up on the couch and gabbing on the phone. Pushing back her curly hair, she perched to take notes, giddy with purpose, and waxed executive. "For Namibia, a cow. And a donkey to guard the cattle. They told the farmers not to poach the cheetah's prey, right?"

Diana was on the line. After reporting the news from F.W.W.P. headquarters, she raised a more challenging subject. "What about the dress code in Pakistan?"

Farraga inhaled. "At least they're already used to wearing a uniform." Then she incanted, "Ladies can make their own rules." Cultural sensitivity was always an issue.

Diana stated the obvious. "If the squad patrols in veil or full chador, they might have trouble seeing poachers. Or predators. Or other dangers, like cliffs."

Farraga looked at the cowboy painting on the wall. "My dream is that they can see the horizon, instead of just the walls of their own hovels." She brainstormed,

"Being covered in red plaid might be useful, like the Maasai in Africa. You know: versus lions. It might work with snow leopards. If you were a leopard, wouldn't you balk at red plaid?" Noticing her own pleasing reflection in the living-room mirror, Farraga imagined the effect of the Pakistanis walking in Himalayan terrain, surrounded by armed women-haters and other predators, while the women's eyes were covered. She tried to Think Positive. "The plus side is, leopards might not attack if they can't identify the veiled ladies as human. Red plaid tents might just look like garish furniture. Maybe even jihadists might not attack furniture."

Unwilling to joke about the Taliban, Diana hastened to the next item on her notepad. "Off the subject: what about ordering fang-shaped pens with our logo on them?"

"Fang-shaped? Clever. Your idea?"

"Not I." Diana grimaced. "A Mister... Sneckfrodpfeffer?" She didn't want to sound anti-Semitic or anything by ridiculing the name. "He suggested inscribing, 'The fang is mightier than the sword. Die by the sword, live by the fang.'" She heard Farraga giggle. Then she heard a door slam in Oregon.

On the other, Left Coast, Professor Vimvole had arrived; he put down his briefcase near the pine console. Farraga beamed at him. Time for a hug! She conscientiously saved the online N.R.A. grant application and set aside her laptop on the couch's rust-brown leather, then wiggled her fingers in gleeful greeting. Professor Vimvole, in response, was more circumspect, wondering what nonsense Farraga was cooking up on the phone instead of cooking him dinner. He couldn't smell anything good, and he sensed his blood sugar dipping perilously, as if he might get dizzy or cranky. Maybe he'd eaten too much fruit for lunch. He tried to keep boyishly slim.

Farraga's body language indicated her call was almost done. Tired, in a later time zone, Diana also was ready to get off the line. To disguise her rude haste, she mentioned, "The old guy also suggested plush bear claws, worn like gloves."

"Oh, for bear hugs?" Farraga inquired insightfully. Seeing the sourness on Vimvole's face, Farraga tossed a gaudy cushion at him. He caught it and kicked off his shoes toward her. "Gotta go, Diana, speaking of hugs. My boyfriend's home." Hanging up, she held her arms open to the professor. "Come here, you mega-fauna, you. Come give a test hug to this prototype jaguar pajama from our prospective clothing line."

The professor stood still, so she jumped up, leaped over, and gave him such a hard squeeze that he had to laugh, just to exhale quickly enough, and to seem congruent with her cheer. Farraga said, hopefully, "I finished your smilodon paper. Do you think it would be good P.R. for my charity if you gave me credit for editing your papers? In a footnote? You usually mention your grad students, when they help."

"They're associated with the university," he differed. "I'm hungry," he snapped, as diplomatically as possible. How soon could she produce food?

"Oh, yes, dear. I was double-checking your reference to fire-pits of the Clovis people, and got sidetracked into the island luau tradition. So I dug a coal-fire oven in the back yard. I made a crock pot of porcini and bison goulash – it's been simmering there for hours. I added fresh oregano a while ago. Peppers, garlic. Does that sound good? In this national emergency?" The professor followed her out to the slate patio. "Watch your step. Don't fall into the *sar*-chasm." She smiled at her own joke. Professor Vimvole's forehead eased.

Farraga planned to ask him again, later, about giving her a byline somewhere, to capitalize on his reputation as a prominent ecologist. Her charity needed any scrap of respectability: anything associated with women was automatically dismissed as ineffectual or shrill. Unless, of course, it was peppery bison goulash.

The ravenous professor was suddenly concerned that the woman had dug a hole where he'd planted bulbs: she should have consulted him before embarking on any alterations to his property. He'd forgotten she'd been a researcher. "I checked your photo album to locate your narcissus bed before I dug," she mentioned, as if reading his mind. "And I fertilized your bulbs, while I was out here, with dung. Not mine. Marion's goat." She lead her boyfriend behind the redwood hot-tub gazebo, near the lattice-top cedar fence. Had he lightened up yet? "Hey... Aren't you presenting at some boy-scout event tomorrow?"

The professor nodded. His eyebrows expressed skepticism at the sight of the rock-rimmed fire pit. Dinner from *dirt*?

Farraga continued, "Marion was chatting with your department secretary. She mentioned how nice if you'll give a quick talk to her *girl* scouts."

Her boyfriend rolled his eyes. "I mustn't overbook," he said. He was a *rock star* of ecology; she knew that. She fed him.

The scout master the next day was a fellow professor, Bernard, whose kid had requested Vimvole's involvement. Weeks earlier, in the childless bachelor's office, the six-year-old son had peeked in the door and saw Vimvole's awards – brass figurines of snarling animals, presented by wildlife conservation societies. Vimvole was secretly charmed by the little boy, but, when approached, he argued, "There's not room for a whole troupe in here. And I don't think kids will understand Pleistocene rewilding. The concept is too easily distorted, or sensationalized."

Bernard, the other professor, was persistent, taking pleasure in opportunities to watch Vimvole – that sanctimonious diva – squirm. "You think it will go over their heads? You can just bring your trophies to show them. The sabre-tooth tiger, the dire wolf. That'll impress them." As encouragement, Bernard got a cardboard box from one of the secretaries for Vimvole to carry the hollow but heavy figurines. "It would be an honor for me to transport them for you."

"My trophies? Just bring them and brag?" Vimvole swiveled in his chair, back toward his desk. His last resort was modesty: "I don't have *that* much to brag about."

Bernard, whose academic career had not attracted nearly as much public or professional attention, demurred. "Your achievement is phenomenal!" He couldn't resist adding cattily, "To get so much mileage out of proving that humans always hunted. True genius finds what hides in plain sight." To cover his cat tracks, the "Tiger Scout" master quickly suggested, "You could meet us in a park, and just hike around with us a little. To satisfy my son."

"Beavers are ancient. I could talk about *Castoroides ohioensis*."

"Yes, just a few details, to pique their interest." And so it transpired. Vimvole agreed to rendezvous with the group near a beaver pond in a state park. Vimvole's colleague was delighted that his son would see how boring was the child's "Rewilding" hero. Something else had dawned on Bernard: one of the other scout's fathers was a loud-mouthed anti-environmentalist, a thug indubitably destined to give Vimvole a hard time.

CHAPTER FIVE

McCARTHY, OREGON, U.S.A.

Indeed, when the day came, that Reich-wing auto detailer, Lucky Williams, showed up, representing his demographic to ensure a "fair and balanced" nature walk. Carpools of electric vehicles dropped kids off. A couple other dads stayed; they gave each other the official hand salute, pretending to be ironic. As the "Tiger Scout" group gathered in the parking lot – the boys swarming in orange striped uniforms – Bernard was especially friendly toward Lucky, and, in anticipation of the Vimvole-baiting entertainment sure to ensue, he even gave Lucky a high-five: "Great weather!" Blinding sun glinted off all the cars; breeze barely rustled the leaves of an adjacent olive grove.

Finally Bernard introduced Farraga's boyfriend. "The renowned... Professor Vimvole!" Taking the heavy objects one-by-one out of the cardboard box, Vimvole awkwardly displayed his brass awards to the waist-high children, then set the Pleistocene menagerie on the roof of his electric car. Vimvole hoped the brats wouldn't ask to touch them. Apart from some shoves and fidgets, the kids were surprisingly attentive. Was their self-discipline due to the scouts' militaristic roots? Perhaps the troupe's hiking and camping in areas with cougars and bears had contributed: Be obedient or be eaten. The children understood that he was like a General, or a lion tamer. Their widened eyes were duly impressed at each object's significance: the statues – tortoise, wolf, sloth, tiger, mammoth – symbolized the honors he'd accrued, public battles he had won, fierce academic opponents he had bested. Vimvole was delighted. The boys seemed to reawaken something in him.

To conclude, "I'll recycle this box when we're done," he commented virtuously, holding up the cardboard. He playfully swooped the empty box in the air, joking to Bernard, "Did *that* go over their heads?" The trophies had commanded the kids' respect; by contrast, adult recognition had never felt so unconditional. Vimvole packed up as the kids drank from juice boxes, quickly sucking them dry. Then the group of males, herded by Bernard, skirted a baseball diamond and headed down a tree-shaded dirt path. Their destination was a beaver dam on a tributary of the Willamette. Periodically one among them flailed his arms, warding off clouds of flies.

"When beaver restore the wetland, that protects our water table," Vimvole said to an attractive tow-headed boy walking beside him. Alert, the boy seemed precocious, reminding the aging professor of his own childhood enthusiasms.

Holding his hands out flat in front of him , the little boy giggled. "How can you have a table of water?"

Vimvole explained, "It's underground, invisible."

The scout master, caught up, joined in, "So nobody's going to think about the invisible water table when the trees in their backyard are chewed down. That's why they hate beaver," Bernard snorted.

"*I* don't hate beaver," Lucky Williams trumpeted, with a lewd guffaw. "I'd like a box of beavers." He stalked along like a gladiator.

Bernard nodded approvingly, though normally he wouldn't acknowledge such crudeness. He pointed out a dam flow device that conservationists had installed. "That's so the dam doesn't cause the parking lot to flood." The group clustered to view the odd construction. "Vimvole, anything to add?"

Vimvole stepped in front of the huffing Lucky and lectured. "Before humans populated the continent, there were about fifty beavers per mile of river. And there were bigger beavers. Over two-hundred pounds, as big as a football player. Mountain beaver are a living fossil, but they're quite small. But fifty times two-hundred pounds – can anyone do the math?"

"One thousand – ten thousand!" A chubby boy shouted out, proudly.

"Ten thousand pounds of beaver per mile," Vimvole grinned. "We think it's normal for a river to rush, and to flood. But the beaver slowed things down quite a bit."

"Just like a football player," the slight, flaxen-haired boy said.

"Linebackers," the chubby boy affirmed, bulking out his elbows.

"Beavers don't respect property rights," Lucky Williams protested gruffly. "And what about river transportation? Boats have to pass."

"Beavers are a keystone species," Vimvole said nonchalantly.

A small voice piped up. "Key-stone? Is that like King Arthur's sword?" The flaxen boy had big eyes.

A father thrust his arm up toward the sky, indicating a raptor. For a few moments, the group watched an osprey circling and diving. The kids were so cute, Vimvole wondered if he should follow through on his relatively hassle-free idea to acquire sons: connecting via the internet, impregnate a lesbian couple. Vimvole ignored Lucky and continued speaking. The tow-headed boy seemed particularly eager to learn. "Wolves and other predators can keep elk and deer from eating all the beavers' vegetation. Carnivores scare deer away from the waterways, hillsides, and other obstacles that slow them down, when they try to flee to safety. Do any of you have questions?"

A spunky Latino boy asked, "How many pounds in a wolf bite?"

"You mean..." Vimvole chuckled. "Oh, about one Big Mac per bite."

A five-year-old murmured, "Beavers are boring. I like wolfs."

At the mention of wolves, Bernard could smell blood: ham-fisted Lucky was primed. The now-sweating father wiped his nose vigorously on his hairy arm, then asked, "Isn't environmennalism the new socialism? I mean, isn't sustainabilly like communism?"

Vimvole didn't bite. "Uh, no... Mister -?"

"Williams." Blue-collar Lucky intended to impress all the little boys by confronting this stuck-up academic. "Weather has natural flukshuations. Like, sunspots. And geologicul differences. Isn't the climate hysteria and Carbon Credit just a way to keep govermment jobs for enviros like you? It's in your vested interest to create panic." He grinned. "No offense intended." At Vimvole's lack of response, he continued, "I just wonder about you animal lovers. What do you think of your *own* species? Not that you do bestiality," he winked. "But maybe people aren't your favorite species. Do you want us herded into human-habitation zones? Do you want a carbon tax on human babies, maybe?"

Though uncomprehending, the kids were intrigued by the change in mood. Then one of the Tiger Scouts gasped. "Look! A beaver!" He pointed. Through the reeds, a dark bump moved. More visible were the satiny ripples in its wake.

The kids hushed each other. A meek dad, who had religious inclinations, started to muse. "The Holy Land had more trees in Jesus' time. Cedars of Lebanon. I wonder if they had beavers there. Beavers on the river Jordan..." He addressed his two wan sons. "Wouldn't it be cool to have Jews and Arabs together, boys, planting trees for the beavers? The Green Dragon in the fertile crescent..." He chuckled at the irony. But at his nod to the "Green Dragon" of environmentalism, Lucky Williams gave him a hard look; in penance, the more saintly dad backpedaled. "Of course, they won't have peace in the Middle East till they accept Jesus."

Lucky retorted, "That's a conversation stopper. Let's go back to talking about how much we all love beavers."

Looking around, Vimvole smiled at the cute kids and tried to think of a joke. "I love eager beavers like you Scouts."

BALKISTAN REGION, PAKISTAN

In a cement courtyard walled in with cinder blocks, veiled Pakistani women cooked, large pots on grills that perched above smoking embers of dung-cake.

Of all things, Ned Lerner entered, nodding to the director of a scuffling camera crew who trailed him. Despite his advanced age, media mogul Mr. Lerner still had the majesty of a lion surrounded by his pride. The matter-of-fact rumble of his commanding voice confirmed logistics: "Angelina wants me to officiate at the funeral?"

The director explained, while simultaneously gesturing shot angles to his crew. "Yeah, yeah. Apparently the poacher didn't realize the women's snow-leopard patrol was armed. U.S. women veterans are the usual anti-poaching trainers in this, uh, Fanged Wild program. But Angelina stepped in to coach target practice when she was filming on location nearby. I guess she's doing a sequel about the widow of Daniel Pearl; something called 'Salt for the Wound,' I think. Mr. Lerner, we'll have you there, by the... canteen."

The men halted to watch the women take flat bread out of a large clay oven, the same way men have observed women do the same thing probably for millennia. But these men were video-recording a documentary about how Pakistani women adapted to modern circumstances like, for instance, the civil unrest and the floods caused by global warming, and household messes caused by splattered anatomy.

The most colorful corner of the courtyard attracted the cameraman; seeing a bazaar of leopard- and tiger-print fabrics, his lens followed unveiled daughters, their tiny, round faces smiling, and their veiled mothers who were applying themselves diligently to sewing something other than veils: gaudy F.W.W.P. garments. The collective's micro-loans had purchased the rustic treadle machines. The women operated them on the ground: furniture might have been burned for fuel. Some women were lucky enough to sit on cinder blocks. Though alert as prairie dogs, the little girls present were oblivious to the lack of luxury; they radiated the joy of being with loved ones while there was something fragrant cooking for interesting guests.

Ned Lerner tried to be approachable with the women without violating local mores. So, animated like Ray Charles or Stevie Wonder, he announced to no-one in particular, "Smells good! Smells like.... curry." Dramatic nostrils waved like a ribbon through the air. "Curry, yes?"

The women nodded, pretending to understand. Then they looked at him as if he were a giraffe.

An American video-journalist, Annette Anillo, part of the film team, had more leeway interacting with the females; she made her way to the middle of the seamstresses. There, she tried on one of the soft Pakol caps that they had stitched together. The veiled women nodded, their eyes modestly approving. The American then encouraged one young woman who, with shy body language, modeled, as it were, a new plaid burqa in Maasai red. Her imaginary catwalk was only one hesitant step, and then she slowly rotated so the flowing polyester barely moved. Afghan Idol, this wasn't.

Ned maintained a respectful distance. He pointed to the seamstresses and their products. "You sell online?" The women kept nodding, joined by the journalist.

The director herded some pushy little boys out of the shot. He whispered to them, "Girls! Girls! Girls! Only! No boys."

Ned Lerner raised his voice, not just to overcome the commotion; when gesticulation failed, loudness was the universal inclination to confront a language barrier. "What's your biggest seller? What's your biggest seller?"

The journalist stepped out of the fray, reaching her microphone toward Ned, then was seized by her early training as an infomercial emcee and quickly held the infidel phallic device to her own mouth. "Teenagers all over the world are ordering them online. They're Fanged Wilds caps, with your own digital portrait on the crown." She turned to display the back of her cap, which happened to have Hina Rabbani Khar's photo. Pakistan's beautiful first female Foreign Minister's full, almond eyes had an expression as remote as Venus. But the face was animated as the journalist, her head still turned, kept talking into the mike: "Predators prefer to pounce if they think prey fails to perceive them. But women everywhere need 'eyes in back of our heads, to deter stalkers.' Ha ha."

Annette Anillo shrieked as she faced forward: Ned Lerner's big, age-shriveled hand lurked, waiting to take the mike. The foreigners laughed awkwardly, while the villagers flinched at the scream, alarmed.

Reviving the professional atmosphere, Ned Lerner entered full public-service announcement mode. "I'd like to emphasize the most urgent reason to purchase these F-quadruple-you-Pee products. In the developing world, where women don't have equal rights with men, where they're uneducated and they don't have access to birth control... and they have more children than they'd like to have... the rich countries have to do their part to help."

While he rattled on about the necessity of conscientious reproduction, a little girl appeared under his elbow and proudly handed the woman journalist a F.W.W.P. shirt patterned with snow-leopard spots. Nestled in the girl's other arm was a white rabbit, another essential feature of the program.

If the camera crew used a more powerful zoom lens, they might have filmed, on the rugged mountainside beyond the nervous crowd, a distant snow leopard. Agile among a tumble of rocks, the leopard descended to stalk the villagers' goats. She detected the scent of rabbit dung.

CHAPTER SIX

SIERRA SAN LUIS, MEXICO

Inching down an arid hillside, a young Latina rode a burro past madrones on rust-colored scree. Frida wore white cotton embroidered with Fanged Wilds and Women appliqués. The colorful stitchery contrasted in mood with the rifle across her saddle. "My grandfather said his mama was with *banditos* in the Sierra Madre." Frida's Spanish rolled off her tongue like the clattering rocks dislodged by burro hooves. The way many women do the world over, she chatted an avalanche. "I didn't believe him! But here I am monitoring my country's wolf reintroduction."

Frida *habla con* Selena, who walked alongside the burro's neck. Selena's slim, short body, also in uniform, fit in the space in front of the burro's thin shoulders. The trio picked their way down the trail. Selena's thumb was hooked above her woven gun holster. "Si, we are observing and protecting the Mexican wolves. And we guard their food, coues deer. If we didn't, none of them would be safe from poachers. If we do our job right, those poachers' children will have much more meat to steal!"

High in the saddle, Frida halted the burro to check the valley with her binoculars. Lowering her arms, she blurted with pride, "If I can learn a job like this, I believe my great-grandmother could have really been a bandita. Maybe I could even be a *bandita*."

Selena tisked. "*Ay, caramba.* This job is dangerous enough, without breaking any laws. My husband worries that deer hunters will hurt me." She glanced up, not wanting to alarm her new best friend. They had already confided in each other about being raped as teenagers, and how they might shoot to kill if any man tried another assault. Selena changed the subject. "But he likes the money I earn. He really likes *cotija* on his tortillas. We get the best *cotija*, not cheap cheese."

Frida didn't respond at once; she just listened to the burro's hooves hit the dry dirt and gravel. Frida thought of her great-grandmother, of the perils she must have confronted. Was there really a moment when her mother's father's mother – an ancestor in olden times, before cars and condoms – was more than a beast of burden? Did she actually have a choice? Was her great-grandmother really... a *bandita*?

Frida finally stopped near some piñon to look through her binoculars again. Holding them to her eyes, she said, "If something happens to me, maybe my son will have a daughter someday, and he can tell her how brave I have been." She pointed to the horizon for Selena, and handed her the binoculars. "Wolves!"

Selena could see the wolves pulling on a fresh deer, dark fangs gnawing on tatters of meat. "My husband would eat that, too," she said.

RICHARD BRIMSTON'S ISLAND, THE CARIBBEAN

Tanning flesh courted the warm globe of the sun: Sir Richard's island wasn't underwater yet. White beach still stretched apart from the glitter of blue, below a vast deck. There seemed to be some sort of bikini conference, a summit meeting of thongs and nipple-triangles, organized into symposia of elongated limbs, emaciated midriffs, and jutting cheekbones, with the keynote: tan.

White cushions gleamed where an array of teak chaise lounges were a focus of activity. One bikini model prepared to give an interview to Annette Anillo, the American video-journalist who had followed Ned Lerner to Pakistan. Anillo was now, with her camera crew, the guest of Sir Richard.

The model clarified, with an Aussie twang, "This is really about the men?"

The journalist nodded, distracted by the camera set-up. "The advertising money is slim for feminine topics," Anillo explained summarily. "But loaded white guys capture everyone's imagination. So our working title is, 'Kings of the Beasts'... a documentary about men saving endangered large carnivores." At the boom operator's shy request, the journalist indifferently strung a mike on the spaghetti strap of the model's red bikini top. "What's your name, again?"

"Shee, my name is Shee." The Australian model smiled at the smitten boom operator and then into the camera. "Are we starting?"

Her beige power suit arranged, the prim Ms. Anillo gave a nod. "Roll."

"Ready?" the model asked Professor Vimvole, who twitched nearby, on the edge of his seat. He nodded the way a puppy wags its tail, all there, and self-consciously touched the mike clipped to his tie. He was the only person present without a tan. Nonetheless, there would be no tan line on his ring finger: he was unmarried. And he was surrounded by beautiful women, all as thin as pubescent boys.

Veteran of Sydney beauty contests, Shee slipped her finger under a red bikini strap and launched into her presentation. "According to Maasai-warrior tradition, red clothes scare off predatory animals." Shee measured a smirk at the Professor. "But I've noticed that it doesn't work on humans that way." The Professor's eyes wandered down to where her velvety bronze thigh pressed against the teak arm rest.

"The professor's research is incontrovertible," the model continued, fawning. "Humans are the reason biodiversity has collapsed. But there is hope. Since before the dawn of history, predators have kept herbivores in check. Put animals back in balance, and more plants can grow in abundant variety. Then *all* kinds of life will thrive once again. With predators, everything flourishes, even in radioactive places like Fukushima, Rocky Flats, and Chernobyl. Speaking of radiation..." The young woman – this was for television, after all – abruptly pleaded: "I come from the hole in the ozone. Butter me, Professor?" With a flirty gesture, she held her jar of organic-coconut sunscreen toward the aging bachelor.

Professor Vimvole took the jar with an ogle of disbelief. His fingers spasmed obediently to scoop into the eggshell-colored goop. His chaise lounge creaking, he applied the lotion to her shining brown shoulder. Her almost-fleshless body was a calcium structure as imposing as the Great Barrier Reef, and as lush with life as it had once been. He dabbed the goop on her back, rubbing it in; his hesitation jerked his hand as if he were a marionette, or Pinocchio.

Shee grinned into the lens, cheeky. "Combine *that* effect with training micro-financed women to manage predators. Money in women's hands promotes civilization. The power of beauty can restore wilderness as well."

Professor Vimvole's feigned scientific application of the sunscreen on her tan. But his attentiveness was punctuated: he also furtively observed the other fashion models. The women were monkeying around, as giddy as a boys' locker room, in anticipation of their own turn before the camera. Like playing touch football, one lithe blond grabbed a bubbly redhead's F.W.W.P. photo-hat and held the safari hat in front of her face like a mask, miming with saucy body language to suggest that her friend, the giggling redhead, was a sexual exhibitionist.

With lightning speed, the freckled mockery victim – unhindered by any clothing to speak of – darted and stole the mimic's own photo hat in payback. The redhead rubbed the hat on her derrière, one peachy, freckled buttock at a time. Vimvole's jaw dropped.

Following Professor Vimvole's eyes, Shee saw the distraction and shouted, "Civilization, ladies!" She continued, "Monkey see, monkey do. Just watching *soap operas* in some countries is shown to reduce birthrate, and to free women from abusive marriages."

Indeed, some months later, in South America and Asia, Ganika and other women whom we meet in the Fanged Wilds Program did get to see the models and Shee on television; they subsequently questioned their own relationship with men, and wondered whether their own lives couldn't be better... or even... more playful.

Shee continued, "Fashion is life or death, too. Research shows that we subconsciously tally how many glances each person gets. Gazes raise status. So if you're looked at, you're not ostracized and abandoned to predators." The model Shee could see in the journalist's eyes that her time was almost over. Preoccupied, Annette Anillo had come to interview Sir Richard, after all. No matter how stunning Shee was, there were a million other women just as exquisite. The power of her appearance was as slippery as the sun screen that she now took from Professor Vimvole's greasy hand.

Shee concluded her sound-bite, "Imagine how much more empowering it is for women to see their sisters on poacher patrol." Trying to keep the camera's attention for one more moment, Shee smoothed the lotion on her fabulous legs. "And the walking is such good exercise," she captioned.

High above, from the villa newly rebuilt after a storm's lightning fire, craggy Sir Richard Brimston strode down the path. At the sight of him, Annette Anillo straightened up, smoothing the tailored linen suit that (surely) made her as sexy as the loquacious model (and other freaks of nature and anorexia: they'd just be sags and bones when she'd become a network executive and proud mother of – did her pregnancy show? She smoothed the front of her tight skirt. Child-rearing would be a great way to bond with other executives.) The ambitious Ms. Anillo interrupted, finality in her voice, to interview Vimvole. "Professor? Any thoughts?"

Professor Vimvole had a stock summation prepared for moments like this. Yet, stunned by the glamor, he just blurted, "What *Shee* said."

In contrast to the bachelor, Richard Brimston was an easy match for all the vivacious beauties. Like a general, Sir Richard lined up the bikini models to face away from the camera, revealing the photo backsides of their personalized "Fanged Wilds and Women" safari hats. He himself looked head-on at the lens and pronounced cheekily, for all the world to see: "I do what I can to help."

Annette Anillo laughed loudly and applauded. "Thank you, Sir Richard. That's it. Perfect. Where do you want your own interview?" The journalist walked up to him while the models dispersed: some returned to sunbathing; some loped down to the water for a swim. The journalist beamed. "Please, Sir. Tell me everything you've ever thought or felt."

Sir Richard smiled wryly. "How about if I just tell you everything I've ever done?" He gestured for her to precede him back uphill to the villa.

Professor Vimvole still perched on the edge of his chaise lounge. Sir Richard had consulted him about optimal locations to effect Pleistocene megafauna restoration and migration corridors where earthquakes had caused the Keester XXXL pipeline spills and rendered the areas unfit for human habitation.

But that only took three hours forty minutes the day before. The sea-plane wasn't returning the professor to the mainland till the next morning. The professor felt as if he'd taken up habitation in an entirely new niche, in an entirely new ecosystem. Could he adapt? He felt like a prey species. If only one of the females would ravish him; sexual union would provide him with protective coloration, as if he belonged in this new herd.

The fashion model Shee returned to her chaise lounge beside him, the elegant furniture complaining as she draped her impossibly long body over it. "Most global-warming solutions seem like moving deck chairs on the Titanic. Lucky we've got such *nice* deck chairs." Shee leaned on the arm rest, curious: "Can the Fanged Wilds program combine with Pleistocene rewilding somehow, Professor?"

The professor found his tongue. "I really don't understand the Fanged Wilds program. It seems too dangerous for women to handle guns."

Shee looked surprised. "I thought you were intimately involved in the Fanged Wilds."

The professor pinched his lips together, staring at Shee's own bulging red ones. *Big lips indicate a high level of estrogen.* He continued staring as her lips spread open to reveal many brilliantly white teeth, monuments to her delight in his company. Shee was pleased with him! And she was so clean, and young.

Dazed, he looked out at the near-pristine beach alive with exquisite females. Their effect was almost hallucinogenic: he imagined each of them mothering a son for him. He pictured a scout troupe with his face. For some reason – although he had paid very little attention to religion in his life – he recalled something about seventy-one virgins waiting for him in paradise. He did feel as if he had a glimpse of Heaven. He wondered if an afterlife existed after all. What if, instead of punishment for sins, he was rewarded for all he had done for ecology?

He recalled that the beautiful Shee had posed some sort of inquiry to which he was expected to respond. He uttered haphazardly, "My expertise, rewilding, is completely different. It reestablishes correct supremacies. The Fanged Wilds program is just a charity run by... a woman I know. A renter."

The fashion model giggled at his awkwardness. Beyond them, the waves etched their mark in the sand.

McCARTHY, OREGON, U.S.A.

Humming to herself, Farraga baked Professor Vimvole a gluten-free welcome-home cake.

CHAPTER SEVEN

MANHATTAN, NEW YORK, U.S.A.

Feeling gritty, dryly scraping away at her eight-hour grind, Diana sat at her desk. The task at hand was negotiation: phone to her ear, she attempted communication with some sort of modeling-agency personal assistant. She described the F.W.W.P. hats. "Professor Vimvole only wants a couple dozen. Can you clear it with Shee to use her photo, to print it on them?"

"Which photo?" The agency underling whined. "Why doesn't he approach Shee directly, if he knows her?"

Diana had a sense that the girlish secretary on the other end of the line occupied the same spot in the food chain as she herself: like a bunny in a burrow, a pawn to larger forces, trying to make sense of the actions of those more powerful than she. "Apparently the professor is..." At that moment, Diana saw Derek the Delivery Guy; the tide was unusually low so just his broad shoulders showed. He waved at her enthusiastically, causing her to stutter as he braced to heft himself in the window. "The professor is... indisposed... to ask her himself."

Derek's face glowed with an amorous, self-conscious grin. After a dodgy scrutiny of the room – seeking perhaps a message of encouragement posted for him somewhere, or maybe an arrow on one of the wall maps, indicating his next destination – he got his knee on the windowsill but caught his shoe toe on the outside ledge and fell face-first into a sack of packages that Diana had set conveniently near the window. Lacking other options, he rolled head-over-heels into the middle of the room. Quickly he stood up, looked out the window in humiliation, rolled his eyes and bowed toward Diana for his performance. Then he proceeded to take the mail sack out to his boat.

Sheepishly, he returned: heavier boxes required multiple trips.

The goods were garments ordered by public customers, and, in the larger boxes, uniforms and supplies for Derek to send on their way to program participants worldwide. He took a second look at the packages, though they were just ordinary elements of his regular, daily job; he studied them as if they might contain something completely novel, something for him personally.

Diana blushed and studied her screen saver as if it were an IRS audit. She knew she shouldn't waste time, let alone get entangled with a delivery boy. But it was almost like when wolves inure prey to the sight of them: Diana was getting used to seeing Derek, so her better instincts, to flee, were being disarmed. "I know how Professor Vimvole feels," she said to the secretary, stealing a lustful glance back at Derek's rear. On his return, he looked at her, hopeful, revealing something for which he yearned from the bottom of his soul. Diana bit her lip and wrote something on her notepad with a fang-shaped pen, then nonchalantly waved goodbye as he took her last box.

KALKATTA, MICHIGAN

Past the city-limits sign, the dawn mists dwelt on the asphalt, claiming the icy road, as if to deny human progress. Ronelle's old Buick careened. She swore, "Just Lord don't let me run into a deer crossing the street. Deer done too much damage to my ass already!"

Her niece Tawona said, "Hallelujah!" She cautiously sipped convenience-store coffee as the balding tires regained traction. "Maybe one more collision with a deer is what I need, though. Whack my body back the other way, maybe: even it out. The chiropractor said I'd always be crooked. I think maybe he was crooked, trying to get me to pay his fee two times a week for the rest of my life!"

Ronelle accelerated and escalated. "Some doctors even more expensive, more worthless. Lyme disease land me in doctor offices the rest of *my* life, for no good, maybe. I'm probably lucky I can't afford 'em." Ronelle squinted, yawned, and added, "Maybe the chiropractor just thought you were cute. How was he?"

Tawona said, "He was a college boy, and disappointed that I didn't have collision insurance. At least chiropractors hug you. He looked like a quarterback. I did feel a little better after he tackled me."

"Goal!" Her aunt howled.

The occupant of the back seat laughed. Also camo-clad, and a new F.W.W.P. participant, Tiara was white and, thus, a minority in the car. Overwhelmed, starting a new job with these two women who were experienced, related to one another, and had matching short nappy Afros, blonde Tiara made an effort at conversation. "You had Lyme disease, Ronelle? What is that, exactly?"

Tawona editorialized, "You know. It's from too many deer."

Ronelle answered Tiara. "I got it from a deer tick's bite." She took one hand off the steering wheel, and pointed to her other wrist. "That's where I saw the tick bite, where he targeted me. Freezes don't kill the critters no' mo'. I was so achy. The antibiotics caught it in time, I guess, for me. Some people can't take enough antibiotics before they get real sick, and it's too late."

Tawona joined in the lament. "There's no cute chiropractor to whack that tick bite back out of you."

Tiara queried, "You were cured right away?"

The tires skidded a bit. Ronelle nodded sideways, as if to say, Not Really. "Nothing cured the doctor bills, and getting demoted at work. I tried every trick, but I got into debt. Bank charged me extra fees for not having any money. Figure that one out."

"I been there. This program is my third part-time job," Tiara said. "At least it's healthy, compared to the other two. No chemicals. No heavy metal."

"Yeah, no heavy lifting." Tawona swigged coffee from her paper cup then said, "This'll be healthy, until it's Miller Time, and we get ourselves shot by some dumbass drunk deer hunter."

"Or attacked by a pack o' wolf," Ronelle optioned, with a flair for the dramatic.

"That's what we have guns for, I guess," Tiara reassured herself aloud, from the back seat. "Besides to bag us some dinner. I'm lucky my dad took me huntin' growing up. The outdoors and firearms and all don't scare me." Trying to sound more casual and sophisticated than nervous, she added, "Even the desperate housewife Eva Longoreglori hunts."

Ronelle amiably found some common ground. "This program was a natural for me, too. In my old Saginaw 'hood, every kid knows how to pack heat."

"Do you still live with family?" Tiara asked.

"Yeah," Tawona sighed: her siblings cramped her style.

"Yeah," Ronelle said, more happily.

"Me too. The weather disasters and floods and everything... it brings families together, huh. For better or worse." She looked at her rough hands. "For poorer, or poorer."

Their car barely in control on the ice, the women reached their destination and parked under the trees. They got out and discovered a deception: dawn's pinks made the outdoors seem much warmer than the frost allowed. With a giggle, one by one, the women jumped up and down in a contagion of abandonment rather than of germs, their breath separating into puffs of steam with each flat-footed landing, like cars of the Little Engine that Could. After rubbing her gloved hands together, each of the three women pulled her rifle out of the Buick's trunk.

Tawona also retrieved a bag of ginseng roots – hairy fingerlings, officially recovered from an herbal-medicine poacher. She'd been entrusted to replant them; there weren't enough government employees to keep up with the task of protecting wild ginseng from extinction, so a ranger had contacted Fanged Wilds.

The women checked a GPS and set off into the forest. As if friendliness would help keep them warm, the three continued their conversation. Ronelle asked, "Do you have kids?"

"Just pets," Tiara answered. "Pets is how I got to love animals like this, enough to, you know... protect them." She wondered how that sounded. "People are okay. But only my cats never abuse or abandon me."

The group walked further. "I like dogs," Ronelle said. "Someday I'll get my kids a puppy."

Tiara asked, "You have kids?"

"Two." Ronelle sighed softly. "My mom is taking care of the my boy and girl while I pay back this loan." She thought about them all at home, eating cold corn flakes for breakfast. She mustered her resolve. "Those kids love when we have deer steaks sizzling on the grill. Maybe we get some venison today. Mama uses Jamaica jerk seasoning."

They stopped to listen for wildlife. They heard birds chirp, and the sharp sound of water. Tawona walked over to a trickling creek, squatted, and jammed a stick in and out of soft earth. She dropped a couple ginseng roots into the holes. Then she grunted. "Speaking of jerks..." Tawona addressed Tiara proudly: "We donated some meat to the battered women shelter."

Ronelle shook her head in woe. "I won't name names... but one sister in our program hid in the shelter where we took the deer venison. She said it never would have happened, she wouldn't have ended up there, if she'd had self image like Fanged Wilds gives her." She bent to brush some burrs off her canvas pant leg. "I was checking that sister's body for ticks after work. I saw what her husband done to her, just because she wouldn't hand over her cash to him when he wanted it." Ronelle concluded, "Talk about a parasite. A little tick sucks you, or a big one." As they walked further, Ronelle started thinking about ticks on dogs. Her mind wandered to the NFL quarterback Michael Vick. She pictured him as a tick wearing a big gold medallion. Vick had been imprisoned for running dog fights. Dogs were maimed and killed; Ronelle imagined, if the giant Vick-tick were helicoptered over and dropped in the middle of the Michigan forest, it would be fair to hunt it down, take aim, and... "Jerk," she muttered to herself.

"You said something?" Tiara asked. Breeze stirred the trees. Leaves rustled as they hit the ground.

Ronelle raised her eyebrows. "It's kind of nice out here, huh," she chatted.

Listening to a woodpecker, Tiara smiled. Tawona said, "You can get birds to come, if you go *pssh*." The rest of the day, when they saw songbirds, the women sounded: *pssh*. Tiny heads cocked with curiosity, and tiny claws hopped nearer, in the vast outdoors.

That night, back home at her mom's house, Tiara brushed her teeth. She reflected: Anyone who pretends life isn't shit is just trying to sell you something. But her day had been as satisfying, if not more, as any day in the army. The army was depressing, especially after her relationship broke up. Holding back her shoulder-length blonde hair, Tiara spat. Sensuously, her two cats – one tabby, one in a dirty tuxedo – took turns rubbing against her legs. They were innocent, free of worries about the future. Her little sister would have to take care of them, if Tiara ended up traveling abroad with Fanged Wilds. Fortunately her sister loved animals as much as Tiara.

Tiara had to buy a portable digital recorder, back when she had to produce evidence to her Army superiors that her ex-boyfriend should be deployed separately from her. (When she mentioned date-rape, her sergeant said, "You're not just trying to get the government to pay for an abortion, are you, soldier? Because they won't.")

The recorder lay on the bedside table. Her bed, made with military precision, opened to the prying of her tired limbs. She curled up with her cats, stroking them and thinking how much she'd miss their simple affection. Tiara felt as if she shared her tenderest truth with their neatly-packaged little bodies. As she pet their fur, skulls and ears, she whispered *à la* Dr. Seuss: "I love my kitties, yes, I do. I would love them in a stew." Like the street light under her blind, the cats leaked love into her life. Tommy was her favorite, a little angel sent from heaven to keep her heart alive; he was a furry presence near her head. She pushed the triangle button and played back the sounds that often lulled them all to sleep, sounds she'd recorded one Sunday morning perched on the roof, with her tabby, Puss Puss, and tuxedo, Tommy, slinking expectantly up behind her: birds singing.

Tiara was a nobody. But to her cats, she was Keeper of the Birdsong.

The warbling drowned out the noises from the other rooms,: her sister's TV; blasts of her brother playing pornographic video games; and the hissing of their propane distiller, their source of potable water during the floods. Trilling and chirps carried her cares away. Along with the recording, the cats purred in and out, as if bliss were a motor fueled by breath.

CHAPTER EIGHT

MANHATTAN, NEW YORK, U.S.A.

Seagulls bickered outside. Sitting in the cold and damp would bother anyone. But her legs felt less achy – why didn't Americans ever talk of rheumatism? – now she had the daily habit of drinking ginger and ginseng tea with a touch of Chinese aconite. Still bone idle, Diana was packing up some F.W.W.P. insignia appliqués when the phone rang. She stuffed the last badge into the bubble envelope, then slipped into her chair and pushed the blinking phone line.

"Fanged Wilds." She closed the sticky envelope flap. "Yes, we are open to suggestions." She peeled the label off the invoice and smoothed it onto the yellow envelope. "Yes, we need all the help we can get." She laughed. The caller was some kind of nut; he had called before. But he was more interesting than packing orders, even when her other task supplied a patrol team in – what exotic destination did this one have? – Chiapas, Mexico.

As her ears attended to the eccentric, coughing old man on the other end of the line, her eyes sought more stimuli. She had vowed, officially, as well as in her own heart, not to do extraneous surfing, social media, or games on the job. Her fingers crawled to her Ukrainian-egg pen jar. She started throwing F.W.W.P. fang-shaped pens one at a time, aiming at the mouth of a Tiki mask. She had placed the mask the day before in the perfect position, propped against a pile of merchandise, after enduring a particularly tedious discussion with a garment silk-screening vendor.

At least this caller wasn't a bore. With muffled pauses – evidently to hack up phlegm – the man described his idea for a new product: "Fanged Wilds and Women brand jerk seasoning. Good for tenderizing jerks."

Diana laughed obligingly. "Got it. I'll submit your proposition to our R&D

department." She wrote, *"F.W.W.P.- brand jerk seasoning. Good for tenderizing jerks"* on a piece of notepaper, then stuffed it with other bumph in a shoe box she had marked "R&D" after a previous phone call from this odd gent. "Our organization relies on grass-roots ingenuity," she encouraged. Closing the shoe box, she made a private joke for her own benefit: "That, and first-rate equipment."

Fondling the woven place mat under her laptop, she considered: this guy was a dedicated supporter of the charity; a moral support, at any rate, if not a financial donor. So Diana launched into a public-relations spiel. "Did you know we teamed with Looms for Wombs, whose micro-financed women weave place mats? They're weaving some holsters for our bear spray."

The old man – hard of hearing – asked, "Hair spray?"

She laughed. "No, not hair spray. *Bear* spray. You know, like pepper spray, to repel an attack."

The old man trumpeted, "Why not... hair spray that can double as bear spray? You want your dames looking good, even in bear country, right?"

Diana envisioned a grizzly bear charging toward a woman who was spraying her bee-hive hairdo. The woman could spray the bear, and the bear's fur become styled. The now-ladylike bear would reach over daintily and get honey from her new friend's bee-hive. Diana threw another fang-shaped pen at the mouth of the Tiki mask. "Just keep those product ideas coming. Might bloom into an ad campaign."

"Bear hairspray?"

"...Or maybe *Fanged Wilds* beauty salons. Fashion tips on how to look less tame."

"Well," he said gruffly, as if detecting her flippancy. "I do have another idea. But it might be expensive and cumbersome."

Diana's aim was getting better. *Thwap!* One pen hit the Tiki's eye. "Talk is free, anyway. But I should make sure you get credit for your ingenuity. What's your name, again?" She was good at vocabulary but bad with names; his was a weird one. "And are you getting our email newsletter, The Ladies' Monthly?"

"Edwin Sneckfrodpfeffer. I don't do email. Okay. My concept is to frighten away large felines that go for the jugular, or for the eye-sockets of their prey." Cough. "A backpack airbag could have a pull-cord that inflates it like a cobra neck."

Diana mulled over the idea, wrote it down with a pen she was about to throw, and put the note carefully into the cardboard R&D box. "OK. Thank you, Mister... Sneckfofeffer."

He hung up abruptly, with a snort.

Diana listened to the water lap outside her office. Any idea was worth considering... all things considered. Her boss, Farraga, seemed to appreciate creativity. Farraga had called it brainstorming, as if it were just another climate phenomenon related to global warming.

GARDINNER, MONTANA, U.S.A.

Beyond the walls stretched grizzly-bear country, and the world's oldest national park. But this was just another tourist motel outside one gateway to Yellowstone. The motel's formerly upscale features barely remained patched together since the Great Recession. It had been damaged by the earthquake that reduced Old Faithful to a skewed squirt, a sort of Sancho Panza to its former Teddy Roosevelt brio.

Amy was moonlighting in pool maintenance. She finished mopping the cracked cement, then stood and stretched her back for a moment. Night outside made the tall windows – where they weren't boarded up, smeared, or opaque with condensation – a mirror to the cavernous recreation area. She carried the bucket to rinse the mop out at the corner faucet, at a drain below the shower head where swimmers would rinse sweat and chlorine.

The splashes echoed as florescent tubes buzzed high overhead. Late cars – motel patrons back from Happy Meals and Whoppers – pulled into parking spaces, their headlights illuminating the steamy pool air. Crickets outside were interrupted by a sudden knocking on the glass door. A cute young woman was holding up a colorfully wrapped package. She shook it gaily, its FWWP label visible, with a charming air of familiarity. Amy unlocked the door for her.

"Hi. Amy Oakley? Remember me? I'm Marla, from training. They sent your uniform in the same box as mine. To save postage, I guess. Do you think they're that cheap?" Marla looked as if she spent high school going to all the football games in a big group of friends. Had she been a cheerleader? As if she might be Italian, she gestured WhatTheFuck and asked vivaciously, "I thought the N.R.A. gave us some huge grant?"

Amy snorted. "I got an 'I'm the N.R.A.' bumper sticker in the mail. Too bad I don't have a car."

"When I was in the color guard, we twirled rifles. So I guess I *do* belong in the National Rifle Association."

So her hunch about cheerleading was correct. "I thought I belonged here." Amy gestured vaguely to indicate the pool. "I'll be happy for a job that doesn't stink of chlorine." She wiped her hands on her T-shirt, below the picture of two huskies: she was busty, so the dogs were displayed in healthy prominence. Her chest was her best feature. She set the package on a deck chair, hoping the shirt inside wouldn't be too tight.

"Yeah. We could make better money fracking. But the fumes are bad. I'm just glad to be out of the army," Marla said. She checked with her delicate hand for moisture, then leaned her thin frame against the fiberglass pool slide. "I miss target shootin', though. Are you pumped for the elk hunt?"

"Yeah," Amy said, "Except it's not exactly cheap calories if we have to carry the meat back out." She noticed a bit of flotsam in the pool, and, unused to idle chatting, hastened to get the pool skimmer off the wall. "I wish we had horses." Wielding the long tool, she added, "I heard that if we get horses we can learn to cut cattle for holistic herding. I guess Fanged Wilds doesn't have money for horses yet."

Marla smiled, watching. "My boyfriend has a four-wheeler. He can haul the meat for us."

Amy maneuvered the aluminum handle of the skimmer, its rickety basket sieving the surface of the water. The floating object was just some cellophane from a pack of cigarettes, nothing too gross. It had probably been stuck to a swimmer's foot. With an incongruous glow of pride, Amy announced, "Yeah, my boyfriend can too. But he might be too busy with his studies." Overriding her intuition, she continued, "He's getting his Ph.D. in forest management."

"No way. My boyfriend is too!" Marla went to a deck chair, sat on its plastic weave, and picked at the tape on the Fanged Wilds package. "I'm so bummed – he's probably moving to Missoula without me." Their eyes met. They froze with a dawning of awareness. Then Marla impulsively ripped open Amy's package. "He says he's afraid of commitment." She gave the colorful F.W.W.P. uniform a vigorous shake to get out the wrinkles, and held it up for Amy to see: blue, with lime-green and magenta rodeo flair.

But Amy had gone back to skimming the water. Marla refolded the shirt. Finally Amy put the pool skimmer back on the wall, turned, and stretched out the front of her husky T-shirt. "Dale said he loved my husky pair." Her lower lip trembled as she stared at the prettier woman.

Marla stammered, "Who picks you up after work?"

Not Dale. "No-one. I walk."

Marla looked out through the dark glass at the parking lot. She shrugged off a chill. "Aren't you afraid, going home this late? ...Unprotected?"

With a clatter of pool skimmer, Amy sat down heavily on an aluminum deck chair. Her eyes hooded in her broad face, she reached over to finger the F.W.W.P. uniform's purplish cowboy fringe. Marla handed it to her. The shirt exuded a cheerful confidence that Amy had never experienced. She stared outside and recited, "I heard, they say to walk as if you have somewhere important to get to."

Marla stood up. "And someone to shoot when you get there. He's waiting for me.

I'm supposed to go to his house. To help him relax."

Amy, face askew, dug fingers into the shirt's denim. "Dale told me he's finishing a chapter in his thesis tonight."

They looked at each other. "He's finishing a chapter." The only movement, at that moment of the night, was aspen leaves falling outside. Marla, without another word, exited out the glass door and walked purposefully to her car. Amy watched her drive away.

The trip wasn't long. When Marla got to Dale's house, the light was on in his living room. The door was unlocked: he expected her. He sprawled in his brown plaid La-Z-Boy, feet up, eyes on a textbook. He held up a finger to hush her as he finished reading. But Marla spoke. "You didn't tell me your girlfriend was in Fanged Wilds, too. Oh, and you didn't mention you had another girlfriend."

Dale looked up, wheels turning. "Uh, who?" He was just buying time.

His #1 girlfriend stamped her foot. "I was in the *army*! I'm trained to *kill!*" Marla hissed. She looked around the room for her belongings.

Dale tousled his hair, slumping with a hang-dog look. "Oh, she's nothing. That was just... that night, when you told me to get lost, y'know, and then... " He hefted his stocky weight and sat up on the arm of the lounger. "Does she think –? It's just a misunderstanding. I was just being nice to her." Marla glared. "She's nothing. She's, like, a *pool cleaner.*" He reached for Marla, weak, his wrists giving up first and flopping like puppies.

She recoiled. "You go talk to her. Amy is heart-broken. Crushed! How could you do that to her?" Marla marched to the bedroom to get her toiletries, snarling over her shoulder, "Stay away from me. I was in the *army.*"

A month later, the two women became best friends. They referred to Dale, their ex-boyfriend, as D-for-Death. But neither of them wanted to kill him anymore, not much... though they discussed him at length, with no affection. "I just wish we could get his four-wheeler."

"He had the nerve to say my haircut could be better. I can't believe how hard I tried to look good enough for him," Amy admitted. "The money I spent on manicures, of all things!" As they hiked, the sound of the women's feet on new snow was drowned out by their laughter. They shouldered their F.W.W.P. rifles like kids on a hunt, surrounded by autumn leaves that glowed golden in the morning sun.

Their uniforms were garish for Montana, but Farraga said there was scientific rationale for lime green vests and magenta fringe. The file of women – Amy, Marla, and several others – looked as if they belonged in Las Vegas; jingling with bear bells, they had an air of absurd Christmas-morning delight, like Rockettes from Andy Kaufmann's Carnegie-Hall special. The camaraderie of the squad was heightened by the two best friends' rapport. "I kept breaking off those damn acrylic nails. What a relief, not to need those anymore!"

"We just need ostrich showgirl headpieces, to go with our uniform," Marla said. "I don't know about y'all, but I would not be caught dead in an outfit like this, if I didn't think it might scare away a bear or hungry pack of wolves."

The others protested, "Wolves are okay. They're scared of *us*."

"Yeah, yeah; wolves aren't that dangerous."

They chatted in the rhythm of their feet. On beat, Amy joked, "Anything that makes me feel like a showgirl is all right by me. Before Fanged Wilds Program, I was a potato, and I'm not even from Idaho."

"You have slimmed right down lately," Marla judged. "Maybe it's that two hundred pounds you lost." They gave each other a triumphant look. "I, on the other hand, feel bloated – must be my period coming. I hope a bear doesn't smell blood and come after me."

Amy listened to everyone's bear bells for a moment, then suggested, "Maybe these uniforms are meant to keep us laughing, and we scare away the bears that way."

Gwen Bumppo, a trainee from Wyoming, piped up. "Y'all know the difference between the scat of black bear and grizzly, right?"

Merrilee, Gwen's sister-in-law from Bozeman, ventured, "Black bear's scat is smaller?"

"Yeah," Gwen nodded. "Smaller, with berries and, like, raccoon fur in it. Grizzly's poop is large, and filled with bells and pepper-spray canisters." She smirked, trying not to squint the painful shiner she had from "Walking into a door." Her husband, Merrilee's brother, was big as a bear and didn't want her to join the F.W.W.P.

Obliviously, Marla chuckled along with the other women, then said, "I heard that some black bears stalk humans. I gotta admit, I like wolves better than bears. I just love watching the wolves. How their family members interact, and play and use strategy to hunt together." The group hiked in silence, till Marla added, "Maybe people find wild animals nice to look at because they exercise and eat right."

Water's white noise made their voices seem smaller. Nearing a river, Amy, walking point, stopped, her broad face open. She pointed up above the next hill at some buzzards hovering and, below them, a couple of swooping, squawking ravens. "Carrion."

Merrilee asked, "So bears and wolves may be close?"

"Probably," Marla conjectured. "Otherwise, the birds would be on the ground. But they might just be signaling the location of prey that the wolves can kill for them."

"Some ranchers bait wolves with carrion," Amy said. She swatted away fluff gently snowing, out of season, from nearby cottonwood trees.

Merrilee, a bit mousy, looked around. "Wolves might run past us any second?" She held her rifle forward, and her fingers checked her woven bear-spray holster. "I guess I want to die young and leave a good-looking corpse, anyway," she joked to disguise her fear.

"You scared?" Gwen teased her. "Of wolves?"

"A dingo ate my baby." Merrilee referred to an incident in Australia, made into a movie with Meryl Streep and a lot of misogyny-spewing extras. And a dingo.

Gwen observed, "At least wolves keep away cougars." After initial alarm, Merrilee fixed Gwen with a wry expression.

"Maybe I can psychic communicate with the wolves so they don't eat you, Merrilee," Amy said. "I took an animal psychic class."

"In Hollywood?" Marla joked.

"In town. At the library." Amy scowled.

Gwen griped, "I wish we had solar ATVs or horses instead of walking. Even in poor countries, they have mules, or, like, camels."

"Farraga from headquarters said there's some transportation for us in the works. Probably not camels, though," Amy said.

Marla snorted. "Camels? Since we dumped Dale – uh, D-death, I could use a hump."

Speaking quickly to abort yet another anti-Dale diatribe, Gwen said suggestively, "Some camels have *two* humps."

"How 'bout it, Amy? We've shared an animal before," Marla joked. "One animal, two humps." Under her breath, she spat, "That prick." She cupped her rifle stock.

Amy resumed hiking and, scanning the horizon, changed the subject. "Some wolves were shot for no reason near here, and they had, like, scientific radio collars on. My in-laws said the wolves weren't even near livestock. It was, like, political assassination."

Following at her heels, Marla was still simmering. "There's only one wolf I'd like to shoot." To make matters worse, Dale was still claiming she owed him some money she'd borrowed.

Merrilee sang to herself, "I feel like walkin' the world, walkin' the world..." She didn't feel like walking at all; she wished she were home in Bozeman.

Gwen, who was in charge of map reading, said, "We're really not that remote, right here."

"Yeah, I went skinny-dipping near here, and a van full of Chinese tourists drove up! Taking photos!" Marla said, "I jumped into the water that fast. It was freezing."

Amy grumbled, "Was that with Dale?" Marla nodded. "He took me there too." She coughed.

"I can't believe I once thought that, if I belonged to Dale-Death, he'd cherish me as much as he loved his four-wheeler." They laughed. "I wish I were joking." Hearing Merrilee hum, Marla marched onward, the rhythm of her feet reminding her of a song from Unsinkable Molly Brown: "If you come from nowhere, on the road to somewhere..." She started to whistle the tune.

"Okay, forget D-for-Death." Amy cleared her throat. "Why don't people take the long view? If wolves keep deer and elk from eating the habitat, the more fish and fowl there are for sportsmen. More species for sightseers to goggle at, more tourist money." She stepped over a fallen branch. Rosanne Burr, the famous face depicted on Amy's hat, looked at the sky. "Then maybe they won't fire me at the motel. They say business dropped off since the earthquake, and then the tornado."

A wolf howled. Wasn't there a song about whistling when you're afraid? Unable to recall it, Merrilee sang cowboy lyrics. "When I die, take mah saddle from the wall. Put it on mah pony and lead 'er from the stall. Tie my bones to 'er back, point our faces to the west. And Ah'll ride the prairie that Ah love the best."

Marla tacitly acquiesced to dropping the subject of Dale. "Let's talk about the weather. What do y'all think, ladies? With global warming, will we get pink flamingos flying around Ole Faithful? And then we'll have to keep an eye out for flamingo poachers. They'll be using those feathers for ladies' hats."

Gwen was part Cheyenne. She said, "There used to be sacred white beavers here. Natives honored them, but I think they ended up as white men's hats."

Marla held up her rifle and quipped, "They won't make a hat out of *my* beaver!"

"Flamingos are cool," Amy mused prudishly, listening to the rumble and toot of a distant train. "Flamingos might bring more tourists."

CHAPTER NINE

NEW RIVER, OREGON, U.S.A.

They could make real money: maybe twenty dollars a button, $100 a pound; it was even more expensive than wild ginseng. Poachers could be desperate in rural economies. Only "magic" psilocybins got them more cash. Farraga pondered. "Where is F.D.R. when we need him? These poachers could be in a W.P.A. Conservation Corps." And amateur mycologists like her could fuel tourism there, just to catch the scent of a matsutake in the wild. Farraga crawled on hands and knees under pine boughs, searching. The ground was raked clean, like a park in England rather than a remote edge of Oregon's coast range.

At Storm Ranch was posted a sign: 'No Mushroom Hunting.' But it seemed every square inch of the wildlife sanctuary was combed. It reminded Farraga of when she was a child, and she thought "rape" was that "bad word, *rake*." Another little girl had written it in the earth of a dirt path, further confusing her. R-A-K-E. Watch out, or they'll *rake* you!

The *matsutake* poachers' rakes sought to harvest the fragrant white spheres before they showed above the surface of the dirt. The fruiting bodies were more valuable before they spread their caps, maybe because – like most babies – they looked so perfect.

But harvesting mushrooms before they'd produced spores was like killing a prepubescent girl; if you wait till she's a mother, her daughters may give birth someday, so that would bring more poundage in the long run. Fungi in the soil was actually necessary to the growth of tall, manly trees. You can't have a forest without living dirt.

A honey mushroom mycelium, a sort of root-mat, was deemed to be the world's largest organism, covering 2,200 acres in eastern Oregon. Raking up bits of the mat may not kill it, but it inhibited fruiting, as if those pubescent girls got no education so just exist and give AIDS to their babies. Or so a depressed middle-aged lady might fancy, if her feminist non-profit venture teetered on shaky foundations. She looked to the earth for answers. Threads of myceliae were like each woman's idea of femininity: they spawn either poison or a feast.

Feeling the sun's radiation, Farraga sighed. Being cooped up with her phone and computer, she'd longed for the wide open spaces. Now she needed to relax and get just one *sniff* of her favorite fungus. She yearned for it. Her craving felt almost like horniness. Farraga sat on a mound of loamy pine needles, in the musk of humus. Maybe she was just frustrated because of her boyfriend, Professor Vimvole, had a busy travel schedule; he'd even become preoccupied and frigid when home. In Japan, *matsutake* was used as an aphrodisiac. Farraga recalled the Japanese myth that women's toes curled when they had orgasm. Should she surreptitiously try some *matsutake* on the professor?

Her toes squirmed in her hiking boots, aching. Oddly, some people thought matsutake smelled like feet. Absurd! The aroma of *matsutake* was divine, in her memory. Like the first time she ever smelled perfume, as she remembered: she was a little girl, and her mother was going out one evening to attend a gala event in the city.

Alone in the bushes, Farraga stretched her neck as if to offer her cheek once again for her mother to pat goodbye with an elegant, white-gloved, fragrant hand. The brushed cotton of the glove still palpable, Farraga could smell that cologne, Chanel Number Five; a glass-stoppered bottle of it sat for years in her parents' bathroom cabinet, dusted with stray talcum from a powder puff.

There in the bushes, Farraga felt paralyzed with the awe that seized her that night, so long ago. It defined *Female*, for her. Her mother towered in high heels; her platinum hair swelled, swept up in a chignon; her white coat was bolstered with shoulder pads; and her petal-soft fingers touched little Farraga like a pungent rose.

Her mother had been a monument to glamor.

But the now-dead lady had been annoyed with the young girl for some reason, and what started as gentle cheek-patting finished with a definite slap. For Farraga, growing up had been loveless. She herself vowed never to inflict childhood on a helpless infant. Maybe Farraga had whined: was it the first time she'd been left with a baby sitter? She remembered wetting her flannel pajamas later that evening, when the teenage sitter, wanting to make a phone call, told her to stay put and watch television: little Farraga's urine had pooled on the quilted vinyl of an ottoman.

That was the best part about wilderness: you could pee nearly anywhere. Squatting now in the underbrush and relieving herself, Farraga looked up to see two squirrels chasing each other, leaping from tree to tree, like an aerial circus. She lost her balance and fell back on her bottom, pant legs in her own puddle. That was another thing about nature: it didn't care how you looked, in a world where vanity seemed like the only way to get love. After struggling back up, she cleaned herself with a tissue that she stored it in a designated baggie. Then she picked pine needles off her haunches. The rodents above chattered.

Squirrel leaps seemed like love, weightless yet descending. What happened to the days when she and Professor Vimvole felt a playful delight with each other? And all the fun they'd had recycling together? Giving all the neighbors CFL lightbulbs when such things were avant-garde? When he kept complaining of "blue balls"? His first kisses were now like Pacific waves crashing into jade tidepools in the memory of someone lost in the desert. How did she lose his interest? Maybe, being devoted to her "cause," she seemed too self-righteous. Was she not enough fun?

Why wasn't she as sensuous and cosmopolitan as other ladies her age? Her friend Marion had just spent a week chanting at an ashram in India, another week learning Thai cooking in Bangkok, and a final week doing yoga on Maui; a potential donor Farraga lunched with, Tonette, had just learned tarantella voodoo in Italy and had an affair with a bi Swede; and another acquaintance went to Tantra retreats on San Juan Island, claiming that the best source of Botox-free renovation was the intoxicating gropes of groups. Was Farraga strange? Why did she spend all her time and money on founding a charity? Her feet still hurt from the high heels she'd worn at the last donors' luncheon, shoes which cost her as much as she'd garnered. Was she too self-negating? Or even masochistic? Why didn't she hobnob her way into the jet-set? Farraga stared at the naked earth. How could she relax and ignore that, even with carbon credits, travel was too polluting?

Anyway, the Oregon State Motto was, "She Flies With Her Own Wings." She pulled and zipped up her pants and, as she stood, idly fondled the F.W.W.P. macrame bear-spray holster looped on her belt. It seemed immoral to seek self-gratification, to become too at ease in this imperiled world. So the Fanged Wilds and Women Program – that happily justified a little expedition, like this foray to New River – was her outlet, and her treasure.

The weekend she had hatched the whole idea, a few years before, she'd also felt neglected. She told Vimvole that she was going to the coast for a couple days of mushrooming. She'd invited him, of course; none of her other friends could understand why she liked crawling under bushes. Vimvole had got a kick out of it, though, a few times, as if he'd been a child at an Easter-egg hunt; of course it took a year to convince him to actually eat any of their gourmet booty, such as chanterelles and morels.

After dinner – oyster mushrooms that night that she'd found near a stream behind the local elementary school – they'd been doing some bed-time reading. Propped on pillows, Professor Vimvole, ambitious as usual, was surrounded by research documents, absorbed in cross-referencing. Farraga had been wearing a negligee, hopeful that his research couldn't compete with slinky pink and tan silk. But he didn't seem swayed by the lingerie, nor was he dismayed by her threat to be gone all weekend.

So she mentioned her fear: "A cougar might land on top of me, fangs first. I'll be on all fours, preoccupied with picking mushrooms... I may be dinner long before I find dinner." Then she'd climbed out of bed and showed him her (bare legs and) solution: she had a Japanese Noh mask, and held it against the back of her head. "Do you think it's just a tribal superstition that lions are fooled by masks?"

But Vimvole went back to scrutinizing some graphs. "I don't know," he snapped. "Fashion means nothing to me." She sighed: he reminded her of her father, R.I.P., when he was brusque like that.

She got back in bed. Pulling the eiderdown back over herself, she settled her cheek into her cool pillow, and lay quietly for a while, stymied, contemplating the Teddy Roosevelt bear on the chair in the corner. Big mustache, tiny spectacles on a chain, floppy Rough-Rider hat...

A masculine voice jolted her back awake. The professor suggested she collect elk-dung specimens. Apparently, one of his research associates had a question: what insects gestate in ungulate dung? Thus, empirical data was in order. Vimvole specified locations up a gravel road that he had once scouted with her. At that time – so long ago, a honeymoon moment, exploring wilderness together – they'd set up motion-sensitive cameras to show how much more vigilantly the elks raised their heads while eating, now that the Coast Range of Oregon had wolves back on the scene. So, half asleep, Farraga had agreed to sample elk dung.

CHAPTER TEN

CUMMINS RIDGE, OREGON, U.S.A.

Wolves weren't what worried Farraga. Driving through an old logging town on a rural highway, she realized that, entering elk habitat in hunting season, she was risking her life. She had brought some size-fourteen flip-flops and empty Coors cans to scatter beside her tent so it would seem as if a man were camping. She'd pieced together hideous "safety orange" clothing: an old baseball cap and one of the Professor's "CVSU Wild Boars" T-shirts. But even taking those measures, she might accidentally be shot...

...Or worse. It was football season. A fierce "civil-war" rivalry existed between vocational, Mormon-fratboy Cow Valley State, versus Mid-Oregon University. The latter's more liberally academic jocks' mascot was an ugly duckling. So a Mid-Oregon Fowl, his blood lust stirred by the gladiatorial games, might savage Farraga like Leda. It was bad luck to be Ducked: the "Hippier than Thou" ganja-&-Ganges gang could worship nature to the point of being completely lax about hygiene and sanitation. The city of McCarthy was a sort of petri dish for anarchists. If only she could explain: wasn't the most revolutionary phenomenon a female being an individual?

But communication may be futile. Despite all the marijuana on that Duck U. campus, dreadlocks didn't ensure any "Peace-Love-Dope" passivity. Those youngsters' blood sugar careened from having the munchies, the true "reefer madness." And some of those kids – the "living off the land" types – might be stumbling through the hills, seeking free meat, shooting anything that moves. Were vegans the pacifists she imagined, as carbohydrate overload wreaked havoc with their insulin? They might mug her for her mushroom harvest.

There were generations of poachers here. In 2011, a poacher's house was searched near McCarthy. Police said a grandchild in footed pajamas offered to show how to hunt a deer: "You've got to hold your spotlight in your left hand and kind of rest your rifle on top of it." The officer asked the boy why he needed a spotlight, and the child replied, "Because it's dark outside, and they'll stop and look at you." Hunting after dark was illegal in Oregon. (They'd apparently averaged sixty deer a year. That family, according to the Register Guard, "forfeited to the government 19 rifles, 1,600 pounds of processed and frozen game meat, and 106 pairs of trophy antlers valued at between $180,000 and $400,000." The father and grandfather were sentenced to four deer seasons in jail.)

Roving red-necks were an issue. Self-defense could be perceived as an arrogant challenge. Some home-schooled hillbilly might just shoot Farraga for being female, uppity, and not Ann Coulter. They might leave her, half-dead, for wild animals to devour. As her imagination galloped, Farraga stopped in a gun shop. Now she was glad to be wearing her orange sports-team shirt. There were two blue-collar guys behind the counter. They both laughed at her when she asked if there weren't a three-day waiting period. "Didn't Reagan back the Brady Bill," she chatted, trying to sound Republican, while her reference to history stigmatized her as effete elite.

She hefted several pistols to determine a reasonable weight. Hoping to seem tougher than she felt, she inwardly recoiled from the pointy metal. She was chary of buying something too cumbersome. But she didn't want her first shot to be from some ineffectual Derringer gnat. Momentarily grabbing a Glock, she joked, *"Thar's bars in them thar hills!"* (The gun-shop guys ended up being quite helpful; one of them did some computer hacking for her, a couple years later.)

Back on the road through the coast range, she had a new *gravitas*. Yet she also felt lightened, as if she'd shouldered and fired up a jet pack. "She Flies With Her Own Wings. *Alis volat propriis.*" She was no longer impotent, on that historic day. Though she had a twinge of self-pity, going to a dangerous spot all alone – without a man to protect her or even to care that she was in harm's way – Professor Vimvole might value her more if she presented him with maggot-rich dung.

Close to high noon, the conventional hunters were most likely to take a break. Farraga drove up the mountain road, parked in a wide spot, and hiked to an "elk plateau." Complacent, unharried elk traveled in larger herds and scoured the high ground to keep the upper hand and eat where they could keep a lookout. They browsed on almost everything but the ferns. What might seem – to the untrained eye – like wilderness, had actually been cropped as flat as cow pasture. To a nature lover, hunters' lobbyists and other human encroachment had "normalized the unthinkable."

Maybe it was just nervousness from its being hunting season – wouldn't it upset anyone's digestion to be shot at? – but the elk had diarrhea. Farraga scooped it up, and, eschewing the security of plastic, conscientiously put the brown messy stench into a cardboard box, to allow air. The precious insect larvae would not suffocate. The lady, however, might.

Despite the disgusting wet poop, and the wet weather; despite the cougars and the trigger-happy rapists; despite her boyfriend nonchalantly putting her life at risk, and ignoring her love... Farraga was filled with simple joy. For this: it felt great to be outdoors.

There was another element, among the elements. While her boyfriend stayed safe and warm, Farraga stayed safe and "chill" with her brand new .38 Special. She felt "present and accounted for" with the metal device. For the first time, she wasn't just an optimistic doormat, begging bullies' forbearance. She could walk where she needed to. And as she helped the environment, she could resist being assaulted, raped or eaten.

That gave her the idea for the Fanged Wilds and Women Program.

What could an aging woman, just a decade or two shy of dentures, do for nature? Give it teeth. More teeth. The biodiversity of the forest was gnawed away by foraging. Salmonberry, deciduous huckleberry, elderberry, service berry: lushness was thwarted before a single berry could ripen. Such fruit, oak acorns, and russula mushrooms were foods that wild humans would relish if deer and elk didn't

decimate them first. Herbivores stunted shrubs and trees with their browsing and –
further inland – ate the bark off endangered aspen trees. A giant Sitka spruce, over
200 feet tall, was aborted as a seedling; where were the Fundamentalist anti-
abortionists for that part of God's Creation?

Tramping along behind the Professor's long legs on expeditions for his research,
Farraga had observed the difference between true wilderness, where hoofed
munchers and herbivore irruption were discouraged, versus places like this elk-
dung plateau. Tourists might visit from SoCal, the East Coast or Europe and not
realize how denuded was even an old-growth stand like Opal Creek. Human effects
had hogged the place, leaving sparse remnants of an ecosystem, the disenfranchised
99.999999% of species. Occupy!

To Farraga, deer- and elk-grazed forest was practically a mono-culture, like Iowa;
only, instead of corn, expanses waved of the plants that herbivores didn't savor:
sword ferns and Douglas fir. It was like a prostitute; humans defiled nature and then
pointed to its fallen state to say, "See? It's a hole, really, for us to use. It's easily
replaced." It might as well be a conscious human campaign to de-fang nature and
render it fit only for temporary human use, like a toothless whore (four-foot tall and
with a flat head where you can set your beer.) The ethos of sport hunting was as
inimical to the prissy, precious, inter-working components of an ecosystem as the
prospect of a proper wedding, commitment and marriage was to a bachelor like
Professor Vimvole.

Four years later, Farraga was mountain-biking up that same gravel road. The habitat
that was now looking (to adhere to the tricky metaphor) more like a career girl.
Clusters of frosty-purple huckleberries had escaped other diners' notice; Farraga
stopped to nibble on their gritty tartness. Farraga suspected the huckleberry bush
remained lush because it was near a cliff, where a cougar pouncing from above
could easily knock a deer off its feet, like a boss seducing a slutty secretary. (Put
that metaphor out to pasture.)

Farraga knew that different predators affected prey in different ways. Wolves dog and exhausted their prey, essentially herding it away from riparian areas and other rough ground where it feared unstable footing. Meanwhile, cougars, bobcats, and other felines sneaked up on prey, preferring the ambush. And bears – omnivorous for side dishes – overpowered their main course, till it was the main corpse. Unlike humans, animal predators hunted the weak and contagious, making the health of the whole herd stronger. Where were the N.R.A.'s family values? Big bucks, patriarchs, and matriarchs shouldn't be prized dead, just alive. Human killers were predisposed to destroy families by disrupting the hierarchy. Otherwise, for instance, orphaned cougars had no parents to dissuade them from stalking joggers. Nature became a 'hood without authority figures.

And wolf packs ended up playing poker in bars down dark alleys, getting painted in anthropomorphous poses by third-rate artists who sold the posters to hang over pool tables.

Or so she mused. As she popped the tart berries into her mouth – thinking of how good their anthocyanins were for her wrinkles – Farraga was off guard. A teenage cougar that had been stalking her noticed a black bear into whose vicinity Farraga had biked. The bear was eating blackberries on a steep incline, a little behind and below Farraga's bicycle. A pack of wolves had also been watching the bear, loping and hoping there would be bear-kill to steal. The wolves were lazy and taking it easy, still digesting the flesh of a murder victim whose body had been dumped near the gravel road.

The cougar, wolves and bear sniffed Farraga's scent. It was not like sniffing French perfume on a white glove. It was more like driving by a dubious but aromatic burger joint and deciding if the possible stomach-ache and eventual self-recriminations should outweigh the temptation to stop.

Only, of course animals didn't have much remorse. They just got scratches, or wasted time on a meal that wasn't satisfying, then they felt a bestial sort of regret about that. They'd think, "I'll remember not to do THAT again," as they picked the bells and pepper-spray canisters out of their teeth. That image flashed through

Farraga's head as she got a momentary sense of being watched. She stepped away from the huckleberry bush, her hand on the woven holster of her .38.

She gasped. What good fortune: she saw some purple blewit mushrooms under the bush! The cougar slinked closer as Farraga bent to pick the mushrooms. Was that her tummy grumbling? The cat positioned its rear claws to leap. But the cougar was wary of poaching in the bear's territory, so it didn't lunge yet.

Poor blewits; their odor and names were so undignified. *Clitocybe nuda* – the Latin name was like a sophomoric joke – nude clit! Har har! Farraga took a lung-full of blewit molecules, its aroma uncannily like canned orange-juice concentrate. She caressed its molded, firm edges; it reminded her of a taffeta and crinoline skirt, with an aristocratic starchiness that might only have received respect in another era, before the ubiquity of freezer Minute Maid and nude clits.

She looked around. If only she found blewits more often. They grew in clusters. Probably animals – deer, squirrels, mice – ate them before she found them. But maybe she'd find more and more, now that there were wolves in the Coast Range, protecting bushes for mushrooms to hide under. Maybe blewits in abundance would gain commercial value. But poachers tended not to take the long view. Meanwhile, wolves and cougars might do some unauthorized harvesting of poachers.

Farraga hid her bike in some rhododendrons. She kicked a burst of spores from an over-ripe puffball mushroom (also called *pedo de lobo*, or wolf fart.) Then she walked up an elk trail into thick forest, looking for more blewits; maybe she'd find enough for a meal. Glimpses of ocean disappeared as she gained elevation.

The bear, wary of the scent, lumbered further away from the human. The wolves, on the other hand, treaded nearer, out of curiosity: that human was slow. And small!

There were some red depressions in the fir duff. Farraga dropped to her knees. Some people liked these lobster mushrooms; there was nothing fishy about that. They did have a good crunch. She dug up a couple, to share with friends, or to dehydrate and package nicely for the gift baskets she occasionally assembled for a generous donor. She put the mushrooms into her fanny pack. Then she stood and took out her .38 Special. Her mushroom collecting, compared to poachers', was like the difference between your boyfriend just flirting with another woman, and sneaking off to some kind of orgy with fashion models on a private island.

Greed was not good. Right? Fanged Wilds and Women Program was for establishing the most basic balance in nature. She idly aimed her gun at a Douglas fir across the road, then, more boldly, shot a round into the air, toward the towering tree tops. She didn't notice the bushes rustle below.

CHAPTER ELEVEN

BALMORAL, SCOTLAND

His Majesty was touring the ancestral grounds with Secretary of State Sarah Pail. She was visiting Britain for the first time. "Nice castle. Those hunting trophies – awesome! And whoever wore the armor had such nice, trim waists." Madam Pail sat up straighter in the car seat, hands on her own perky figure.

The King averted his eyes, gazing longingly out at the pines of the last remaining wilderness on the Isles. Their cavalcade followed an upland dirt road, toward an outlook point. "Indeed. Did you know? We'd like to reintroduce wolves in Wales. To help manage the holistically herded Carneddau ponies on Snowdonia's upland," the King chatted. "To keep them in tight formation."

"I love tight formations." There was a silence. "Not near as *much* landscape here as Alaska," Madam Pail commented, swaying as their vehicle wound its way between blunt crags. "In Alaska, we have more room for animals," she said, breath held till an expulsion: "Right beside the mash potatoes. I tell my vegan friends, if God didn't intend us to eat animals, why did He make them out of meat?" Her hillbilly hoot filled the small space.

The King nodded, chuckled, and said to his guest, "Ah." The vehicle, a Land-e, rounded another curve. Conversation lagged. But, as their Land Rover came to a halt, as if jolted into action, the King stated, "The glens are growing into dells as our new wolf packs keep the red deer light on their feet."

Sarah Pail leaned forward, making sure she heard right, then commented conspiratorially, "In the States we have a phrase, 'Light in the loafers.' It means..." She snorted, "The sort of person who doesn't go in for anything rough."

A Royalty Protection constable opened the door for her. Apart from the security detail at attention, everyone stretched their legs, ambling around to admire the vista. Then Madam Pail returned to the King's side. She put a hand on his back. The King's eyes became saucers at the touch: detectable through the melton wool, she was running her fingernails up his spine. "It it so gracious of you to let us hunt your property, Your Majesty. I only wish you and the princes were coming along."

Reined with practiced affability, the King quipped, "Well, Madam, it's not that we're 'light in the loafers,'" he reassured her, "We love a good hunt as much as anyone." He glanced at Dick Chainey, who had circled purposefully, squinting in all directions, and was now walking toward the aide's arsenal, arm outstretched. The King knew Chainey had shot another hunter in the face. Surveying the heath diplomatically, he continued, "Hunts can be perilous, though. I do hope the only thing that gets shot today is the deer."

Madam Secretary laughed and said, "Oh, that thing about me shooting wolves, that is so overblown." She gave him a grin. "It's not like this is Alaska."

"No," said the King. "It's more like Canada, I suppose."

A special agent handed Madam Pail a rifle, which she shouldered with an imperceptible wince: she'd had a hard work-out at the hotel gym in Jerusalem the day before. Behind her, an English constable spoke *sotto voce* into his microphone. "I thought Dick Chainey was out of commission. Over."

Royalty Protection's radio response cackled, "They cloned him in the '80s. Karl Rove's brainchild. So to speak. Over."

The English agent sternly tested radio communication once again. "I wish they'd clone Mrs. Pail. Over."

On his earphone, Royalty Protection's command control said, "Roger that."

The constable said to himself, "I'd roger that, all right." He'd heard Pail was opposed to abortion under any circumstances, so he momentarily had a fantasy of her carrying his spawn. Twins ran in his family, so – as his conscious mind focused on detecting any suspicious movement in the forested hills – his unconscious had him lounging in a hunting lodge in Alaska while Sarah - that maverick Joan of Arc - breastfed their twin girls, whom he also, as his fantasy proceeded, eventually impregnated.

Then Dick Chainey accidentally shot the constable in the face. Later, as the ambulance drove up, Chainey commented to Pail, "What's the big deal? Medicine is free in this nanny-state." Pail shrugged. The clone turned toward the red of the setting sun to warm his blood.

MANHATTAN, NEW YORK, U.S.A.

Fang-shaped pens were stealth missiles: Diana was surreptitiously flinging pens at her Tiki-mask target as she talked to her boss Farraga on video chat. "No," she said, "not too many people have trouble with my British accent."

"I should have put you on conference call." Farraga had been arranging a training weekend – a demonstration – for interested parties in England, "And I kept being proper, saying, 'I beg your pardon,' so many times, I finally switched back to your All-American '*What?*'"

"Pardon me?" Diana was distracted by her penmanship.

Farraga explained, "I could understand a completely foreign language better than that partially foreign one!"

"Well," Diana attempted a stereotypical Briticism: "I do so look forward to our rendezvous, ever so." She added with Victorian flourish, "We'll take tea."

"Right-o," Farraga giggled. "And what's your cell, M'lady, if we need further coordination?"

Diana was abashed. "I'm sorry, I don't have a new cell phone yet." She looked at her shabby surroundings. "I'm short on cash."

"Oh, you poor dear. I know we should pay you more. But you know, we have to help buy new uniforms for the Armed Forces." Farraga laughed. "Taxpayer humor, there."

"Yes. I know my salary's as much as possible." Diana grimaced, the last pen flung.

Farraga tisked. "Do you at least get some time to further your studies, in the lulls? How is your Portuguese?"

Diana uncovered her flash cards, piled loosely in their carton under some invoices. "Yes, my Portuguese is coming along." She pulled one card out: *Mentira*/Lie. Before she realized what was happening, with a thump and a splash, Derek appeared in the entrance window. He bent out of sight to tie up his boat but soon clambered closer. He waved and took the packages from inside the ledge. He studied each address as if merely being conscientious in his job, ensuring that no irregularities would hinder prompt delivery. But his eyes betrayed him, after seeking her in the dim light, by lingering when they locked on hers.

Startled, she pretended to listen to Farraga. Diana was shy. She pulled the flash cards out and held them up, arranging them according to an imaginary system. "All the romance languages come more easily, once you survive the first. The first is the beast." She ultra-casually waved goodbye to Derek, elbow down like a royal's, accidentally knocking the carton over the edge of her desk and spilling the Portuguese flash cards onto the floor. Did Derek see her clumsiness betray her infatuation? Maybe his eyes hadn't adjusted from the bright sun.

FORX, WASHINGTON, U.S.A.

Rain drummed on the awning outside. A falter in the rhythmic splashing syncopated with a light bulb's flicker on the twitching wet shine of a newcomer's face. The bar patrons halted their desultory drivel. Cyrene, tending the bar for reasons unknown even to her, nodded at the new arrival. "Been huntin'?" she asked casually after a glance at his soaked camouflage jacket.

The hunter grunted an affirmative and added boldly, "It's not the same since those damn wolves took over the Olympic range." He took his beer, looked at a chair, but hesitated, opening the floor to a response that might herald his arrival among like minds.

Near him at the bar, a burly beer-drinker, Ted, was complicit. "That elk carcass I just found sure wasn't killed by vampires."

The bartendress gave Ted a tepid, familiar smirk. Cyrene challenged the beefy man: "Hey, those are my ancestors you're talking about."

Ted answered, buck-toothed, "Vampires?"

At his attempt at a Dracula accent, Cyrene chuckled. "No. I'm part Quileute. So wolves are my ancestors." She moved some glasses off the formica counter-top. "If white men don't like my wolf relatives, they should give them their own rez." Finding an unexpected source of power in her own words, the bartendress softened the politics, reassessing her own situation: "Just like you keep me behind the counter."

The wet stranger removed his coat and took a seat, his back turned, so he didn't see the bartendress defy her stiff jeans and leap preternaturally lightly onto the bar. She tightened the flickering light bulb.

Having watched her levitation, slack-jawed Ted leaned back on his stool to regard Cyrene. "How in *hell* did you do that?"

The bulb burned out with a flash. "What? Destroy light bulbs?" Cyrene towered over him, unscrewing. "I guess it's finally time for one of those new, sickly blue ones." Bending her denim-clad legs, she jumped back down, tossing the used bulb in a trash can behind the bar. Reflexively, she grabbed a rag and wiped the counter where her feet had been, as clean as a cat.

The wet hunter turned to watch her rear and asked, "Do what? What did she do?" His grin was ill-at-ease, since his curiosity implied ignorance.

No one answered. The silence was like at a family gathering, where a child, as if psychic, mentions something no-one wants the patriarch to know: the locals instinctively hushed. The newcomer let it drop. More than answers, he craved a sense of belonging. And he did fit in: since he'd taken off his camo coat, everyone in the bar was uniformly sporting plaid flannel. Their colors were traditional reds and greens, as if in a fairytale about Little Red Riding Hood and the Wolf that Ate Christmas.

But Cyrene's plaid shirt was pink and purple. She smiled over her shoulder, revealing unusually large canines. The men in the dark bar all watched her on her way to the storeroom to get a compact florescent bulb. Something inexpressible was afoot. The men, feeling vulnerable, acted bored.

CHAPTER TWELVE

OREGON COAST STATE PARK, U.S.A.

Campfires helped illuminate the road as they walked from the restroom. Hans and Greta Hütte of Duisburg were sixty-ish, semi-retired, and sightseeing through Western Oregon. They had toured California a decade previous: San Francisco, Hollywood, and the Monorail through Yosemite. Now they were seeking an experience even closer to nature. Towel and toothbrush in hand, the solid couple were almost back to their tent when a bike light approached them, dancing as the rider avoided potholes in the parking lot.

Farraga passed her car with its bike rack and rode up to the tourists, hyperventilating. "I just saw a cougar!" She ejaculated, "Up there!" She pointed up the road, gasping with glee and fright.

The couple was oddly unmoved.

"I just saw a cougar!" Farraga repeated. The tourists stared at her. Straddling her bike, Farraga steadied her feet on the ground. She calculated. On a hunch, she asked, "*Sprechen Sie Englisch?"*

They nodded, and Hans Hütte said with a heavy German accent, "Yes. Vve speak *Englisch*," as if refuting an accusation. "Yes. Vvhat is... cougar?"

Farraga defined, "Mountain lion."

The woman confirmed, "*Loewe?"*

"Yes! *Loewe*. Lion. *Ich hab'ein gesehen! Gerade gesehen!* I just saw my first one!"

The couple still seemed strangely unimpressed. Farraga giggled at the contrast between her agitation and the couple's phlegmatism. It was as if the campers were half asleep already, in the womb of their tent, instead of exposed, along with her, to the jaws of night.

It reminded Farraga of when she'd called an acquaintance – a wonk from the university administration – near a state park to warn, "I just walked behind your house and smelled a forest fire!" And the home-owner dismissed, "Oh, you probably just smelled someone's chimney." Farraga of course then called 911; the dispatcher said that tree-fellers were burning slash, smoke that smelled like an inferno, not like someone's Yule log. But her acquaintance had acted as if Farraga were crying rape while pointing at a dildo. Why were some people so phlegmatic? Was it Prozac? Did their Personal Savior make them so significant that catastrophes, even global ones, would only happen to someone else?

Maybe the wonk's automatic reaction was that Farraga, being female, was a hysteric. At the possibility of immolation, might one not give even Chicken Little the benefit of doubt? Was it like an injured bird being attacked by her own flock, pecked into silence for squawking lest she attract predators? Was that the rationale for "shooting the messenger"?

Climate deniers: with civilization at stake, might they not have made a few allowances? It's a faulty mental model: "I'm in my home, therefore I cannot be in a forest fire," or, "That alarm sound is annoying, so I'll destroy its source rather than seek its cause." Or, "I'm relaxing on vacation, therefore I cannot be eaten by a lion."

The campground was quiet. These unreasonably reasonable Germans seemed to regard her as untamed. *Order, vvee must haff Order.* But she'd just seen her first cougar! Was a lion too uncivilized to be acknowledged, too challenging to the status quo? Farraga attempted to convince: "A cougar is dangerous, you know. *Gefaerlich. Loewe.* Lion."

The German camper shifted his toothbrush to the other hand: Hans was preparing his English to pronounce a statement. After an interpreter's time lapse, he scoffed, "They have posting warnings about many things here. Poisson oak. Tsunami. I see no warning of lion."

Did he think she was some kind of anarchist? Farraga's adrenaline was still churning from being too close to a predator. Didn't the Germans want to share the most thrilling event of her animal-loving life? She said with finality, "Well, they're rather rare. I just had to warn you. Now you can help me warn your fellow campers." She pointed to the other tents, then up at the line of trees leaning over the road. "*Sie warten in Baueme*" – she acted out pouncing – "*und bissen Sie im Kopf!*" She clawed toward the blameless woman's head; such was the pecking order. "The cougar I saw was stalking, though. Walking." Her hand crossed like an animal in front of the balking couple; her middle finger lurked and looked at them insidiously.

Greta Hütte finally spoke. "What you call this animal?"

"Cougar."

"*Kuger.*"

"Mountain lion. Puma. They hide in the trees, and jump on you." She observed their continued disbelief. "Someone should have warned you. Do you know where is the park ranger?"

The man pointed down the road. "Oh, there is an old man and old woman in *ein* R.V."

"Ha!" Farraga sat and put one foot on a bike pedal. "Volunteers. No budget for pro's anymore." She faced them but was talking to herself, for want of better options. "And those park rangers looked so good in their uniforms. You like uniforms too, *nicht*? *Jawohl*. Did you see the research showing that just wearing a uniform increases a person's attentiveness? Well, campers have to look out for themselves, now. And for one another. Predators do promote situational awareness, so you pay attention to your surroundings. Too bad for kids with earphones blasting." She gave the tourists a little scowl. Why did they treat her like a ninny? How many ninnies spoke German on the fly? She grouched *auf Deutsch,* "Don't thank me. I was just excited to finally see my first mountain lion. And not be eaten." Farraga bared her teeth and pointed up at the trees, nodding.

Nazis had exterminated her relatives, after all. Yet her blood no longer trickled within a helpless herd: I am woman, hear me roar. Farraga quipped, *"Kuche, Kinder, Kirche... Kopfgebiss."* Dredged from the archives of her brain, her reference was to the K.K.K. of German sexism: women's lives were supposed to be comprised of only Cooking, Kids and Church. Farraga added, "Bite to the head." She gave the tourists a wave and biked back to the parking lot, calling over her shoulder, piqued, *"Schlafen Sie gut.* Sleep well."

She loved to bike. It was so lovely to unwind and smell the night air, rather than always using the car. But she hadn't driven to the coast with Professor Vimvole just to enjoy nature. She'd biked from house to house to interview prospective sea-otter monitors. The F.W.W.P. recruits would help protect the local Marine Reserve's kelp forest from urchin infestation. Some fishermen sabotaged the Reserve, feeling that they themselves should be protected as an endangered species. Fishing gear could accidentally entangle otters, animal acrobats who competed with humans to eat the sparse remaining mollusks and crustaccans. The otters, in turn, were like Chiclets for killer-whales to chew. So Farraga recruited compassionate ladies, retired to the coast, who had time and boats for ocean commotion. One rollicksome lady was even an animal psychic who tried to convince the orcas not to eat the "wacky water weasels."

Farraga put her bike on the rack on her trunk. Then she drove her air-fueled car through south Newerport to pick up Vimvole at a Climate Change event of the National Oceanic and Atmospheric Administration. He'd forgotten to get her a ticket to the banquet. But she didn't mind: the former $38 million NOAA Center had been built on the land-fill of the Yaquina Bay flood plain in a tsunami zone near the Cascadia fault. The new facilities were on a federal wharf on the sand. Driving down the narrow access road, Farraga was glad she'd just spent the day taking tea with ladies in their modest living rooms: they all had the common sense to live above the high-water mark.

ASTURIAS PRINCIPALITY, SPAIN

The sun rose over misted mountains. An amorous shepherd lurked, his whistling of *Capriccio Espagnol* drowned out by disturbingly human-voiced bleating of his flock. Inside, senoritas' red bell-bottoms rustled against each other: inserted down the pants sides were taffeta flamenco ruffles trimmed with black lace. The Spaniards' form-fitting fabric had, instead of traditional polka dots, jaguar rosettes. A carved claw – a tribute to the endangered Cantabrian brown bear – adorned each glossy black chignon. Chilled in the dawn dew, the shepherd hoped one of these beauties would somehow hear his whistling, look outside, and notice him. He could brag to them about his sustainable grazing technique, keeping his sheep close together.

But the ladies' attention stayed within the neighborhood *taberna*. Over tiny espressos, these women of the F.W.W.P. outpost in Villaviciosa were preoccupied with examining a package. It was apparently intended (as the internal invoice indicated) for North Carolina. The size-zero natives removed what they first thought was some sort of banner or tent. The bartender protested: "But it's shaped like a shirt."

As the others held up the denim shirt in disbelief, Ofelia Del Toro phoned the New York headquarters. The chica there said not to bother returning the erroneous mailing. "*No importa, diga la chica Di-anna.*" Later, up in a meadow, Ofelia and the other young Spanish women made tripods of branches and, on the crossbeam, nailed the voluminous garment up to provide shade for their wolf patrols.

Iberian wolves, numbered around 500 in the 1970s, now roamed the mountains of Spain in the thousands. Back in 2000, Asturian farmers submitted compensation claims to the government for sheep killed by wolves. The record claims numbered more than the tally of sheep actually in the region. Some of the non-existent sheep might have been killed by domestic dogs (known worldwide as "Rovers") who also may or may not have existed. No sheep pierced by unicorns were found, which is fortunate because no compensation program was in place for such an eventuality.

However, possibly due to Salvador Dali's legacy, the love-starved shepherd discovered a large watch melted, sizzling, over a leg of mutton. Its ticks talked. The shepherd wished one of the beautiful F.W.W.P. would look at him someday, so he could tell her of the miracle.

CHAPTER THIRTEEN

SKAGAFJÖRDUR, ICELAND

True story: the first polar bear in fifteen years swam 300 kilometers, or two hundred miles, to get here. Since polar bears can only swim about fifteen miles at a time, he hitched rides on ice floes, apparently, from Greenland. Police killed him.

Then, one month later, another polar bear made it to Saudarkrokur. She was bolting back toward the sea when police shot and killed her.

Another polar bear came to Thistilfjordur, making the tally three polar bears on Iceland in twenty years. Police killed it.

Diana fell asleep at her desk one day and dreamed that a crowd of Icelanders wearing bulky hand-knit sweaters were preparing to protect themselves from polar bears. They lit sparklers. With a shout of warning and exuberance, someone set off some firecrackers. Then a man ignited the bonfire, its blaze illuminating a ring of smiles in the world's oldest democracy.

An avuncular man announced, "This is how we can be safer around the next polar bear. And Morlocks." The crowd cheered. Apparently everyone there was familiar with The Time Machine; when night lasts several months, you watch a lot of old movies (Diana reasoned, as she slept.)

But a bonfire could be just as fun, and therapeutic in the winter. Some Icelanders roasted marshmallows; some sat and knitted with bone needles; while others – trigger-happy, Viking types – went off to hunt the greedy bankers who caused the "bearish" economy...

Then Diana woke up. The Icelandic commotion was really a flock of seagulls outside. She wiped the drool off her desk. The office was unbearably muggy.

CRAWFORD, TEXAS, U.S.A.

A rancher and his hired hand were clearing brush. Jorge, the hired hand, didn't talk much, since it was expected he'd put all his effort into the labor of his sweating muscles. Anyway, Jorge knew that talking would just parch his throat.

But that was no deterrent for the rancher, who filled the scorched, still air with his own opinions as if they were nectar. "Them folk that like bears and wolves so much, should just have wolves and bears in their apartment buildings." He cackled, then coughed and hacked. "Gummint wants me to herd my cattle packed together like they're chased by wolves. Say that'll rebound the grassland and the aquifer. My cattle won't get fat if I run them like that! How 'bout a herd o' them politicians come stampede the draws like they chased by wolves? Hell. Churn the dirt and shit fertilizer? Politicians can just *talk* fertilizer."

Jorge nodded with a smile. His feet crunched on dry leaves as he went to throw a dead sapling into the back of the pickup. It would be kindling for his friend, Mrs. Inez, to use in her grill. She liked to sear meat before she put it in the chili in her solar oven. Jorge's dry mouth watered at the thought of all the types of peppers she grilled with drippings from the meat.

With a leather-gloved hand, the rancher swatted a fly perched on his nose. He elaborated, "I mean, the gubmint should put wolves and bears in the middle of cities...'cuz that's where all the wolve and bear lovers are." He spit a mouthful of dust. With Jorge as audience, he held his pitchfork like a weapon, and took a stance. "They threaten my livestock, I shoot 'em. Wolves and bears, too."

The older man bent back into his work. His pitchfork got stuck in a clump of twigs that he had aimed at the burn pile. He kicked it with his foot, detonating a satisfying explosion of dead leaves. The rancher started to feel as if Jorge were almost a buddy. He grew more intimate. "Nothing personal, but – they call 'em Mexican wolves, they belong in Mexico. Immigration is fine, within reason. But like Ma Ferguson said, 'English was good enough for Jesus.' Those wolfs don't howl in English." Pleased when Jorge laughed, the rancher boldly admitted, "I leave meat out to get those wolves in rifle range."

Jorge nodded. He knew the rancher was a lousy shot, especially when he was drunk. And as targets, Mexican wolves weren't much bigger than coyotes. He smiled at the thought of his boss's over-confident potshots.

Encouraged by Jorge's amusement, the rancher got giddy. "Maybe I should put one of them Starbucks here to get those city enviro-mental-tists to come 'round closer. Eh? Just put a Starbucks a couple hun'erd yards from my front porch." He was still chuckling as he fired up his chain saw.

Then Diana woke up again. A speed boat whined past, outside the window. What was that dream she just had? How could she revive? Tea was no longer enough to keep her alert. Diana yawned, trudged over to the office cooler, and filled her ceramic mug with water, then added a teaspoon of organic coffee powder. The particles swirled before they dissolved into coffee darkness, its fragrance making her sigh.

CHIAPAS, MEXICO

The foreman looked a little like Juan Valdez. But the coffee beans he was sniffing were not destined for a Folger's can. They were shade-grown, and subsidized by Starbucks. The shade was not just a tax shelter, but a genuine ecological windfall. The coffee shrubs hunched under mango trees, crowded with fruit, the air rich with its tang; above spread a canopy of hardwoods alive with birds.

With a cry from its beak, a resplendent quetzal darted overhead. Shafts of daylight flashed on its iridescent feathers. In a former civilization, headdresses featured blue-green plumes stolen from its tail. The bird was worshiped as a divinity, and any Mayan or Aztec who killed a resplendent quetzal faced the death penalty. Such quetzal killers might be decapitated on a temple pyramid while, nearby, bright red quetzal breasts, still living, winged aloft like splattered blood. Or the hapless hunters – poachers, as it were – flung down a pit to drown, might look up to see aqua tail-feathers trailing across the sky, blues that disappeared from the men's last sight. By ancient tradition, entrails of such criminals could be fed to animals in the royal zoo. History abounded with such brutality... and snacks.

Modern protection for the quetzal bird now involved, standing under the mango trees, a woman whose colorful uniform was resplendent in its own way. Its feather and animal patterns identified her with the F.W.W.P. The woman, Maria, shouldered a rifle. Her mother had been a Zapatista rebel; experienced since childhood with warfare, Maria carried the gun with a relaxed readiness. She didn't lack investigative acumen: she asked the coffee-plantation foreman, "Seen any jaguar?"

He shook his sombrero. "No. Just lots of birds and monkeys, come to steal berries!" His teeth showed white as he squinted toward her breasts. Voice deepening, he added, "I want to nibble your berries."

Maria was glad to have a gun. And her patrol partner Juanita would be back soon, when she was done peeing behind a bush. Maria made a show of scrutinizing the trees as she observed, "Jaguar eats the animals who eat berries." She walked away.

Monkeys squabbled in the jungle beyond them. The foreman scowled at the eyes on the back of Maria's hat. Those Fanged-Wilds women were too stuck up, he thought. But their microfinance was a clear benefit to the crops, which were suffering in the unrelenting heat. He himself didn't feel at all well. The foreman wondered if he drank too much coffee. Listening to the monkeys, he wondered if they, too, were caffeine-frenzied.

A flock of buntings chattered, fleeing from a tree below which Juanita emerged between two coffee bushes. "*Hola*. Where's Maria?" Juanita adjusted her scarf, spreading over her collarbone its print of the Virgin of Guadalupe or – to be more authentic – Coatlaxopeuh: She Who Crushes Serpents. Under it, hidden in her ample cleavage, nestled a ripe mango that Juanita couldn't wait to eat.

The foreman saw that the second woman wasn't armed. "Wouldn't you rather stay here with me?" he asked. His heart wasn't in the proposal; he felt ill, with a burning in his chest. But it was expected of him as an *hombre macho* to make advances on any attractive or unaccompanied woman... Especially if she wasn't carrying a gun. Little did he know that Juanita considered beaning him on the nose with her soft, warm mango. She picked a likely direction and set off to find her friend Maria.

KAA-IYA GRAN CHICA NATIONAL PARK, BOLIVIA

The thorn scrub made for rough going, even where there were trails. The Bolivian women had the brightly colored canvas legs of their F.W.W.P. uniforms tucked into the tops of thick, red socks; their boots protected their ankle bones. They marched in line, the rhythm of their steps syncopated with bursts of conversation. Ahead of them, many hooves tapped the tired earth to awaken: their herd of alpacas munched on the run, the grazing method approved by the Savory Institute to encourage vegetation. Softly barking a word, the professional herders warned one another of obstructions in their path – rock, branch, cracked earth – and avoided brushing against scrub that might be crawling with bugs.

One woman, Pilar, commented to the others, "Never mind the many jaguars, and the many poachers... What bothers me is so many ticks." A few steps further on, she repeated the word with revulsion: "*Garrapatas.*" She elaborated, "The poachers have guns; the jaguar have big teeth..." Her companions turned to look at her as she pressed a finger to the skin of her brown arm. Her face puckered like a demon child nursing. "Ticks have little, *pequeñitos* hungry mouths."

The corners of their mouths upturned, the women marched on; they were unified in humorous indignation at their tiny adversaries. Finally, with ironic lilt, Luisa, the woman ahead of Pilar, said, "Poachers eat birds; birds eat ticks. Ticks eat everyone."

"Si." Her friend laughed and held up her gun. "*Quiero fusilar garrapatas.* I want to shoot ticks."

Another woman said, "The jaguars eat what eats the birds." She portrayed with a flopping-noodle arm what animal she meant.

Luisa confirmed, "*Una comadreja*: a weasel." Joy released, the women mimicked weasels like a wave.

They resumed their progress. Pilar nodded. "The jaguars eat poachers and weasels. But they won't eat us, as long as we stay close together!" A large bush scratched their pants, one woman's leg after the other. They kept walking, all in rhythm, many short women, as if one long body.

MANHATTAN, NEW YORK, U.S.A.

Diana yawned and stretched, from her fingers to her toes, Doc Martens knocking on the enclosed confines of her desk with a hollow sound that surprised her, as if she'd forgotten how long her legs were. She struggled to wake fully. Her boss was coming the next week; Diana had to get her act together. But all she wanted to do was nap.

CHAPTER FOURTEEN

MANHATTAN, NEW YORK, U.S.A.

In syncopation to the percussion of the water lapping outside, a brand-new aquarium bubbled across the room from Diana's desk. In and out of the beam of a spot light, piranhas' tails wiggled, propelling their search throughout the tank. Their lower jaws jutted as if to pout at the lack of meat: they would rather be swimming in a fresh carcass, rather than in a glass box.

Diana surveyed the new (used) furniture. "Oh, Farraga. This is so much nicer. Thanks so much." Diana took an armful of Fanged Wilds clothing from her short visitor. The tall employee piled it on the highest shelves of just-constructed cabinetry, its wood reclaimed from empty offices in the building.

Farraga set the postage meter on the new table. "Volunteers should be able to handle mail orders from now on. The system is all set up. It should be easy to understand, even for transient volunteers. So you won't have to juggle everything, the way you've been doing, dangling from our shoestring. I am so impressed with your organizational skills. You will go far, young lady. I can't believe you kept up as we got more and more orders."

Diana choked up with the praise. "I was starting to feel as if I know the delivery boy better than my own family," she admitted. "Of course, my family is back in the U.K., which seems more distant by the day."

"How are they?"

"Capital. My mum is learning a little Urdu and getting to know some Paki neighbors. I met them on video chat."

"I bet you'd love to pop over for a visit." Farraga tilted her head in sympathy.

"But it's terribly dear."

"Unless you know someone with a private jet," Farraga joked enigmatically. "Aw, you must miss her. That's what having a career will do for you. Hearth and home come second. Well, think of me as family. Grab a pal and come have dinner with us – me and my boyfriend – tonight." She went to fuss over a wall map, brushing the sag out of it. "He – Professor Vimvole – is speaking at an environmental conservation conference here, as I think I mentioned. They paid his expenses. So I saved money on the hotel! He's a renowned scientist, but he spends as if he were still penniless in grad school. The professor could probably fund our entire program himself! But – well, I did get a free hotel room."

Farraga repositioned pins in the map to mark locations of patrol units: Japan, Russia, Spain. Then the older woman took a deep breath. "We might have to find a restaurant that is inexpensive." She blushed. "Can you recommend a bistro that has vegan food? Imagine this: the professor said he loves my cooking *too* much! So he became vegan. I told him too much raw food is making him too thin. And he needs cholesterol to think clearly." Farraga clapped her small hand on her mouth. "He took that as an insult. Sometimes I wonder if gentlemen of a certain age can receive input, or if that's just a function of estrogen. What do you think? You know: yin and yang? Yin can adapt, like water?"

Diana shrugged. She was evidently not getting a raise.

A boat grew louder then killed its motor. Splashing from the floating dock slapped the wake as the boat glided, then from outside came thuds. The open window soon framed the angular, eager face of Derek. He extended his long arms to present a bulky, battered package tied with rough yarn. "From Namibia. More holsters, do you think?" He grinned self-consciously – was his desire too transparent? – as he climbed inside quickly: if Diana didn't have time to reach the window, he could approach her with the package to prolong their time together.

Diana pursed her lips, detecting his attempt to expand their daily exchange. She took the package and weighed it casually in her hands. "Holsters? Maybe. It's from the cheetah lady."

"It's marked, 'Acacia Eco-block,'" Derek said with some genuine curiosity.

"Probably a thornbush fuel sample. Thanks." Diana blushed, to stand so close to the warmth of his body, as if she'd ignited a novel sustainable heat source of her own.

Farraga crossed to the young man to shake his hand. "Yes, *thank* you for all your hard work. Diana mentioned you. This struggling enterprise is dependent on you, and your efforts!"

"It's just a job." Derek noticed the new décor.

"Just a job." Farraga handed Diana scissors for the twine. "Well, that makes it infinitely harder. If you work for a worthy cause, each day flies by on the wings of your heart." She put on a F.W.W.P. hat and gave him a military salute. "Nonetheless, you show dedication. I wish we could afford to give you a real tip." She took off the hat and looked at its photo. "I would give you this, but with Barbra Streisand as Funny Girl on it, you might not get the desired response. Not at all. Not unless you're in a Pride Parade!" Faced with the young people's blank stares, Farraga just digressed. "Barbra has incredible eyes, doesn't she?" Farraga had registered Derek's chemistry with Diana, and her wheels turned. "Derek, won't you come to dinner with us tonight? Diana, would that be *de trop*? Then Diana can tell you more about our worthy charity, and how her language skills hold it together."

Derek and Diana glanced at each other and nodded. Derek spurted awkwardly, "That would be great." Diana had nodded! So as not to stare at her, his eyes wandered around the room. He was surprised to see some four-foot tongs sticking out of a box in the corner. He picked up a pair, inspecting the plush bear-claw pads on the end of each prong. Delighted, he stuttered, "A new product?"

Diana suddenly turned to her boss. "Oh, Farraga, I almost forgot. Please tell Professor Vimvole that the printers are sending his hats right to the hotel." She looked down at her waist: Derek was tenderly squeezing Diana with the tongs' soft bear claws.

At Diana's disclosure, Farraga balked. "Oh, that funny boy. Vimvole! He didn't tell me he'd ordered any of our hats. He wasn't enthusiastic about... our... hats."

Diana seized the giant bear-tongs with her elbows, wrenching them away from Derek and – since she was not getting a raise – giving in to a unprofessional giggle. Via elbow-clench, she wielded the handle and bonked Derek with it. Her weapon swayed from her rotating ribcage, hands clenched to her sternum; she would look robotic if not for her beaming face. She and Derek scooted around the room, he, pretending to evade, and she, pretending not to be in avid pursuit.

Finally Diana responded to Farraga, who was discreetly inspecting inventory and unpacking some culottes from India. "Yes, twenty hats."

Farraga mused, "He wouldn't use his own photo. Goodness, whose – oh, maybe he meant to surprise me. Gosh, if Vimvole used a photo of me, I hope it's a flattering one!" She set down hats graced with Dian Fossey and Joan Root, and vainly touched her hair, daring to be pleased, as if discovering a secret admirer. Love was in the air.

Diana set down the bear tongs, catching her breath. "Oh, don't worry, it's of someone else. He sounded excited. It's –" The situation dawned on her. "Oh, uh – maybe I shouldn't say..."

Derek was also out of breath. He gaped at the piranhas and commented festively, "I like the new additions in here."

Farraga caught his reference to the aquarium. "Now she won't be lonely. Every girl needs her interior decorated," she said absently. Trying to divine Professor Vimvole's strategy, she pressed, "Whose photo adorns his hats?"

"The fashion model, Shee," Diana mumbled. Should she change the subject? Intuition insisted on action. Diana shuffled some invoices on her desk and announced, with an incongruously martial tone, "The anti-poaching units in the field are what warrant all attention." She sat down purposefully, as if in atonement for her recent glee and carnality.

Farraga gazed at her and stepped nearer to pet her silky hair. "You are the nucleus of the operation, my dear! Without you, we will collapse." She looked around the room for another chair. If they couldn't find more chairs in one of the abandoned offices in the derelict building (she thought, with sudden exhaustion), she would have to make another trip to the third-hand store to buy a chair. Feeling faint, she sat on the floor beside the new cabinets. An avalanche of Fanged Wilds clothing fell off the top shelf onto her.

Diana leapt up. "Oh, I'm so sorry. I didn't stack those too well. Here, sit in my chair. I need to fill some mail orders, anyway."

Derek helped replace the inventory, then hesitated before he climbed back out the window. "I can come back later today, if you need me to pick up late deliveries."

Diana pushed the clothes securely above Farraga and then offered the boss a hand, stalling before she answered Derek. "Oh, well... if you happen to be in the area."

Farraga interjected, "Don't forget dinner! Shall we all meet here at seven? I'll show... Professor Vimvole... the office. Now that we've got it looking so attractive. Till now, it looked too old and shabby." She laughed with determination as she re-folded some colorful shirts. "He likes pretty things."

CHAPTER FIFTEEN

BALKISTAN REGION, PAKISTAN

Hand up to protect his pomade-sculpted hair, Senator Pickfawny ducked into the dim entrance to a cave, nearly bumping his head on the butt of a Kalashnikov held in the joyless grip of a Taliban guard. Inside the cave, swaths of gold-threaded silk hung to form a tent, creating an Ali-Baba opulence that veiled the stone walls. Senator Pickfawny bent again into a formal bow as he saw his *al-Qarnas* hosts. The sheik and the mullah were men whose religious fervor could present an obstacle to the Senator's plan. But the Senator knew that, with God on his side, all was possible, praise the Lord. Senator Pickfawny obsequiously introduced himself to both men, shaking the sheik's hand. He bowed again, as if ironically honored, when the mullah's robes didn't even rustle: rather than a handshake, the bearded man failed to offer anything but a scowl. But the swarthy elder had reason to be proud: he had once met with Ronald Reagan.

The three men sat down on nomad-style ottomans stuffed with chaff that crunched with their weight. Senator Pickfawny launched into his plea. "Your people have good reason to distrust interference from our country. But there is an undercurrent in the U.S. that is perfectly aligned with what you're trying to accomplish, as far as oil; promoting morals; and keeping women in their place."

The Senator glanced around at the exclusively male constituent of the room. There were only seven Muslims, all in black-and-white al-Qarnas kaffiyehs, impeccable except for the rough-looking guards. Brad, his own Senatorial aide, shifted tensely, standing beside the tailored but greasy-faced Arabic interpreter.

Senator Pickfawny continued valiantly, "In the U.S., women can drive in NASCAR. Far worse, they can get drugs that prevent them from having babies.

That is the most unnatural thing in the world." He warmed to his sermon. "It completely subverts what God has intended for man, and for families. A cantankerous woman who needs a baby to settle her down – she can pick and choose whose baby she has, and when she has it!" To conclude, he garnished his argument with a campy mimicry of hoity-toightiness: "She can decide to be the Speaker of the House instead, if it's in her mood."

The Mullah stroked his beard, scrutinizing the clownish American before him. With a British inflexion in his voice – he was Cambridge-educated – he finally said, "I know that woman. Such a woman should stop speaking and start *listening*. At least Hillary Clitown only got a secretarial position."

Senator Pickfawny missed the joke but was heartened that the Mullah was in agreement with him. He opened his hands in supplication. "This is tearing my country apart. The perversions of Hollywood and Las Vegas are just fruits that Eve has picked from the tree. And your people, and my people, can stop it, when Christianity and Islam join together like the children of Abraham that we are. As President Ronald Reagan said about you, 'You're the moral equivalent of our founding fathers.'" The American clasped his hands together dramatically, and brought them to his lips. "Even Saudi women want cars. When women's role is secured, and women can no longer drive, there will be plenty of oil for us men."

A disturbance at the entrance was just a Muslim servant carrying a tray past the guard. Shuffling to where they were sitting, he served each of the three men a cup of sage tea.

Senator Pickfawny held up his tiny teacup, as if proposing a toast. "You and I agree on the most fundamental issue. And we can work together. We Americans have technology. And you have the soldiers with the commitment to do what's necessary worldwide." He gestured toward the Taliban guards, who perused his every move with glinting hatred. Beside him, the Senator's aide Brad mirrored him as the Senator lifted his cup toward the uncomprehending men. "In my culture, that kind of commitment is rare. Boys would rather play pornographic video games, or watch football. They just care about what's in their underwear, and it's not bombs. That's why we really do need you."

The Mullah nodded. The sheik said, "Jewish materialism is another enemy we share."

Senator Pickfawny's forehead broke a sweat of excitement. "Yes! Materialism is a cancer, opposing true godliness! How is a man free to pray... if a woman is nagging in his ear that she wants a new kitchen!"

The interpreter tried to translate; none of the Muslim men understood the word, "Nagging." At the eventual Arabic interpretation – asking for ovens! – the cave full of men rumbled with their unanimous amusement at female triviality.

CHHARATPUR, INDIA

The smell of cooking signaled the return to the heart of civilization. The women passed a woodsman's water-buffalo cart, its small bed waiting to be filled with kindling. Beyond, a goat stared at them, pissing. Ganika was getting used to leading her patrol group through the edge of the jungle. But it was always a tremendous relief to be back on the road to home. Her canvas boots pinched her feet with each step, and her sweaty culottes were more binding on her legs than the sari she was used to wearing. But physical discomforts framed her sense of accomplishment. Helpful was the women's agreement that, whenever anyone felt like whining, they would sing a Bollywood song. Ganika learned new lyrics.

But her feet felt as if she were walking on embers of fire.

She put a brave face on it, though, when her little brother and other children she knew ran up to greet the squad. Her favorite, a little girl named Aashi, was particularly excited. "Did you see a tiger?" the child asked.

Though weary, Ganika wasn't going to disappoint such a breathless question. With uncharacteristic playfulness, she answered, "There was *something*. I could feel eyes on me, following us through the jungle. Was it a sloth bear? I don't know what was watching us. Maybe it was just monkeys."

Aashi walked beside Ganika's hip, pensive. "Maybe it was my mama," she suggested.

Ganika laughed, trying to divert a sad subject. "Maybe your mother was reincarnated as a tiger!" Ganika steadied her holster with one hand while she lunged playfully at Aashi, teeth bared, and grabbed Aashi's thin shoulder as if clawing.

Aashi squealed, her face filled with a rare, startled happiness. Ganika reached for her again, more gently. They walked, holding each other's dusty hand. The rest of the group spread abreast of them, accommodated by a rare moment when there was no other traffic on the rutted road. The little girl Aashi looked across at the other women in the squad, feeling as if she belonged with the adults. They were all too tired to notice her, except for Ganika, who squeezed her hand.

Ahead was a crowd in fuchsia saris. The patrol resumed single-file to make room for a Pink Gang; these vigilante women were on a campaign to confront abusive men. A flurry of gossip revealed that today they were off to label with graffiti a house where "bride-burning" murder had taken place with impuny. One of Ganika's companions waved her FWWP hat with its photo of the "Gulabi" (Pink) Gang founder, Sampat Devi Pal. Despite the seriousness of their cause, all the women smiled at one another as they passed. Those with *laathi* poles saluted each other. Despite the dust, Ganika felt a second wind revitalize the end of her day's journey.

Traffic and noise increased as they neared their village. Ganika handed her canteen to Aashi. "Here, fill this for tomorrow, please."

Aashi pointed at the logo on the canteen cover, sounding out the title, learning to read. As the women neared the water pump, the little girl asked, "Do you think my mama would be in the Fang Program?"

Aashi's mother had been a vacant sort of person; if Ganika or anyone asked her a question, her face would seem to groan, "Why should I know anything?" Ganika, exhausted, sighed. She admitted to Aashi, "Your mama might not like walking so far with a heavy gun." The girl's dulled expression prompted Ganika to qualify: "But she would do it to pay for your school." She paused as Aashi waited her turn at the pump. Madhya Pradesh state government offered poor families with daughters a few hundred dollars for every few years of schooling, and more than 100,000 rupees ($2,250) when the girls graduated high school, but relatives – or loving strangers – had to ante the initial financial investment.

Aashi held the canteen out under the spouting pump, its handle complaining of rust and dust, as usual. As if to agree, the little girl grieved, partly to herself. "If only that old stove hadn't fallen over. I wonder if my papa bought his *new* wife a new stove." She looked up inquisitively at the women, in case anyone knew her stepmother.

Ganika took the canteen silently, thinking of Aashi's mother. As a teenager, Ganika had attended the wedding and been dazzled with the days of pomp and delicacies. Aashi's parents were only married for a few years when a fire had unexpectedly broken out in their kitchen. And for some reason, the young wife hadn't been able to escape.

Ganika could picture her over her stove and remembered how diminished Aashi's mother looked a few days before her demise. Maybe she was just too tired to fight the flames.

Aashi went to join her stooped grandmother. Ganika waved goodbye to Aashi and headed for home, to the comfort and mouth-watering, spicy smells of her aunt's kitchen. Her little brother – showing unusual deference – ran ahead to announce Ganika's return. Ganika recalled how she had waited in her own kitchen for her husband – may he be free from rebirth – and how his eyes would slip over her as if she were a built-in part of the house. His gaze always settled on the plate of food she gave him.

Now Ganika was the one to return and to be fed. As she reached her doorway, she turned and waved at other women from the squad still trudging along the road to their own homes, using their *laathi* weapons as walking sticks. Ganika patted her holster and nodded to remind them: they would meet after supper to store their gun at the police station. And then, at long last, Ganika would be able to sleep.

But her evening was not as restful as she needed. As they ate lentils and potatoes together, Ganika's aunt speculated, "Aashi's mother would be alive if she had ultrasound, and no daughter." Hindu custom dictated that only sons could light their parents' funeral pyres, one tradition making daughters disposable. There were less than nine hundred girls for every thousand boys under the age of six.

The aunt's comment was upsetting, and the night, sweltering. When her day was finally done, Ganika, sheet tangled, was too tired to sleep. Toward morning, she had a nightmare that she was a tiger devouring Aashi's mother, the woman's body evacuated but the eyes still alive and watching. Ganika wanted to protest that she did not eat meat. But her mouth was too full.

CHAPTER SIXTEEN

BALKISTAN REGION, PAKISTAN

The lid of a battered metal pot clattered as it boiled, balanced on a sterno burner. Haadiya sliced root vegetables with a curved knife, then lowered them with a wire skimmer-ladle into the hot froth. She glanced across the narrow cooking shelter. Mustache bristling, the full lips of her brother, Ashfaq, tugged at a cigarette, as if nursing to milk the right words to say. Finally, after a long, slow exhale of smoke, he snapped: "The *al-Qarnas* jihad will not allow you women to continue in that micro-finance program."

Their nephews shouted outside as they herded the goats into the pen that abutted the cement-block building, both structures in the shade of a cliff. In another enclosure, puppies yipped; the F.W.W.P. was also addressing the culture's aversion to canines, the tip of the wedge being Pomeranians. Haadiya had already fed the furry balls some half-cooked stew. "Mohammed said even a prostitute was forgiven her sins, just for giving water to a dog," Haadiya recited inaudibly.

With the handle of the ladle, she lifted the hot lid and dropped some greens in through the steam. She had gathered the greens from a mountain crevasse where the omnivorous goats could not reach. This gentle, resourceful Pakistani glanced at the door and hoped for a miraculous arrival of someone who would argue with Ashfaq, to persuade him to help the women – her sisters, cousins, and friends – instead of obstructing and harming them.

The pot continued to boil. Haadiya tapped the sterno tin almost shut. Smoke mingled with savory steam. Ashfaq's cigarette was almost gone, the brown of its paper barely showing between his bulky brown fingers.

Unrescued, finally Haadiya blurted, "Ashfaq, we protect your goats for free. And we are trained to defend ourselves. Our puppies will defend us, too." Modestly she turned back to add delicate fronds of fresh herbs to the stew, their fragrance vaporizing in the heat. "Still, you can kill all of us. The dogs we raise for patrol, you can eat as meat." She carefully ladled a crisped chunk of salted goat fat onto the edge of a plate, where Ashfaq wouldn't miss how big and juicy it was. "But if you leave us alone, we will keep protecting your goats for free." Haadiya spooned out more stew; set a browned, chewy chapati on top; and handed him the steaming plate.

Her brother's eyes were on the food, so Haadiya felt unsure of his reaction to her bold statement. But he stubbed out his hand-rolled cigarette and, instead of arguing, ate. Puppies kept yipping.

TOMAR, PORTUGAL

The patron saint of Tomar, Irene was born in the dark ages and tutored to be a nun. If she went out of her parents' house, it would be to visit elderly cripples. On such excursions, a nobleman saw and soon fell in love with her. Her tutor, a monk, also made advances to her. But Irene just wanted to be a nun. So the monk spread the rumor that she was pregnant, and the nobleman had a henchman strike her with a sword and throw her body in the Tagus.

Down river, Benedictines found the body "uncorrupted." (What that specifically meant is up to the imagination. Was it that the murdered woman hadn't committed unauthorized pregnancy? Or did "uncorrupted" mean her dead flesh was still alluring?)

The Knights Templar castle had been interesting, looking down on the red tile roofs. Marion was enjoying the quiet town, away from the urban commercialism of Lisbon. Her travel companions acquired a local tour guide who had accosted them in the plaza. The olive-skinned young man was one of the many local descendents of "New Christians," the Jews forced to convert during the Inquisition. Enterprising, he paraded Marion's party along the cobbled streets to the historic synagogue, and then crossed over a picturesque bridge spanning the river (no virgins currently floating in it) to the oldest Catholic church in Tomar.

"Aren't you coming in?" the Oregonians asked the multi-lingual tour guide.

The Portuguese's eyes grew beady as he strained to disguise revulsion, looking up at the rose-windowed facade of Santa Maria do Olival. "I am born again, madame," he said. "I will not enter where they worship... that woman. She isn't even in the Trinity. *I* worship Jesus."

"This will make a good story for my feminist friends." But when Marion got home to McCarthy, her audience was diminished: uncharacteristically, Farraga was out of town. "The way that do-gooder talks about 'carbon footprints,' her shoes probably leave black smudges when she steps off a plane," Marion told her husband. She unpacked her platform wedgies that had been hellish on the cobblestones.

"*Why* are you friends with Farraga, again?"

"My doctorate. She's a textbook case of misguided idealism. My thesis hinges on her, however unhinged she may be. Though it is annoying when she harps that planes waste fuel."

"Just remember, when your carbon footprints don't show in the sand, it's because God is carrying you." He watched her pull out some souvenirs. "They're mailing the tiles for the kitchen remodel?" her husband asked: Portugal was famous for glazed tiles, perfect for a backsplash.

"They were a steal."

He smiled. "You deserve it." She put on her fuck-me wedgies, their heel height copied from guru Marianne William-Son. Her husband nodded appreciatively: they made her buttocks look pert. "Yeah, you deserve it."

"It's great to be home!" Farraga didn't understand that Marion *had* to travel, to keep her marriage solid. How else could Marion make her husband miss her, and keep him wanting more, despite her sags?

MANHATTAN, NEW YORK, U.S.A.

The samurai armor, Noh masks, and other décor of the sushi restaurant lent an operatic clash of elemental drama in the spare style of Asian art. A gold, black and red parasol hovered over the dining table. Black, gold and red demons' faces bedecked tiny plates, as if their dabs of wasabi taunted with infernal pungency.

"What's that you got?" Diana leaned toward her boss, wondering how she afforded such a nice tiger-pattern jacket. *"Enoki miso?"*

"It's just regular miso soup. With velvet-foot mushrooms," Farraga answered drably. "They can reduce tumors," she added, almost apologetically.

Professor Vimvole scrutinized his own dinner, green with algae.

Chopsticks poised like preying mantises, pausing to admire the artistic sushi on the table between them, Diana and Derek selected the first piece to eat. "Looks delectable," Derek said. "I do miss shellfish, though. Ocean acidification happened so fast; I wish I'd eaten more oysters." He added, daringly, "Not that I needed them." He waggled his eyebrows.

Diana coyly disapproved of his allusion to aphrodisiacs. She looked away and grinned. "Cheeky monkey."

Farraga took some Sustainable Sardine Sashimi with her chopsticks, dipped it in wasabi-spiked soy sauce, then tried to focus on how delectable it was. The horseradish distracted her for a moment, burning her mouth better than whiskey. She sucked on and spat out the tiny bones. Professor Vimvole was her primary concern. After fortifying herself with a swig of saki, she asked him, "How is your vegan sushi, darling?"

Professor Vimvole ruminated, chewing and looking blandly at the Pollan Sushi on his plate. Anxious to project ease, Diana chimed in, "Yeah, how is that?"

Derek, having ordered the "Octamom," was gnawing on the legs of a baby octopus. He swallowed and asked doubtfully, "Yeah, is that any good, with just soy beans?"

Waiting for the professor's answer, he scooped up and planted a mouthful of wasabi; his face bloomed with the condiment's piquant heat, puffing, puckering and blowing.

Diana tried not to be mesmerized by Derek's antics. She leaned closer to Vimvole to analyze the soy and algae sushi. "It *looks* good."

Knowing about the fashion-model hats, Derek gently teased Farraga. "Looks deceive. And just beans might not satisfy for long. And bean-poles shade the rest of the garden." Having captured the women's attention, he rhapsodized. "Even if you're a bean counter, or a human bean, beans are worth beans."

Diana smiled at his silliness out of the corner of her eyes. Pretending still to be preoccupied with the professor's dinner, she said, "I think they're called *edamame*. I just remembered a Chinese saying, *da dou fu*: 'Beat tofu.' It means to have a weak opponent. Like, are you made of muscle, or just soy?"

"You don't know your own strength, until you stumble into a snake pit," Farraga snarked. Vimvole just looked at his food and chewed.

The date was not going so hot. Derek wondered if the professor was autistic in some way. What was that condition, Assburgers, that some smart guys had? Whatever. Derek was undeterred from his campaign to cheer Farraga as well as to attract Diana, digressing: "You ladies are so phenomenal at languages. I have a hard enough time with English. Or should I say, *American*? It's *Diana* who speaks English." He tensed his mouth to sound foreign.

Diana hesitated, intending to give Farraga opportunity to respond. But the older woman just toyed absently with a piece of jellyfish in her sesame-seaweed salad. So Diana said, "Oh, maybe it's just a girl thing. You know how we love to communicate, like always asking, 'What are you thinking?'" With affection, she pursued, "What *do* you think, Farraga? Is that why we love languages?"

"Curiosity about languages is like our love for animals. It's the desire to connect with a consciousness different from us. Bond over the divide, linking all creation."

Farraga's lips pursed, as if constipated.

"Even Nazis loved animals. Nazi scientists tried to teach dogs to talk." Derek chimed in. "What do you think, Professor? Are *you* bilingual?"

Professor Vimvole was gobbling his food, and only raised his head to show his mouth was full, mumbling, "Oh..."

Farraga tried to laugh. "Derek doesn't mean, do you have a forked tongue. We all know the answer to that." With a flutter of her cloth napkin, she burst into tears. In one movement, she pushed back her varnished black chair and rushed off toward the restroom.

Professor Vimvole observed her departure with detachment. Calculating, he picked up the last piece of his sushi with his chopsticks. "This bean sushi is fine. It's practically fat free."

Derek looked back and forth at the professor and the dark recesses of the restaurant, where his hostess has vanished. "Is Farraga all right?" he asked, and looked helplessly at Diana, whose jaw had dropped.

Soy sushi poised at his lips, Professor Vimvole said, "Women are like that," and popped the food into his mouth as easily as switching channels on a remote. He was going to present the keynote eco-ethnopaleontological speech at the next day's conference, and his career was only going to soar after that. For now, he just commented, "She's sensitive to alcohol. She didn't drink when I met her. She's changed." Farraga had menopausal mood swings, or maybe she was already completely infertile. At any rate, he was safe because he wore two condoms secured with a rubber cock ring and organic cotton shorts – guarding against herpes as well as impregnation – when he fucked her.

Brows knitted, Diana said, "Excuse me," stood, and followed Farraga. The men heard a dull crash as Diana's passage accidentally knocked a glossy enamel mask from the wall beside the restroom. Waiters slinked to the rescue, snickering at the scene. Other patrons craned their necks to look.

Derek sat, flummoxed, and watched Professor Vimvole wipe his mouth with a red, black and gold napkin. What was that label.... his sister's Ex, the psychologist, used, a word – what was it? – when she was emotional. "Women are from Borderline, men are from Asperger's; isn't that what shrinks say?"

The professor nodded. " Women breed complications. Things can just be... pure."

The young man's beloved was disturbed, and it was this old fart's fault. Unsure of how to proceed, Derek chewed on some calamari steak and washed it down with the acrid unfamiliarity of saki. Then he attempted a rebuttal. "Maybe women's complications are that they see relationships we miss."

"Things can be simple."

"As simple as soy." Derek was upset. "We men feel smothered, muscling to reach our destination while females point out what we're stepping on. We may call them over-emotional, when they're just preventing us from causing harm. To them and... you're an environmentalist, right? You dis women when they represent delicate beauty and nature..." He sipped saki. "Women give up. They make themselves trivial. The polar ice caps' melting may be due to too much female passivity, and too much male virulence. I mean, virility." Derek looked longingly toward the restrooms, and then down at his Octamom tentacles, waving off a black fly. "Life without women would be like sushi with all wasabi and no fish."

"This soy sushi is fine," Vimvole said, studying Derek's face with a shrewd attentiveness he had not exhibited previously, lingering.

Derek could see: this was a Famous Scientist. He wrinkled his nose. "Who wants a woman when you can have a little boy. I mean, *soy.*"

In the restroom, Farraga was re-doing her make-up, leaning over a basin. "Are you sure you're okay?" Diana asked.

"Yes. Grooming is so soothing." Farraga blotted mascara. The belt of her tiger-striped coat was cinched at the back to make her look slim; the belt had hung down like a cute feline tail, swinging right into the toilet when she'd peed. Now it still dripped, dark and wrinkled where she'd washed it. "I'm overworked. And the professor's conference tomorrow – there will be so many influential people, it's a daunting opportunity. They could keep our program afloat. I'm nervous – I might have a chance to plug Fanged Wilds at the banquet; that could be our ticket to survival. Might even ensure our fashion show." She looked at Diana confidently, then burst into tears again. "Oh, it's my friend – my *friend* that's the problem."

Five minutes later, Diana made her way back through the tables of other diners. "She's okay," she said reassuringly. She reclaimed her red and black napkin from the floor and sat back down. "A friend of hers was diagnosed with terminal cancer, it turns out."

"Professor Vimvole and I were just discussing how women are sometimes emotional for good reason."

"Emotional? Science proved you can detect the emotional impact of an image a fraction of a second before a computer randomly chooses it. So emotions can make you psychic." She wiggled her fingers playfully at Derek's cranium. "*Arigato*," Diana thanked the snooping waiter refilling their water glasses. "Neurologically, you can't organize memories without emotions. I don't think I could bounce between languages if I didn't have emotions about the peoples who speak each one. So even stereotypes serve a purpose. They're like flavors for mental associations." Derek chewed some rice. "Like, the Japanese vocabulary I know, I associate with neat little packages, because they're so aware of presentation in Japan. So my brain assembles a sentence in Japanese like a platter of sushi." She glanced back at the restroom. "Maybe emotions help women multi-task. Well, at least it doesn't matter that Farraga's food is getting cold."

Derek pointed out, "Except the soup."

Diana looked slyly at him. Something about Derek made her feel daring. "Don't tell!" She reached out and brought Farraga's lacquered soup bowl to her lips. "*Enoki miso!*" With a naughty wink at the appalled professor, she sipped a taste. A salty mushroom tasted earthy.

CHAPTER SEVENTEEN

KINKIMAN ISLAND, JAPAN

Geisha girls passed around a bowl of Japanese rice crackers with *nori obi*. They were watching an old samurai movie. "This, my favorite scene," one, Kayoko, giggled and bowed. "Oh, Toshiro! Curl my toes!"

She was referring to Toshiro Mifune, the actor who played the toughest samurai. On the television, he asked the servant girl Koiso to remain incognito, to keep working in the house, to spy on and sabotage the villains. He was asking a lot. "Koiso, will you go back?"

On screen, Koiso answered bravely, "Yes. I understand."

Toshiro Mifune's character watched the servant girl return to possible brutality, rape, and death. He chastized the other male witnesses: "Now *there's* a samurai. More reliable than all of you." The other samurais in the film looked ashamed.

The Geisha holding the crackers set down the bowl with precision, grabbed the remote, and paused the film. "I am more reliable than all of you," she teased. "We should go do the evening patrol."

The other girls chimed in, "I am Koiso!" Each girl vied to express greater Samurai conviction. "*I* am Koiso!"

Kayoko exclaimed, "I am more reliable!" The girls put on their traditional platform shoes, and each armed herself with a sword, rifle, and parasol.

Women used to be banned from the island of Kinkiman.

And there used to be sixty sika deer per kilometer at this famous, tsunami-lapped tourist destination. Local men celebrated a bullfight-like festival of cutting off deers' antlers. Now, beneath the picturesque sunset, the girls herded tourists away from packs of sometimes-snarling wolves on the hunt. The wolves steered the deer away from bushes that had been bonsai only a year or so before. And the fanged animals halted contagion by culling the sick and elderly deer, as the pack eyed the sick and elderly tourists.

Many tourists bought a souvenir parasol to shoo away any threatening beast. Some Japanese men even bought the parasols to identify themselves as "herbivore men," Japanese slang for those who eschewed traditional machismo. The girls all agreed that they prefered carnivores. Unlike most, these Geishas weren't trained to please men, but rather, sought what pleased them in men. When they saw a man who met their approval, their immodest signal to each other was to howl like a wolf.

Sometimes, real wolves answered them. Mists of dusk shrouded the windswept trees of the island. The girls hushed.

MANHATTAN, NEW YORK, U.S.A.

"Howl! Howl!" The elegant crowd in the banquet hall yipped like coyotes, spurred on by the ebullient, tuxedoed Emcee, Scanlon Neroe. Neroe stood with his microphone at the center of the table on the dais, nodding and chuckling, "Good job. Just like the real thing." Theatrically, he queried Professor Vimvole and Farraga, who sat at the table near him: "Don't you feel as if you're in Yellowstone, or Yosemite?" Neroe prompted, falsely casual, as if he weren't speaking into the mike, "Listen to that pack of wolves."

Less conspicuous in the din, one woman returned to her interrupted disinformation, straining to be heard. "Bush's CIA ordered Daniel Pearl beheaded because he knew Omar Sheikh murdered bin Laden in 2001," she shouted. "Osama paid Bush to wire Building Three. The CIA also arranged for Marianne's movie to be – " The woman yawned, palm tapping her mouth then flopping open, vacuous.

"The Pakistanis gave Obama Osama – he'd outlived his usefulness," her dinner companion argued with the undercover CIA operative. Then he joked: "Wonder what the seventy-one virgins looked like in hell." Most of the crowd continued to participate in the yipping, sounding even more like little dogs in their excitement.

Alluring in lace and sequins, a roving woman squatted to talk to someone at another table. "How's your wife?"

The man responded, "Compared to what?"

Another, more inebriated women delivered at the top of her lungs, "Used air filters from Fukushima. Through the mail." Her table hushed for a moment, to her embarrassment. "I'm not radioactive," she stammered, and her neighbors resumed howling politely.

A picky eater, sniffing his wine, was saying, "Denmark doesn't just kill whales and eat the mercury. They also are high on the global polluters list, per person."

His trophy wife commented, "I bet they cut a lot of forests to make their wooden shoes."

Tension in such a celebrity-studded crowd felt like alley cats in heat. Some attendees couldn't stop preening. "The personal is the political. The personal is the planet," a woman ejaculated incomprehensibly, straightening in her chair as she tried to relax. "Whoever invented yoga is a genius."

Her ascerbic date replied, "My cats pay royalty when they stretch. But I haven't seen who they make the check out to. Bikram, I guess." He noticed, with satisfaction, another man lasciviously watching his escort's yoga pose.

Another conversation started innocently, a woman's forkful of bison *mignon* poised midair as Exhibit A. "Since most biodiverse habitats are in private ranches, it protects more species to eat grass-fed meat than let the land go to other uses. And vegans forget that some habitats only produce meat," posited the woman in white, voice chiming above the ruckus as meat juice dripped on her bosom.

Her black-tie neighbor nodded. "Especially cities, after the collapse of civilization. Vegetarians are going to think they've gone to Uruguay to play rugby in the Andes. At least most people are decent enough to wait till their neighbors are dead... to have them for dinner." He held his wine glass in a mock toast, red liquid swirling.

Scanlon Neroe, the Emcee, finally tapped the microphone to quiet the vocalizing mayhem. "Lastly, ladies and gentlemen, I'd like to thank our keynote speaker, renowned eco-ethnopaleontologist Professor Vimvole."

Professor Vimvole stood and bowed gawkily, his napkin falling off his lap. The Emcee added gallantly, "And his lovely companion, Farraga."

Farraga rose, showing off her long, gold-orange dress striped with claw-marks that formed a tiger-print heart. The effect of the heart was gashed, as if to express a mourning for all tigers lost. Unbridled in her devotion to her cause, Farraga reached for Scanlon's microphone to put in a plug for species' conservation that would empower half humanity, too. "I'm Farraga Dentata of the Fanged Wilds and Women Program, the F-quadruple-U-P." she announced boldly. "What a great group. Now we need to quadruple you."

Her slogan-slinging was distracted for a moment by the activity of Professor Vimvole: he pulled from his briefcase a pile of F.W.W.P. caps in a variety of colors. Farraga continued, "We can redeem the integrity of ecosystems..." She saw all the photos of the young fashion model, Shee, on Professor Vimvole's caps. What was it Farraga wanted to say, again? She tried to exterminate the frog in her throat before she lost the crowd's attention.

Fawning, wiry Vimvole ducked from table to table to hand the hats out to the celebrities in the audience: Harrison Prius, Pop Elliott... And, exuding pizzazz, Vimvole's associate Richard Brimston chatted at a front table with Ned Lerner. "If the Occupy movement had taken other species into account, the percentage would have been ninety-nine point-nine- nine- nine- nine": Ned gestured infinity as he received his swag. Nearby, Leonard DiScorpio, Ed Norsol, and Ed Begfor Junior, all modestly held court with George Clowny. At another table, Ted Dancing playfully held his new cap over his face, Shee's features on it exaggerated as if they were a minstrel's. Looking at his own cap like a mirror, Will Feral smooched her lovely likeness.

Robert Bedford laughed at him. Woody Harrelsin, the actor wearing an Armani hemp tux, fingered the textile object and kept asking sardonically, "This is hemp, isn't it? Isn't this hemp?" Shrugging, Kenny Logsdontli put on his cap and self-consciously scratched his Grizzly Adams beard that had grown sparse and grey. Flashing her famous smile, Cameron Ladette beamed kindly at him, "You look great!"

The celebrity wattage was blinding. Farraga valiantly maintained her composure – if only she could explain what the F.W.W.P. hats really represented – as her boyfriend flirted with Trudie Stylish and Skyjourney Weaver.

The professor bowed and presented caps to Laurie Exdavid and Roxanne Hannah; Roxanne saw poor Farraga's discomfort and quipped to O, "Those Fanged women are flying by the seat of their pantyhose." Lady Haden-Guest nodded sympathetically.

Oblivious to their comments, Vimvole backed away officiously, hamming it up, as if American environmental philanthropy had royalty and he were petitioner at the palace court. These people could send his career through the roof! The sky was the limit! All the while, he'd ignored Farraga's attempt to get the spotlight. Vimvole was still abashed, caps in hand, when approaching Ashley Muddinpalini. The gorgeous (despite being puffy-faced) Ashley whispered appraisingly to the even more breathtaking Rosario Awesome, "These hats are hot. The kaffiyeh is dead, as a fashion statement. These *Fanged* caps are *in*." The two ladies accepted the headwear but just held them near their ears for photographs, to avoid messing their delicate, glossy coiffures. Emboldened, Vimvole posed behind the actresses' chairs, clearly enamored. How could he get a copy of the photo? He fumbled to hand his business card to the photographer, and ended up handing them to every celebrity within reach.

In climax, rising like Venus out of the audience, the model Shee waltzed up to Vimvole and planted a goddess's kiss on each of his cheeks, and then – unbelievably – on his mouth. The crowd made appreciative noises. What a night!

People pulled out phones to photo, text and tweet. "Hot model smooches eco-nerd!"

Humiliated by the display, Farraga forged on. The Emcee, increasingly annoyed at her, stretched his hand out for the mike. Teetering on her Schieferstein heels, the F.W.W.P. founder beseeched, "Redeem the ecosystem by learning to *live with predators* throughout our country and our world... not just in places like Washington D.C. and Hollywood..."

As the professor, still with Shee, returned a peck on the towering beauty's fully augmented lips, Farraga cleared her throat and added: "Live with predators, even in our boudoirs." She smiled with false levity.

The crowd interpreted her statement as saucy, and, all eyes on the triumphant Shee, celebrated with more yipping. Farraga let loose a low, mournful moan worthy of a lost wolf. When the audience's coyote imitations finally subsided, Farraga's howl filled the rumbling hush.

Obliviously glowing with delight, Professor Vimvole put the last Shee cap on his own balding head and, with a wave to his glamorous new friends, returned to his seat soon after Farraga had sat down and chugged his glass of wine to follow her own fortifying beverage. The Emcee's was neglected so she drank that too. Was this how Hillary Clitown had endured Monica Lewdinski?

It was a lively evening. To renewed applause, Chris Marten took the floor with his guitar to sing his hit, "Ten Thousand Dead Mango Trees."

CHAPTER EIGHTEEN

MANHATTAN, NEW YORK, U.S.A.

A few miles away, Derek escorted Diana on their own Friday-night date. This, their second dinner in row, was a barbeque on his boat, suggested by Derek as a sort of decompression from the sushi fiasco. They found a secluded spot to watch the sun set. He dropped the mainsail – his "Diluvial Delivery" logo crumpling – and set anchor near Ellis Island. The charcoal grill hung off the side and soon hissed with marinade. Diana wondered about the hand-stenciled name, *Dolfinesse*, on the transom; did Derek know dolphin was really spelled with -P-H? She was in shock that apparently he slept on the cushioned bench of the tiny, tidy cabin. Could he really live here? She had to admit, the brass gimbaled hurricane lanterns did make it cozy. And the duck was delicious with mandarins, zest, and fresh greens. He showed her his Mason jars of sprouted seeds.

Diana liked him *too* much. But fortunately he didn't make any moves. Analyzing the options, across from him as Dolfinesse gently rolled, she avoided his eyes. Instead she looked at his T-shirt on which was pictured a bison butcher's diagram with the caption, "The Future of our Planet is at Steak." She thanked him for dinner. "This was much nicer than some stuffy restaurant."

The New York skyline towered around them as he took her home. The night-slicked water rocked them in a wake: a cruise boat, loud with raucous women's voices, celebrated under strings of holiday lights, their reflections like a million sequins. Shyly, Derek ventured, "Hey, the Empire State Building isn't too far out of the way. Have you seen the view?"

Hoping for good timing, Diana dropped the bomb: "I guess I should go there, before I go home. I mean, did I tell you? I'm thinking of going back home to

England."

Derek cried, "What! Why?" He doused the motor, its fuel spurting indignantly. Their wake sloshed and flailed. He turned away. The wind had picked up, prompting Derek to raise the sails.

As he worked, Diana stated apologetically, "I might get a better-paying job doing import-export there. Now that the Gulf Stream is stalling, with Britain's weather extremes approaching another ice age, our national sense of humor has really blossomed."

"Yeah?"

"So the BBC is marketing gag items."

"Like what?" He pouted, trimming the jib.

"You know, Survivalist Beatrix-Potter rabbit snares. Tear-away Full-Monty kilts for blue-collar men who moonlight as strippers. "

He cracked his neck and snarked, "Beefeater hats? For thugs who'll work as police for a taste of beef?" The wind changed direction, and as the boat jibed, Derek gently pushed her head down so the boom would miss her. "...Bearskin hats that explode into four-and-twenty blackbirds?"

She was startled at the sail's snap. Derek's inventiveness also surprised her. "Blackbird pies, maybe. That sort of thing. Nostalgia, plus the all-essential comic relief. It's already a commercial success. Entertainment and humor sells in a depression, same as a hundred years ago."

Derek sat down, dejected. "More money. Can't argue with that."

Diana attempted to distract him. "Did you know, that nursery rhyme is really about Blackbeard's pirates?"

"No... Four and twenty...Blackbeards?"

"'The maid is in the garden' means there's a ship nearby, to plunder. You think we Brits are all tea and crumpets." She gazed toward the gondola station at the end of her street, near her studio apartment. She *could* be descended from adventurous seafarers. "Nay, laddie. We're bloodthirsty. Sir Walter Raleigh was a swashbuckler."

Her admiration for that notorious daredevil confirmed that Derek wasn't in her league. When the sails loughed, Derek tightened the sheets and they proceeded without speaking, till he eventually asserted, "Well, you'd better go see the Empire State Building before you go. Now that you're just a tourist here." She agreed diplomatically, and they changed course.

Fins of two sharks cut the black water; Derek steered clear with a pull of the rudder to starboard. He trimmed the sheets again. As they neared the partially submerged Empire State Building, he loosened the halyards, lowered the sails, and glided. The new entrance marina thronged with passengers boarding and disembarking from water taxis and tour cruisers. Popular with out-of-towners, rich bankers, and others at leisure, many gondolas had been imported from Venice, an Atlantis which no longer had use for them. Slipping into a vacant spot, Derek jumped off and tied his boat to the end of a pier. Then, with a hang-dog focus on her delicate, pink hand, he helped Diana up onto the long platform. They made their way through crowds that herded one another in each direction, one clamoring, clustered mobs coming and going to and fro.

In the huge elevator, they poised like flamingos over baby strollers. "A female terrorist with a stroller full of explosives is a metaphor for what humans do to the planet," Derek blurted morosely. The bustling – tourists of every nationality, and pickpockets – gave Derek the anonymity to mope. Moments later, he grumped into the stifling din, "Someone plunged seventy-five stories down an elevator shaft here, and lived."

The people were transported as if up a seminal vesicle. At the ejaculation, Diana grew demure, letting families exit before her. The blast of chill hit them like a cosmic vacuum. In conciliation, Diana put a quick, warming arm around Derek's waist. She regretted upsetting him. The two young people walked the spaceship-like observation deck of the Empire State Building. All around was a galaxy: millions of lights reflected in the glistening canals of Manhattan. Derek wondered if he could learn to navigate via the stars.

Diana and Derek completed a circuit and lingered, side by side, searching the horizon for landmarks. Finally Diana asked him, "Do you have ambitions in life?"

Derek shrugged wistfully. "I try to be happy with what I've got." He gazed out, then focused on her. "It would be awesome to make a really special delivery someday. Like, something big, to somewhere exotic..." Was there any hope? He glanced at her sideways, deflated and out-of-his-league, but optimistic: "With someone special beside me to help out."

"Like, someone to help you carry it?" Diana gently teased him. "Someone really strong? Better find someone who's not klutzy like me."

She was, indeed, inclined to be clumsy. Derek countered, "Maybe someone special could just help me find the destination. Like, say, it's an export," he elaborated, "And she translates the packing label for me."

Diana palliated him. "You do have to read labels carefully. Otherwise you could have a disaster." She playfully gave him another one-arm, comforting hug.

As they squeezed together back into the elevator, lust began to glimmer in her. She looked up at the line of his jaw. As long as she might move back to the U.K., and he knew that, maybe it was safe to become more intimate.

Back at sea level, the evening was too warm, but at least the sun was gone. They were walking past a boutique hotel near her Greenwich apartment building – she had a garret studio –when Diana saw something beneath a tree at the edge of Washington Square. On the dirt was a pair of fur-toed orange high heels. She pointed and said, "Someone left their shoes!"

Derek bent to look at them more closely. Diana picked them up thinking that, with prominent silver claws protruding from the tops of the toes, their straps like curling tiger tails, and revolver-barrel heels, they were just the sort of shoe that Farraga might be seeking for the product line that F.W.W.P. was developing for high-end fashion. Then she got a whiff of Chanel No. 5, and they heard a rustle above. Derek and Diana looked up to see Farraga sitting on a branch, her face barely visible in the leaves, and her orange dress hanging down with its tiger gash-mark design.

Diana gasped. "Oh my gosh! Farraga? Is that you? What are you doing?" She stepped closer to see. "Are you all right?"

Purposefully, Farraga pronounced, "I'm waiting for someone."

Diana had never encountered a boss before in a tree. She averted her eyes and said, "Oh. Okay." It occurred to her that Farraga was drunk again and possibly endangering herself. Weighing the fact that Farraga had burst into tears the night before, she pressed, "Are you sure you're okay?"

"You mean, apart from Nature being Anne Frank, and thugs everywhere marching to trample her with their shiny boots?" Farraga sniffed, defying her precarious position. "All the Good Germans and collaborators. Eugenics – ha! Good women die because they can't afford medicine or education. Life, blossoming into fullness... while selfish, wicked men..."

Derek suggested, "Maybe we should help you down from there."

Farraga snarled, with teary determination, "Vimvole is bigger than I. So I'm going to get the drop on him. Then I'll scratch his eyes out." She squeaked with a sob. "That – wolf. He could have promoted our ladies' charity, and instead – he kissed that... model." She cried, "A mannikin, flawless in all her glory! Right in front of me. He wanted the whole world to see. And then I left behind my nice tiger coat."

"Back at the banquet?"

Farraga shrugged, regretting the need for their concern. "Oh, you kids run along." She tried to reassure them. "If it weren't for him, I wouldn't have had a place at the head table. Or been invited to the gala at all. I should thank the stars. I just... I thought... Farraga Vimvole would be such a cute name!" She giggled apologetically. Her branch creaked; leaves shimmied and fell.

Diana looked into Derek's eyes, sharing compassion, and then said, "Oh, Farraga, it's not worth it for that old fart." Derek reached his arms up, to encourage Farraga to descend.

Pleased, Farraga prodded, "You think he's an old fart?

Looking into Derek's eyes again, Diana confirmed flirtatiously, "Yeah, you could definitely be with a guy who's... younger and... handsomer."

Farraga snorted, "I'm no cougar."

Derek tugged affectionately on Farraga's bare foot. "You're waiting in a tree to ambush prey. You have cougar traits."

Shifting on the branch, Farraga admitted quietly, "I want to kill him."

Derek laughed uncomfortably. "Again: cougar." With outstretched arms, he helped Farraga swing down from the branch, lowering her flaccid weight back to earth.

Diana handed her the shoes, and steadied the woman's tipsy recalceation. "There are so many women in the world who can only dream of wearing shoes as cute as these. Focus on the women. That musty old professor is not important. Anyway, I have a premonition you'll find a cuter guy, one who's younger than that... mangy old wolf." Farraga stood tall again, almost five foot four in heels.

Diana and Farraga hugged, breast to breast, and breast to breast. Watching with satisfaction, Derek said, "You probably could have met a nice policeman if you'd stayed in that tree." Over Farraga's shoulder, Diana gazed at Derek, trying to communicate discreetly with only a wiggle of eyebrows: Let's take Farraga to her hotel, and then go to my place, to be alone together. Derek stared at Diana's eye language, detecting an auspicious turn of events. Then he noticed police flashers reflected on her irises. "It's time to move along, I think, ladies!"

Startled, Farraga hooked an arm on each young person's elbow. "I'm so sorry to cause trouble. These shoes are too spiky. I may need you to help me walk, if we're to escape the law expeditiously."

Diana rearranged Farraga's shoulder strap to secure it, and patted the older woman's back reassuringly as she teetered along the sidewalk. Farraga, dissemblingly normal for a moment, queried, "What on earth are you kids doing here?"

Joyfully, Derek explained, "Diana lives near here." He couldn't believe Diana had become so friendly. He started whistling *On the Street where You Live. A*s they distanced themselves from the mounted cop riding through Washington Square, he sang: "Can you hear the lark in any other part of town?"

Her warning lights blinking, the mounted officer was only now visible behind them, her mule clopping at a modest pace with a pause to nibble some nasturtium flowers in a cement planter. Farraga gauged their safety from police apprehension and moaned, "Oh, Diana. I've maxed my credit cards for the charity. The cow and the donkey for Namibia – how could I say No? I can't afford a hotel. Not a safe one, anyway. And I can't face my boyfriend... Vimvole. Diana, do you have a sofa I can sleep on tonight?"

So much for Derek going upstairs for "tea." Diana looked at him, then her fallen face feigned eagerness for her hapless boss. "Farraga, of course! I mean, no sofa; I just have a single bed. But we can share. You said I'm family, right?"

Derek's shining eyes spurred her valiance. Was he admiring her graciousness? No, he was wondering nervously if they were going to have a threesome. He gulped, horny. Diana continued, "This is great; we'll make the most of your being in town. Didn't you say you wanted to buy another chair for the office? Tenants in my apartment building sell all their belongings all the time. We can look together tomorrow."

Farraga was uncomprehending. "They sell *all* their belongings?"

Diana shrugged. "If they can't pay rent. Sometimes they just disappear, and the landlord sells their stuff."

Farraga sighed. "Oh, if only we could develop a program for inner city folk. Nature strengthens community, and lends meaning. Give women an option so they don't swoon with irrationality, and silly choices."

Diana was saying, "There are poachers and foragers in Central Park," when Farraga burst into tears and blubbered, "Oh, people do suffer so."

The *ménage à trois* seemed safely impossible; still strung along, Derek put his arm around the older woman's shoulders. "You're upset. You'll feel better in the morning." To Diana, he mouthed, "Apart from the hangover." He continued quickly, "Hey, that would be great to have a Fanged chapter here. It could be like the Guardian Angels, only, instead of red berets, they could wear tiger caps with Diana's ferocious face on the back. They could escort ladies like you who are out at night."

Diana batted eyelashes at him and said, "Yeah, Farraga. You know, that was dangerous for you to be alone."

Farraga let go of Diana's arm long enough to pat her own bodice. "Oh, I try always to have a derringer. Cleavage is not just a fashion accessory. Push-up bras are fabulous as a holster." She clucked, her tongue still loose from the alcohol. "To think, my boyfriend thought I wore this bra just for him. I guess tonight, I did." She showed shame. "Diana, he'll never know. You might have saved his life tonight. I'm still not sure that's a good thing."

Diana lightened the subject. "Wolves like him have a place in the ecosystem. We just need to learn how to co-exist, with no harm to either party, right? Do you think we should call – anyone? ...Call Professor Vimvole, so he knows where you are? Farraga?"

"I can't bear to speak to that beast."

"If I had better self-esteem," Derek admitted tentatively, "I'd swear he made a pass at me last night. But we'd probably better... I can call him," he asserted. It was his reflexive habit to verify location of deliveries. "What's his number?"

Farraga recited a cell number that Derek dialed. He made a humorous horse face to alter his voice. "Yes, Professor Vimvole? This is the New York Palace Suites." He puffed out his chest. "Ms. Farraga Den-ta-ta asked us to inform you that she will be staying with us. Yes, sir, I will pass on your message. Good evening." He ended the call and said, in the same pompous tone, "The professor will see you at the airport. Shall I call him back and say you've chartered a Lear jet instead?"

"You've no idea: if only I'd schmoozed better at the banquet, a Lear jet might have been a reality." This triggered remorse. "Diana, I'm so sorry you don't get paid enough." Farraga slurred, "But you know how, at get-togethers, or at a bar, or wherever – the people you're introduced to always ask, without fail, 'What product are you affiliated with, and how do you market your personal brand?'" Diana nodded. "I hope you're proud to say, 'F-f-f-" She hiccuped and gave Diana another hug as they all came to a halt, having arrived at Diana's building. "Fanged Wilds."

Diana took a step back. "Fanged Wilds and Women is more than just a job. It's my passion." Continuing this diplomatic tone, Diana added, "Thanks, Derek, for dinner, the Empire State Building, and everything."

 Hair fallen over his eyes, Derek stuttered, "I thought I was coming up for tea?"

Diana pouted. "Oh, we'd better all call it a night." Her eyes lingered on him.

Derek held his hair back from his forehead – and his brain from exploding – and watched the two beautiful women climb the brick stairs. "Well, give me a call when you're all tucked in. So I know you're safe."

"Oh," Diana melted. "OK." To mirror his tenderness, she lisped, "After he tucks us in, I'll have my teddy bear report our status to you."

"Oh, Diana, you are so sweet," Farraga said. "I'm so glad you're my friend. I have few true female friends. I'm usually more of a man's woman. Men aren't such feline canines." She snickered, then hiccuped again. "The best women are bears. You're a teddy bear. A sleek, honey sun bear." As they disappeared into the building, Farraga waved to Derek and started singing *Teddy Bears' Picnic*. "If you go down to the woods today, you'd better not go alone. It's lots of fun in the woods today, *oof*! Safer to stay at home..."

Derek whistled along. "I've always wanted to learn the words to that," he called to

Farraga.

"Come on up," Farraga replied. "Come on up and I'll teach you while Diana tucks me in." So it was that Derek found himself in Diana's tiny apartment. The two young people put the heart-broken drunk into one of Diana's flannel nightgowns and into bed. Farraga propped an eye open to see Derek take Diana's hand and kiss it. Selfishly Farraga blubbered into the pillow: what could she do to make Vimvole love her again? At her sob, Diana sat down on the edge of the bed and sadly waved goodbye to Derek. The young man went back out into the clammy night.

Vimvole, in the meantime, was still wired from his thrilling evening. Farraga would ordinarily give him a vigorous back-rub and ease all his tension, were she along on a night like this. But she had become unpredictable. The eco-ethnopaleontological presentation and subsequent socializing having been such a worthy success, Vimvole decided to call the concierge. "I'd like an in-room, one-hour massage." From her desk in the lobby, the woman's voice affirmed that the service could be available in twenty minutes or so, only one hundred dollars fifty plus gratuity.

Vimvole hung up and efficiently channeled his excess of excitement using some exquisite photos kept in a secret file in his laptop. Then he showered using organic verbena soap prudently brought from home; even nice hotels didn't always have organic soap.

When the massage technician arrived, she was attractive enough that he was glad he'd taken precautions, to curtail any embarrassment. The thirtyish woman's relaxed face and straightened, flaxen hair reminded him of the youthful vitality of the tow-headed boy scout and his rambunctious troupe, back in McCarthy. The young woman's gentle professionalism, as she set up her table and instructed him what to do, made him feel as at ease as when he'd had crushes on his teachers in grade school. He grinned, happy.

She went into the bathroom to wash her hands while he stripped and stretched under the flannel sheet. The faucet ran for a minute, then was shut off. Loud, so she could hear, Vimvole proclaimed, "I gave a lecture today about ethnopaleontological rewilding. And was honored at a banquet. So I'm still wound up."

"Rewilding?" The massage technician reappeared, squirting some lotion from her tool belt into her muscular, shapely hands.

"Ecology," he explained modestly, then put his face down in the toilet-shaped flannel cradle, aligning his arms under the sheet, on the soft table beside his bare hips.

"Wow. You're saving the world." Her cool hands touched both of his shoulders at once, slipped down his arms to his elbows, then scooped back toward his neck. "If only Gore had made 'Inconvenient Truth' earlier. There might be hope." Her kneading of Vimvole's neck muscles almost made him gasp with pleasure. She worked down his spine, toward his tail bone, her fingers seeming to weave him back into one piece. All his frayed ends were smoothed by her hands.

As she returned to his triceps, Vimvole mumbled into the flannel, "Do you believe that massage therapist who said Al Gore molested her?"

The professional clucked her tongue. "Maybe. I get why she waited to report him. She didn't want to lose her job *or* an environmentalist."

Vimvole, face down, let his arms hang over the edges of the table, "accidentally" letting his forearm brush against the woman's thigh.

CHAPTER NINETEEN

MANHATTAN, NEW YORK, U.S.A.

Late the next day, the headquarters of the Fanged Wilds and Women Program thronged with law enforcement. One officer checked a new wicker chair in the corner for evidence. Another cop furtively tossed a piece of jerky into the aquarium, where piranhas swarmed the meaty treat.

Outside, Diana sat on the deck of a police boat. Above her on the floating dock, an enterprising journalist in a stylish houndstooth pantsuit and sensible shoes, name of MacDoogle, interviewed a detective. MacDoogle asked, "Why was such a small non-profit organization targeted with a sophisticated parcel explosive, in your opinion?"

The detective felt around in various rumpled pockets of his mildewed trench coat, seeking something. "Hard to say. It's hard to imagine anyone targeting a ladies' organization, as such. Ladies helping third-world girls? Not likely. Too trivial. So it probably has to do with their nature-conservation policy. Hunters and ranchers, maybe, got peeved."

"Isn't that too obvious? It couldn't be a rival of this...F.Q.U.P. I mean, F.W. –? Other organizations? Should I look into that angle?" As the shrugging detective was consulted by another cop, MacDoogle googled on her hand-held. Who else was horning in on the market? Wilderness Stewardship Network... Fauna Forever... International Society to Conserve Wildlife... Earth Club... National Habitat Preservation League... Friends of Natural Resources... Biodiversity United... Charitable Ecology Brigade... World Environment Coalition... Wild Animal Protection Fund... The list continued, with individual conservancies and rescue programs, global and local, for every imaginable species: Hares Today... Fawns

Tomorrow... Dolphins and Other Non-Human Persons.

How many passionate animal lovers could there be?

The industry was apparently thriving, to allow so much competition. And competition got testosterone pumping; then things could get vicious. What was that, *Do-Gooders of Wildlife?* Were they as popular as *World Life Wildfund?* MacDoogle checked online, tapping on her tablet. She saw the latter, WLW's, net assets of $227,351,912; and its male CEO's salary of $465,427. She read further: DGW's assets were $21,137,679, and their CEO got... (she added $255,994 + $45,759) ...like... over $300K per year. MacDoogle prodded the detective, seemingly lost in thought: "There's significant money at stake. Any idea who's in the ring wrestling with these gals for their pet cause?"

The detective touched MacDoogle's shoulder, in confidence. "Be careful, snooping around these righteous types. Ends justify means. They're animals. Like, PETA – Ethical Treatment of – you know. All fighting over the same carcass."

"Thanks for the warning." The journalist glanced around suspiciously. She wondered if there weren't some way for all those organizations to cooperate and even pool resources. But competition was the norm, in this dog-eat-dog world. She herself was eager to scoop this story, as she rushed to get enough information. "And what exactly was the damage here? Old building. Looks pretty rundown already."

"It's apparently a grassroots operation." Rummaging again in his coat-pocket contents, the detective shifted from foot to foot. A light dawned: he leaned over and found the pack of gum that he had been seeking; it was wedged in the side of his shoe. He offered some gum to his interviewer; the up-and-coming journalist, making the diplomatic choice, gingerly accepted. They stood facing each other, man and woman, and crushed the gum with their teeth. The detective dropped the crumpled wrapper in the murkywater. "Fortunately the detonation was halted by their aquarium." He smirked. "One of the staff members, that young woman sitting there, *'Had an intuition'* to throw the parcel into the aquarium."

A sailboat motoring toward them had Derek at the helm. His face distraught, he spotted Diana and idled toward the boat she sat in. He held up a broadsheet with the URLs of news stories, the top headline heralding:

PIRANHAS RESCUE CHARITY: Anti-Poacher Pack Dodges a Bullet.

The journalist saw it and cursed. MacDoogle complained to her new acquaintance, "That Ruptur Murdrech! He's like Hearst; he hacks the story before it even happens."

Diana locked eyes with Derek as he glided nearer. She slowly stood up. Derek roped his boat-cleat to hers and climbed over. When the police Zodiac boat steadied, Derek clasped the beautiful, traumatized office worker in their first, wobbling, embrace. As they hugged, he pressed his lips against her silky hair. Then the young man kissed Diana's fragrant head compulsively, over and over, almost frantically.

MacDoogle, the newswoman, rolled her eyes and activated the wifi on her tablet again. "Listen to this," she snorted to the detective, and read: "'Armed Women: Legs aren't Enough?' *Ha!* 'Microfinance: Risking more than just Money with Poor Females?'"

The detective stood beside her and kibbutzed more Tweets on the tiny monitor. "ECOLOGY = Danger?" He grunted. "Ladies, go Back to yer Kitchens where yer Safe!"

To get the unfamiliar – perhaps overly friendly – policeman to step away, the journalist read another posting out loud. "This sexist so-called charity doesn't trust women to know when they want to be home-makers. Elite, frigid debutantes are exploiting poor women with the claim it helps the environment. To 'help the environment' means it takes food out of people's mouths."

Looking at MacDoogle's face in disbelief, the detective folded his arms. "That's nuts."

She shrugged. "This writer has a huge audience. People love him." The two new friends exchanged a look of understanding. "To get a following, I should write polemic drivel like that. The rough-hewn buddies pressed closer together to read more. "Oh, a Hyena News exposé of the founder! 'Farraga Dentata didn't finish her doctoral thesis at Mid-Oregon U. yet still feels qualified to push her elite agenda on uneducated women whose children need them, born and unborn.'"

Derek huddled down with Diana on the moist aluminum bench seat and gazed at her with furrowed brow. "It was a package I brought you, yesterday?" She shrugged, exonerating him. He hung his head and tenderly prodded, "Are you okay?"

Diana shook her head. "This is freaky. I mean, they just don't pay me enough. We've had hecklers but we've never been attacked before. I'm not sure if I should stick around. I should quit."

Derek looked grim. "What are you saying? Are you really going back to Britain? Import export? ...Kilts? ...Four and twenty blackbirds?"

Diana sighed, "I just need a better job." She looked at his sailboat. "Maybe I can find one around here. Like, as an interpreter, or a tour guide." She curled closer to his warm chest, as chill set in from the metal seat under her mini skirt. "Poor Farraga. She must be heartbroken. And terrified. But she just doesn't pay me enough. Not for this... death threat."

Meanwhile, in the spacious lobby of Professor Vimvole's hotel, Farraga was holding an impromptu press conference. Still in her orange evening gown, her push-up bra pinching her ribs, she talked into a journalist's microphone. "With spare lunch money, folks can employ poor women to protect cheetahs, snow leopards, sharks, otters – key species world-wide – and, in the process, grow respect for Mother Earth and all her daughters."

Another slickly-clad journalist confronted her. "But... women and guns? Does violence invite violence?"

"We can stay in denial, or we can defend our lives." Farraga quipped, "Women and guns is the perfect balance of nature and nurture. Women hold up half the sky, by tooth and claw." Her spunk could be explained by the expression on her handsome boyfriend's weathered face: he looked repentant. Would he cherish her, now she was threatened? The professor stood holding their two small suitcases, his, of brown recycled rubber, and hers, blonde leather hand-trimmed with pink fur. Farraga indulged in a moment of sentiment, looking at her increasingly famous paramour. Then she declared, "Whoever thinks they can stop the Fanged Wilds and Women Program may be dead meat. Be sure to print that."

Professor Vimvole interjected, "Don't antagonize anyone." He trembled with indignation. What if the unknown aggressor knew Farraga lived in Vimvole's house? What if a bomb was sent there, too? "The women's charity may have to rethink its entire –" He spurted, "This could be the end."

The hotel lobby's attentive crowd snickered and murmured. Farraga pulled out her compact and outlined a defiant smear of lipstick on her moue. "Professor Vimvole does not speak for the Program. For the record, his contribution to the charity has been the scientific inspiration of his rewilding research. That, and, of course, his unflagging support of me as his domestic partner in our homemaking and... our abiding passion. Together we're committed to nature's survival as well as to each other." She smiled at the journalists, avoiding the professor's eyes. "Please be sure to print *that*, too, along with a mention of Fanged Wilds' line of eco-chic fashion apparel and accessories, whose sales, along with your donations, provide the bulk of our non-profit budget."

"Is that what you're wearing?" asked someone behind a microphone.

"How will this affect your personal life?" dug the journalist with the most polished hairstyle. She exchanged a glance with Vimvole. He sat down on the arm of one of the lobby's comfy chairs, melting a little: was the woman with the microphone flirting with him?

Farraga shivered in her sleeveless gown. Her phone rang. "Oh, I must answer this." She looked at the screen. "It's our poor little office manager who discovered the explosive." The journalist shrugged as Farraga stepped between a potted palm and a pillar.

"Farraga," Diana's voice was excited. "I logged on to my laptop to update our website and tell my family that I'm safe, and... You wouldn't believe all the feedback we've got! Listen to this: 'I'm doubling my cash contributions! Nature is worth it! I ain't L-I-O-N!' Edinburgh has a campus support group that says, 'You grrrls R Grrrrrrreat!'" Brogue trilled her tongue. "And the tweets: TIGERS Luv U fiercely & SO DO I! Don't let BAD predators win!'" Herds of well-wishers clustered online; Diana recited more encouragement. "Oh, Farraga, people are pledging to send us thousands of dollars!"

"Don't count those chickens," Farraga wept, trying to stay calm, but unable to suppress tears of relief.

"Well, some nice massage therapist just arrived in a gondola and handed me, in person, a check for one hundred fifty dollars. And a confidential note addressed to you."

Unbeknownst to the women, in the offices several floors above Diana, the account executive with the sleekest, fastest motor boat was listening over his earpiece to the taps he'd put in Diana's desk and phone. His investment banking colleagues and superiors had no inkling of his extracurricular capers. But they were consistently impressed – though they only showed it via one-upmanship – with the young executive's apparently endless supply of ready cash.

"Early lunch," Glen mouthed to his boss over the walls of the cubicles. He grabbed the keys to his cigarette boat from the NASCAR™ ceramic holder. As he headed to the stairs, he planned his attack. "Know a good sushi place? I'm one of those guys who loves raw fish," he'd say to Diana, when he asked her out. "I just love the texture of raw fish on my tongue." He'd monitored her conversations with her "mum" and Farraga, so he knew the best approach to sweep her off her feet. With an expense account like his, the sky was the limit. The one thing she secretly desired most in the world: a safe place to raise kids. Glen's triumph over Diana was one helicopter ride away, to Connecticut. She would probably take one look around and put out on the nearest well-trimmed lawn. She was probably well-trimmed, herself. He relished the escapade.

He got to the ground floor and made his way through the corridors, past the mostly unoccupied office space at water level. When he got to the F.W.W.P. office door, police tape sagged across it with a flutter. So Diana's new suitor backtracked and got his cigarette boat from the marina at the main entrance. Glen's wake incurred obscenities from a gondolier as the banker's vehicle hastened around the building to scope out Diana's little pier. There she was, like a flower box, perched on the window sill! Waiting, as if for him! "She's my property," he incanted to himself, using a dating affirmation that had always worked like a charm. He feigned surprise for her as he slipped hear. "Need a ride?" He flashed a hopeful smile.

"I've called for a gondola-"

"Jump in! I need some air. So you'll be doing me a favor, to let me be your chauffeur." He judged her expression. "Do something dangerous; it'll make you feel alive." Glen saw that the low tide had increased the distance from the window to the dock. "I can help you down." He motored closer and made as if to tie off his lines.

Diana looked down at the platform rocking on the water. Then she saw the gondolier appear around the corner, still scowling, the same, lascivious old guy who'd fondled Diana's posterior on an earlier occasion, months before, when she was new on the job. "There he is," Diana said unenthusiastically but firmly.

"I'll give him a consolation prize. Come on – I'd love someone to talk to, as long as you're in need of transportation." The grimy gondolier looked about to give Glen an earful for speeding, so Glen whipped out his wallet and waved a hundred dollar bill. "Something for his trouble."

Diana's eyes bugged out. She clutched her laptop satchel to her chest. "Are you crazy?"

"Come on, he'll use it for his kids. Trickle-down works. This is proof of trickle-down in practice." He stood up sufficiently to hold out the bill for the gondolier to reach it. "One for the Gipper."

"Oh my gosh. Today has just been too much," Diana said. She watched the astonished gondolier accept the pay-off; he tucked it into his shirt pocket with a familiar grin to her and a thumbs-up nod indicating her "catch." Or was it her john?

Glen helped her get in. "Hey! I skipped lunch! Got a dinner date?" Diana settled into his sun-warmed, cream leather bucket seat. "Thanks. Diana, right? Help me. My mom is hassling me to have kids. And I don't even have a girlfriend. I need to confide in someone, my hopes and fears. You seem like such a sympathetic ear."

This charvy guy was a bit of a berk. Diana noticed four slender fingerprints on the chrome of the dash: traces of a woman's hand lotion. So he probably did have some sort of a girlfriend. "Sure."

The gondola out of his way, Glen brought the six cylinders up to a purr, a match for his lung-power as he chatted the young woman up. "So what happened to you today? I bet you need to talk, as much as I do. Everyone needs a shoulder." He shouted as he sped up, "Do you know a nice sushi place, by any chance?" He rubbed his six-pack abs with one hand, glancing at her carnivorously. "I could murder some raw fish."

CHAPTER TWENTY

NANIRAUÁ, BRAZIL

Piranhas boiled the water in a feeding frenzy. Motors whined as two boats engaged in a chase: Fanged-Wilds women were after some poachers who had netted, but not reeled in, a thrashing dolphin. A Fanged-Wilds woman shouted through a megaphone, "*Gostariamos so falar!* We just want to talk!" With the typical male response at such a proposition, the poachers made themselves scarce as rapidly as possible. "Just talk! Just talk!" the woman bleated, as the men roared off. Another woman shot a warning shot into the air, barely holding on as overhanging vegetation whipped their boat. One poacher brandished a machete and cut loose the dolphin-dragging net.

The woman pointed: half-hidden by foliage, an orange jaguar was running through the lush green of the riverbank. "Jaguar looks hungry," she murmured.

The poacher who wasn't manning the motor pushed away from projecting foliage. Snagged on a branch, his shirt stretched but didn't release till too late: the man fell out of his boat. His dodgy accomplice motored away, abandoning the floundering poacher. He splashed toward shore, unaware of the predator. Meanwhile, the small pink dolphin broke loose from the net and disappeared into the depths of the river.

The women slowed their boat, unable to see through the dense undergrowth. Rain had begun to pound down. Through its static hiss, a wail from the man confirmed that the jaguar had seized him.

The women stared at one another. What should they do? Human hunters competed with the jaguar for deer, capybaras, tapirs, peccaries, caimans, anacondas, monkeys, and fish. Jaguars didn't usually eat humans. But the last, interrupted cry of the poacher implied the worst.

The women turned their motorboat around in the water. As they returned to their longhouse, one Ribeirinho-tribe woman reasoned, "We will spend our pay on the children's education. They will never have to be cat food for a living."

Rain poured off the roof thatched with açaí fronds. The women's families were preparing leaves to use as disposable plates for their dinner of fish. Everyone gathered closer to hear the women's recounting of the day's events. "We chased two dolphin netters, and then we saw a jaguar who.... may have attacked one of the poachers." Not to appear too eager, one man disguised his curiosity and primed the conversation with a mention of the weather: "The rain is fierce tonight. Less wildfires this year, maybe."

Then a renowned peccary hunter asked the Ribeirinho women point blank, "Did you shoot the jaguar?"

Her mouth filled with red fruit, the Ribeirinho woman who carried the gun that day glanced at her team members. She finally said, "The poachers hate 'Fanged Wilds' program. The poachers don't want us women to have any gun in the first place."

Her comrade extrapolated, "So the poacher must not want us to shoot." The entire tribe ate pensively. The loudest sound was rain falling. A baby cried.

As they finished, licked the leaves, and discarded them, a husband of one of the F.W.W.P. women walked through the tribe to the Shaman. He asked the wizened, aloof figure, "Did the women need to shoot the jaguar?"

Her obsidian eyes obsequious, a half-naked, cinnamon-skinned maiden held some berries for the Shaman, delaying his response as he picked them, one by one, from her hands. He chewed them. The husband waited respectfully till the Shaman pronounced, "That man would kill the jaguar if the jaguar not kill him first. The forest needs jaguars. And we need the forest."

Later that evening, as the fire died down and the Shaman was smoking a pipe, one of the Fanged-Wilds women pushed her little girl toward the elder. The woman announced portentiously, "Dilminha has dreamed of the jaguar. She wants to be your apprentice."

A couple other men heard this and laughed; two boys jeered, egging each other on. The little Ribeirinho girl pouted for just a second at them, then stated, "Jaguar is the national animal of Brazil."

The Shaman gazed at the little girl.

The next day, the Shaman meaningfully put a Fanged Wilds and Women hat on Dilminha's little head. The little girl smiled knowingly and turned away, her face aglow with confidence, like a cat that had eaten a mouse. The photo on her hat was of Dilma Rouseff, the first female Brazilian president.

NORTHERN CAUCASUS, RUSSIA

When she was in the army, after experiencing combat as a convoy driver, Alice had been recruited for the "Lioness" program. That was a system designed to acknowledge Muslim gender polarity and sex-segregated modesty. Alice was trained to search Iraqi women at forward-unit checkpoints, the imperiled front line where American females were otherwise not deployed. Iraqis appreciated the women's training in Arabic and their efforts to communicate in the native language. But the Americans' diplomacy was mostly unspoken, and broad: they modeled equality not just to the women in veils, but to the other infantry. Their presence proved that females volunteer for danger.

An aborted, retrieved "suicide vest" that Alice saw – home-stitched tan canvas – reminded a fellow Lioness, Nicole Estrada, of the belts worn by newborns when they needed their umbilicus protected. Considering the suicide vest, Nicole said, "Think of all the mothers who may have lost someone in this war. They could use their anger as an excuse to make something like this."

The soldiers' nickname for suicide-bomber females was "Pop Tarts."

But the Lioness program evolved to improve public relations with Iraqis by capitalizing on the presumed nonviolence of females. Janis, Carylyn, Lynndie,

Megan and Sabrina – the five women from the U.S. who were entangled in the Abu Ghraib scandal – didn't help the cause. But Alice could sympathize with a soldier slipping into outrageous behavior. The suicide rate for female veterans doubled that of civilian women. Out of over 200,000 American women who had served in Iraq and Afghanistan, over eleven thousand had been diagnosed with post-traumatic stress; before her new lease on life had brightened her options, Alice reckoned that the pay-off for her army years would only be free brain-numbing meds and disability benefits for PTSD.

Alice hadn't imagined that she could get a real "Lioness" job, using her military skills constructively. Emerging from a heart of darkness that threatened to break her, she found a career to brake Earth's apocalypse. Unemployed when she heard about the Fanged Wilds Program, Alice was now a trainer. Under her guidance, local women regenerated grasslands by herding flocks densely while also protecting leopards, wolves, bears, and other dental marvels.

The Fanged Wilds program finagled clearance into the war-torn Caucasus region. Officials peremptorily perused the documents, pretending action was impossible. "VVhat iz thiz, another Puzzy Riot?" But the papers were couriered by a curvaceous, F.W.W.P.-uniformed representative who filled out not just her dress but – in neat, flowery handwriting – each newly proffered triplicate-form. The officials saw that the Fanged Program was merely women, giving jobs to other women. The amused apparatchiks judged that, in essence, the girls would be doing nothing but "holistically" herding bush-meat on the hoof and selling cute para-military costumes. Too trivial to be opposed. Priority for nothing but Slavic shrugs.

Recruited online, with flyers, radio ads, and also by word of mouth, more blousy representatives came to the nondescript administrative buildings. They promoted their cause in a Dickensian fashion: "Rather untidy about the shoes and stockings. They were not exactly pretty, perhaps; but they had a great deal of colour in their faces, and looked quite stout and hearty."

Liquor appeared in the highest official's office. Soon, with a few rounds of vodka and an anthem – lead by the first, voluptuous F.W.W.P. representative, Olga, belting out the melody à la Nancy in Oliver Twist – the politburo practically welcomed Fanged Wilds, with mutual promises of festivities to come.

Civilian locals were friendly; they liked that F.W.W.P. brought in jobs, even if it was only for women, for a couple dollars a day. Negotiations were launched for the women to deploy to Chernobyl, which had become a de facto wilderness preserve. (Horses trotted; bears lumbered; boars squealed... *and they lived half-lifely ever after.*)

Meanwhile, the Caucasus mountains needed wildlife management.

The animals' habitat was beautiful. But the humans' lodging was more rudimentary: old army barracks had only an occasional rose bush, apricot or apple tree to slow the gusts of wind from the mountains. Shutters and screen doors banged if not closed carefully. The women sometimes wore kerchiefs over their noses like bandits when they had to be out in the swirling dust.

But today the weather was mild. Outside the old army barracks, Alice and Tiara – both Americans in leopard-spotted, pink trimmed uniforms – cleaned their M-4 rifles on a wooden table.

Blonde hair in braids, Tiara's history was similar to Alice's. Her "female engagement team" in Afghanistan worked beside indigenous female police and explained MQ-1 Predator drones to villagers. As she bent down to pet a stray tabby cat, Tiara felt comfortable reminiscing with Alice. "I remember an old man said, 'Your men come to fight, but we know the women are here to help.' Now we're ambassadors with our historic enemy, Russia. You know, the Cold War? Women coming out into the world is like the Warm War."

Alice smiled and oiled her rifle stock, her face uplifted with an expression of growing satisfaction. "Ahhh." Her movement became more and more suggestive, till Tiara squealed, uncharacteristically girlish, and picked up the cat to hug. Alice joked, "Men will stop waging war when their women can oil their rifles right. With our army skills, and some grease, we can show women how to give a new meaning to 'global warming.'"

The women made a few increasingly obscene comments – more like sailors, really, than soldiers. They curtailed and stifled themselves at the rickety approach of a babushka, the elderly local waddling up carrying a straw basket filled with home-grown produce. Some of the participants – Abazins, Adyghey, Kabardians, and Circassians from former Soviet satellites like Moldova – followed the old woman, discussing what to pay for the arthritic babushka's vegetables, and how to fix them: cabbage rolls? Stew? Vegetables were so complicated: roasted turnips, or borscht? Translating, the locals explained to the Americans what the options were for dinner. Raising her arm with effort, the babushka presented pungent herbs for them to sniff. She followed the traditional Abkhazian nature-based religion in which the supreme god was Antzva, meaning "Mothers." (Lesser gods ruled the weather, forest, wild animals, and hunting.) As the others smelled her herbs, the old woman murmured in her language, "Praise Antzva."

Tiara smirked and addressed the cat in her arms. "*Pussy.* Did you ever see that T-shirt, 'I've got the pussy, I make the rules'? And some guy photo-shopped it to say, 'I've got the pussy, I make the food'?"

Alice laughed. "I've got the M-4. Now make me stew." They moved their gun components to make room on the table for the vegetable selection.

The hearty Russian woman, Olga, spread a lacy pink paisley kerchief to set the food on. "Rutabaga, my favorite," Olga said without irony in Russian, then explained to the Americans, "Yum yum."

Someone went to the canteen deep freeze and brought back a soup bone wrapped in oilcloth. Its cartilage collagen and other nutrients would keep the women athletic; it was cheaper than glucosamine supplements for their joints, and the high-calorie marrow was good spread on bread. More immediately, a Chechen participant brought a tray with a colorful pitcher and tin-handled glasses. "*Kombucha chaga!*" she exclaimed, implying an inherent warning that the tea was more medicinal than delicious. The F.W.W.P. women and the babushka all imbibed, swigging and puckering at the sour, earthy flavor. "Some mushrooms radioactive. Not this *chaga*," the Chechen reassured them.

"Refreshing." Tiara, wiping her mouth, proclaimed, "Puts hair on your chest. Better'n steroids." She thumped her sternum as a translation to the natives. Then she distributed to each participant three clips of ammo.

Having completed her gun maintenance, Alice offered around some local cigarettes. Her mom and brother had died of cancer, due not to smoking but to chemicals. The F.W.W.P. participants were like a replacement family to her. "I'm nobody," she whispered to Tiara, who also didn't smoke. "But to my corps, I'm queen." She didn't know she was Tiara's hero, too. Tiara noticed a flock of birds crossing the sky above, and sighed, contentment filling her like the chaga tea in her stomach.

The Chechen participant piped up, spurring a flurry of translation among the women. "Women are like mushroom fungus. Treated like rot, but indispensable to life." The other women soon parroted the statement triumphantly in all languages. "Poachers in my hometown sell bear organs to Turkey and China, for folk medicine. I heard that some women in Iran are copying our program. They want to increase their population of cheetahs. Russia wants to get cheetahs when there are enough to share. Russian and Iranian women are cooperating."

The Chechen nodded as more of their team joined them, some casually putting an arm around each other, to draw the group closer; their situation had infected them with touchy-feely informality. The Chechen said, "I think women can get along better than men. Or at least we fight with less explosives. Sometimes only with fingernails." She humorously formed her strong hands like claws. "Groups make better decision if women involved – that's scientific research. Better decision than even one smart person all alone, it's proven. Science say women can stop people so don't act like small children. Because women are democracy more than bullies."

Magova Yevloyev passed around a snapshot of her children. "Now Chernobyl is radioactive. Could be worse. Territory will be nothing if there's no tree or animal. Our children will need bezoar goats, Dagestan tur, saigak and boar. Leopards and bears too, in wildness. Poachers take them all, like weasels and foxes."

Pressed against Magova's soft hip, Alice added, "Females need to take the long view of things. I think I'll keep working here till I'm really ready to emit kids." She waved at the cluster of children watching idly from outside the chain-link fence.

The women fetched bowls and arms and crowded around the table together. Some cleaned their guns; some peeled turnips or chopped cabbage. The communication difficulties had tired out the conversation. Then a Ukranian sang, "I hear if from ze pipple of ze town."

Tiara joined in, trying to sound like Cher, "They call us –" Everyone sang *Gypsies, Tramps and Thieves*. "Ev'ry night the men'd come aroun'... and lay their money down."

As the song died out, a local reporter showed up. His rather dapper suit was frayed at the cuffs. The women had him sit down for a cup of tea, a splash of vodka, and, when it was ready, a plate of savory sage stew. He gave them good press. They let him shoot an M-4.

CHAPTER TWENTY-ONE

DROUGHTERBERG PLATEAU, NAMIBIA

The hacking sound of bird calls was syncopated with the rhythm of Lydia's sawing, as she prepared to remove the big horn from an anesthetized black rhino. His second horn was too stubby to saw, Lydia figured. Behind their de-facto leader stood her fellow F.W.W.P. participants, their uniforms now faded, with ragged cuffs and gaudy patches sewn over threadbare knees. Lydia assured the other young women, "This is a sure way to keep poachers off him." Seeing their hesitation, she added, "He'll not wake up for a while."

Severed, the horn dropped off into the riverbank's mud. One of the bolder women, Chantal, snatched it up. Chantal brandished it and joked, "I am not afraid of him now. Now I am his equal!" Then she held the rhino horn in front like a penis. "Who needs a gun? If I have this weapon." Chantal had been born in the Congo, where she'd watched Ituri militants hack off and eat her mother's arm.

Lydia was the only one who didn't laugh. She had been somber since her parents' death, and preoccupied with finances; she frequently checked her savings balance on her cell phone. She lectured the group, "If they sell it as aphrodisiac, that one horn can pay for our entire program." At a cloud of dust, she squinted suspiciously: a truck passed, a mile or so away, on its way to the diamond or uranium mines in the national park.

The light-hearted woman handed the horn over to Lydia. Lydia wrapped it in faux fur before she pushed it into her sack. F.W.W.P. headquarters had (for some unfathomable reason) sent the Namibians yards of metal-embossed, plush cheetah fabric for the local micro-financed seamstresses. The Namibians couldn't use much on the uniforms without making them too hot. But they hoarded the fabric as if it were Golden Fleece, and brought it out of storage only for ceremonial purposes.

They'd made a throne of it when a shaman had come to consult with the tribe on whether the program was an advisable enterprise, or whether (as some local officials contended) it was dangerous and misguided. The shaman had looked very comfortable on his throne when he pronounced the women's behavior appropriate for a drought year. He recommended that they invite him to return when the climate had improved, to reassess the situation. His assistant bundled up the glittering fur and took it with them upon departure; all the supplicants agreed that it would not have been seemly to leave it behind in the impoverished village, having been sat on by such an august personage.

But Lydia had enough remaining plush pelt to package the invaluable rhino horn till her brother got it to a buyer. She surveyed the mountain of unconscious rhino. The idle women inched away from the soon-to-be-dangerous beast.

Lydia raised her saw. "We shall clear thornbush and collect branches for the kraal till he wakes up." Invasive acacia thornbush harmed cheetahs. The women also slashed thick reeds and gathered saplings to strengthen the livestock corral. The more the women helped the nearby farmers, the less likely there would be an inquisition when the rhino's nasal stump was noticed. When they'd sent the tranquilizer cartridges, headquarters had advised Lydia to use her own judgment and intuition for decisions. Somehow she had the feeling that headquarters would approve, if they knew that, since her parents got sick, she hadn't had any joy in life, not until she felt the strength of her own biceps severing the rhino horn.

GIRLL FOREST, GURAJAT, INDIA

The brigade was well-established and effective, though the women occasionally had to venture out armed only with sticks: there weren't enough shotguns to be handy in an emergency. Yet the ladies were resourceful. Manesha Vaghila, at twenty-three, tracked down a gang of nine antelope poachers. The men were on motorcycles, and she was alone. Yet she managed to apprehend them. She and other Girll Wildlife

Sanctuary "van rakshak sahayaks" became world-famous for maintaining the habitat of the last wild population of Asiatic lion. Global warming hit hard where the temperature often reached a hundred-twenty degrees. Animals and people suffered from hunger and thirst.

Tourism put the wildlife on display. More "lieutenants" on the beat could referee the animals' interface with human activity. People living within the reserve were allowed to herd livestock and gather dead wood. Negotiations were launched with Maldhari nomads: F.W.W.P could help train tribal women to protect the hundreds of lions in the 877-square-mile reserve. The women might also stop timber smugglers; respond to fires; and monitor the thousands of open wells in which lions sometimes drowned.

Villages ringed the forest. Farmers jury-rigged electric fences – juiced by overhead power lines – that incidentally killed stray lions, though the fences were intended for keeping the Girll herds of blue nilgai from eating crops. On the phone, Farraga tried to establish rapport with the Maldhari coordinator. She mentioned local ungulates: "The lions keep down the population of the *nilgai*, right?" Farraga had seen photos of the targeted animals whose appearance inspired her to joke wanly, "How can any antelope be so ugly? It's a mercy killing: *nilgai* look as if God crossed Quasimodo with a mule."

The local organizer lilted, "Nilgai are like cows, madame. So they are sacred." He was trying to cow the charity founder, a world away in Oregon, and milk her for funds.

Farraga sighed, patting her buxom chest. "To get more respect, maybe women in India should moo." She changed the subject to sloth bears.

McCARTHY, OREGON, U.S.A.

Sipping organic merlot in Professor Vimvole's living room, Farraga steeled herself. Her non-profit organization needed money. She surfed on her laptop for inspiration.

Should she borrow a page from one of the vastly more successful charities? They knew that enlisting public support was as important as substance. Cribbing from them, Farraga prepared a questionnaire to mail to supporters:

- Which of these is your favorite wild animal?

    Polar Bears   Lions   Sea Otters   Tigers

    Cetaceans   Wolves   Cougars/Panthers

    Leopards   Cheetahs   Wild women

- Which of the following needs to be protected?

    Cheetahs   Sea Otters   Tigers   Polar Bears

    Eagles   Dolphins   Wolves   Girls

Farraga poured some more scarlet wine. Why couldn't she dwell on happy thoughts, like her friend Marion? She forged on, depressing though it was to think of any living creature losing its freedom, prevented from being wild. Her plagiarism grew fecund:

- Do you believe governments should stop using deadly toxic poisons like Compound 1080 and sodium cyanide on wild lands, indiscriminately killing wolves, rare swift foxes and even pet dogs, while also outlawing a woman's right to own her own uterus?

                                        YES ___ NO ___

- In your opinion, do you think wild wolf pups should be gassed in their dens, while women worry how they look in the mirror?

                                        YES ___ NO ___

• Should Big Oil be allowed to sell the Arctic-tropical National Wildlife Refuge, America's greatest wildlife sanctuary, to Saudi Arabia, and indenture displaced indigenous women for harems?

YES ___ NO ___

• Should wealthy trophy hunters be allowed to shoot polar bears in Canada just to use as decorative carpets – no matter how stylish – or have trophy wives?

YES ___ NO ___

Farraga's draft avoided some of the biases in the original Do-Gooders of Wildlife survey from which she was cadging ideas. Beyond the emotional blackmail, the Do-Gooders' lists of "Favorite Wild Animals" who needed protection were curiously constricted, almost as if the purpose of the questionnaire were really only Question #12:

Would you be willing to show your concern for defenseless wolf pups and other endangered wildlife by helping with a tax-deductible gift?

___ YES – I want to do all I can to save the lives of wolves, polar bears, manatees, sea otters and other charismatic animals threatened with extinction. Send me Free Gifts in exchange for my donation of:

$20 ___ $30 ___ $40 ___ $50 ___ $100 ___ $500 ___ More $_____

Do-Gooders of Wildlife must have been effective, since behind her desk was her year's collection of their copious fund-raising mailers, enough to keep Georgia Pacific afloat. The stack – in a corner of Vimvole's spare bedroom – was over a foot high, thick with free address labels, stickers, and boxes with a Do-Gooders of

Wildlife pen "with which to sign our petition."

Farraga tried to craft a version of their insatiable plea for her own organization. But it just didn't seem ladylike to beg for money. And offering "Free Gifts" possibly made by political prisoners in China or under some other repressive and/or environmentally feckless regime... that just seemed unethical. Farraga ended her own version:

Please do whatever you deem appropriate at this juncture. Thank you!

RICHARD BRIMSTON'S ISLAND, THE CARIBBEAN

Seagulls hopped over obstacles on the sand, looking a little rattled and reluctant to fly. A hurricane had left debris scattered everywhere. The billionaire's staff was still removing it – throwing pieces into picturesque carts pulled by picturesque miniature donkeys – when a different demographic populated the deck and narrow beach: some fashion models had come to work. They were working on their tans.

Not only that: they had been charitably reviewing new styles produced by Fanged Wilds. Shee exhibited a straw hat with mylar fringe at the back: "This one is called the 'Topanga Canyon.' It's for ladies who jog in the evening when the cougars are ready for dinner. Cougars just love those overhanging rocks." Shee was familiar with Los Angeles, often stopping there on her way home to Australia.

Her friend Jooci, who lived in Santa Monica and had a part in a reality show called Ah la Mode, spoke up knowledgeably in Valley Girl tones. "Topanga Canyon? That's all crunchy granola? They won't wear mylar unless it's made from organic hemp? What is up with – Sequins? Lime green and aubergine? Hideous. I thought this was about being natural?"

Shee shrugged. "There's neons in nature. Bright colors on prey are associated with inedible toxins. Anyway, Withdru Tarrymore already gave us positive feedback on the Topanga hat." The other models perked up at the celebrity's name. "Withdru said you can move the fringe to the front if you have flies in your face. Or paparazzi bugging you. Cate Blanchreef wears one with Aung San Suu Kyi's photo, just for bangin' around Sydney. She's a Fanged fan. She told me, 'Contempt for women wastes our greatest natural resource.'"

A servant wheeled a rattan drink cart out to the sun-drenched beauties, then, with barely a clink, distributed their favorite drinks: a Midori spritz, here; an açaí smoothie there.

Shee had a degree from the University of Sydney and could be pedantic. "Mylar is essential. Chinese folklore says that mirrors and reflective surfaces scare off demons. That legend probably stems from lions and tigers being wary of flashing lights. Maybe the animals think it's a wildfire, or a flash flood."

Igiri, the Brazilian model drinking the fat-free smoothie, took off her Topanga hat and grimaced. "Mirrors sure don't scare away *my* demons. They stay right in my saddle bags and make faces at me." Her sloe eyes glared at her slightly non-linear femurs.

Shee took a tall-stemmed glass of pomegranate-cranberry juice (with a sprig of basil) from the servant. "Your demons are all behind your eyes, Igiri. But if you're worried about your so-called saddle bags, you can go field-test the hat in the Santa Monica mountains. I guarantee you'll jog faster if you have a constant reminder on your head that a cougar may be right behind you."

Igiri lay back, black against the white cushions of her teak lounge chair, and slurred in her Portuguese accent, "I want to help, Shee. But I'd have to hide in the bushes. I couldn't wear lime and aubergine anywhere that anyone I know might see me. Everyone knows the colors this season are Prague."

Kayoko, a model from Japan, tried on a Fanged Wilds tiger-pattern shirt over her bikini top. Shee adjusted her friend's shirttails, cinching them empire-style above tiny ribs with a tie. Kayoko said, "I like the vertigo stripes. They make me look taller, no?" Shee nodded. With much less curiosity, Kayoko also asked, "There are real animals this color?"

Shee explained, "The colors are what animals seem to perceive most clearly, so they make you look bigger. We went with stripes instead of jaguar spots, because... well, polka dots don't have the right effect on humans."

Igiri noted, "They're kind of scary on a real jaguar, though." She'd heard tales of the Amazon.

"Yeah," Shee agreed. "Fanged Wilds does use spots for the ladies in the Caucasus region. Being a little clownish defuses tension. There are volatile elements there who need reminding that the ladies are just there to patrol for animals." She sipped her purple juice. "Just walking in the forest, protecting the world against the most dangerous threat of all, habitat destruction. They say that the Fanged Wilds participants are reducing friction between the sides."

Igiri stopped analyzing her hated thighs and lay back on her cushions. "Women are social lubricants." She yawned. Maybe the subject of detente was inherently soporific. Around her, the models stretched out in the sun; Aisha from Ethiopia was already gently snoring.

"Estrogen is a social lubricant," Shee agreed. "It's *yin*." She caressed a silky tiger shirt. "Sensuality starts with hugging a baby. Bodies to touch bypasses male posturing." She wanted to talk and tried to keep Igiri awake by saying, "Women of color are exoticized in, like, Sports Illustrated, having dark-skin models in animal prints and poses. So having all women in animal patterns is like wearing a yellow star in Denmark. It's like telling Hitler, 'We are all exotic animals.'"

Sir Richard strolled down to the sand and, pausing at the mobile bar, accepted an cocktail, ice tinkling, from the attendant. At the sound of his "Thank you," the models revived. From the box of clothing, Shee donned an actual lion-tattered negligee and twirled in it for the nobleman's benefit. "The Chicago zoo is helping Fanged Wilds producing these," she told him gaily. "Each one is thrown in the lion cage with bunny urine on it! They're a specialty item."

"And they're selling well?" Sir Richard asked, answered by her nod.

"They're washed."

He commented, "Investing in this Fanged program certainly seems more organic than, say, pumping sulfur dust into the stratosphere. That hat is hideous, though."

"Flashes, and lime with eggplant stripes, deters attacks..." Shee gave him a come-hither glance. "From *animals*, anyway!" She dared him with her eyes. But he was preoccupied, giving the okay nod for a damaged palm tree to be felled.

The other models roused themselves in Sir Richard's presence. Jooci (of San Fernando Valley and, lately, Beverly Hills) said, "Lemme try on those leopard pants? I love those, like, panther cats. I can't believe they shot another one in Santa Monica?" Her friends nearby made supportive sounds of disgust. She wriggled into the pants, giving everyone a show. "I think the same pleasure people get looking at me, I get looking at cats?" To compensate for her audacity, Jooci added diplomatically, "I like looking at you chicks, too, though." Turning her back, she batted her long eyelashes and flirted over her shoulder with everyone.

Shee teased her, "Thanks for not being too catty." She and Jooci began to hiss at each other. "Baboons use babies as shields to deter attack. Maybe you should try that, Jooci, if you're old enough to conceive. Or are you too skinny to get your menses?" The two models circled each other and scratched the air. Other women joined in, getting physical. Shee and friends sported themselves, imitating cats and play-wrestling on the sand, while Sir Richard supervised the last of the hurricane clean-up. Workers in cover-alls raked the beach clean.

CHAPTER TWENTY-TWO

TOPANGA CANYON, LALA-LAND, U.S.A.

The California Conservation Corps, in conjunction with F.W.W.P., had a "lion brigade" hike Dirt Mulholland and the trails branching off it. One morning, the brigade, from a vantage point on a hill, spotted a cougar. They whispered to one another and agreed that the lion was stalking a jogger. Visible through the trees, the jogger's lime and purple sunhat bobbed, its brim's Mylar fringe shimmered in the glow of dawn. The C.C.C.F.W.W.P. women made a ruckus, throwing rocks and shouting. They didn't throw far enough yet still scared off the big cat. Afterward, they claimed the cougar had already been hesitating because of the hat. The jogger, the popular comedienne Louise DreiFüße Julia, gave a television interview. "The hat is ugly, but it seemed to work. Ugly is the new black."

The meme of the comedienne spread. Sales of the hat increased dramatically in the Greater Los Angeles area. The hat became a phenomenon like the old-fashioned gas-guzzling sports-utility vehicles, or SUVs, that implied a life of adventure, even for relative stay-at-homes. Guys bought a "cougar hat" for their significant other, in a veiled suggestion to jog, or "The fringe can hide your face when you don't have make-up on." Fat women wore one, maybe to imply that they may not be out-of-shape forever, so "Get it while the gettin's good." Or maybe it indicated, "Delectable meat!" Or maybe they wore the Mylar-trimmed hats to imply, "I don't care what I look like; my life is clearly too exciting for me to care."

When a cougar was shot by a homeowner in the Hollywood Hills, sales skyrocketed: the hat became a symbol protesting cruelty to animals. Louise DreiFüße Julia was interviewed again for local news. "Animals have just as much right to be here as we do. They were here first, according to the Bible. Or one of those books. Darwin, and all that. Can anyone validate my parking?"

A campaign developed to reintroduce grizzlies to the hills. Didn't the California flag showcase the species? Yet grizzlies had been extinct in the state's wilderness since 1889. A trained bear named Ben G. was released in Topanga Canyon. High-profile supporters – several, landowners whose mansions had burned in wildfires – stocked their relic swimming pools with fish for Ben G.

DAM BEAVERS RANCH, NEVADA

The sun shone, intense. In a desert wash prone to flash floods, in a restored riparian zone, the frumpy Madam joined Shee, the sexy Australian model, beside the willows surrounding a spring. Gears were grinding; the twp women watched a hulk of a hauler position his dump truck. He backed the electric vehicle up to where the cracked earth turned moist. The hauler got out and, as he lowered the tail gate, noticed the ladies peer over their sunglasses, playfully lascivious. Bashfully, he rolled up his T-shirt sleeve and flexed tanned biceps for them. The three all cracked up. Blushing under his sunburn, the man ducked back into the truck cabin to flip a lever. The hydrolics of the steel bed groaned, hoisting the load of aspen branches till they rumbled and tumbled in an avalanche out the back.

The hauler produced a long prong with which he yanked the branches that lagged behind, coaxing them onto the ground. The women were riveted. "I like a man with a long stick," the Madam declared. "You can haul me anytime, big boy. Haul me to heaven."

Shee smirked. Looking outdoorsy in a F.W.W.P. safari hat – crowned with Wangari Maathai – and cotton khaki cargo pants, she pushed a few willow sticks into the mud. The willow would take root and expand the damp area. She pulled a baggie of spore out of her pocket and sprinkles it so mycelium would grow through the soil; the absorptive fungal mat would help hold water in place. "Nevada needs resilient root diversity. And beaver wetness."

The Madam laughed. "So your scientist friend will bring the beavers *when*? In a year?"

Shee nodded happily. "In winter," she said, with her Southern-Cross accent. "Then the wetness will spread, and the beavers will have babies. They have matriarchal colonies that disperse when the matriarch dies. It's like a Queen *Bea*-ver. Like you!" Shee affectionately squeezed the older woman's flabby arm.

"You're the queen. Where you jet-setting to next, your Highness?"

"I'm flying to China and India next month to help their beaver populations, to save top soil. It's almost like here, where floods just wash people away. Here, it's folks living on commercially developed, paved wetlands. There, it's farmers and their fields. Then they sell their daughters. Hey! I bet Nicholas Christer could help me get some trafficked girls back to the land, working outdoors, restoring beaver."

"Saint Nicholas. I heard of him," the Madam guffawed. "Some of my girls send him money for, like, whatever the hell he does in Africa."

"Maybe we can get some sort of trans-global alliance. The Alliance of... Damned Beavers for Beaver Dams."

There was a commotion at the house. At labor with his prong, the muscular hauler's eyes popped as several toothsome females appeared, mostly in silk teddies and stilettos – a stand-out was a red-head in black leather chaps, red hair above and below. The curious prostitutes observed from the deck of their quarters, which was a sprawling structure with solar panels on the roof: the world's first eco-whorehouse. Not far from the crumbling ghost town of Las Vegas, Nevada had several oases, areas like the Dam Beavers Ranch, and was still world-famous for supplying "comfort" to men from all over who were otherwise suffering from climate collapse and the ensuing economic crisis. Even environmentalist and "chemically sensitive" men desired such services and would pay handsomely – what would be a month's rent for many people, or a year's rent for many more – for the organic experience. Oh, yeah.

The busty red-head in her leather push-up bra shouted to the fashion model, "Shee! You're so gorgeous!"

Shee answered, "Maybe. The only rack I have is where I hang my coat. Or the occasional rack of lamb." The prostitutes chuckled hungrily.

The hydrolics of the dump truck sighed as it clunked flat again. The hauler saluted the Madam. She responded suggestively, "You'll get your payment inside, okay?"

The handsome hauler tisked, and held up the hand that sported a wedding ring. "I'm making beaver happy. That's payment enough."

Shee ran into the house and returned to give him an autographed Topanga hat, for his wife. "Activism may be futile," Shee said, with a dazzling grin. "But you do meet the best people."

MOUNT ARARAT, TURKEY

An Anatolian leopard was poised among some grey boulders. Unidentifiable humans filed through the scrub nearby, their pace rhythmic. The leopard's spots changed: its skin rippled over its tensing muscles. One by one, the humans disappeared behind the pine trees. The leopard followed them, silent behind the marchers' footsteps that crunched as they trudged through grey remnants of snow.

The last human crouched to fondle a tree seedling. Her voice sounded, but in response, her companions only hesitated briefly to acknowledge her before, with grunts, they sluggishly continued onward. The last woman still bent low, obscured by foliage. The leopard got near enough and swayed side-to-side as it braced to pounce. But it cocked its head, confused. The eyes on the woman's F.W.W.P. hat seemed to be fixed on him. She stood up to walk behind the others, startling a rabbit from under a bush. As the smaller prey scurried away, the leopard paused; the cat stealthily repositioned its body to stalk the rabbit. The team of Turkish women continued through the forest.

A third of the earth's landmass still had trees.

THE OUTBACK, AUSTRALIA

F.W.W.P. "Cowgrrrls" simulated the effect of predators on herds as they drove dozens of kangaroos to churn the desert, strip by strip, back into lush rangeland. Remote and desolate corners remained on their route. Sleeping in an abandoned school bus was a madman who lived on dingo meat and lizards. As he snored, he snared a 'roo. Waking to the commotion, he stumbled out to his eucalyptus grove and saw, silhouetted in the rising sun, a cowgrrl galloping toward him on a barely tame black brumbie. Long hair whipping into her face, she slowed, dropped her reins, and raised her rifle. With one shot, she put the snared game out of its misery. "Tend yer tucker, mate," she yelled churlishly, then turned her horse and rode off to rejoin her leaping livestock.

HUNGARY

1914 to 1929, the "Angel Makers of Nagyrév" were women who poisoned dozens of abusive and boring husbands. A few annoying parents and progeny were also fed the arsenic skimmed from boiled flypaper that the housewives concocted. Just a "hiccup" in history: 1914 – 1929.

ARKANSAS, CALIFORNIA, COLORADO, DELAWARE, LOUISIANA, MARYLAND, NEW JERSEY, NEW YORK, NEW MEXICO, OHIO, PENNSYLVANIA, TEXAS, WEST VIRGINIA, WYOMING

In fracked states, doctors found themselves asking the patient's spouse to step out of the room, please. Behind them shut the doors. Then, with chagrin, the doctor asked the sufferer, "Is there any chance your wife is poisoning you?" Gas-drilled drinking water contained arsenic, along with solvents that could dissolve a marriage.

BOORATISTAN, U.N.D.R.W.R.

Holding a gun by its barrel, an official in a blue polyester suit sat at a desk emblazoned with a large nameplate: "Rakhat Ratbore: Deputy Minister of Foreign Affairs and Swim Wear." He was edifying the (male) director of the newly formed Office of Glorified Womanhood, which had formerly been the Department of Swim Wear. Deputy Minister Ratbore explained, "Women can *hold* a gun. But they never shoot it. If you want their gun, you just take it away." He had invited one of F.W.W.P.'s recruits to assist in his demonstration. Ratbore got up, walked to the center of the office area rug, and handed the gun to her. "See, I just grab her gun and take it away," he said, stepping toward the recruit. The woman flipped the Minister over her back, onto the rug. A blue button popped off his blazer. The Minister jumped up. "See? If she were a man, she would have shot me. Women are weaklings."

CHAPTER TWENTY-THREE

KALKATTA, MICHIGAN

Alice was finally on leave back home in bed with her fiancé, Steve. His pale, burly arms embraced her on top of their camouflage sheets. She tickled his tattoos festively. They entwined fingers and both let out a big sigh. Alice said, "Wow. That was weird."

Steve was taken aback. "Weird?"

Alice turned somber. "Yeah. While we were making love, I really felt as if I was a leopard."

Steve concured triumphantly. "You really were a lioness! I'm so glad to have you home."

Alice shifted and touched his hair. "No, really. I think about the big cats so much when I'm out working, patrolling the forest. It was as if I became one, letting you ride me." She wriggled till her chest was in his armpit. "Do I seem different?"

"You have pimples on your ass." Steve feigned disgust.

Alice gave him a playful punch. "I don't like the soap they have over there. It's like carbonic borax, or something."

Steve hugged her. "I missed you."

"I missed you, too. But if I stayed here, I'd probably be snorting Oxy. Or doing meth like Carylyn." Her thumb indicated the direction of the next-door neighbor.

"I don't want you to go back." Steve stroked her arm. "I thought about reaching in and pulling out your diaphragm so you get pregnant and don't leave me." He grimaced, emotional. "But with those muscles, you'd probably fight me off." Alice punched his shoulder. Steve protested, "Hey, whites are practically a minority now. We have to keep up the race."

Alice jumped out of bed. "Lighten up. Let's go get pizza! I'm starved!" With a furtive double-take at Steve, she pulled a denim jacket over her T-shirt.

They went out the door. From the front steps was visible Carylyn, the skinny woman next-door on her porch. Alice called out, "Hi, Carylyn! Want to go out for pizza?"

Carylyn swatted a toddler on the head and smiled with meth-damaged teeth. "No, thanks. Have fun." Carylyn picked up a tabby kitten and held it to her T-shirt, printed with the message, *"TH3 POWER is yours. LUV thy neighbor. B3 the CH4NG3."*

Alice ran over to hold a kitten for a moment. "Maternal instinct should be for all species, right?" Several kittens sprang and tumbled around the toddler's feet. Carylyn looked perplexed and eventually asked, "When are you going back to – where is it? Moscow, Idaho?"

"Russia." Alice said, "I'm here for a whole month. There are local people here for me to train, before I go back to Russia." Carylyn picked a smokeable butt from the full ashtray and, as Alice and Steve left, she waved, the butt clenched in the wound of her mouth.

Once out of earshot, Steve snorted, "Now there's a 'Fanged Woman.'"

Alice differed, "More like the opposite. *Fangless* woman!" She waited for the gust and noise of a passing Kalkatta Transit Authority bus to pass, then observed, "I think it feels good to say the 'F' word because it makes you bare your fangs."

Steve experimented. "Fuck. Ffffuck."

Alice discovered a righteous glimmer of hostility in her emotions. "Fffuck." They laughed, for different reasons. Alice pulled Chechen cigarettes out of her jacket pocket and offered one to Steve. "I smuggled these in. Careful – they're strong."

Steve joked, "Nicotine stains will help us fit into the neighborhood." The depressed-looking buildings didn't disprove him; the rows of houses seemed to be waiting for something to happen, as if they'd stepped out for a coffee break and, in that brief interim, been laid off and shut out with nowhere else to go. There could have been ghosts of union organizers curling out from behind their haphazard, yellowed-white shutters. But there was no movement.

CHIHUAHUA, MEXICO

The corrugated tin roof shone with the last of the orange sun. In her F.W.W.P. uniform, Frida arrived home and greeted her family. She announced with spunk, "Chihuahua used to be famous for little dogs. Now we are famous for little wolves!"

Uncle Tio mumbled about the apparent self-contradiction of "*Lobos pequeños*," as if Frida had said, "Cute grizzly." But he focused on food. Abuela had pots of greens, long-grain rice, chilis and beans simmering on burners. Banging the aluminum door, Frida's son ran in. While Frida hugged her little boy, Diego, Abuela put some tortillas on the table and watched the young mother and child with a look of satisfaction.

"Com'estan los conejitos?" Frida asked Diego. "Did you help?" Abuela was participating in F.W.W.P. by raising rabbits.

"I put one on the grill outside," the boy said, pointing to the charred meat already on the table. Abuela nodded proudly. Then Diego pulled at the wooden slapstick that hung from Frida's belt. "What is this?"

Frida ripped the device from its Velcro fastener. "Try it!" Diego shook it; it clicked. Frida spurred him: "Give it one big jerk." The slapstick's report seemed as loud as a gunshot. "It is to scare off a predator if he gets too close!" Diego snapped the slapstick again. Frida jumped as if frightened, whimpering. Diego chased her with it clacking. She yelped like a dog. Uncle Tio leaned over in his vinyl-padded chair and caught Diego in his sinewy arms. Frida turned around, grabbed the little boy's ankles, and pretended to eat his thighs.

Eventually Uncle Tio and Frida let go. Diego collapsed onto the dirt floor. When they all sat down to eat, he set the slapstick on the table beside his plate. "Isn't this like the stick that the clowns use?"

Frida asked, "Do you think I am like the clowns? *Soy una payasita?*"

Diego looked at the gun that she still had on her hip. "You are like a *bandito*."

Frida pulled a lock of her black hair under her nose, like a big mustache. "I am Pancho Villa!" Diego stared at her, then smiled, eyes big as sombreros.

THE LAKE DISTRICT, ENGLAND

Climate change moved diseases to where hosts, having grown without previous exposure, had few immunities. The United Kingdom was an example. Despite a concerted attempt to increase fish stocks in all standing and slow-moving water, a malaria outbreak spread from the Lake District. It inspired an understandably anonymous poem:

Mosquitoes wander in a cloud

That floats on high o'er vales and hills,

When all at once I saw a crowd,

A host of people fallen ill.

Those whom tidal fever kills

Shall soon push up the daffodils.

ARGYLL, SCOTLAND

Attending the races at Ascot, her garden hat was blown off by a small tornado. That was the last straw. Diana's mother moved north to Scotland, where there were fewer tropical diseases. The change frazzled her nerves, so (without telling her daughter) she had an affair with the postman. She did urge Diana to get a boyfriend. "It's the most important thing."

MANHATTAN, NEW YORK, U.S.A.

Diana checked in with the "troops" in Bolivia, and gave them a light-hearted English lesson via video chat. "Birds eat ticks," she said with a giggle.

KAA-IYA GRAN CHICA NATIONAL PARK, BOLIVIA

The Bolivian women shook out their colorful woven ponchos and stood in their F.W.W.P. uniforms, searching each other for ticks. One woman was practicing with the others the few phrases Diana had taught them in English. "Birds eat ticks," she repeated.

Probably no-one from the United States would recognize the meaning if they heard the interchange of the three indigenous Bolivians, picking at each other's clothing, trying to pronounce, "Birds eat ticks." A Texan, for instance, might query, "Beery teak? Bee sticks? Bear steaks?"

MANHATTAN, NEW YORK, U.S.A.

Diana checked the web-cam of the Namibian squad. They had claimed she might see a cheetah at dusk. But the view was not exciting: she only saw a few acacia trees near the river, some livestock, and the women resting.

OKAVANGO RIVER, NAMIBIA

In that classic scene once exotic to the eyes of twitchy Westerners, an African ignored flies crawling on her skin. In this case, Lydia was also wryly hosting a bird on her head. She was sitting with the other F.W.W.P. women on her team, waiting out the heat of the day under a tree beside the languid river. Birds pecked on the backs of hippopotami. The squad was also keeping an eye on a rhinoceros who grazed in the brush. He too had a bird on his back.

Beyond him, a kraal built of camel-thorn branches corralled karakul sheep, a breed adaptive to the harsh terrain due to their ability to store fat in bulbous tails. Fetal pelts made prized garments on colder continents. The sheep were guarded by a donkey. Like the women, also wary of the rhinoceros, the donkey and sheep peeked through the breaches of the kraal.

The other F.W.W.P. participants observed Lydia's bird-harboring experiment. They fanned themselves languorously with large leaves, too slowly to disturb the bird on Lydia's head. Lydia inchanted, "The birds wait till the ticks are full. Then the birds eat." Through the sun's glare, she squinted at the red light on the web cam.

CHAPTER TWENTY-FOUR

WASHINGTON, D.C.

On the sidewalk, humming to herself, a panhandler sat beside a hand-lettered sign propped up on a parking-fee machine: "Politicians should wear uniforms like NASCAR™ drivers so we know their corporate sponsors." Sewn on her hooded sweatshirt were cloth patches penned with the word "YOU." Heels clicking as they walked, some crisply clothed professionals passed her, exchanging wry comments. "*Poly* means many; ticks are blood-sucking parasites. *Politics*."

The panhandler shifted to get more comfortable on her cardboard. Using felt-tip indelible ink, she wrote on the bony knuckles of her left hand: Y – O – U.

Inside, the hotel lobby was crowded with too many jaded Beltway insiders; even an ex-President failed to cause a stir as he passed through. And Bill Clitown's entourage was down-home enough to diffuse any remaining White-House glamor. The restaurant's lavish fare having sated one of his appetites, the elderly former President drawled, "Ah'm just fuller'n a tick. My digestion isn't what it used to be. Greenhouse gas emission imminent. Ah ate enough to choke a horse."

Ned Lerner glanced down at his dining companion's belly and made a pointed comment. "My bison steak is leaner than ever, nowadays. They tread lively now, with their heads up, sniffin' lions on the wind."

"Hope they're upwind of me," Clitown joked. "The EPA would have cited me. Now, about emissions... National and international governments have failed. They will not make any serious progress before it's too late," he summed up the dinner conversation. "It would obviate the need for China and India to sign any accord – like that would ever happen anyway – if we address the problems of individual cities."

"You may be close, but no cigar. How about we address the problem of individual women?" On cue, Ned Lerner's natty assistant opened a briefcase and out of it handed Mr. Lerner a F.W.W.P. cap printed with Hillary Clitown's photo. "Y'know, C40 isn't the only climate advocacy group around. Heard of these gals?" Mr. Lerner presented the hat to the former president, joking, "If you're sluggish after our meal, better wear protection. You never know what's gaining on you."

Jovially, Bill Clitown smiled at his wife's photo and put the cap on his balding head. "Ned, you are right on the money. If I'd worn this in office, I'd have evaded a peck o' trouble."

"Pecker trouble hunts you down," Ned Lerner responded, his expression inscrutable but his eyes lingering on a particularly statuesque woman sashaying across the marble floor. She stopped to speak to the concierge. The hem of her blazer was chevron-tailored to accentuate her tush. Mr. Lerner, charmed, added, "I'd have been fond of a solution myself. At least, in our day, our wieners didn't tweet much." Bill Clitown followed his elder's gaze approvingly but was suddenly distracted from the beautiful woman the way an amorous shepherd might be by a wolf: Senator Pickfawny had emerged from the elevators and was also navigating the lobby. Supporters who recognized him from Hyena News waved and called out right-wing slogans.

The statesman's coterie was much more populous than theirs, perhaps because the ultra-conservative constituency campaigned for large families. The homogenous white-bread contingent was wrapped up in their own spirited discussion. But Senator Pickfawny, alerted by his aide Brad, acknowledged the liberals. "Gentlemen," he sneered, *pro forma*. His fraternity of supporters adopted impish expressions at the sight of the promiscuous ex-president, as snide as if the ex-president himself were wearing a semen-stained blue dress.

Bill Clitown removed his cap in a gesture of respect, one battle-hardened warrior to another. Bill and Ned muttered a baritone chorus of greeting, "Senator." They watched him walk away. Ned Lerner asked, without urgency, "We haven't had mischief from Pickfawny lately, have we? Since he abolished the EPA?" The Environmental Protection Agency had been privatized and was now run by Halliburton, with Ralph Nader as the figurehead. "And his bill to outlaw education for girls? Just the usual pro-fetus stuff?"

Bill Clitown joked, "Yeah. He's quiet. Too quiet. Except for bragging that he's never set foot out of the U.S. Sounds like he's covering up some trips to Tijuana, if you ask me." He looked at Hillary's cap. "Not to dis Barrack – I'm obviously biased – but if Hillary had been elected, she'd have made short work of Pickfawny and his ilk, I wager." He donned the cap again. "Maybe our daughters' daughters will have the answer to fundamentalist oppression. Eh, Ned? Or do you think they'll just devolve to be Mad Max's chattel, and be sold for gasoline?" The men and their entourage all guffawed at the idea.

McCARTHY, OREGON, U.S.A.

Police found what they took to be a makeshift yoghurt factory in the housing of some foreign students. The FBI had alerted the local constabulary to suspicious online activity, so the officers confiscated the computers in the apartment. Then one policewoman thought to expedite some yoghurt samples to the CDC. The substance being cultured turned out to be a bacteria already detected on doorknobs throughout the university, discovered after an outbreak of debilitating leukorrhea that ranged from custard to cottage cheese.

In custody, the foreign students boasted of their tactics: while male enemies should be engaged with violence, it was not dishonorable to attack "Western whores, like Monica Lewdinski" with biological warfare, since they were already "VD-oozing." Strains of infections were developed to target only females. As the news spread, women in America started to wear white gloves again, like in the nineteen-fifties.

Following the trend, F.W.W.P. came out with a line of white snow-leopard patterned gloves. The fingertips were decorated with claw-like seed pods, each claw sewn on by participants in India, for instance, Ganika's aunt. The label tag announced that the seamstresses were actually paid in vegetable seeds. In the place of chain-stitched mirrors – traditional decor in India – the gloves featured more functional knuckle protectors of brass, à la steampunk. Women in big cities world-wide were seen more and more often wearing the Fanged Wilds line of "tactical fashion."

MANHATTAN, NEW YORK, U.S.A.

Fans of the charity donated artisan samples that might be of use or inspiration. For instance, Maoris in New Zealand (along with a plea for their predatory kea parrot) sent a mask. Diana had propped the Tiki mask about eight feet away, among the F.W.W.P. caps in the inventory on the shelves; when she wasn't using video chat, and thus remained safely invisible, she dispersed the aggravation of long phone calls by aiming pens like darts at the Tiki's mouth. More and more, she succeeded in hitting the mask somewhere on its face. Fortunately the cracking sound of the pens striking the wall beyond or landing on the linoleum floor had not, as yet, elicited any comments from the other end of the phone line. Questions from her boss Farraga could be particularly embarrassing. While they were co-conspirators, maintaining the illusion that Fanged Wilds wasn't a shoestring operation on the brink of chaos, the women were not intimate enough for complete frankness.

Interactions with the public, on the other hand, allowed for more leeway in shading the truth. Diana's conversation currently underway was with a gentleman who seemed part deaf and in other ways oblivious. He had insisted that F.W.W.P. manufacture jockstraps adorned with Hillary Clitown's face. Diana reassured him, "Our R&D department will look into that." She flung a pen at the Tiki mask. "But it might seem..." The pen skittered along the shelf into a pile of cheetah-print shirts. "...Inappropriate. Any more ideas?"

The old man wheezed something about an alternative: jockstraps with Bill Clitown's and Arnold Spermenegger's faces. Diana picked another projectile from the mug of F.W.W.P. pens. Since this eccentric phone-caller was potentially a rich donor, she had to remain as encouraging as possible. So she checked her notes for his name and then ejaculated, "Yes, that might be more to the point. As an object lesson. Excellent! But I must say – please forgive my familiarity – you sound awfully hoarse, Mr. Sneckfrodpfeffer. I hope you're in good health."

With what sounded like his dying breath, the old man protested that he was fine. "How about charcoal-color baby booties imprinted, 'Carbon footprint'?"

She coughed, "Great. Thanks for all your suggestions." After hanging up, Diana mumbled in disbelief to herself, "Jockstraps? For a ladies' charity?" But who knew? Maybe it was a product that would appeal to a new demographic, say, the rowdy investment bankers upstairs. She put a synopsis of her notes into the shoebox marked "R&D."

The map on the wall caught her eye. She wondered if she would be more spiritually at ease living in Scotland or back home in England, where it might be more acceptable to file using old shoeboxes: it seemed unAmerican not to have shiny file cabinets.

The investment bankers from the penthouse office had let her into the building once – when she'd dropped her keys into the Hudson, and couldn't get in her window entrance – and hadn't spared her any ridicule about her professional accommodations. Their office, eight floors up, couldn't be much more luxurious. It didn't need to be, of course, since business clients communicated via video chat and apparently only saw a wall behind their account executive. But the bankers all wore impeccable, silk-wool blend suits and arrived at work with a roar in NASCAR-like, glossy racing boats.

The bio-fuel that powered their boats was probably from food crops, she thought, with a twitch of disapproval. And the speed-boats were so noisy, she had to close her window to hear phone calls when the bankers pistoned off anywhere during the day. She suspected that, on their way back from a three-martini lunch, some of them caused a wake on purpose, to tease her, just so her tire-pontoon dock would smash into the building. She jumped when it happened, and muttered to herself, "Testosterone poisoning."

Still, she had been grateful for the boisterous bankers when she'd lost her keys yet again that morning. They'd let her in and humorously showed off their "Putting green" in one of the abandoned "ground" floor corridors. They said they also used the empty second floor when they played paintball, a possible explanation for occasional mysterious thumping and creaking above her. "Come join us, if you want – we have plenty of paintball equipment." They also invited her out, with locker-room bravado, for "Steak and drinks sometime, or maybe a round of water golf." One man pressed, "Why work so hard? The world is going to shit, no matter what you do." Scatalogical escatology, Diana thought.

When they'd herded upstairs to their cubicles, she'd scratched a spare key out from where she'd hidden several, in the crack between the wall and the floor of the sinking building.

She wondered if she should try to be more sociable. It would be good exercise to dart eight floors up the dank stairs, see the macho mens' office, and cadge a cup of espresso from them. But she was shy... and felt safe at her desk. So Diana updated F.W.W.P. social media, surfed, and then read an online magazine, The Diplomat, about animal smuggling rings: "Authorities a found a tiger cub that had been drugged and hidden alongside a stuffed toy tiger in the suitcase of a Thai woman flying to Iran from Bangkok's international airport. Later, officers caught a 36-year-old man from the United Arab Emirates bound for Dubai with suitcases filled with drugged wildlife, including baby leopards, panthers, a bear and monkeys." Another article, about the Russia/China border, listed, "1,041 bear paws, lynx fur, unspecified claw parts and five tusks from the extinct woolly mammoth.... The elk lips alone weighed 143 pounds..... 'China is a vacuum cleaner for Siberian wildlife,' said Aleksei L. Vaisman."

Aleksei was a nice name. It sounded handsome and dashing. Diana imagined meeting him, gazing into his piercing ice-blue eyes, and asking, "Is there a connection between human rights violations and animal abuse?" Outside, a speed-boat snarled while a barge sounded its horn. The phone rang again. "Yes, hello. Fanged Wilds," Diana said, tossing a pen. "*Oui, bonjour. A votre service.*"

CHAPTER TWENTY-FIVE

ARGYLL, SCOTLAND

The burbling stream broadened into a pond. Beside it, the tall, handsome Gamekeeper paused to await his hiking companion. His tie matched his sage-green vest, tartan cap, and sporran kilt-pouch. The Scotswoman who joined the "ghillie" was attired just as carefully in a weasel-trimmed, plaid F.W.W.P. uniform.

The Gamekeeper, Bert, pointed to the beaver dam on far side of the pond. "When Scotland reintroduced beaver, folk were rightfully worried."

The F.W.W.P. ranger scoffed. "Scared of beaver? Are ye scared of beaver, yourself?"

Bert the Gamekeeper slanted her a glance. "Not I. But beavers topple wood."

The woman, Marina, asked, "Scared for the wood, then, are ye?"

They watched as a moving lump revealed that a beaver was swimming. The dark protrusion headed for a copse of willows near the pond. Bert said, "There'll be enou' wood now the red deer are hoofin' more lightly."

"So ye're not scared of beaver, then?" Marina prodded.

Handling his shotgun, the Gamekeeper teased her back. "Wolves hereabouts, now, y'know. Are ye not a bit skittish about the wolves, yerself?"

"Ah am, indeed; in fact, Ah am," the Scotswoman said. "That's why Ah have my weaponry." She produced small bagpipes from under her arm and inflated first her lungs, then the instrument. With an anguishing sound as harsh on the ears as haggis could be on the stomach, she played a tune.

The beaver halted by the willows, listening. In the underbrush, a lynx cocked its tufted ears for a moment, then fled. The bagpipes wail on. In response, wolves howled over the Highlands.

When Marina was done, and a hush settled, the gentleman said, "Beavers mate for life, didye' know?"

"Do ye speak of country matters?" the lady replied, in a reference to the naughty bits in Hamlet. Bert's only answer was to hand her a wildflower. Arranging her woolen kilt, Marina eased her bum down in the grass while her instrument wheezed to rest at her side. "Don' ye care for a sit-down?" Bert knelt, looking pleased. She continued, "Ye may lie in my lap. Yer head in my lap." She pointed at his ginger hair, released as he removed his tartan cap. "Yer urbane head, not yer country one."

He loosened his tie. "Reminds me of how hedgehogs mate."

"How do they?"

"With great care." Bert the Gamekeeper complied with her instructions gleefully, stretching out. She stroked his forehead. "How do men with turbans do this?" he wondered aloud, looking up at her. He was getting very comfortable indeed. "That's surely one of the tragedies of mass turbation."

The Scotswoman swatted him on the nose with the flower. "Failin' means yer playin'," he countered, to compensate for his bad joke. His shrug nestled him deeper, and he quietly started to sing, "I would walk five hundred miles..."

TALYSH MOUNTAINS, AZERBAIJAN

"How far?" the Zoroastrians eyed the horizon. In this predominantly Muslim country, they were a minority with a proud history of honoring nature, with all its reasons and seasons. They'd heard that, over the border in the neighboring Kavir Desert, near the Iranian Oil Ministry's exploratory drilling, some women who shared their own faith were joining together to assist game wardens, the women's purpose being to protect endangered Persian leopards and Asiatic cheetahs and their prey – especially goitered gazelles – from poachers.

Over steaming, cracked cups, this news was discussed in the local tea houses, the men's clipped bursts of enthusiasm skidding on the caffeine. To celebrate the ecological aspects of Zoroastrian culture, the men organized their own patrol to protect leopards and cheetahs. The day was marked on the tea house wall calendars.

The Zoroastrian men who had rifles brought them on the expedition; in a particular order, its hierarchy dictated by social considerations, they set out to climb the hillside trails. Thousands of years of history had led to this moment, when an ancient form of worship confronted new realities of ecology. As they hiked through ravines near the petroglyphs of Gobustan, the men talked about what they would do if they confronted a vicious feline, or if they had to combat other men whom they might encounter hunting for illegal pelts or bushmeat. The Azerbaijanis did come upon a trio of hunters. But the strangers only held up a few rabbits that they had snared, and proclaimed that they knew of no big-game or gazelle poachers in the region.

As the scorching sun mounted higher in the sky, and their tin water bottles emptied, a schism developed in the Zoroastrian contingent. They stared up at the crags. One or two of the men contended that they needed to venture to higher altitudes, where a greater abundance of wildlife would have attracted more ambitious trappers. Others in the patrol adhered to the opinion that the majority of poachers would be closest to population centers. Suddenly, an explosion made everyone else jump, the report ricocheting off rocks: one man shot his Azerbaijani Defense Industry rifle. A fleeing rabbit twirled into death.

Back home that night, at the end of the expedition, the discussion of its success did not directly involve the community's women. They contributed by barbecuing the rabbit on a rustic spit along with a butchered goat, basted with pomegranate juice. Smudge-faced children looked fixedly at the delicious meat. The men celebrated their excursion in traditional ways.

RICHARD BRIMSTON'S ISLAND, THE CARIBBEAN

The Director and his assistant held up their Virgin Piña Coladas – sprinkled with fresh grated nutmeg – and toasted: "To the hurricane-free weather!" Palm trees barely rustled in the warm air. What a perfect day for filming! The fashion model Shee and her friends had arranged to create a public-service commercial for the anti-poaching micro-finance charity. "Fashion models are *role* models, especially for impressionable teenage girls." The cinnamon- and chocolate-legged women were wearing pelt-pattern, fur-trim linen F.W.W.P. mini-aprons over their cave-woman semi-bikinis. Faces painted like ferocious animals, they had already nailed a scene of barbecuing at the gleaming grill; the shoot was almost complete.

They took positions to capture the punchline: Shee pronounced saucily, "Fanged Wilds and Women Jerk Seasoning tenderizes on its own... But if you want, you can aerate the meat first." On cue, the Director's assistant sling-shot a photogenically charred meat-roast into the air. Shee blasted a shotgun at it.

"Cut!" the Director called.

One of the fashion models squealed. "I got bits of meat in my hair!" She dropped her tiger oven-mitt and ripped off her soiled, shaggy apron.

"Hold on," the Director called to her. "We'll film the dogs on you." The model acquiesced tentatively. Wolf-like dogs were released by a handler. The cameraman repositioned himself to document the women, who posed giggling with the silvery dogs licking splatters off their bodies and faces. Then a few models ran and dived into the jade blue sea. Standing in the waves to wash off, two of them scrubbed each other's grease spots meticulously with fine-grained, white sand.

When the young ladies returned, the Director got one last inspiration: he had the models pass the roast like a basketball, each female ravenously ripping off a juicy mouthful. Then, oven mitts up like outfielders, they tossed the meat across the circle, in a keep-away from the dogs. Over feminine noisiness, the handler's commands, and the dogs' joyous yips, the Director finally shouted, "That's a wrap!

Let's eat!"

Servants instantly mobilized. Platters of fruits and vegetables appeared.

"I'm already full," one of the models, Jooci, said. "That roast volleyball is the most meat I've ever eaten?" She rubbed her flat stomach, lubricated with beefy marinade drips which she then sucked off her bony fingers. A sleek dog approached her tentatively, licking his chops. "But it was for a good cause."

Shee had her eye on the table of food. "Maybe better for you than that raw juice you live on. All that juice dilutes your stomach acid; probably that's why you have trouble digesting meat," Shee teased. "You probably piss away an African village worth of vitamins with every twenty-dollar glass of produce that you drink. Good thing you're doing this for Fanged Wilds. You need better karma."

Jooci responded, "Oh, Shee! Look! You have some meat on your thighs. Can you wipe it off, or is it stuck there?"

"It takes a barbie to make a Barbie," the Australian riposted on her way to the barbeque with an surreptitious glance down at her long brown legs, checking to see if there were indeed any splatters left. "If they took the word 'fat' out of our vocabulary, I bet women would have fifty percent more vitality overnight," she mumbled. "Our I.Q.s would shoot up, and we'd solve all the world's problems. Your brain needs cholesterol."

The film crew was packing up. The cameraman commented sheepishly to the boom operator, "Well, I don't know how it'll play in Nebraska, or Berkeley, but that scene definitely adhered to our theme of 'wild.'"

Shee picked up a basting brush in one hand and, with the other, helped tend the smoking charcoal with a poker. "Farraga will love the PSA. She sent us Oregon *matsutake* to grill! They're so flavorful. Talk about wild; she swore the mushrooms are stolen. Like she sneaked through someone's back yard."

"Stolen?" the bikinied Jooci asked, intrigued. Under Shee's watchful eye, a sous-chef salted and oiled the *matsutakes*.

Placing the mushrooms on the grill, Shee elaborated. "Farraga insisted it wasn't from a public park. It was from *private* property." The food sizzled with tendrils of steam, marinade hissing as it dripped on the coals. Shee lamented, "Poor city people eat junk food because there's no good shops nearby. Just canned peaches and Spam. We should teach them to find edible mushrooms on lawns. A lot of them are edible if you cook them long enough, or boil them first."

"Mushrooms... *boiled*?" Jooci made a face.

"And rinsed to leach out the poisons. Like with acorns. Anyway, poor people should be allowed to pick them in parks."

A commanding James-Bond accent turned pretty heads. "Gleaning is legal in many parts of the world," Sir Richard commented, emerging from a dressing cabana in his turquoise Speedos. All could see: he was hung like a billionaire.

"Eat the rich," Shee said hungrily.

"Shee, you slut, he's married," Jooci protested, giving Sir Richard a big smile.

"He bought the cow, and I love sausage. So what?" Shee snapped, having just burned her finger, poking at a *matsutake* to see if it were cooked yet.

 Jooci turned to the dog following her. "Speaking of cows, don't you have to go get airbrushed, or something, Shee? Or get caps on your bulimia teeth?" The dog started to lick Jooci's twiggy abdomen. "That's carcinogenic, doggie! Meat *bad*," she baby-talked.

Sir Richard watched, amused, and shared a laugh with Jooci. He sat down on a chaise lounge near the barbeque to pet the promiscuous dog. "Humans have canine teeth for a reason," he commented, looking at the flesh all around him.

Shee growled playfully. "Watch out for all that carrot juice and fruit in your raw diet, Jooci," Shee persisted. "All that sugar can make your moods unstable." She handed the basting brush to the sous-chef. "And blood sugar exacerbates mutagens *in vivo*."

"Say what? My yogi would say that's just meat toxicity coming from your brain, out your mouth," Jooci declaimed. The dog abandoned Sir Richard. Jooci lay back on the sand so the dog, long tail wagging, could lick her more easily. "My yogi is so wise? And raw vegan? Anything cooked has, like, no life force."

A servant gave Shee a small raku plate. Shee forked a *matsutake* onto it, strode over, and ceremoniously handed the fragrant delicacy to their entertained host. "You'll love this! Of course, if it weren't cooked, it would make you ill." Shee winked at him.

Sir Richard smiled, relishing his bite of chewy fungus. A servant handed him an appropriate vintage. "Divine," he finally pronounced, toasting Shee with his crystal glass.

"Fortunately our body is built to shed toxins of all sorts. And all plants have toxins to discourage over-predation by animals, as my friend Professor Vimvole told me." Shee sat. "He's so wise, and vegan. Though I'm trying to cure him of that. Maybe I'll ease him back with a nibble of me."

Sir Richard mused, "Is it a rigid diet that makes people feel good, or the zealotry needed to stick to it that gives them the rush? Sado-masochism has many faces. But I envy the unquestioning devotion of the fanatic... Now that I've lost my own religion, capitalism."

"Don't worry. Someone will sell you a new religion," Shee wisecracked.

"Maybe I'll become a cooked-food fanatic," he said, taking another mouth full of savory mushroom.

"Professor Vimvole admits that hunter-gatherers were probably thrilled to find roast animals in brush fires. Or they set fires as part of the hunt, and killed two birds with one stone, so to speak. Our Aborigines have traditionally cooked some roots that otherwise make your throat swell shut, you know, when raw. Aborigines probably agree with me: fire pretty much defines civilization."

"It probably will again, now that peak oil has passed," Sir Richard said. Then he scanned the sky beyond the palm trees, squinting from the glare off the sea. "Hurricane weather coming," he said. "Let's live it up while we can!" If lightning struck twice, it might burn his mansion down again.

CHAPTER TWENTY-SIX

GARDINNER, MONTANA

The barbed-wire fence stretched for miles. Bobbing in the wind, a hand-lettered wooden sign hung: "National Forest Service Conservation Corridor. NOT Private Property." Branded cattle grazed inside the fence. The sound of their ripping grass and cow bells joined in symphony with a flock of crows. As unexpectedly as the 1812 Overture, a lion roared.

Along with corporate and church subsidies, taxpayers' revolts had reduced exploitation of public property. Grazing rights, increasingly restricted, now required that ranchers make accommodations for predation. Since a pride of lions neared in sight of the herd, cowboys unwound long strips of flagging – its reflective material flashing in the breeze – to deter the lions from getting closer to the cattle. The lions watched, curious as cats, but eventually went to hunt wild bison that night instead.

There were other innovations on the range. The Fanged Wilds and Women Program had coordinated efforts with Pleistocene re-wilding organizations. One aim was to mimic lost species like mammoths' and mastodons' effect on the ecosystem. So Amy and other F.W.W.P. participants now had elephants as transportation. The towering animals also served as shooting platforms if the squad needed to use their rifles. Zoos donated the elephants after "natural" disasters like bankruptcy due to climate change effects. Pachyderms controlled by riders constituted a compromise with locals, who still balked at all the new (older than ancient) residents.

The other women rode ahead; Amy slowed while her elephant defecated. In reference to the fertilization, Amy announced, "More big seeds get a head-start in life!" She rode over to Marla.

Her face was level with the height of Amy's leg; Marla stood on the ground, looking through binoculars. She lowered them, reached behind the elephant's ear, and affectionately petted the wooly chap on Amy's shin. "Don't wear these if you go to Idaho. They're as good as a blow-up doll there." They snickered at the sheep joke.

"How's the view?" Amy squinted toward the grassland's horizon.

Wide eyed, Marla said off topic, "Can you imagine when Montana was full of fruits like osage oranges?" Osage-orange trees were a species encouraged by the Pleistocene re-wilding proponents, along with other big-seeded fruits like avocados.

"Everything was bigger then," Amy said, "I think. The original American lions were much bigger. But those zoo lions are big enough." She tapped her elephant's left shoulder so it would turn to where she had a better view of Marla and the immense terrain.

Marla observed, "Bison *needed* a predator. They are more lithe now." She looked through her binoculars again, at the lions stalking the bison herd.

Amy joked, "Yeah, they're svelte."

Catching on, Marla said, "Slinky."

Amy posited, "Supple."

Marla concluded, "Bisonly." The women burst into giggles. Marla added, "I wonder if those cowboys have noticed."

Amy bent over in a show of confidentiality. "Unless they're from Brokeback Mountain, I think they've noticed *you*."

"Uh, huh." Marla snorted. "Hey! Did you hear? The fashion industry has gotten involved with Fanged Wilds. They're mounting a 'Predators are the new Black' show for next, uh, season. In Italy, Milan."

Amy joked tentatively, "You could go model. You're so beautiful." To deflect any pain, she added, "I'll take care of the baby."

At the sound of crying, Marla bounced her knees, soothing the infant in the carrier on her chest. "D-death wants to name my son Aslan, did I tell you?" She referred to their Ex, Dale.

Dale was a sore subject for both of them. Amy grew rambunctious with frustration. "Not... D-daniel Boone? Or... D-davy Crockett?" Amy pursed her lips, then pried, "Did he send support yet?"

Marla scowled. "He needs it for tuition, he says."

Amy wrinkled her nose. "I'll pray to ask his guardian angel. Tonight, after work." Her elephant shifted his weight and curled his trunk restlessly.

"I'm sure he'll support us someday. He's a dedicated professional. Big bucks in logging."

"And you're a professional mom now. It must have been handy, back when the government gave food stamps to professionals like you."

Food was an issue. The grounded woman's stomach growled. "Can you shoot a squirrel or rabbit for us?" Marla begged, embarrassed. She thought about Dale and how he talked about God's grace. Looking up at Amy, Marla thought: grace could only be defined as feminine.

"You know I'm a lousy shot," Amy warned. She tapped behind her chap, her rider's crop slapping the grey hide of her elephant's shoulder, to prod her ponderous steed onward. "But I bet maybe I can get a garter snake. They're slow." All the woolly-chapped women waved goodbye to Marla, who bounced her carrier. The mounted women spurred and rode their elephants over the grasslands, in their new career.

The sun in her eyes, Marla looked down and said to her baby, "I'm the whole world to *you*." His eyes perused her face. The baby was a tiny version of her: they were like two mirrors folding in on each other. Further afield, pachyderm eyes rolled, looking for mice. Holding on tight, gun ready, Amy bent and looked for a snake in the grass.

KOREAN D.M.Z., 38th PARALLEL

After a refreshing lunch of *bo-shin* dog stew, Ned Lerner rode in a swamp boat with Kim Dong Ill. Their silent party motored along past reeds. The engine cut, and the boat glided over glinting ripples. The North Korean head-of-state announced in unintelligible English, "We have black bear, Amur leopard, and Korean tiger in the demilitarized zone. Barricaded over sixty years. Not many people here. Now these Fang Wild women." He gestured to indicate the two stunning Korean women in matching silver-blue Fanged Wilds uniforms, looking like a team of dolphins manning the motor.

Ned Lerner nodded politely. He understood a few words. "Well, as I've said before, I want the UN to recognize this as a World Heritage Site. Global warming dictates it."

Kim Dong Ill nodded. "Dictation is good. But I not worried about globe warm in Korea." He thrust his fingers toward the scrubby land.

Ned Lerner's handsome, craggy old face betrayed surprise. What had the dictator said? The Korean women, practically in unison, explained reverently, "Dear Leader can control the weather with his mood."

Kim Dong Ill nodded. "I can control women with my mind, too. That is why I may let these patrol. It will look as if they are unsupervised, but I will be controlling them."

Mechanically, one of the women pointed at a black bear near the furthest shore, fishing. Looking at the sexy fish-costumed women and contemplating mind-control, Ned Lerner said, "That's a nice trick. I'd like to learn that."

Kim Dong Ill stared. "Fishing? I thought all you cowboys go angle. Rod and tackle. I know these things. You cowboy want to fish like bear?" He swatted with a hand.

Straightening to see the bear splash the water with its paw, Ned Lerner said, "Ya gotta admire that, controlling fish with barely a flick of the wrist."

BLAGOVESHCHENSK, RUSSIA

Carrying carbines that were heavy enough to make their rawhide snowshoes sink with each step, three Russians hunted for bear. Bear paws fetched about 1,500 rubles a kilogram. The smugglers were on track to find a bear's den. One man croaked in an excited whiskey voice, "Four paws! Plenty of vodka then!" A set of paws would bring the hunters about fifty dollars, with even more cash for fresh or dried gallbladder.

Another smuggler, Krin Staader, shushed and pointed to the base of a big tree, where tracks of the lusted-for paws lead to an aperture in the snow. They pointed their guns at the darkness as they sneaked closer. A wooden limb cracked from the weight of winter; the men jumped. Silence again; they eventually ventured to examine the snow around the tree more carefully. The gruff-voiced man man picked up a fallen branch and poked it into the snow drift. He finally declared, "There is no den. Bear was here to catch a hare, maybe." He shrugged.

The minute they relaxed their vigilance, a frozen limb fell behind them with a crash of cracking twigs. They turned their backs, guns pointed outwards cautiously. They swayed slightly right and left at each new sound, as the forest around them adjusted to the breeze. The men were facing away from each other when a shower of snow was released from a lofty tree crotch at the same moment that they backed into each other, Three-Stooges style, and all discharged their carbines at once. The blast drowned out their shrieks; they fell face-first as if to take cover in the ice-glazed snow. The gun reports echoed through the forest as more snow and exploded twigs dropped onto the prostate, bellowing bodies.

After taking stock of the humiliating situation, they stood up and dusted crust and clumps of ice off their pelt coats. With bravado, Mikhail Brink, the most garrulous, saved face by announcing, "We could get a leopard or tiger here too. They are worth much more money."

Gregor Kristensen, his less-experienced companion, bleated, terrified, "There are leopards and tigers here?"

After a look of superiority at the third man, who also feigned insouciance, the first smuggler ignored the outburst with a change of subject. "Too bad we don't have helicopters like Sarah Pail."

The smugglers guffawed with tight throats. To redeem his virility, the cowardly Gregor Kristensen insisted, "Too bad we don't have Sarah Pail."

Unbeknownst to him, fear was justified. Curled up in her igloo-like home, a bear was awakened by the gun blasts. She snorted to warm her nostrils, and stretched stiff joints, preparing to investigate the enticing smell of edible animals.

Gregor Kristensen pursued his topic. "We get maybe millions of rubles to smuggle a fine woman like her to the right buyer," he said. The smugglers leaned against the big tree, in an unspoken agreement to have a smoke of the blunt, harsh cigarettes they'd got in trade for a pelt.

The most talkative man, Mikhail Brink, boasted, "No joke. I sell a woman once in Hei He; bought these guns." The other men had heard the story, which explained their inattentiveness as the erstwhile human trafficker described the transaction; instead, while passing a flask of vodka, the quieter men alerted to a noise.

They had misjudged the location of the bear den. It was just inches from where they'd first supposed it to be. The bear dragged Krin Staader under the snow beside the tree. His companions shouted helplessly, their cries growing more desperate as a leopard dropped from the tree onto the boastful trafficker.

His hat falling off, the third and last smuggler, Gregor Kristensen, stumbled in horror through the snow to escape the scene of carnage and carnivory. His snowshoes were awkward; he was almost back to the outskirts of Blagoveshchensk when a Siberian tiger leaped from behind vegetation and sunk its teeth into his bare head.

The animals were satisfied by the unexpected mid-winter meals.

MOUNT RUSHMORE, SOUTH DAKOTA, U.S.A.

High above the flood waters, a hum filled the corridors of the extensive underground facilities. The entrance was disguised by a fracking rig at what was essentially the nucleus of the nation's military-industrial technology. In one warehouse-like compartment, Dick-Chainey clones waited, jaws clenched, an army ready to be mobilized, their fingers on the levers of their Barca-loungers.

For lunch, they were each served a liverwurst sandwich with iceberg lettuce and a gherkin, which they ate mechanically under the buzzing lights. Unexpectedly, as their dishes were cleared away, a solar flare knocked out the power grid. The generators, as it happened, were already out of gas; the clone project wavered as a priority of the current administration. The room was pitch black.

"Fuck!" the clones said in unison. (The original Chainey's obscenity on the Senate floor must have been genetic expression.) Then the clones lay back in their easy chairs, awaiting further instructions.

In the silence, each little sound dwindled, diminished by the high, corrugated ceiling. Someone cleared her throat. The servants could hear each other setting down the dirty dishes in the dark, clattering on nearby cement floor. Slowly they fumbled toward the sound of each other's voices.

"Hell-o?" They tried to remember each other's names so they could call out. "Lizzie?" Someone ventured, "...Stella?" Other employees chimed, "P-patty? Sylvia?" Their eyes quit straining, and brains adjusted to blindness. The servants reached for each other and touched for the first time.

CHAPTER TWENTY-SEVEN

PLEISTOCENE RANCH, SIBERIA

Across the steppes, abutting one another, herds of horses, bison, antelope, caribou and musk-oxen multiplied like cells smeared on a vast petri dish. Tiny colonies of macrophages hunted: packs of wolves infiltrated the herds on marshy Mammoth-tundra. This laboratory was for the manufacture of an Eden.

Too gross for the Heisenberg principle of uncertainty, the observers in this experiment did not alter the results; in fact, the sight had become so commonplace to these science-minded researchers, they barely registered the occurrence of what in Yellowstone would be an occasion for dozens of loud-panted tourists to post identical, jerky videos to Youtube. Hand-held cameras, in this case, would have induced sea-sickness in viewers: the humans pitched and rolled, transported over the grasslands on the backs of Bactrian camels. At the sight, summer-brown ermines slinked into their holes. A red fox, peering curiously, skulked behind a shrub.

Astride the much larger, gangly animals rode Sergey Zumorof, the ecologist who spearheaded the Pleistocene Ranch. Accompanying him was a Russian team of F.W.W.P. uniformed women in fur hats. Flapping in the breeze, the women's long Cossack coats had a picture of Catherine the Great on the back. Their fur hems revealed tiger-print pants tucked into glossy black knee-boots dangling high above the ground against the camels' tawny flanks.

The undulating party halted where tourists would take a picture. But Sergey Zumorof just chatted. "I have dined with your product." He licked his sunburned lips. "Your jerk seasoning is *khorosho* on reindeer steak. Not so good on goose," he admitted amiably, head tilted. "Good on seared boar."

The anti-poaching ranger closest to him, a bronze Amazon of a woman named Verushka, said, "When I grill meat, I shish-kebab the mushrooms that fight cancer. That counteracts the carcinogens in charred protein."

The loll of his camel seemed to dislodge a non-sequitur, or maybe he was spurred by the sun: Zumorof mused, "Radiation: causes cancer, cures cancer."

Another, less sanguine warrioress, with long platinum braids, called, "If you're worried about cancer, wash your meal down with green tea."

Zumorof quipped, "Wash down with vodka. That cure *anything!*"

The women gave each other a look as if to scoff, "Men!" The tea-teetotaler, while not a vodka fan, wished to mitigate any discord so hospitably suggested, "We should raise a glass. To celebrate how our Pleistocene-Ranch biodiversity reduce greenhouse gasses. A glass, to grass! And its fibrous root mats! They sequester more carbon than trees, no?"

The group grew ebullient at just the mention of vodka. "Human habitat will be destroyed by our own greed, ego, and cuntiness. We must be like Zumorof. To Sergey!" Broad-faced Verushka shouted. "Men should be like him, and women, too." Back when Soviet athletes used steroids in the Olympics, the stage was set for Russian women to consider strength normal. These women were all robust. Yet they admired Zumorof for his idealistic principles as much as for his prowess, back at the barracks, at leg wrestling. He was indeed a great man.

Acerbically, Verushka broached the "Altaigate Scandal," an incident where local politicians treated Russian government VIPs to helicopter-poaching, shooting protected animals and causing a Mi-171 chopper to crash in 2009. "We wait to get drunk. Wait till after our women's brigade to protect snow leopards in the Golden Mountains, no?" Verushka patted her camel's neck.

"Yes, leopards. And sheep. Fluffy, horny sheep," her tea-loving friend said to her companions. She released the reins and held the tips of her blonde braids up like horns. She gave Zumorof a coy glance, then exhibited remorse. The women had applied themselves with Slavic intensity to their business of keeping environmental devastation at bay. Speaking of vice and misbehavior, the virtuous camel-rider added provocatively, "I heard news about folk-medicine. Smuggled from Blagoveshchensk."

Verushka confirmed, "Blagoveshchensk?"

"Just north of Hei He. There's a new illegal trade, in poacher parts. Poacher gall bladders sell to people who want a lot of gall."

Missing the joke, Verushka struggled. "Black market just sells their gall bladders?"

The humorous woman responded, "The rest of the poacher parts are too small." When her companions looked askance, she held up her pinkie finger and nodded meaningfully. "Real men follow the law."

They noticed a smug look on Zumorof's face as he gazed at a grazing horse's backside to feign obliviousness. The growling females showed each other a meaningful forearm to suggest abundant virility.

The party rode further. Astride, the women swayed and seemed to teeter as they positioned their camels on a bluff from which they could survey the herds. The animals grazed amid fields of flowers near a river. One of the women started to sing a Russian folk song: By the Long Road. "*Yekhali na troike...*" Its tune was stolen for the sixties' pop song, "Those were the Days, My Friend."

"Those days will come again," Zumorof said. He joined in, a beloved baritone among boisterous sopranos.

ETON, ENGLAND, U.K.

On a background of kelly green, earth tones bloomed with disarmingly rosy accents. The famous playing fields of Eton College were adorned with dozens of multi-cultured women in F.W.W.P. get-ups, some with faces painted. Shark outfits, exotic-animal prints, mushroom-dyed pink rabbit trim, and furry bunny boots clashed with the participants' no-nonsense expressions. The situation was intimidating. Teeth flashed white with determination.

Cockney, Jamaican, and Pakistani heritages mingled into the organized mayhem, an orchestration of activities possibly seen in one place only in the heyday of sunny Silicon-Valley dot-com team-building days. In the warm drizzle, facilitators assigned and delegated to co-captains. To soothe feelings, they gave hugs, transplanting Californian touchy-feelie Life-Coach techniques to the playing fields of Eton.

As the day progressed, stiff upper lips, cynicism and British reserve melted as if Michelle Obama's hand were gently resting on the small of each woman's back, a statuesque guardian angel whispering in the back of consciousness that they could lightly steam garden-fresh organic vegetables instead of boiling them *à l'anglaise* to mush and ending up with muscles to match.

To be fair, some of the exercises were strenuous, quite. Yelling their lungs out, the women with lighter complexions went from peaches-and-cream to strawberry tarts. In the Four-Way Tug-of-War, the aim was to pull the center ring over your team's goal (in this case, four cloth polar bears, nestled in divots in the ground). Loosely grouped, it was the Africans opposite the Greater Europeans, and the Asians against the Americas. The women made transient alliances with teams on either side who shared their own team's incentive to swivel. "America left," pleaded Europe, for instance. Strategically most important may have been communication with ones own team. For instance, the women shouted when to take advantage of a lull or momentary weakness with an unexpected assault of yanking: "Now!"

Leadership developed as someone felt inspired to command when to swerve left or right. Fellowship was unspoken when team members agreed, via body language, to sand-bag. In that last technique, team members who otherwise might not be appreciated for their low center of gravity were suddenly recognized for the bulk of their attributes, as a holding pattern (like the Dao's "yin within yang") was revealed, in an instant, to be the key to survival.

From nearby Windsor Castle arrived a special observer, His Majesty, the King of England. Amid the participants' squeals of anguish and ecstasy, he stood stiff-legged and cheered for his subjects' team. "Make like George the Third. Yank the yank-ees!"

As if she were at a Los-Angeles baseball game, "Yankees!" parroted Jooci, the fashion model, born in L.A. She was serving as his guide through this photo-op. Her main function – besides wearing an elaborate F.W.W.P.-theme Ascot hat and smiling for the cameras – was to explain the rules of each activity to His Majesty.

The tug-of-war protracted into fruitless skirmishes and gruesome trampling of polar-bear goals. So Jooci steered the King away. "Over there, you might want to observe the Survival-Tool Selection." In this more cooperative venture, the women debated the merits of each object, the premise being that they could only choose three objects to keep them alive in a given situation. One woman held up a toilet plunger, while the others listened to her rationale with skeptical expressions. Bear Gyrlls stood nearby at the ready as survival consultant. Giving the buff TV star a smile as luscious as water in the desert, bridging the distance between them with laser-like magnetism, Jooci then officiously checked her notes. "I think this group is supposed to imagine they're in the Antarctic."

"Antarctica?" the King confirmed companionably.

Yes," the spokes-model said. "Ew, I hate ants. Shall we go see if they, like, get to choose bug spray?"

Their trek detoured around a "Minefield," where a woman was shackled in pink, fluffy handcuffs. Her aim was to use only her voice to direct her blind-folded partner past "Mine" obstacles. When the partner reached the finish line, the blinded participant would discover a punchline as well: the "mines" were pictures of tyrants like Stalin, Idi Amin and Pol Pot, and her blindfold was a mask of media ogre Ruptur Murdrech. A cream-pie wielding ninja disguised as his adopted wife, Wendi Dung, added to the challenge. A historian from Oxford was stationed at the finish line to answer any questions. "There is no 'mine' in 'team'," he quipped.

Near him, at the far end of the field, informal spectators lined up behind the kind of flagged ribbons that the Fanged Wilds program ordinarily used to ward wolves and other predators away from livestock. On their first foray from Michigan, Ronelle and her niece Tawona were demonstrating a three-legged race. As they paced in rhythm, their sororally matching natural afros bobbing, they juggled silk scarves to each other with their spare hands. Ronelle yelled, "Pull!" Simultaneously she and Tawona stopped and dropped the scarves. Ronelle pulled forward the shotgun strapped behind her back; they held it together, barrel and stock, as the skeet was flung through the air ahead of them. The blast knocked the two women backwards onto the grass into a pile. They screeched with triumphant laughter; the skeet exploded. Pieces of shattered clay fell toward the distant lawn.

"I say, that is smashing," said the King.

"Oh, only when they hit the target," Jooci the spokes-model said, adjusting the killer-whale tail on her extravagant, animal-themed hat. "Sometimes they miss." A dozen adolescent boys in tennis whites ran from behind a blind to pick the hot-pink shards up off the lawn. The more polite of the spectators applauded, while some rowdy ones cheered and, straining at the ribbon, started heckling the spectacle of Tawona and Ronelle still on the ground. "Break's over!" Jooci yodeled to the hecklers, "Girls just wanna have fun..."

Tawona tried to use the shotgun as a crutch. But the two Americans from Michigan, still tied together at the ankle, were giggling too hard to stand up. Distracting the crowd from the skeet-shooters' indignities, a royal dog handler paraded some stunning Great Pyrenees towards the King. His Majesty saw them and explained to his companion Jooci, "I wanted to show you our breeding pair of guard dogs."

Jooci gasped. "But – the corgis! I have to see the corgis, too!" The Californian pleaded greedily. "I just love dogs?"

The King looked accommodating. "I'll see what can be done. I just wanted you and the other ladies to see the guard dogs we use for the flocks. Corgis can herd our sheep. But we need these big fellows if we're going to reintroduce predators widely."

He watched the spokes-model lavish affection on the robust breed, who succeeded in displacing her urgent need for corgis. Jooci mewed, "I wish I had these love-muffins to protect my wool." The dog handler coughed and cleared his throat but no words passed his stiff upper lip.

Ronelle and Tawona removed their leg bondage and shyly approached the monarch and the F.W.W.P. designated spokesperson. His Majesty gave a meaningful glance to an aide and suggested, "Surely the ladies would care for a spot of tea? Organic?"

"Or some raw meat to gnaw," the spokes-model whispered loudly to the King, before Ronelle and Tawona reached them.

"We do have steak and kidney pie." He smiled. "Not raw. Quite well-done, I'm afraid. That's English cooking for you. The closest tradition we have to raw food is warm beer."

After Jooci made formal introductions, Ronelle turned to her friend and said, "Tawona, what you say we have one of those skinny gals for a snack?" She'd heard Jooci's raw-meat comment.

Tawona looked at the Lion of Zion decals on her polished thumbnails and declined. "I get them twiggy ones stuck in my teeth. I guess I could use Kate M – her Highness – to floss."

His Majesty chuckled obligingly at the quaint ex-colonists. He said, "I appreciate ever so much your showing these lasses what's what. I say, it's capitol. Top notch." He beamed at the pair, then mumbled, "Great Birnham Wood shall march to victory indeed."

Tawona studied him. "You sure y'all ready for wolves on this island, sir?"

Meanwhile, holding her Ascot hat, Jooci kissed a Great Pyrenee on his big nose and told him, "You're as cute as a wolf. But what I'd really love is packs of corgis running through the hills here, like, chasing the deer and bunnies. Corgis belong in the ecosystem."

Seeking refreshment, the Americans joined the Royal entourage at the gazebo. Just then, Diana called them on her video-phone. "Tawona! How is it going?"

"We're having real English tea with the King!" Tawona reported. "I think our team-building exercises have won him over to our program!"

Ronelle called out, "Hi, Diana," toward the phone. "Why aren't you here with us?" But neither she nor Tawona heard the answer, as they were ushered to seats of honor and handed rose-scented hot towels with which to refresh their face and hands.

CHAPTER TWENTY-EIGHT

MANHATTAN, NEW YORK, U.S.A.

Diana tossed a fang pen, hitting the Tiki mask propped on the inventory shelf. She wished she worked for an organization that could afford to send her back home to England for the special event. Outside roared the speed boats of the investment bankers, probably late for work. If only Diana worked for NASCAR, or the National Football League, or the World Wrestling Federation. They could afford a hop across the pond, probably in private jets. Many corporations nowadays had solar-powered sonic hydroplanes, she'd heard. She sighed, bored, tapping another fang pen on her desk, syncopating a rhythm to the bubbling of the aquarium.

An hour later, she was panting at the entrance to the bankers' penthouse. "Good gracious, you guys! There are orcas swimming near the building!"

Trimmed and crew-cut tops of banker heads appeared over the chrome-framed cubicles. Several heads bobbed up and down with laughter. Glen came out to greet her, an inscrutable stare fixing his blue eyes on her. "You just ran up eight flights of stairs to make that story more believable, right?"

"No, really! And it's dangerous. Be careful in the marina; the tide is up. I was just standing on my pier, getting a breather. An orca could have easily nudged his head out of the water. He could have dragged me in and eaten me!"

Another cubicle released an inhabitant from former colonies. "Fanged Wilds. You want it, you got it," an East-Indian imported executive teased the prissy English girl.

"This isn't orca territory," Glen said, somewhat respectfully. He smoothed his hands over his pressed Oxford shirt as he stepped nearer to the window, looking out.

Diana joined him, still catching her breath, noticing the office's panoramic view. She could see along canyons of buildings where the avenues sloped down and became waterways. But she didn't see the whales. She insisted, "They could be the orcas that were washed away in that tsunami over Sea World."

Beside the expansive pane of glass, Glen looked doubtful. "Sea World whales? Those couldn't swim this far, with those droopy fins." He flopped a wrist above his head; his cuff fell back and revealed his Tag Heuer watch beside his thick neck.

Others in the office came closer, like a locker-room congregation, conspicuously checking out her miniskirt. A wag in a black suit, his own wrist limp above his head like a dorsal fin, blurted, "The other whales would think they're gay!" The bankers cracked up. Then shushing came from one corner: an executive was still on the phone in his cubicle, selling futures.

Diana continued in a stage whisper. "These guys' fins looked healthy. I mean, not that there's anything wrong with if they *were* gay. I mean, those Sea World captives were practically living in a bath tub. So what, if they had to resort to something just to keep their spirits up. More power to them." Diana by this time was beet-red with the whole situation. She strained her voice, trying to say the right thing. "Or if they were born that way, and just happened to find each other in the same bath tub. Not that it's statistically likely. But you never know. It's none of our business, anyway. Consenting whales should do whatever they like. Especially wrongfully incarcerated."

Glen rolled a fancy desk chair to her. "You need a rest. Sit here and watch for whales. I'll get you an espresso." He looked at her cute legs as she sat down.

DAM BEAVERS RANCH, NEVADA

Meanwhile, in America's rugged desert, mirages shimmered in the sun's ruthlessness. The whorehouse was a sort of oasis, in the metaphysical sense, for hungry men in a flesh drought. In an increasingly polluted world, maybe their wives or partners were too exhausted to have sex willingly. Or where the customers were from, female infanticide had made it impossible to find a mate. Whatever their situation, the Ranch offered the men a place to feel in command of themselves.

But Vimvole was wary of indulging any personal urges. He considered himself to be present purely in an academic capacity. Shee, the internationally respected fashion model, had solicited his involvement on this mission. He was solely a concerned, brave eco-ethnopaleontologist overseeing the reintroduction of beavers at a flood-prone spot. A dangerous flash flood could appear at any time like a wedge of tsunami; the professor had binoculars out and was in fact riding shotgun. His colleague – the efficient, goal-oriented and trim District Wildlife Manager, who drove the pickup – joked, "We'll just get in and get it done. Just a quick in-out mission."

In fact, Vimvole was fascinated and mortified by the well-proportioned prostitutes – surprisingly attractive, one dressed like a cowgirl – who came out to greet the men. "We've got the baby beaver in my bath tub!" a snub-nosed, vivacious blonde announced with delight to the air-conditioned men who had opened their doors to the heat. Nodding politely, the men headed back to the beavers that they'd transported in secure, cushioned cages roped to the pickup bed.

Two slightly less appealing Working Girls – blemished skin, flaccid muscles – brought out handfuls of apple slices for the animals. The three youngest professionals noticed that the professor was handsome and probably wealthy; they vied with one another to be the most irresistible product. "Is that a tampon string hanging out?" the fake-blonde cowgirl said to disadvantage the real blonde.

With barely a sneer, the real blonde pulled up her pink silk negligee. "Ha!" Ignoring her, the cowgirl and the brunette stood on tiptoe in high-heels to lift up the green tarpaulin. It was weighted with dripping bags of ice to cool the animals. The girls pushed the apple bits through the wire.

"Some beavers only eat meat," the brunette snarked, with a glance at the real blonde. "Snatch it right up, that's what they do."

The beavers huddled at the far side but soon waddled to the food. "I just want to cuddle them," the real blonde giggled. Vimvole blushed to his own grey roots, looking at the brunette's blue-jean posterior as she strained over the side of the truck, her daisy-duke cut-offs riding up.

The District Wildlife Manager had promised his wife not to linger. He opened the creaking tailgate with a jangle of chains. "Can you girls go get the kit?"

"I love when a man in uniform tells me what to do," the brunette, Sorraia, flirted.

Emotional, the real blonde protested, "I want to keep him forever! My fuzzy baby beaver!" Watching the older animals eat, she predicated, "But my bathtub can't be occupied, when my clients want to take a shower. They're shy about going to some sleazy girl's bathroom instead." She looked pointedly at the cowgirl, Sorraia.

The Wildlife Manager pulled one of the cages off the truck and interjected Family Values. "We'll put him with his folks. The relatives work together the baby's first two years."

"How sweet!" the real blonde, Honey, said, catching Vimvole's eye and smiling at him. Vimvole remained skittish but for some reason felt protective of her.

The Madam appeared out a side door of the eco-brothel. Her rusty curls were piled up over an extravagant hairpiece in an impressive construction that seemed to scoff at gravity, as did a recent, brittle face lift that spread her smile. "So good of you boys to do this," she pronounced grandly. "You gentlemen know we're all organic, right? And tokens of our appreciation are inside, whenever you're ready. Unless there's some healthy treat right here that's piqued your appetite," she added, with a wink to Honey, her favorite.

"I'm on state business. And I'm slaked at home, thanks," the uniformed administrator responded, with a gracious chortle. He tucked his thumbs into his neat waistband, abundantly virtuous.

"That's not what I hear from the fillies at the Wild Horse Ranch," brown-maned Sorraia teased him, giving a high-five to her Madam.

"Saddled up a ride to the Big O corral, did you, cowboy?" The Madam snorted. The women were trying to get a rise out of the official; playfulness usually payed off as a challenge that male ego couldn't resist.

"About those feral horses," Vimvole stammered. "And native burros. Now that there's hardly any livestock exploiting public lands, private guardians of wild horses can release them to interbreed and improve the genetic stock. Can you tell that to your frrr –" He cleared his throat. "Your friends, those ladies at the Wild Horse Ranch."

The District Wildlife Manager concurred. "Ideal herd size should be one hundred or more, for genetic viability. They only have a few dozen at Wild Horse." He added an innocent, "Right?"

The convivial Madam shrugged and put her shapeless arm around Honey's tiny waist. "Rangeland Repubicans okayed birth control for wild horses at the same time they tried to close Planned Parenthood. Makes you wonder if they fuck horses, don't it? That'd explain Anne Colter's long face. Colt, my ass. Long in the tooth, as well."

The crass harlot brayed gleefully, causing Vimvole to shrink away. He gestured to the D.W.M. to help him move the closest cage.

"No, I'm kidding," the Madam touched his arm. "Repubicans come here by the busload, and they pay us better than liberals," the gaudy woman confided. "Right Wing understand commerce." Seeing that the men wouldn't become customers, she ran off at the surgically de-wrinkled mouth. "Maybe it's the religion; it makes them feel guilty, so they fork it over, like penance. Like the pope that sold indulgence. I even keep a couple disabled girls, the kind that parents see on sonograms to abort. Some conservatives like 'em here; must be why they're for breeding 'em. I heard they get more by fracking their drinking water. Sarah Pail was on TV about that, and how proud she is to be a bucket of baby batter."

Vimvole, raised Catholic, had turned red as a tomato and backed further away. As the men carried the beaver cages over the dry soil to the stream, the Wildlife

Manager said to the Madam trailing them, "You're in a dirty business, Phyllis...
Mrs. Shaftly."

"Most of my girls are healthy, clean and organic," Mrs. Shaftly reassured Vimvole.
"Just a few 'specialty' girls, but they're all natural, too, apart from the frackin'
water." She stopped smiling. "Men make fortunes on objecting... girls into objects.
Why shouldn't a woman cash in, for once?" To convey earnestness, she pursed her
lips. Unfortunately, the muscles pulled at the thin skin near a face-lift scar, and
blood trickled down her powdered face.

CHAPTER TWENTY-NINE

COAST RANGE, OREGON

Salmonberry bushes rustled. Elk browsed skittishly, unseen by human eyes. But monitoring them was a pack of wolves sauntering in the vicinity, rabbit blood on their muzzles. The adolescent wolves, still hungry, longed to lunge at the nearest elk. But the grey alpha male and female were demonstrating an important lesson: how to select the easiest catch among an ungulate herd.

Then a subordinate, darker wolf halted, nostrils twitching: it noticed the scent of a cougar. The alphas ignored the distraction. But the adolescents sniffed the air in imitation of their humble, black-brown elder, whose pointed nose indicated that the cougar was up in the trees. The dark older wolf and his juvenile gang wanted to harass the feline. But – with no provocative hissing from above to make the urge irresistible – the dark wolf, with a backwards glance, obediently followed the alpha members of the pack: the hierarchy had its rationale. The youngsters again took his cue, despite the interesting scent. A lack of respect would be noted by all. Their paws proceeded to tread silently on the wet earth.

The cougar slept, oblivious to the lupine soap opera unfolding down in the bushes.

Also oblivious, but much lower than the lion, Farraga crawled nearby. She was searching for delectable mushrooms. She only had a vague, abstract awareness of nearby wildlife. She would never guess their proximity, beyond what was suggested by glistening, fresh elk dung, around a pile of which she scrupulously picked her humble path, on hands and knees. Did she hear a noise? Probably a raccoon. She was prepared for an encounter with a cougar, though: on her rear, appliqued with impressive teeth, was a silk-screen of a face. The face – George W. Bush, as Alfred E. Newman – was intended to function like the ones on the back of the F.W.W.P.

hats, as a deterrent, like the two big dots on a butterfly's wings.

Her wardrobe choice might have been constrained by vanity. Her hunting expedition was partly inspired by the concern that, if she didn't exercise more, Vimvole would say she was fat. And she needed recreation so stress wouldn't give her wrinkles. Anyway, an aging woman in America was marginalized, trivialized and basically invisible (except to marketers, who promise to sell her something – anything – to make her seem youthful). She may as well wear what she needed to, to survive, while she had fun in the sidelines of civilization, a clownish hag: rubbish in the shrubbery. Why was she trying to compete with fashion models, anyway?

If the cougar nearby hadn't been sleeping, it might have been confused about where to attack the two-faced Farraga. It might have actually been intimidated by the size of her pseudo-head. The ersatz Bush mouth, with its silver-threaded lamé "What, me worry?" teeth, might even look big enough to bite back.

It was her turn to be impressed when Farraga spotted a boletus edulis mushroom. Its cap looked like one of those sourdough boule loaves in which some restaurants served a hearty soup. Not anemic like them, though, it could be bread baked with an egg-white glaze to give it a brown gloss. Still admiring it, mouth watering, she reached for it only to see someone else's hand extend toward it through the undergrowth.

"Oh! Good heavens!" Farraga cried, never having encountered another mushroom hunter in that remote ravine. Half-expecting the hand to belong to a ravenous cougar instead, she instinctively reached for the release of her patent "cougar-spooking collar." With a whoosh, it sprang above her head, its ripstop stretched on a flexible stay of bent fiberglass.

Hearty laughter announced the slightly foreign-looking younger man who appeared through the foliage. The man pointed at the huge, quivering nylon collar and exclaimed, "You heave parachute?"

Shaken, Farraga stuttered, "Heavens, you scared me. It's just an invention..."

The stranger was handsome and Aryan. "*Invenshone*," he mimicked.

She tried to place his accent. How to explain to a non-English speaker? "I thought you might be something dangerous," she finally spurted.

"*Dangeress!*" He scoffed, as if she were describing breakfast pastry. " I am ghentle as a lamb." He pronounced the word "gentle" with a hard "G," as if he'd never heard the word in conversation and had only sounded it out from a book.

The pronunciation gave him a childlike quality that made Farraga's humiliating appearance more bearable. She reached for the ties on the cougar-collar and returned the contraption to her back. With a touch of *noblesse oblige* to restore her dignity, she gestured with her chin: "You can have that mushroom."

The blonde foreigner waved his large, strong hands. "No, you keep." He pointed to her collar. "You have frighted me away."

Farraga stood up and velcroed the edges of the collar back down, pouting. "Aren't you afraid of cougars, around here?" she asked, seeking to justify her so-called parachute.

Still on his knees, he said enigmatically, "I think I... like cougars." Sociably he presented a European-style string shopping bag from behind the vegetation and showed her its clusters of brown-paper, the contents, presumably, his cache of mushrooms. One packet was stained with huckleberry juice. "*Mustikkapiirakka*," he said to himself, with a self-conscious eyebrow waggle.

Farraga furrowed her brow. "Where is your accent from, if I may ask?"

The young man said, "I am Finnish but be living in Bavaria."

Farraga knelt back beside the *boletus edulis*. "Do you know there are dangerous mountain lions here?" She made herself look small, to emphasize vulnerability, and to vindicate her eccentricity.

The man made an extravagant show, cutting and trimming the dirt off the mushroom stalk for her. With a sly smile, he said, "Yes. And cougars, too." He handed her the kilo of meaty fungus. "I was bear hunter in Europe."

Farraga had a vague recollection of a black bear who'd shown up in Germany in 2006, only to be shot by authorities. It had been the first bear seen in Germany for decades. The public had nicknamed it Bruno; in Farraga's mind, Bruno was assassinated by a Nazi firing squad. She blurted, "Good heavens. You're not here to decimate keystone species, are you?"

His sable eyebrows arched, uncomprehending; he asked gamely, "Can I have you for dinner, and tell you about it? My name is Sauli."

After her accusation, Farraga didn't want to be rude, having had her catharsis. "Well, my hobby is foreign languages. But I have to admit, I don't know a single word of Finnish."

Sauli stood. He said, "I will introduce you to a new foreign tongue."

"Well." Farraga looked at the mushroom. "We should cut this in half and share it. But you know, the center is probably teaming with maggots."

"Teaming – like *football* team?" he asked, charmingly.

She tried to explain, holding the mushroom up, and displaying her pen knife in the other hand. "We can enjoy its beautiful outside. Or we can cut into it and see all the bugs and insects and rotten parts. If we dive into it right away, we can save the best of it, before they eat more."

"I want to go inside. Hidden secrets, I am not afraid. We will share what's good." He pulled a piece of brown paper out of his bag in anticipation of the autopsy.

Farraga got her bearings. "Bugs might ruin our appetite for dinner."

"Then we go right away to dessert," he proposed. At his unmistakably lascivious tone, she gave him a chastising look. So he boyishly suggested, "Berry pie? Maybe?" They dissected the fungal microcosm. But the mushroom had hardly any inhabitants at all.

And they ended up driving to a restaurant with an enticing menu that banished all maggots from their minds. Or so Farraga calculated, as she wondered why the food tasted so delicious. Each bite was more satisfying than anything in recent memory. The meal was almost an infantile comfort. It felt as if her digestive juices were flowing after being undetectably impaired. Undiagnosed remission – spinsterish, she wondered, had she eaten beet greens for her gall stones lately? – possibly explained why this seemed the most delectable dinner in her life.

As she savored each morsel, Sauli told his life story. "So after we shot the one and only bear in Germany, I to Slovenia to learn a better how to manage beasts." To be funny, Farraga bared her teeth and growled at him. He smiled at her slowly. "Bear Gyrlls say, wilds create strong bond between people."

Farraga was still getting used to deciphering his accent; she wondered what *grilled bear* had to do with affection. She didn't watch much TV, too busy even to see nature shows. The sunset over the ocean was her idea of entertainment. Through the picture windows, the surf was audible, even in the crowded restaurant. Maybe the hushed whispering was due to the spectacle of her George Bush pants.

The younger man continued, after an awkward pause, "Really, with some women, it's market or it's free, but... their companionship is like meat. This evening with you is more like..." Sauli's handsome face softened. "I approach a forest."

Farraga, taken aback, quipped, "Old growth, presumably."

Sauli tried out some vocabulary. "Lush. Mystery-ous." He grew facetious. "And I maybe consumed."

Farraga aided him in joking away the topic with a reference to cougar behavior. "I could just nibble a bit, and hide you under a bush till I'm really famished."

Mistaking her joke for flirtation, Sauli said, "You have big eyes. Bigger than stomach?" He added, "Big eyes help you hunt in the dark."

Farraga took an unexpectedly deep breath and cast caution to her exhalation. "Hopefully I wouldn't have to hunt *too* hard, Sauli."

He leaned back in his chair, with a tiny smirk of self-satisfaction. "I am experience to guide hunters." He gazed at her hungrily.

Farraga filled the air. "The top of the food chain is a good place to be. Like amorous birds of prey... *Tear our pleasures with rough strife...*" Why did she feel poetic? After a last sip of wine, she attempted sanity. "Sauli, you are quite young. And I have been seeing someone. For years." She sighed, "I think he still cares for me."

Sauli challenged her. "You *think* – ?"

Farraga elaborated. "We've been very busy. I, with charity. I'm coordinating a green micro-finance project with the fashion industry." She set her knife on her plate. "And the... gentleman... has been very dedicated to ecology, advising on Pleistocene re-wilding."

The technical terminology, intended to serve as a barrier, failed: Sauli snorted. "This man you see, he Pleistocene? Maybe he is a cave-man himself, that he cannot show that he loves you?"

"My dad withheld affection, too. You know how girls marry their dads. So to speak." Farraga was embarrassed at the intimate turn of events. She felt blinded in the spotlight.

Sauli shook his head. "Forgive. I make you unhappy. Tell me about your charity."

Farraga stopped holding her breath. "*There is a wolf in me* ... fangs pointed for tearing gashes ... a red tongue for raw meat ... *and the hot lapping of blood*—I *keep* this wolf because the wilderness gave it to me and the wilderness will not let it go...'" She had regained equilibrium. " '*I am a pal of the world:* I came from the wilderness.' American poet: Carl Sandberg."

"Poem," Sauli nodded.

Back in her element, communicating *à la femme*, Farraga, his date, continued. "You know how it takes relatively few predators to maintain a forest? Predators focus women's primal mind, igniting their passion for preservation. Danger hones your intuition. And research shows that imagining issues geologically distant – far away – increases creative problem solving."

Sauli tried to follow. "International..."

"Yes. The women advise one another from across the world, and thus grow more inventive with their own dilemmas." She sipped the last of her cherry-rich wine. "Predators are like global warming; you may *think* you have other priorities. No! Avoid death! It's as if a mad gunman is *in the building*." She paused as the busboy bobbed nearby, removing their dishes and eavesdropping, his face growing less bored.

Sauli discreetly pushed a couple dollars into the jeans pocket of the now-smiling busboy. "Help to poor people is not for them. It is for us, privileged. *Starke fressen Schwache?* Help them, or be animal." Sauli looked earnest.

Farraga agreed. "But terror capsizes rationality. Fear sabotages enlightened self-interest." Sauli seemed to be letting her language wash over him. "A woman can think things through – not just rely on animal reflexes – if she's equipped to protect herself." She thought of the .38 in her knapsack. "It just takes a few brave women to realize that, and organize, and rescue their own habitat."

"Rabbit hat?" Sauli said innocently. They sized each other up. The waitress put the check on the table. In a tone of sweet lamentation, Sauli admitted, "It would take only one woman to change everything for *me*."

Farraga paid her half of the bill and stood up. "I've enjoyed the thrill of the chase, but I have no interest in a fling."

"Love is like danger-ress rock climb. Rules are: *commit* to next move, and..." He stepped up and took her two hands. "Always maintain *three-point* contact." She didn't back away; he felt nice. Sauli persisted, with a note of macho whimsy: "I could move to Oregon. You never know. While I wait for work visa..." He cogitated. "I can remodel your kitchen." He helped her on with her coat. "No hurry, just take time, think about what color paint you want."

CHAPTER THIRTY

DAM BEAVERS RANCH, NEVADA

The smell of water-based nail polish filled the office. Mrs. Shaftly was getting an in-house pedicure when she dialed Farraga's private number. Outside, the hunky District Wildlife Manager's truck was driving away. He'd brought back the beavers that had been washed away by a flash flood. The willows and other vegetation had mostly held, but the hauler brought a load of aspen branches to help the animals get started on rebuilding their dam. The event reminded the Madam of that charity, the Fanged Wilds and Women Program. "Yes, Ma'am, I'd like to help," she told Farraga, after introducing herself via telephone.

"Oh, I am delighted. We don't have much support from the Nevada area," Farraga admitted.

"Not too many people here, anymore, since the drought. Our clients come from out of town. Even royalty, all the way from Scandinavia. My friend Shee, the model, was breezin' through and told me about you. Her scientist pal helped us set up a beaver dam. We're the nation's first environmental brothel and the best in the West."

"Oh, you must be so proud." Farraga was typing on her laptop to check the Ranch's website. "Thanks for your interest. Naturally we're always begging for contributions, on our knees..."

"I've spent a bit of time in that position myself," the Madam said.

"Yes. Ah." Farraga, in Oregon, on Vimvole's leather couch, blushed. "Life can be humbling." She repositioned the decorative cushion balancing her laptop on her crossed legs. "We do have a very glamorous event coming up, though, through our contacts in the fashion world."

Mrs. Shaftly took her completed, first foot off the stool and offered her second foot to the beauty technician. "I can make a donation, and some of the girls might, too. I've had a bout of illness lately, and want to make a difference while I still can."

"Oh dear. Something serious? May I ask?"

"Oh, just what you'd expect, born near Rocky Flats and growing up with my dad working at the nuclear facility."

"Oh, Mrs. Shaftly..."

"Call me Phyl."

"Do let me mail you one of the shiitake logs I have in the yard. Fresh, simmered mushrooms can be quite medicinal. Just keep them moist in your bathroom till they're all grown out."

"Oh. Okay." The Madam snorted. "First a beaver in our bathtub, now this."

"Mushrooms are such a solace to me. Mushrooms symbolize life emerging from decay. What for a fungus seeker like me may be a gold mine, looks to anyone else like a dank, overgrown old crotch of land."

"Damp old crotch – You gettin' personal there?" Mrs. Shaftly chortled. "No fungus here, I hope. Though, who would notice, lately..?"

Farraga tried not to balk. "Mushrooms symbolize regeneration emerging from devastation. Maybe they can inspire you too." She heard the other woman take a painful breath; she leavened the tone. "And supporting our fashion show in Milan might brighten your day, as well. It will most likely be a tremendous load of fun."

"Would you name us in the program? Like, in the brochure?"

"Well, I know you're not exactly girl scouts..."

"Actually, I was," Mrs. Shaftly interrupted.

"Me too!" With a deep breath, Farraga ventured the campfire song, "Make new friends, but keep the old..."

"One has silver... with a heart of gold," the Madam sang, completing the couplet. They both laughed like old friends at her inventiveness.

"Oh, heavens," Farraga finally said, thinking of the fashion show publicity. What would having a whore-house as sponsor... do? "I don't see why not. I'm a one-man-woman myself, but I try not to be a prude about consenting adults, you know, and what they do with their own – what we used to call their 'bathing suit areas.' I suppose nowadays it's called the 'thong area.'"

"Well, you see plenty of thongs around here, when the girls are feeling modest." The Madam nodded hello to a passing prostitute in a nurse costume. "They do a lot of dress-up, to keep competitive. They would get a kick out of our Ranch being mentioned at a fashion show."

"Okay." Farraga bit her lip. "We'll just have to negotiate what kind of donation we're talking about, to determine the level of sponsorship."

Madam Phyl laughed. "I'm used to negotiating price."

"You're probably far better at it than I. But, no matter what we agree on financially, I hope we can be friends. You sound like a very interesting and kind-hearted woman."

"Heart o' gold," the Madam repeated herself.

MILAN, ITALY

The panels of the stage backdrop clashed tiger stripes with cheetah, ocelot, jaguar and leopard patterns, all oversized and tinged with reptilian iridescence, as if skinned from dinosaur mutations of the beasts. The music enhanced the effect, with bass beats thundering as urgently as if chased by mega-monsters. Shee's celebrity friends adorned the audience. Rock music blared from speakers. The fashion show was underway.

Keeping up with fashion and trying to establish a trend could be cut-throat. So the

Fanged Wild Board of Directors called in some favors and arranged – as budget allowed – for elaborate showmanship. A huge circus cage on shoulder-high wagon wheels waited in the wings, containing a grumpy-looking, thin, yellowish polar bear, lent from a nearby zoo. A stage hand dollied a pallet of rabbit cages into place beside the bear.

Farraga tried to communicate with the stage hand, using the rudimentary Italian she mostly learned from singing along to Puccini. Her hand flapping like a big ear, she whispered to him, "*Coniglio?* Bunny? *E coniglio?*"

The stage hand, eager to please, waved toward the dozens of bunnies twitching and hopping to the side of their cages furthest from the bear. "*Si, si, coniglio.*" He made a buck-toothed grimace in an attempt to wiggle his nose like a rabbit, proving to Farraga that Italians don't only gesture with hands.

Confident in the effectiveness of their sign language, she continued with a stiff whoosh of her arms, saying, "Let them all go when I wave at you. *Quando faccio così con la gelida manina, Lei fa tutti liberi. Bene? Capisce?*" Still waving, she peeked out from behind a panel, calculating how many outfits remained in the line-up. Then she held up four fingers. "*Quattro minuti.* Oh, I'm all nerves." How could she calm down? She quietly stamped her platform boots, trying to get grounded. She readjusted their claw-foot clasps. Then she craned to see Professor Vimvole in the VIP section, hoping to catch his eye and get a reassuring smile from him. But his gaze was glued on the stunning fashion show.

Wary Dearie from Somalia and other models, faces painted like animals, had prosthetic teeth, glued bits of fur, and feather eyelashes to accentuate their already exotic looks. These confident professionals displayed all manner of F.W.W.P. clothes including a naughty burqa. They strode in clawed footwear and wore accessories like the "cougar collars" and boron-carbide parasols. The lithe demonstrated noisemakers; the lissome, mylar pom-poms; and the svelte lit sparklers: all things that could be used to dissuade predatory animals, wielded by erstwhile prey. The usual haughty expressions of the catwalk – implying that the women floated, untouchable – were replaced by earthy grins. Why act remote when you're secure and confident?

Jooci – feeling no pain thanks to medical marijuana – swung a hemp-strapped transparent shoulder bag like a censer, showing how to carry a firearm without a concealed weapons permit. She removed the paintball gun and playfully shot a splat at a decorative side-panel that shuddered. Paint dripped.

An experimental item was the transparent top hat worn by Shee, its construction accommodating a functional rabbit that theoretically would thump its back feet in alarm if a carnivore were nearby. As Shee strutted the runway in recycled-fur-trimmed jaguar boots, however, the rabbit looked remarkably at ease, possibly sensing that the majority of animals present were anorexic and threatening only as competitors for a carrot.

The music morphed into "Peter and the Wolf." Unwinding ribbon, Shee and the other models extended anti-wolf flagging between them. Those without top-heavy headgear bent over and wagged flirty no-no fingers at any apparent "wolves" in the audience. Aisha and Igiri handed a few of the grinning males lollipop-handled masks with big noses, big ears, big teeth, and other unmistakeably lupine characteristics. Other men received hats bearing photos of well-known international playboys.

All the models were on stage. Farraga gave one last smile and a wave to the cute Italian stage hand and, smoothing her silk gown, stepped out toward the microphone. On cue, rabbits liberated from their cages began to appear and hop from backstage. Emerging opposite, from behind the sophisticated audience, theatrically tattered Italian urchins approached and climbed onto the catwalk. "*Viva gli bambini e la preda!* Children and prey are the future," Farraga announced.

The children dodged between the improvisationally voguing models, to catch the rabbits. "Bravo! *Bravissimo!*" someone shouted. A couple hundred wrists jingled with jewelry as the audience applauded the novel spectacle. This wouldn't just make the news – it would go viral! Farraga waited for the clapping to subside, then announced, "It takes very few apex predators to balance an ecosystem." She looked expectantly to where the stage hand was due to roll out the polar bear.

The Italian did appear, but wheeled an empty bear cage to center stage. Farraga recoiled at the bang of the swinging, iron-barred door. Staring she tried to disguise her horror. "Where is the bear?" she gasped to the confused looking Italian. *"Dov'e orso?"*

The stage hand was hesitant, his big brown eyes betraying calculation. He tried to figure out who else could be accountable for a mistake. He seemed to conclude that Farraga must have instructed someone else to free the bear. *"Tutti sono liberi,"* he confirmed, as if liberating a zoo were surely delineated on the printed program.

Farraga froze with a rictus that belonged in a cockney farce, not the gonzo phat-def-eco-chic fashion event of the year. In a Basil-Fawlty falsetto, she squeaked, "Run. Our ecosystem is balanced. Ha, ha. Run to the exits. No, don't." Trying to prevent panic, she intoned more deeply, "Walk calmly. *Orso.* Bear. *Via andante, pianissimo.* Walk away from the bear." She listened for growling backstage. "You've all bought our bear spray, haven't you? Ha ha ha ha." She grabbed an urchin who, uncomprehending, had come to hand her the struggling rabbit in his arms. "Grab the children and leave. Stay calm. Don't... PANIC!"

The cosmopolitan crowd finally made sense of her babbling when a child screamed and pointed to thigh-high jaguar-boots on impossibly long legs that were disappearing: a model's body was dragged backstage. Wasn't it just a stunt? Mayhem broke out all at once, with the crashing of chairs to the floor as the aisles clogged. Gallant Congolese Sapeurs – dandy Africans imported to add color and panache – pushed aside everything to create new throughways for the flood of the event's audience-*cum*-participants.

Some children dropped their rabbits, and the prey animals became role models for the spooked humans. Professor Vimvole, outdoorsman that he was, assessed the situation before some others. Kicking away a rabbit, he halted by the exit. To Shee, he barked, "Shee! Run! BEAR!"

Shee was unprepared to drop her mannequin sangfroid, face painted like a cheetah, as she strode toward him. In a practiced, reality-TV voice, she scoffed, "The fashion industry has always been vicious."

Her nonchalance was shared by others at the butt end of the upscale refugees: they were more voyeuristic of others' reactions than concerned for their own safety. It was all part of the spectacle. On Fahbulous Fahbio's bulky shoulders were draped several ragged urchins he'd picked up, perhaps inspiring a new interpretation of fur stole for some designer the next year. (Their destination blocked by many specimens of well-maintained flesh, the Yes Men discussed devising a Modest Proposal for human hides, a sort of companion to their suggestion for Big Oil to market human tallow.) Flamboyant dawdlers were already sharing via cell-phones their own impressions of Surviving the Escaped Bear episode. Fahbio calmly commented to Stella McPaul, "When fur start flying, I think Naomi Campbell caught up with Mia Farrow"; he was referring to a gossipy court case where Mia claimed Naomi got a "blood diamond" from a warlord.

"Who knows what lawsuits are in the works, after this," Stella said. "Fanged Wilds will be ruined. Those bloodthirsty witches." An animal-lover, she balanced a rabbit on her shoulder like another version of stole, while a second bunny, cradled in the crook of her arm, was protected from the crush of humans.

The bottleneck at the doors suddenly reversed: Lady Gagg's escort, a famous American football player in mink coat and hat, had briefly been mistaken for the bear. Pirouetting, a diva removed her hat pin and jabbed a man obstructing her change of course; his frantic lunge pushed more fashionistas toward another red exit sign that was revealed when a decorative backdrop panel set sail off the stage with a majestic flutter, like a manta ray, slowly crashing into the tumble of chairs. People herded toward the new exit, tripping and swearing, forgetting what the real threat was as they tore silk stockings or bruised million-dollar shins. The actual polar bear, and Farraga, were nowhere to be seen. Then from somewhere came a crunch of bone.

CHAPTER THIRTY-ONE

WHERE?

Echoes of activity reverberated through the hollow of a cave. The location was hidden high up off a winding road somewhere in the crags of the Alps. Farraga regained consciousness, seeing Vimvole's concerned expression – a delirious dream – turn into the glare of a dark-eyed foreigner. The lower half of his face was covered by his black-checked kaffiyeh. Other blurred faces around her were similarly covered, the hostile eyes watching her with unfamiliar squints like strange animals. One man, incongruously in a chair and holding a cell phone, spoke in some sort of macedoine of Mediterranean accent, saying, "We've got her. Yes." Farraga struggled against her bondage, trying to cough away the rag in her mouth. She looked for an escape in the wet cave walls. To Farraga, her captor snapped, "You will demand all your women relinquish all weapons. You must."

In defeat, her eyes rested finally on the English speaker. She glared at him. With a sneer, he approached, and his uncaring hands removed her gag. Farraga worked her dry mouth, then said, "*Salaam aleikum.*"

The foreigner responded automatically, "*Salaam –*" then changed abruptly to insist, "Command your women –" Behind the houndstooth cloth, he cleared his murky throat. "You women must relinquish all guns."

Farraga stalled, her head swimming. "I've no authority. My guidance is just suggestions. Our program is democratic. Decentralization is popular in the States. Directors like me are monitors rather than managers. Our organization is patterned on Paul Van Riper in the War Games of 2002. They're independent. Each group is autonomous, once trained." She coughed. "We just delegate responsibility, and then after that we trust the women's intuition."

From behind her, the man accused, "Women's... intuition." He hissed, "Weetch! Sorceress!"

What was covering her thick hair? The men must have put a scarf over her offensive curls. Farraga whined, "Call our headquarters in New York." The office manager Diana could alert Interpol, at least; the resourceful young woman had the sense to do that.

Stepping in front of Farraga and cocking his gun, the terrifying stranger gloated, "We have secured your staff there also."

Farraga wilted with anguish. "Little Diana? Oh no..." An escaped polar bear had seemed like the worst possible catastrophe. And now everything she cared about was at the mercy of jeering fiends. Farraga hadn't slept the night before the fashion show, fretting about bison kebabs and boar canapes, re-gluing wolf masks, and fussing over a million other details. Now she slumped, her silk-gowned knee hitting damp, cold rock. "Please. Don't hurt little Diana," she begged, all hope extinguished by exhaustion. "Diana is nothing. Please just let her go. She can do nothing for you. I will do anything you ask. Please don't hurt her."

MANHATTAN, NEW YORK, U.S.A.

A pair of terrorists in sealskin wet suits and dripping, race-car checkered kaffiyehs had tied Diana around her thin chest, then looped the rope around her hands held behind her chair. A salty, oily hand clapped abruptly over her mouth. Hairs of his beard protruding under his pin-holed polypropylene face cover, the tallest terrorist snarled in practiced English, "Do what I tell, and you won't get hurt." Diana seemed to recognize the phrase from a movie. She felt unsure whether to scream for help. This wasn't a joke? She'd stepped into a predicament worthy of Hollywood. Was this real? She'd just been griping by video chat to her mother that, by not being invited to Milan, she was missing all possible excitement. "A polar bear in a cage!"

She felt detached, as if in a video game, watching the bizarre scuba-diver grope a plastic pouch belted to his waist. He pulled out a document and barked, "You sign this statement." He produced a recording device that he held toward her mouth, its green screen glowing. "Read it aloud. We distribute it in every manner to control your satellite outposts and duped minions."

Diana leaned forward and read, "Relinquish weapons – "

"Sign!" the man snapped.

She shrugged, impeded. "My hands are tied."

The second terrorist stepped awkwardly behind her, his swim flippers slapping the floor, and released her hands. The first man pushed the Tiki mask of pens toward her. Diana took a fang-pen and looked at the statement on her desk. She suggested helpfully, "Maybe our Board of Directors should sign this instead."

The foreign-sounding man growled, "Who, and where, are these Bored Directors?" He really seemed interested, as if she were slipping into a trap he had set: he was getting information out of the prisoner without having to waterboard her with his kaffiyeh.

But she answered honestly, "I don't know. I've wondered." In the back of her mind played the image she had constructed in idler moments, a surreal scene around a conference table with a shark, orca, dolphin, lion, bear, wolf, and tiger facing one another, discussing the Fanged Wilds Program, while a bounding sea otter served tea from a goatskin bodega bag. The picture, formerly a source only of leisurely amusement, gave her an odd burst of determination. She loved animals, and felt driven to protect them from these men's violations. With a deep breath, Diana faked hysterical weeping, shook her head in defeat, and started to sign the piece of paper. She pretended the pen wasn't working – she hadn't clicked out the tip – and sobbed again. With each heave of her ribcage, the rope at her chest grew more lax.

Diana reached for a second pen. Faltering, she started to sing the little Arabic she knew, Uum Kulthum's *Rubáiyát el Khayyám*, as a valiant distraction:

A Book of Verses underneath the Bough, A Jug of Wine, a Loaf of Bread, and Thou,

Beside me singing in the Wilderness. Oh, Wilderness were Paradise enough!

The men stood stunned at her Egyptian song. They had thought macho intimidation was enough to silence and paralyze her. *"Enta omri,"* she added: *You are my world.* With careful aim, she flung each pen into the two terrorists' wondering eyes. Her arms and legs were almost free! She slipped like a fish under the rope, ran to the window, and vaulted out. On her heel she felt the rubber of a terrorists' swim flipper as they chased her, shouting in Arabic. But she had escaped! She leaped off the pier and plunged into the water for salvation.

Cold engulfed her. Diana swam through the frigid murk. She surfaced for a desperate, salt-strangled breath and started to follow the wall of the building. Then she froze: in the dim depths shimmered a long, black and white submarine. Through the portholes, she glimpsed a checker-headed soldier and, beside him, Senator Pickfawny's aide. The American's expression was the essence of melancholy, his blue eyes wide with grief and – with a glance at the swarthy man beside him – a lip-loosening tinge of lust.

But the deadly gaze of the terrorist struck Diana like lead shot. The suffocating gloom also revealed the oblong of a shark slipping through the sub's headlight. Kicking with all her might, the lonely office worked struggled to gain distance despite her need for oxygen. The submarine engine grew louder, vibrating not just on her eardrums but against her burning chest wall. She had to breathe!

She willed herself to thrash till the dusky light and wet gasp of air gave her temporary license to live. Below her, the shape of an artificial reef swirled with shoals of fish, obscuring sight of the submarine and the shark. Diana treaded water. A pair of fins cut the choppy waves in an unexpected direction. More sharks! A familiar, sputtering motor was perceptible somewhere. At the risk of annoying her, Derek had made the habit of passing her office and clanging his brass bell on his way home. Unwilling to die unnoticed, she screamed as Derek's boat – unmistakeable with "Diluvial Delivery" written on the sail – appeared briefly behind a wave. Only the back of his head was visible, only for a moment. She spit salt water, retched, and accepted: the sharks would grab her numb legs any minute, or a skin-diver – intent on destroying the women's charity – would shoot her. She couldn't feel her legs, anyway, from the cold water; they were just dead weight. Breathing was rendered almost impossible, hypothermia crushing her chest. Diana began to sink, heavy with doom.

Derek glided to her as he dropped the sails, almost drowning her with his wake. His muscular arms pulled her aboard, his strength supernatural compared to her leaden incapacitation. Diana collapsed on a bench seat, gazing at him in wonder. Weak, she looked around the boat as if still in danger, chattering, "So many sharks..."

Derek wrapped her in his coat. "Sharks? It's New York." Derek sized up her condition and quickly raised the sails. Then he set the rudder and superfluously gunned the engine. "Hold on tight!"

Clutching both bench and coat, her numb cheeks growing immobile, Diana mouthed at him, "How did you know I was–"

He shouted, "My womanly intuition. I sensed your alarm. I'll get you straight home. I just have one quick delivery, for the cop station." He indicated boxes of Qrispy Qremes.

Diana said to herself, "I have to tell the police! Terrorists are in my office!" In the off chance that the phone in her wet pocket still worked, she fumbled brittle fingers against razor-cruel fabric to call Farraga. She could barely move, as if imprisoned in stocks. With a jerk of the boat, her phone was flung out of her hands into fathoms of oblivion.

Derek doused the sails as they neared their destination and motored the last few feet. By the time they moored at the police station, Diana was too chilled to have control of her muscles. Derek assumed she was just coming inside to get warm. He helped her out of the boat, then grabbed his delivery. They made their clumsy way up the front steps past a ragged homeless people who camped there, hoping to get arrested and fed.

Derek squeezed her arm. "I'll be right back!" Misconstruing Diana's situation, Derek left her while he jogged away down the hall to deliver the Qrispy Qremes to the snack lounge. When he returned, Diana had approached a sergeant and was just shuddering and dripping. She set eyes on her returning friend with an authentically hysterical gurgle, teeth clenched.

"What is this girl trying to say?" the sergeant asked Derek.

"She works for a women's charity, Fanged Wilds," Derek ventured, reaching for a pen and paper. With one warm arm around her, he turned over an incident report form for her to explain herself in writing on the back. But to his surprise, she put it right-side up on the counter and hunched over to fill in the blanks, still almost paralyzed, commanding her stiff fingers. *Diana Mountbatten.* She looked at the sergeant's badge and wrote his name, too, at the top: Flop Williams.

Derek pulled off his "The Future of our Planet is at Steak" T-shirt to towel her hair a little. Flop Williams was impressed with the young man's bare-chested physique. Looking at the bulging, cut pecs and biceps, he stammered, "They – those women? Fanged Wily Women? Didn't they pull some publicity stunt a while ago, with a bomb?" The sergeant smirked toward Diana, who became wild-eyed. "I heard about that, the miraculously defused bomb. Pretending piranhas saved you. Clever." Flop Williams walked away, the rolls of his neck smoothing flat as he stifles an outright laugh. "What women do for attention!" He hoped Derek noticed his well-shaped gluts.

A female detective had monitored the situation at a distance and asked Sgt. Williams, "Another 'splasher'? Trying to act helpless in front of her boyfriend?" She tisked and looked past the young people as she headed for the snack room. She needed some calories to stoke her for her weight-lifting session.

CHAPTER THIRTY-TWO

PARIS, FRANCE

LHOOQ. *Ou là là.*

Voilà. Vive la différence.

SOMEWHERE IN THE ALPS

Farraga was still tied up when she noticed that the chieftain of her captors was receiving what looked to be an upsetting phone call. The chieftain shook his head. At the message's odd conclusion, the strange man murmured to a muffled comrade, "New York... aborted."

Farraga thought to herself, "Abortion? Yea!"

But the foreigner quickly recouped his vigor and raged at her, in barely comprehensible words, "You, command your women to relinquish all weapons! Your entire organization must be aborted! Rich Jewish *con.*"

Con was the French obscenity that gaped like anemones in a sewer throughout many a conversation in France, not just discussions of female genitalia. At their leader's outburst, all the other kidnappers rushed closer. They pulled out tiny scimitars that glinted, knife points drooping downward toward Farraga, the *con.*

She prepared herself to die. How did they know she was Jewish? "Only on my mother's side," she argued silently. Maybe they had made the obvious deduction: mass extinction was like the Holocaust to the Nth degree, so who but a Jew would risk everything to stop it? Farraga wondered if the terrorists would dispatch her right away, or bury her to the waist and stone her. Stoning would make an ugly corpse: a lifetime's primping, gone to waste. She thought of Vimvole, how she always tried to be pretty for him, and how much she loved his dedication to ecology, as well as the Professor's firm jaw line. The aging woman wept. Her only hope was that she thought she'd heard the word, muffled in facial hair and black and white kaffiyehs: "Ransom."

FOREST PARK HILL – BEAVERTON, OREGON, U.S.A

Out of the trail-crossed forested heights west of Portland ventured a cougar. It had been glimpsed and already blamed for a few months of disappearing cats, two small dogs, and a ferret. Cleaning out her pool with an aluminum skimmer, a mom looked away from her toddler; blood froze in her veins when she heard the outrage of her child being dragged away by the tawny lion, jaws locked around the small, surprised skull.

The mother's husband – one of Forest Park Hill's Asian population of East Indians, Hong-Kong expatriates and P.R.C. tycoons – ran out from his den, planted his feet, and repelled the wild animal using distance Qi Gong with both palms. The hundred-pound cat leaped back over the rattled seven-foot cedar fence beside the pool. The little boy, rushed to the hospital, had only suffered lacerations and an eye twitch that soon healed with acupuncture. The father was swayed by local encouragement to teach Qi Gong at the subdivision's palatial recreation center. But he was too busy with his position as VP at Insourcetel.

More residents installed motion-detector sprinklers. The cougar was not noticed in the neighborhood again. She went back to eating indigents and other forest-dwellers.

As the news of the situation spread to their packed shelter, the Church of Saint Francis arranged to distribute baseball caps with Jesus's face on the back. In a similar spirit, a local naturopathic college organized volunteers among its preternaturally healthy students; they demonstrated basic "Wrestle the Tiger" Qi Gong for the homeless living in Forest Park and other wooded areas of the urban greenbelt. The casualty rate decreased, as far as most humans knew.

NORTHERN CAUCASUS, RUSSIA

Alice's trip home to Kalkatta, Michigan, complicated her relationship with her boyfriend Steve. But it cemented her friendship with her next-door neighbor Carylyn. Alice treated her with a ticket to the GlobalCitizen concert in Flint. (The stage and awnings collapsed in high winds, but that was normal for the climate. The event raised $2,034 for a desalination plant in Somalia.) Carylyn, a true lover of music, considered it the best day of her life. She slept deeply that night and had vivid dreams infused with sensations she'd never felt before: sisterhood and belonging. Alice and she bonded over beers on her porch the next afternoon. That evening, she accompanied her new friend and Steve to provide moral support at a tattoo parlor: Alice got a longhorn bull on her left deltoid.

Months later, after getting clean from bath salts and methamphetamine, Carylyn applied and was accepted into the (as Alice joked long-distance over the phone): "F. Quadruple-U. Program. Quadruple *you!* You're four times the woman you used to be. You're a *Fanged Woman!*"

Feeling more like a question mark, Carylyn packed old army clothes handed down to her from a dead cousin. Leaving her kids with her long-suffering sisters, Carylyn took the grueling airplane trip to Russia. The transition was difficult. Substance addiction was replaced with jet lag, culture shock and homesickness. The days passed, during which Carylyn followed Alice around like one of the mongrel dogs that the local Russian soldiers fed scraps. Assigned to assist Alice in the last stages of the Chernobyl cadre's deployment, Carolyn resented her tasks. Alice directed her to read the instructions for decontaminating their Geiger counter. "And can you not glare at me," Alice asked. Her hometown friend continued to glower, her idol-worship of Alice's "True Grit" increasingly strained.

 Minor crises were magnified for Carylyn and all other participants when the founder of the Fanged Wilds program was kidnapped. They all had thought the fashion show would be the program's saving glory, financially speaking. How could they even function now, without Farraga? Alice's confidence crumbled. Overnight, the brigade leader grew withdrawn.

Losing role models was the start of their problems. The women contended with a new challenge. With a blanket draped on her thin shoulders, Carylyn found herself listening late the next night to a language hodge-podge: the other Americans, Alice and Tiara, argued in spurts of translation with Magova Yevloyev and the Slavic women. Assembled in the common room of their barracks, they perched on rickety chairs around the rough wooden table. Alice stood. She found her voice. "You train for precise execution so that, when you end up in a situation like this, you can operate on the right side of chaos." Alice looked into their doubting faces. Rubbing her eyes, she pleaded, "This is exactly the sort of catastrophe we've prepared for. We just didn't know what the details would be. We *have* to do it. To save Farraga, for headquarters, for our program... and maybe to save all Mother Nature."

Magova's face glowed by the light of the hurricane lamp. She said, "Ukraine, *Femen* women protest by going topless. They say it proves woman need no become like man, to make change happen." She lifted her .45 sidearm, brandishing its weight. "Woman need no become like man, if she is equipped."

Aliced nodded. "The great equalizer."

Tiara whined, "But... our families." The camp cat trotted toward her, and she picked it up and hugged its folding body familiarly with her knees and arms. Her own cats were being cared for by her little sister; Tiara thought of her, chubby, in pajamas, safe at home in Michigan, playing with F.W.W.P. paper dolls. The tabby's head squeezed out under Tiara's elbow. Tiara didn't want to mess up, now that her family was proud of her for the first time.

Carylyn agreed with Tiara. "Don't you worry what Steve will say?"

Alice drank from her glass of *kvass*, counting to ten. Then she ranted, "How can you mention men when we have a crisis on our hands? Steve tried to get me pregnant just to trap and domesticate me. *That guy!* As I was leaving, he said my job isn't important." She got up and paced, glancing at the clock: past midnight. "When we were young, we were trespassing – looking for magic mushrooms – and accidentally ended up in a field with some bulls. Steve started rubbing my shoulders, telling me to *relax*. What does it take to get us to recognize a desperate situation? What kind of example are we for future generations? Will they even survive?"

"God made us. We have to survive." With a meth-mouth grimace, Carylyn stammered, "Humans are part of nature."

"Like cockroaches are part of a kitchen," Alice grumped, bitterly. "Humans are so stupid, they'd shit in their own mouths if they could reach. Sure, I'd love to be a happy hole, back with Steve. But someone has to be accountable, at some point."

Carylyn stood up, hysterical, screaming, "We can't do it!" Alice stepped nearer and slapped her, then squeezed her shoulder, an instant comfort. The other women stared. "Thanks," Carylyn said, rubbing her cheek as she sat back down. "Ow." Her head sunk forward. She started to pray quietly, "Hail Mary..."

The night stretched into a tug-of-war between fear and duty. By dawn, they reached a hard-won consensus. They geared up with heavy coats, backpacks, rifles, pistols, and parasols. Plan B was underway: they grabbed several four-foot long tongs with plush bear-claw pads on the ends.

BALKISTAN REGION, PAKISTAN

Haadiya's burqa was light blue covered with mirror eyes. It was sewn as a prototype and then given to her as a gift by a F.W.W.P. friend – and English tutor – after Haadiya posed in the burqa for their online catalog. Of course only the seamstress and a couple villagers knew it was she, Haadiya, in the photo. Even her own family members could look at the catalog and think it was just a plastic mannequin modeling the item.

Haadiya hastened into a crouch, lifting the garment's cotton folds to keep it from getting tangled. Under its tent-like billows, she was awkward with the cell phone. But the voluminous fabric was handy to conceal her clandestine call. If discovered, she wouldn't automatically be distrusted just for being hidden: invisible females were the norm. Her unseen whispering might only be chastised – if she explained it away as prayer – as a waste of time. "Praying that Allah make you tend the animals, clean more and cook better? Allah smite you for not getting to work!"

She was deficient as a wife, and in other ways as well. But Haadiya's bad English was adequate for the situation at hand. "Boxes come from Ashfaq. Many box. One hundred. Heavy. Heavy more like water. Wait soon." Her Pomeranians yipped outside in their enclosure. The Taliban had made hats out of some of them but the remainder were tolerated by the men for their commercial potential as guard dogs.

KINKIMAN ISLAND, JAPAN

The F.W.W.P. Geisha girls dressed in their cute, boron-carbide samurai armor, walked to the ferry, and paid ¥1,600 for tickets. Tourists snapped photos, and oohed-and-awed. "You look really hot," one squirrely guy said in English.

"Not ret," Kayoko answered enigmatically, with round, animé eyes. Her companions giggled. But they *were* warm. The cool sea air on their voyage made their armor more comfortable. The ferry rocked the girls toward their destination.

NANIRAUÁ, BRAZIL

The Ribeirinhos' longhouse was quiet without the men, who had gone hunting and fishing. The tribe women involved in the F.W.W.P. washed their uniforms and hung them to dry on hammocks near the fire. Then they went to dig a secret bunker under the new guest house that the men had built for the program. For shovels, the women used canoe paddles: headquarters – Diana – had forgotten to arrange for them to receive real metal shovels. But the damp ground was soft, and the women strong. And determined.

KAA-IYA GRAN CHICA NATIONAL PARK, BOLIVIA

Less garrulous than usual, despite chewing coca leaves, the Bolivian contingent of the F.W.W.P. slowly put on their holsters and collected their guns. One woman lifted four-foot long F.W.W.P. tongs with bear-claw pads on the ends. They set out, chewing more coca leaves.

FORX, WASHINGTON, U.S.A.

Her trip to Hanford had been fruitful. Heavy backpack pulling back her shoulders, Cyrene the bartendress turned the door sign to CLOSED. She locked up. It was normal for citizens to wear guns in plain sight, so she didn't bother to hide her holster. Probably no-one would notice that hers was a paintball gun. They probably wouldn't even wonder why she was in full combat gear, carrying a gas mask. FORX was fun.

GARDINNER, MONTANA, U.S.A.

Near the barns, Amy Oakley and Gwen Bumppo loaded saddle bags on elephants and cinched the straps. The elephants' ears flapped at an approaching ruckus. A cowboy ran down the hill toward them: it was Gwen's ex-husband, screaming. "A grizzly got Dale!" At the women's perplexed expressions, he explained, "He was four-wheelin' with Marla!"

Dale the Ph.D. Forester had moved back to town. He had reconciled with Marla by convincing her that Amy was a lesbian who had poisoned Marla's mind against him, Dale, the hard-working, environmentalist father of her tiny, brilliant son. [Aslan's first words were, "Goo goo warming."]

"Marla is okay?" Butch nodded in response to Amy's concern. With a silent glance, Amy conferred with Gwen and her sister-in-law Merrilee. Her voice husky with remorse, she immediately insisted, "We have to focus on this, Butch. Sorry! It's *beyond* urgent!"

Determination speeding their movements, Amy, Merrilee and Gwen climbed up rope ladders that hung from the loaded cargo platforms. Slipping onto the swaying elephants' necks, they rode away, trying not to look back. They didn't see Gwen's ex-husband surrounded by snarling wolves. The hungry pack possibly felt threatened that the man might compete for the bear's leftovers, as more and more humans had become scavengers in the worsening climate, with its ensuing failure of agriculture, murrain of livestock, and famine.

The women spurred their mounts on with switches that trembled in their hands between each frenzied strike. The tottering heft of the majestic elephants suggested maharajahs going to battle wearing colorful cowgirl outfits.

GOBI GURVANSAIKHAN NATIONAL PARK, MONGOLIA

The *amanita muscaria* was taking effect. To a small tree near the petroglyphs, the shamaness tied the Bactrian camel she'd ridden from her yurt. From behind its yarn saddle, she retrieved a frame drum.

The shamaness beat the taut drumskin till, above her, on the petroglyphs' boulder, the reverberations summoned a Siberian tiger. The feline stared as the camel's hooves thumped the dry ground: the tethered animal looked aghast. The shamaness laughed to herself as the tall, knock-kneed camel eructed a belch of protest and tried to skitter away. Kindly, she went back and fed the camel some *fu shen* poria fungus to calm him. "It's just a meeting of the Board of Directors," she said to him, in her own musical tongue. "Shush."

CAPE TOWN, SOUTH AFRICA

African folk healers gathered at the strange summons. Those of them hale enough to stand were in a semi-circle on the beach, waving totem wands of animal parts. A crone sat at the center, facing the surf; her body was deformed with age and oppression, but her voice rang strong as she chanted, "Sharks, heed a woman's touch. Sharks need a woman's touch."

Apparently in a trance, no-one seemed surprised when sharks frothed the water, their dorsal fins, tails and snouts visible. Further down the beach, sea lions flubbed nervously away from the tide. More of the sea mammals torpedoed out of the water and squirmed away in a panic as the shark numbers grew. The human voices crescendoed, ceremony becoming trance. The crone proclaimed, "Good and evil; known and unknown. These are the coordinates of the map of consciousness. Travel with me. Become one with the cosmic Fuck-You." Nodding and slowly falling limp, the folk healers let their spirits enter the sharks, leaving the prostrate human bodies behind in the blistering hot sun. The water was cool; it felt like liberation.

OUTER BANKS, NORTH CAROLINA, U.S.A.

Hurricanes had destroyed most residential constructions; the shifting terrain had gone back to nature. Wild ponies grazed, their long swishing tails near the loblolly pines and newer rainforest overgrowth where a cougar stalked. Near the horses, a salt&pepper-haired woman leaned against a live oak. She wore comfortably loose, Dixie-style F.W.W.P. clothes. She had noticed and pensively observed the cougar. As she bit into a Qrispy Qreme, the wild lion saw her. The woman impassively released her "cougar collar," which unfolded with a pop above her head, making her look like an Elvis impersonator. The snap startled the horses. Their eyes rolled as they instinctively moved away from the steamy shrubbery.

The cougar swallowed its feline indignation, backed deeper into the vegetation, and made itself comfortable: new opportunities would arise. The sound of waves lulled it into a nap.

Her donut finished, the F.W.W.P. member, Shawna, licked her fingers. Then she reset her specialized collar, twisting the brim and fastening the Velcro above her shoulder blades. The proximity to danger inspired her to say a prayer for Farraga. "Please protect her from those wicked men." Shawna had already donated guns – sneaked from her husband's Tea-Party Second-Amendment arsenal – for the cause.

She was grateful for the sense of belonging with her "partners in crime." Some of her dearest friendships had bloomed in the organization. The other "Wild" local ladies and she took overnight retreats together at Nags Head Woods. They shared a true love of animals, like the red wolves at Alligator River as well as the majestic horses running free. "Poor Farraga. Please let her get away safe." Shawna felt as if she'd do anything for Fanged Wilds. From the dune top, she discerned in the choppy Atlantic waves a pod of dolphins leaping one after the other. She felt as if she were one of them: happy. She had found her pod.

McCARTHY, OREGON, U.S.A.

The phone rang in the kitchen: the Senator's aide Brad got ahold of Vimvole at home. The professor was snacking on gluten-free toast, leaning over his kitchen sink instead of using a plate. "Yes, Brad?"

"The Talibangelicals are asking for ransom," the government employee warned.

Vimvole grunted and then didn't stifle a laugh. "Maybe those Fanged Wilds girls can hold a bake sale." After they hung up the phone, he slapped the crumbs off his fingers and laughed even more generously.

CHAPTER THIRTY-THREE

SOMEWHERE IN THE ALPS

It seemed to be night, colder than ever. Farraga was tied to a hard chair. Where was she? She shifted her hips. The chair felt more Swiss than Italian, she conjectured, more functional than stylish. Maybe collaborating in the plot against her were anti-Semitic Swiss bankers. Switzerland hadn't given women the right to vote till 1971. So maybe "Kinder Kirche Kuche" misogynists were involved in her kidnap. How pervasive was this conspiracy? Were neo-Nazis supplying aide? Why else would contempt for women be so ubiquitous, and sex slavery, if not aimed at a concerted Final Solution?

Paranoia, being uncharacteristic, suggested to Farraga that she might be delirious. Maybe she was in shock from low blood sugar. So the chair might be Italian after all. Wasn't it wood? If her captors were able to spirit her further away from Milan, to somewhere in Libya or Iran or Syria, wouldn't the chair be plastic, or goatskin? She heard... a sound. Hardness had its own tone. Stone was her captor, muscled with machismo; hunger was another enemy, a fifth column, weakening her body and mind.

Judging the few clues she had, she tried to guess where the foreigners were from. They were slumped against the crevassed walls, amorphous, dozing in the dark. One by one, they started snoring, till the echoes sounded like a far-off train. Could they be Taliban, making themselves so comfortable in a cave? But their leader had a bit of a German accent. And he called her the French obscenity, *con*. She thought about the last thing she'd heard the chieftain say: "The women will put it... where? *Ces putes de cons.* Our opium fields...and forests? For... cancer?"

A shuffling behind Farraga drew her attention. She analyzed but couldn't place it;

what was that inhuman quality? What could be more ominous than these men? She choked: the dark hulk of a bear lumbered from the back of the cave. More rank than a frat-house sofa, the bear sniffed Farraga like a warm hurricane in her ear. Her scream was stifled by the spit-soaked rag gagging her. The frat sofa's sinuses rumbled beside her; heat from his breath felt moist. She shut her eyes and played dead.

The bear padded further forward, clattering a pebble. Gargled grunts suggested a sleeping man being gripped, shaken, and mauled before he could express alarm. In moments, the cave was awake and echoed with the startled cries of wakening men and angry bear growls. Briefly the noise was deafening. The bear roared. A bullet ricocheted. Then the shouts and men's footsteps faded toward the cave entrance, noise distorted with echoes.

Farraga was abandoned, helpless. Yet someone behind her sawed at her bondage. Her hands suddenly free, she tore rope off her torso and pulled the gag down around her neck. "Who -?" It was Sauli! He pulled her, whispering, "No worry. Follow me."

Farraga leaped free, stumbling behind him deeper into the cave. Thank goodness she had worn boots in the fashion show. But the boots' platform soles made each step unstable as she followed the firefly of Sauli's flashlight. Its jiggling beam suggested possible paths through fang-like stalactites. Blades of calcite and crystalized minerals glittered. After what seemed like interminable slipping and tripping; wrenched ankles; knees and elbows pummeled and scraped; pain searing her Chanel-perfumed skin; the captive and her savior attained a glimpse of liberty: stars appeared through a crack in the earth. The fugitives emerged in rocky terrain. Sauli's hand pulling hers, she scrambled over moonlit scree, grabbing at bushes that tore her gown and ripped off her scarf. The couple didn't stop till they slid down the steep bank of an alpine stream. There, Sauli and Farraga crouched and splashed icy water into their mouths, gasping. Sauli dried his hands on his pant legs and reassured her, "We safe now. I called army. They come."

Shaking, Farraga looked back behind them. The bushes were still. "The bear won't chase us?"

Sauli shook his head. "He has enough to eat. Or maybe he is she, pregnant and hungry. But full now."

A few miles away, the bear pursued the fleeing kidnappers down the mountain. The militants discharged firearms, to no effect. The bear mauled yet another of them. After that – even when one righteous soldier tripped, or another dropped his gun – none paused willingly; the prey kept scrambling down the trail and through the brush as fast as they could, propelled by an extraordinary force: terror.

Piss-pantied terror.

One man reached a tree and hoisted himself up on a branch. The others ran past him. As the bear got close to the tree, the huge animal held her nose up. The scent in her nostrils irresistible, claws sinking into bark fiber, the bear clambered, preternaturally swift, up the trunk. She pawed the man's legs. At his screams, his chieftain reluctantly halted. Could he attempt intervention? The chieftain shot a .45 pistol. But it was too late, he saw. Observing, the chieftain's face registered a perverted curiosity at the shaking of the branches and voiceless butchery.

Then the bear crashed down out of the tree. The chieftain, again a choice on the menu, shot his last rounds. But the towering bear just scratched at the wounds as if at nicks. The annoyed animal then swatted the erstwhile survivor, whose shrieks terminated in a rasp heard only by ants in the scree.

Nearby, a man's foot got stuck. He stabbed at his shoelaces with his tiny scimitar, trying to cut free. Enticed by the movement, the bear ambled over to him. The terrorist jabbed at the living monolith. The knife barely penetrated the thick fur. Immense force descended. Human agony echoed down a ravine as that kidnapper (a sophomore, Economics and Business, Arizona State) was torn apart.

Turning to judge the gruesome scene behind him, another fleeing kidnapper got clotheslined by a branch. He fell and became tangled in brambles so he could barely move. He looked up, his face registering each heavy step that brought the excited bear closer to him. The man's struggles only entwined him more completely in the thorny vines. When he realized he was doomed, he cried, *"Allah achtung!"*

Then there was silence. Not long after, a rhythm pulsed. Causing a swirl of stunted tree limbs, a helicopter swooped along the mountainside. Airborne, an Italian army officer adjusted and pointed a spotlight to survey below him. Soon he called into his radio, *"Veo un' orso. No veo gli uomini.* I see bear. No men!" Someone far below launched a flare. Illuminated, the bear's haunches disappeared back into the cave. On the ground, at the tree line, Italian infantry in glossy mountain-climbing garb searched the underbrush. In the light of a second flare, a soldier found bloodied remnants of kidnappers' clothes; among them, checkered scarves looked like NASCAR ambitions wiped out at the finish line.

The Italians conferred via radio: Where did the terrorists go?

The bear arranged human meat, her winter provisions. Then she clambered to her favorite spot in the back of cave. As she curled up, sleepy, she belched. She shouldn't eat so quickly. But her instincts were confused by the altering seasons. Should she even hibernate this year?

Back at the stream, Farraga shivered with shock. Sauli held his arms open to her. Losing all composure, Farraga threw herself at his merino wool-clad chest. She wept in his arms. He pulled her to sit on the rocks, huddled together, just the two of them, safe. The distant throb of the helicopter in the dim sky reassured them. Calm consolidated her with the warmth of Sauli's body. As her fear dissolved, she finally regained rationality. What exactly happened? She asked, "How did you find the cave?"

Sauli shrugged. "I am bear hunter. I know all these caves. After Alps glaciers melt, expose more rock. I many times think this cave be perfect for criminal master mind. Lucky guess. I be through all caves."

That moment, Farraga fell in love. Surging with vulnerability, she blurted, "There's one you haven't explored... if you're loaded for bare." She blushed. "B-a-r-e, bare.

Oh dear. Linguist jokes will come between us."

Sauli sulked. "I can be cunning linguist. What can that come between?" Despite – or perhaps because of – their language difficulties, they kissed. Their lips formed that delicious sort of suction that, in another context, might be released at the opening of a jar of tart berry home-canned preserves... or by popping out exotic, vacuum-packed coffee beans on a Sunday morning. The suction lingered, as if to hold back the dawn. The suction prolonged their anticipation of delicacies, holding tight the promise of domestic bliss. They made a home together in that kiss.

Unused to physical affection, and unsettled by her urge to suck and swallow his saliva, Farraga, flustered, finally interrupted. "What's your last name, again?" Her eyes crossed into a Picasso perspective, looking at his chiseled face so close.

After lingering kisses to her cheek, Sauli clarified, "Last? Family name? Varvio."

She thought to herself, "Farraga Varvio." Sheer poetry. She gasped, "Oh, Sauli, how can I feel so good, and so awful?" The immensity of sentiment had to be reduced to words. Farraga stuttered, "I mean, the last thing I remember is that runway model whom the bear... got. Jooci. That poor girl. She was just skin and bones."

Sauli raised a bushy blonde eyebrow. "Eat, or be eaten."

WASHINGTON D.C.

Senator Pickfawny looked out from his office window at the flooded Mall, peppered with gondolas and other small and nimble craft. The robust man disabled the speaker-phone on his desk and, surreptitious, talked into the receiver with a tone of disbelief. "Those Fanged females have radioactive material from Chernobyl, Colorado and Fukushima? They'll place it in all the opium fields, coca fields, and remaining old growth forests? That's their threat?" Hands trembling, he crossed to his mini-bar, grabbed a quart carton, and poured himself a tall glass of milk. "Well, at least that last one isn't an issue. We – I mean, Kock Industries – finished harvesting the old growth."

"Those Wild women demand that the hostages be released," the caller exclaimed in strangely accented English.

The Senator answered in inadvertent falsetto. "But the girl already escaped!" He cleared his throat. "I can't get contact with the other operatives, who have the old woman!" He took a sip of cold milk. "Oh, I can't bear this." Out of a drawer, he got a rubber nipple that he fit over the lip of the glass. He sucked greedily on the false teat.

HARTFORD, CONNECTICUT, U.S.A.

Also sipping milk – or, to be specific, a commercial fluid including bovine growth hormone, antibiotics and feedlot pesticides that had been in cows' bodies – was Glen's mom. She was recovering from surgery: ovaries and tumors were removed and were now several stories below with other people's body parts in the hospital incinerator. The surgeon said radiation and chemo could improve the prognosis. Glen kissed the wrinkles of her wrist. She moved her hand to fondle the investment banker's crew cut. "Your sister says I can fix this just by drinking raw juice," she said to her son.

He snorted, shifting on the edge of the bed. "Jooci is anorexic." He looked in his mom's bleary eyes. He had to shield her from the news that her fashion-model daughter had been eaten by an escaped polar bear. "You're going to get the best care that money can buy, mom," Glen sputtered, shedding a tear. "I'll even sell my boat. If I have to."

His mom had him return her glass of milk to the side table. "I'd feel easier if you'd get married and find Jesus," she said with phlegm-thick effort.

Glen patted her pillow. "I do want us to pray together, mom," he said. He reached into his blazer that hung crisply on the back of his chair; from the pocket, he pulled out the print-out of an email from a frat brother. No stranger to homework, he had prepared for his mom's religious entreatments. "Let me share this with you from...

Pastor..." He unfolded the paper and read: "Pastor Joe Nelms of Tennessee. Heavenly father, we thank you tonight for all your blessings. You said, 'In all things give thanks.'" Glen looked at his mom lovingly. He choked back a sob, shaking his large head at her frail condition. Then he took a deep breath to complete Pastor Nelms' prayer, with a quick explanation, "This was at NASCAR before the Daytona Speedboat races were in Orlando:

"We want to thank you tonight for these mighty machines that you've brought before us. Thank you for the Dodges and the Toyotas. Thank you for the Fords, and most of all thank you for Roush and Yates partnering to give us the power we see before us tonight. Thank you for GM Performance Technology and the R07 engines. Thank you for Sonoco racing fuel and Goodyear tires that bring performance and power to the track. Lord, I want to thank you for my smokin' hot wife tonight, Lisa. My two children, Eli and Emma, or as we like to call them — the little E's. Lord I pray you'll bless the drivers as usual tonight. May they put on a performance worthy of this great track in Jesus' name. Boogity boogity boogity. Amen."

Glen's mom's jowls went slack, as if the sulphur of Hell now smelled of car exhaust. Then the mother and son shared a warm chuckle. "Praise Jesus," Glen's mom said. The Lord would find a parking spot in her son's heart.

CHAPTER THIRTY-FOUR

BALMORAL, SCOTLAND

The King of England and his family invited Ronelle and Tawona on a "red deer" hunt. A knock on the door was the B&B owner giving them the early-wake-up call with a tray: teapot, hard toast and marmalade. Ransacking their luggage and producing some clothes that were still clean, Tawona ended up wearing a tight crimson epaulette shirt and an ermine-style fur headband that pulled her natural up like a crown. As she admired herself, she sang, "I'm looking at the man in the mirror. I'm asking her to change her ways." Ronelle wore a Outback hat with a photo of Australian ex-prime minister Julia Gillard above the F.W.W.P. logo.

Apart from Ronelle's roguish hat and Tawona's sassy fur, the two American F.W.W.P. rangers forsook egalitarian principles; since it was their last full day in the British Isles, the Yankees succumbed and gave themselves over to being star-struck with royalty. When the expedition set out, it was still dark but for a glimmer of hero worship. The King bounced in front of them on the leather seats of the Land Rover. He announced, "We'll hunt till mid-morning." With clear enunciation, he proceeded to delineate the strategy that promised success. The women's attention was unwavering, apart from a few yawns. Turning to talk with them, his arm on the seat back, he concluded jauntily, "If we don't get a buck, I'll take you to Loch Ness and we'll try for a shot at Nessie."

Healthy and handsome, a Prince sitting beside them joked that his family's hospitality had an ulterior motive: angling to get invited for the renowned hunting available in Michigan. "Or maybe we can all go hunt in Alaska!"

"Alaska. Yeah." Apropos, Tawona asked, "So y'all met Sarah Pail?"

His Majesty nodded amiably. "She wasn't quite the Mama Grizzly I'd expected."

Everyone chuckled. The headlights showed they were driving into the hills. Dawn beginning to outline the trees, Ronelle, still sleepy, had a daydream of Sarah Pail as a big flower on a bush. Ronelle pictured deer nibbling on the growth, and Sarah Pail squealing, "Ouch! Hey, watch it. I'm a mama grizzly! Ouch!" Didn't she encourage inhumane, aerial wolf gunning? Wolves would watch Pail being eaten, sit on their haunches, then stroll off like the freedom train passing the lynching of a plantation owner.

The Land Rover came to a halt. At their destination, the welcoming party consisted of some middle-aged ladies who spearheaded the Fanged Wilds Program in Scotland. They stood beside a lantern and a picnic basket. As everyone mingled for introductions, Ronelle acknowledged the locals' tartan twist on the F.W.W.P. uniform. "You ladies look fabulous."

The more wrinkled character, Abby, bent to pour cups of tea from the basket, its thermos clad in plaid, and said, "Fashion is important when one can't afford cosmetic surgery like you American Hollywood types."

"Don't be rude." Martha, her colleague, shrugged apologetically and explained away her friend: "Arsenic and old lace." She presented the King with a porcelain cup of tea which he deferred to Tawona.

Abby gave tea to the Prince. "Old lace, guns and fur." The red plaid of Abby's jodhpurs set off the style of her flared blazer, trimmed, as it was, at the hip pockets, with black-tipped grey fur.

Birdsong filled the air.

Martha collected the used cups as each person finished the milky, sweet tea. As everyone else shouldered a rifle, Martha touched Abby's fur. "We raise the bunnies ourselves, give them the lives of kings, and then make cauldrons of stew for the homeless," she commented. "Sometimes we sell one to a visiting Londoner, for the red foxes down there. Cities need a bit of nature." The back of Martha's velvet riding helmet sported the steely gaze of Queen Elizabeth I, the theme continuing with a white lace ruffle around Martha's neck.

Queen Elizabeth the First's mom, Anne Bolyn, was on Abby's shiny black bobby helmet. The freewheeling Scotswoman, registering Ronelle's questioning expression, pointed at her partner's hat and quipped, "An old battle ax needs a touch of varnish. Q.E. knew that. Feminine beauty is a currency, you know."

The expedition was ripe to set forth. As the hunting party fanned out over the terrain, the idiosyncratic pair of locals inexplicably burst into the French anthem, the Marseillaise. "*Aux armes, citoyennes,*" the old ladies sang, voices quavering.

Tawona carried her rifle cushioned on her crimson epaulette. She felt relieved that the demand for conversation had ceased; she was pensive, having exchanged a flirtation with a Prince.

Somewhere on the heath, a wolf howled.

NORTHERN CAUCASUS, RUSSIA

Outside the wooden barracks, Alice, Tiara, Magova Yevloyev, Carylyn, and some local participants – including ever-passionate Olga – set out on patrol. As the other women walked ahead, Alice quietly confided in Tiara, "Headquarters called. Farraga and Diana escaped! Maybe... I guess we shouldn't have been so hasty with that... stuff."

Tiara felt sheepish. Having been trained to handle nuclear warheads in the army, she had nursed reservations for days. Did they overreact to their administrators' kidnapping? They'd been so emotional when they heard that the Milan fashion debut had been sabotaged and F.W.W.P. members taken captive. Tiara reasoned, "Farraga and Diana's escape was unlikely. Al-Qarnas likes to assassinate. And the chances of those men actually doing what we asked..." She adjusted her backpack. "I mean, when have men ever listened to *you*?"

Magova Yevloyev overheard the conversation. "You have doubts, no? But we did what was good. Now the opium fields and cocaine will become nature preserves. Timber will be forest again." She slapped her leather-gloved hands together.

Curls bouncing as she nodded, Olga agreed. "Like beautiful Chernobyl."

On their route to the forest, they stopped in to visit an ailing Ukrainian woman they'd befriended. [Name redacted by State Security] had been instrumental in their acquisition of the radioactive "Missing Unaccounted For" material. Already diagnosed with lung cancer, she had convinced other sick women to join her sortie. "We are needed. That alone gives us strength," she croaked, while Magova and Olga translated in the crowded, small room. "Women give their bodies for others. It is our nature." The elder gasped another breath, to continue: "When we choose to offer it, our body is perfect." She cackled. "No matter how many tumors."

Grasping each other's hands, Tiara and Carylyn burst into tears. The Caucasus F.W.W.P. contingent also started wept at the old woman's speech, each tear contagious from eye to soulful eye, cups that runneth over with gratitude. The poorly financed "Fanged Wilds" members repaid the frail local women's sacrifice the only way they could: with love, admiration, medicinal herbs, fungi from the forest, and fresh meat. Oh, and the locals' favorite gift. The Ukrainian woman's face lit up, ecstatic, at the sight of the Marlboro cigarettes. With great effort, she sat up in bed and clutched the cellophaned carton in her arthritic hands. "*Bolshoia sposiba!*" Cheekbones red with emotion, Olga ignited a match from the coals in the stovepipe brazier, bent, and lit a cigarette for the thankful invalid. The babushka's parchment lips sucked in where teeth were missing. Smoke veiled her grateful, bleary eyes. Her head bobbed on her thin neck to nod, "*Khorosho.*"

Alice had Olga and Magova explain that the M.U.F. material was dispersed as planned, and the victims were freed. A success! Tiara added conscientiously that the intensive smuggling effort might not have actually been necessary. "Radiation may have been avoidable after all." But the locals didn't translate that for Tiara, not initially, not without some prodding, till the ailing babushka's sharp blue eyes demanded explanation.

She listened, puffing. "Not necessary?" the old woman scoffed. "We have made it harder to turn leafy green nature into noisy markets. Something is better than nothing. Before going to Chernobyl, I was just an old woman with cancer. Not even obliteration gave me significance. I was nobody. Now I am a fighter for Fanged Wilds."

Magova added to her translation, proudly, "I too am a fighter for Fanged Wilds."

Tiara put an arm around Magova and exclaimed to the elderly Ukranian, "You deserve a bear hug!" Since the sick woman was too radioactive to touch, Alice and Tiara maneuvered their giant tongs with the plush bear claws on the ends to hug the heroic Ukranian who beamed at them, her cigarette erect between determined, buzzard-skin lips.

CHHARATPUR, INDIA

Cool water wasn't all that flowed one morning within the gritty curb of the local hand pump. Sun-struck, a jealous neighbor watched Ganika's aunt walk away: the F.W.W.P. participant proudly wore an eye-arresting ocelot sari. The observer lingered at the pump, her envy transformed into conviction.

As the sun rose higher, the villager gestated the rumor that Ganika's proud, aging relative was a witch. "Just look at her. Haven't you seen her? Dressed like a wildcat. The old woman's eyes look like a cat's, too."

"A *tonhi*?" Another housewife gasped. Black magic could be grounds for village exile and often even murder. The growing crowd dawdled, arranging pots and urns, adjusting saris, waiting to hear further information or corroborating opinions. There were so many ways a witch could trick you; a woman's sorcery could even turn your own family against you.

Then another villager, an admirer of Fanged Wilds, twitched her sari back from her face and contributed pointedly, "Doesn't Ganika have the gun today?" The gossiper's sense of self-preservation stifled her vicious calumny. Frustrated, she just banged her water cans together as she stalked back to her own hovel, baking in the blazing heat of day. That night, her husband mentioned that his cow seemed more calm since the women started their tiger patrol. His wife decided to be nice to him, thinking how she herself could get an ocelot-print sari.

CHAPTER FORTY

MANHATTAN, NEW YORK

Her houndstooth blazer buttoned up, MacDoogle headed out, clambering into the metallic air of the dawning city. Her mood was foul. She hadn't had a good scoop for weeks. Maybe getting up early would get her a worm. Yeah, a worm was probably the best she could hope for. More likely, her free-lance prospects would shrivel, and she'd soon be begging for a job hacking phones for a Murdrech. Motorboats honked a block over in the morning stillness. MacDoogle fastened the window's padlocks from the outside, trying not to clank too loud and disturb her neighbors; they didn't seem obnoxious, so they deserved consideration.

Descending her fire escape, she startled two raccoons foraging. Beedy eyed, they stared, then scampered out of the brownstone apartments' trash cans. Odd that they'd escaped urban "bushmeat" hunters. As the journalist jumped several inches to the pavement in the alley, the scavengers escaped in their tiptoed, monkey-like gallop. One of the animals dropped a piece of paper.

It wasn't a food wrapper. Why was the animal eating paper? The journalist wondered, interrupting her impromptu morning stretch. A rat scurried away as the young woman neared the trash cans. MacDoogle's investigative instincts compelled her to scrutinize the note paper. She bent down. Though written on, the paper was apparently discarded after catching the drips from some sort of greasy, barbequed meat. The sauce actually still smelled good, MacDoogle was pleased to notice, as she crouched closer: citrus, and pineapple, as well as smoky caramel, chilies and of course catsup. So few things in the city smelled good, apart from fresh food. Or fresh garbage. Ha ha. The journalist coughed, thinking she would hunt down a decent deli for lunch, get something grilled, and then just skimp on food for a few days.

Pigeons flushed from the eaves high overhead, awakened by the peeking sun. The journalist did a double-take and her surprise grew as she deciphered what was scrawled on the paper. Wasn't there a transvestite who'd just moved into the building, who used to work for a senator? Brad, but he was changing his name to Brenda? It was his! Hers! This was news!

WASHINGTON D.C.

On the steps of the Capitol Building, filling a carefully constructed red business suit, the flawlessly coiffed Annette Anillo filled her new job as Hyena News correspondent. She licked a manicured pinky finger with which to smooth her dark, plucked eyebrows, then reported to the camera. Her journalistic enunciation embellished with inflections of scandal, she said, "Senator Pickfawny was taken into custody, a surprise after his allegations that it was a ladies' charity that distributed radioactive material to sites throughout the world."

The correspondent paused for effect, her tone implying discrepancies. The camera light blinked. "An aide of his provided contradictory testimony: the aide claims that the senator may have assisted *al-Qarnas* allegedly to render certain wilderness areas uninhabitable by humans, but useful for terrorist training camps. Other high-level officials are implicated and expected to resign, unless – as per the bill that Senator Pickfawny sponsored in 2012 – their priest or pastor absolves them. " Annette Anillo modulated her voice to imply that she herself was a good Christian, as was her network's target demographic, and that her pregnancy – should it be discernible – was legitimate. She continued, "As a key witness against al-Qarnas, the aide could go into protective custody. But instead he's chosen to disguise himself with an Arabic woman's purdah. Burqa. Head hood."

BALKISTAN REGION, PAKISTAN

In fact Haadiya, of all people, had made friends with the Senator's aide, Brad. The relationship was born when her brother Ashfaq brought the Americans to stay overnight in their hovel complex, conveniently remote and protected by a cliff. At their request, she showed the strange Westerners the Pomeranian puppies she was raising for the F.W.W.P. leopard patrol. "Infidel mongrels?" the Senator had joked. Haadiya had of course been veiled as she served them what the aide called "the best goat stew [he had] ever eaten." Ashfaq kindly translated the compliment so Haadiya was sure of its meaning.

Unused to praise, Haadiya invisibly blushed. But, growing accustomed to affection from puppy licking, she unthinkingly gave the aide an immodest gaze. His remarkable blue eyes bore into hers. That one moment changed the course of history, as far as the F.W.W.P. was concerned.

At a later date, Haadiya answered Ashfaq's cell phone for him. To avoid GPS – Global Positioning – Ashfaq had left it with her. That was when Brad, the Senator's aide, called. She practiced her English: "Hello, mister." Haadiya made noises to indicate sympathy, as the aide unburdened himself of some of his frustrations and doubts. He had clasped right-wing fundamentalism to his breast, he said (as she mewed), because he had deny what was fundamentally right for *him*: he was a woman in a man's body.

He said he was going to get a sex-change operation and join the Fanged Wilds Program to raise puppies. He said he too would be wearing a veil the next time their eyes locked. He said he could tell from her eyes that she could accept him as he really was. Haadiya didn't understand many of the words he spoke. But she'd sensed the meaning through the emotions. And she recognized one of his phrases: "*U'hebbiq.* I love you."

Haadiya knew that her husband and the other men might rush into her dusty cottage at any moment. They may torture her to divulge where Ashfaq had gone. She didn't have the means – a woman, alone – to escape. But, to face any dawn on the horizon, she had been given the strength: the infinite summer sky of that gentleman's eyes saying, "*U'hebbiq.*"

MANHATTAN, NEW YORK, U.S.A.

Love was all around. Derek sailed through traffic, headed for his favorite stop of all: Diana's building was in sight. Among other obstacles, a boat was already docked at his destination. As another sailboat glided out of the way, Derek could see people on her pier. His heart tilted. She was hugging some big guy in a suit! A businessman! Clearly visible against Diana's black slacks, the guy's hand slipped down intimately to the curve of her hips. Derek dropped his sails, his legs wobbling. The businessman helped Diana into her office entrance, then climbed down into his gleaming, ostentatious speedboat. The interloper blew Diana a kiss, revved his loud motor, and pulled away, churning and rocking the floating pier. As Derek watched, Diana disappeared over the sill into her office.

Derek clenched the steering wheel. His own little motor sputtered as he pushed the throttle. He turned and drove aimlessly back the way he came, squinting into the afternoon glare off the water.

OREGON, U.S.A.

The unrelenting attention to detail and dogged scholarship of his sixty years was finally paying off: Professor Vimvole was finally enjoying the kind of discipline he had really deserved all along, administered at the hand of an unsurpassed beauty. Her perfection embodied the kind of purity he'd always sought. His dreams come true, the fashion model Shee started a slow strip just for him as he gaped with glee.

She had tied him to the bedposts with sensuous organic rubber strips from an Amazonian plantation; now, as he flinched, grinning, Shee threw her silky safari shirt onto his bare chest. Vimvole made a show of inhaling its aroma of perspiration: after they spent that day hiking together with a scout troupe in the national park, Shee had told him that he was naughty. And Shee – his longed-for dominatrix – would punish him by not showering. He really didn't like the scent but, after all, he was naughty.

Shee turned her back to him and threw a brassiere that, thankfully, was not like one of Farraga's silly, bulbous F.W.W.P. contraptions. No zebra-fur trim or Kevlar padding with secret compartments for ammo or cyanide capsules! Shee's bra was just like tawny, sheer skin, shed like a reptile's. Her long back dimpled and flowed with ribbons of sinew as she flicked her smooth hair back and forth past her spine, sinuous as a cat's tail, tantalizing him with the swaying flanks in her organic cotton trek pants. The pants – as narrow and adorably cargo-pocketed as a boy scout's – fell suddenly to the floor. Vimvole moaned, "Come closer!" The rubber pulled his wrists as he stretched his arms, straining fingers, hoping to pull her thong down over her sharp, puerile hip bones. "Please," he begged, digging his bound feet into the mattress and thrusting his throbbing pelvis.

Then Vimvole's lust changed to horror. Shee had transformed into a white lioness. The huge feline paced around the edges of the bed. From its fearsome mouth, it growled something that sounded like, "Honestly, little man. You thought I was a mere human?"

The rubber stretched but, inflicting rope burns, held wrists and ankles as he flung his hips toward the side of the mattress, helpless to escape, his ass now dangling toward the floor. Where he peered past his shoulder, the lion's whiskered face loomed close to his. Vimvole lost control of his bladder as he gurgled at the beast's fangs, "Don't eat me!"

Then he noticed a person at the foot of the bed. She looked as if she could be Shee's mom or an aging fashion model. She proudly announced, "I'm Linda Plucky, a trans-dimensional shaman. Please donate generously to the Galactic White Lion Trust. Canned hunting should be banned hunting. Fear the lion gods!" Her mouth expanded to show inches of incisors as she roared.

"Help me!" Vimvole shrieked in ascending octaves. "Help!" Between him and Linda Plucky, tigers started crowding over the bed. Kicking his legs frantically, Vimvole woke up in the act of throwing off his tiger-print sheets.

Vimvole spat, "Farraga's sheets!" His head was spinning. He swung his legs to confirm that his feet could touch the ground after all. His sigh turned into a strangled moan. He was clearly not at ease sleeping alone. He was freezing; he grabbed his bathrobe. He picked his Teddy Roosevelt bear up off the floor, straightening its spectacles. Then he put on his own eyeglasses and went to piss, glancing at the bathroom counter now absent feminine toiletries and cosmetics. Farraga's heirloom boar-bristle hairbrush was gone now, too. But the latest eco-fashion catalog was in the magazine holder, better than ever: the models held the garments to the side, on hangers, so as not to conceal their naked bodies.

And the toilet seat was conveniently up. Bladder relief revived the professor's fortitude. Since Farraga had moved out, he would have to get more aggressive on the online dating site. His reputation might be in jeopardy if he didn't get a new woman soon; he'd been too picky, avoiding bossy types, waiting to find a female who was educated but still clean and malleable, one not inclined to snoop or have suspicions. Of course it was impossible to find one who wasn't too experienced.

He washed his hands and face. Then he checked the time on his phone, as he dialed it. While it rang, he took a hand mirror from his bedside table. There were bags under his eyes. He'd like to date a much younger woman; was he still handsome enough? Was his confidence rattled from Shee's confusing flirtation with him? In the back of his mind, a remnant image of her turning into a lioness made him shudder. Did he have a bad dream?

Vimvole shook off the nightmare with professional brusqueness. Emotions had no place in this dog-eat-dog world, where the sharks you were swimming with had teeth disguised as sexy smiles. The "pretty woman trap" was everywhere. Be devoured from the penis up, or keep pacts with like-minded men, bond together to keep each other's vision as clear as eagles', and maintain youthful ideals. Or else be emasculated. "Hi. I heard the news. Brad, what can I do to help the Senator?"

The professor dropped his mirror on the bed. Brad, Senator Pickfawny's aide, explained that he was resigning. "The Fanged Wilds scandal. I just can't go on," Brad choked, apparently trying to hold back but overwhelmed with sentimentality.

"Take a deep breath. Brad, we have to keep up the fight! We need your strength!" Vimvole felt closer to Brad than to almost any man in his life. He couldn't bear to lose such a soul mate, especially at a vulnerable time. He clenched his jaws at a fleeting memory of his restless sleep. Vimvole griped, "That Fanged Wilds is an iceberg that won't melt." He walked with the phone to go seek comfort by making his morning cocoa. "Get a grip. Hang in there. The al-Qarnas fiasco – that was a misfortune. But there are other avenues – like Pleistocene rewilding." He microwaved a mug of almond milk. "You and the Senator can be of service – indispensible. Predators can scare Breeding Units" – his word for women – "into staying at home. Cooking us dinner. At home, in the kitchen. And out of our... private business."

"Yes," Brad agreed, with a caveat tone. "Controlling women is tricky."

Vimvole looked out the window at his bed of white narcissus along the fence. His bad dreams dissipated with the comfort of talking frankly with another male, one whose clandestine phone calls he'd cherished now for years. He stirred organic cocoa and stevia powder into hot almond milk. "Brad, think. If we let women get the upper hand, it will make us resentful. Brad, harboring resentment is proven to correlate with cancer! Prostate cancer, testicular cancer..." He took a deep breath. "*Rectal cancer*! You can't argue with psychoneuroimmunology. Men must band together. Literally, to save our asses."

Brad stuttered, "Yes. I just need a... break. Don't worry about... the... pristine photos. I've got your back. Always will. Confidential. Discreet. I understand better than anyone how you need them, to relax. But I've got to take a break from all this. It's been too much." Vimvole sipped his breakfast drink. After an uncomfortable silence, Brad confessed obliquely, "Your involvement with Farraga really backfired."

Vimvole thought of the tiger sheets and asked, "Where is Farraga? Have you heard anything?" She had been monitored closely by the Senator's contacts, with Vimvole's help. He leaned against the bedroom door frame, then sat on the tangled sheets. He'd mail them to Farraga, to feign conciliation and nurture her as an information source... Or – he thought, with an urge for ritual – he might burn them in the back yard: her solar oven would work as a fire pit.

Setting his cup down, he reached for his big, worn Teddy bear, shocked by what Brad divulged: "Farraga's on Sir Richard's island. Dying of cancer. And I – I want to start a new life. As Brenda. Please, call me Brenda. You understand."

"Brenda?!" Vimvole was perplexed. But Brad's explanations – over an hour of question and answer – led to no satisfaction, only the blank stare of Teddy's spectacles, and the comfort of Teddy's soft little body. "Let me digest all this." After the call, Vimvole didn't leave the house. He just put the cold mug into the sink and then paced like an animal in a cage. Superstitiously, he piled the sheets and Farraga's gaudy sofa cushions on a chair by the back door to incinerate when the weather dried out.

It rained in McCarthy that whole day long. With eighteen feet of snow pack in the Cascades, a sudden freeze followed a sunny day. As night again fell, icy rain pounded the roof like a fusillade from Rambo clouds. Rain added to snow melt, all sliding off slickly frozen ground, unable to seep into parking lots and streets. The Willamette River flooded.

A year before, a wildlife organization, with pomp and fund-raising, had erected a bronze bust statue to Professor Vimvole. The location was in the park where the "Tiger Scout" troupe heard him lecture about the beavers. Vimvole fretted as the water rose; he had to access his laptop's secret photos to calm himself. Then he gazed at photos of the statue, with satisfaction, dismay, and other mixed emotions: the bust had already been bullet-riddled rambunctiously by anti-environmentalist hoodlums, till its chest looked like brass Swiss cheese.

Vimvole anxiously ransacked his kitchen that night, nervously hungry. He looked in the fridge for something to eat, to soothe himself. He spooned out the tail end of a jar of cashew butter; the gritty paste stuck to the roof of his mouth. As he waited for his gluten-free bread to toast, it occurred to him to check the freezer. There, along with baggies of local huckleberries that she had picked, sat a custard cup of some vegan mushroom paté that Farraga made for him. As he removed the plastic wrap, he noticed she had typed a sticker on it: "To the Vegan, the Spoils! Best served cold." So he barely microwaved it to thaw before he spread it on his toast. The savory scent was irresistible, with thyme and a vineyard pique of sherry. Farraga had been an undeniably great cook. And she really knew her fungi.

He was blissfully unaware by the time the Willamette's level immersed his statue; its metal crumpled when a branch floated into it, its pedestal soon giving way at the impact of more lumbering flotsam, a hapless delivery van. The van – decorated with air-brushed leaves, and identified on all sides as Eco-Diaper Service – lodged on top of the Vimvole replica, taking its place on the spot.

CHAPTER FORTY-ONE

RICHARD BRIMSTON'S ISLAND, THE CARIBBEAN

Farraga, meanwhile, was indeed on the island in the Caribbean, lying in a bedroom of the luxurious villa. At her side was an attentive curandera. The prune-faced healer stood over an enamel basin and squeezed the aromatic drips of nutmeg poultice out of a chest compress. The steam didn't seem to bother her work-hardened hands. The woman's reputation as a witch doctor was reassuring. She came on a schooner all the way from Jamaica to nurse the impoverished philanthropist. (...Philanimalist? Philgaiapist? *Mensch*?)

Her cancer's recurrence didn't depress or scare Farraga. All things considered, she felt grateful to have it in her life. Didn't she need an excuse to rest? A gust of sea breeze lofted the gauzy white curtains. Lulled, Farrage reflected on all the other sufferers – wonderful, courageous women, from the Ukraine to Nevada, from ex-nuns to the Madam, Phyllis Shaftly – whom the Oregonian wouldn't have befriended if her health hadn't been as challenged as theirs.

Bonded via affliction, inspired to see beyond their own inevitable deaths, the diseased discovered unforeseen, mind-expansive options. Mortality revealed a path that they otherwise wouldn't have followed: to cure the cancer of the Earth if not their own. Their undertaking, while it didn't defy reason, certainly defied convention: women thinking for themselves, conscious of the sea of radiation that was Modern Life. Their action gave meaning to the mutagenic rays obedient breasts absorbed from the crush of mammograms. Cheap microwave ovens, WiFi hotspots, flat-screen TVs, cell-phone tower frequencies... Ladies in agriculture, toiling exposed in ozone-lasered fields while shady husbands spent the money on whores and cold cerveza... And sororities marching out to the sidelines to get sporty suntans while cheering frat boys. What radiation made the most sense?

Shee knocked. The statuesque charmer entered at Farraga's invitation. "I'm not bothering you?"

"No, please." What a beautiful relief from mental stewing! "I always love to see you, Shee." The curtain rippled as the curandera closed the door behind her.

"Oxytocin and a sense of belonging enhances immunity," the model opened.

"I'm not on Oxytocin. I'm not doing meds."

"You're thinking of *Oxycontin,* Rush Limbag's drug of choice. When calling us femi-Nazis isn't enough of a high for him. That oxymoron *needs* oxytocin. Oxytocin is the bonding hormone. Very feminine. So..." Shee stretched her arms languidly, "Why do you think men hate women?" They both chuckled.

The flippant question deserved conjecture. "Probably every man has been rejected by a woman who's too good for him." Farraga relaxed into her pillows. "So it's *your* fault. Yours, and goddesses like you." She mimicked Cat Stevens/Yusuf Islam and sang, *"Here comes my baby... with a love that's oh – so fine... Never to be mine, no matter how I try..."*

"So if beautiful women just put out, the world will be at peace." Shee unfolded her seemingly endless body onto the empty side of the bed, raising into a sideways plank to adjust her muumuu flat under her hip. "Maybe we should start a charity of free whores for all. Like vestal virgins. Start in the rainforest, with the loggers."

"Make love, not war. It didn't work in the 1960s, and it *ain't* gonna work now," the older woman scoffed amiably. She looked at the ceiling, thinking of God and country. "With all the feminizing xeno-estrogens in the environment now, men probably don't even want sex anymore. They just want to show off to other men. If you gave each man a beautiful concubine, he'd probably start a war to get the next guy's."

"I was a procurer for my sugar daddy, the guy who got me into fashion. He paid my way to the U.S. That's how I met the bunch at Dam Beavers Ranch. He brought me, to prove he didn't *need* whores. Lord, did he strut for them, as if he hadn't a clue they were creaming over his cash, not his ass."

"Men pay women to fake it, and then suspect all women of being false." Farraga smoothed the sheets. "Sex is dynamite. The kind that kills you." Farraga held her breath: Sauli was on his way, hitching a ride on a freighter from the Mediterranean. Could she handle the excitement? Would he be the death of her? Should she tell him not to come? She was scared of her own feelings.

Shee sighed. "Sounds like you need a good lay!" Languid on the bed, they spent an hour in girl talk. "What did you see in that twitchy old professor? Apart from his having *fantastic* bone structure?" Shee wagged a long, manicured finger: superficiality! "You fell for a pretty boy."

"We did have a good time, long ago. Championing nature together. Passion for the cause got confused with lust," Farraga confessed. "You know how, with a certain lover, it's as if you're devouring each other?"

 The Australian's smooth face lit up, the whites of her hazel eyes brilliant against her tan. "Oh, *yeah!* It's like tearing into a big, juicy steak! ...And then, after a while, you ask, 'What am I doing with this... Twinkie?'" They pealed with giggles that brought on a fit of coughing in the invalid. The curandera, Char Wallah, heard and brought some hot broth, balancing it in feather-light Dansk cups on a tray. The grateful ladies toasted the medicine woman and sipped sensually. "Mmm. Mushroom, sage, and something else." Shee moved her pretty mouth, tasting.

"Do you like it? Me, too. Medicine should always be like this." Farraga smiled. "Anyway, since I'm an American, food is well nigh the only health care I can afford. But Sauli says he'll marry me, so maybe I'll get treatment under his nationalized plan. Yea for the nanny state!"

"Who doesn't need a nanny, to remain presentable?" Shee joked.

"You don't... you bitch." Farraga smiled again. Her phone rang. With air kisses, Shee followed the curandera out, swishing in her aqua-tone, mermaid-tailed muumuu of jersey-knit hemp rayon. The number on the phone was unfamiliar, but the whiskey voice was not. "Phyllis, how are you?"

"I'm at the hospital. How are *you?"*

"I'm on a cleansing diet, that sort of thing."

"You're not turning vegetarian on me, are you?" The Madam's laughter was parched.

"No, Phyllis. Still paleo. It's heaven to emulate neanderthals. How about you, dear? Are you juicing, in honor of Jooci, rest in peace?"

"Those vegetarians get on my nerves. Save the environment, ha! I'm not going to give up meat just because their cunts are incontinent."

"But you did switch to organic, didn't you, dear? Did you insist, to the hospital kitchen?"

Mrs. Shaftly coughed. "If my mama had nagged me the way you do, I probably never would have become a whore."

"Tell me more about your childhood. You know that's good for your immune system."

"How about... I tell you about my old age instead. I'm getting the hell out of this place. The gal in the next bed got cancer from being radiated for lymphoma as a kid. They just cut her tits off. All the chemicals and shit they want to do to my dying body, that cost a fortune – these ghouls remind me of what you said about predators: they target the sick."

"It seems like the opposite of nature."

"I'd rather the money go to Fanged Wilds."

"At least we've lived...well. The medical industry is built on hypnotizing women that we're heroes and champions for being victims of cancer or, you know, M.S., or whatever. I'd rather be a hero for making a stand." The two women talked for a couple hours, both dozing off intermittently till the last mumbled goodbye.

Farraga was woken from her nap an hour later by a call from Marion, in Oregon.

Marion had got a cheap face-lift in Cuba and was donating the money she saved to F.W.W.P.: she was stalwart. Her voice was effervescent. "You can beat this, sweetie. You did before," Marion cheered. "Cancer is just fear. Find what's on the *other side* of your fear. Do you want me to come visit?" Marion was in a vigorous mood because she'd given up on completing her PhD. Her thesis had been on misguided idealism. And now, instead of dreary typing and research, she might be invited to Sir Richard's island. Her friends would be so impressed! And she'd be such a blessing for Farraga. "Just remember: what you resist, persists."

"I don't resist my own extinction," Farraga admitted, giving in to fatigue. Char Wallah – who had heard the phone ring – brought in a *demi-tasse* of roast-root espresso. The old curandera's tanned face was business-like: she wanted to keep Farraga alive. "Mass extinction is another matter."

"You've done so much." Fanged Wilds had been the focus of the PhD thesis.

"Life devours you. The choice is what flavor you are." Farraga took a deep, wheezing breath. "Please, I beg you, be the standard bearer when I'm gone. Before civilization exterminates itself, we must redefine it to include other species. Non-human persons, that is." The drink revived her. And her feeble ranting was an invigorating release; Char Wallah saw, smiled triumphantly, and left the room. In her honor, Farraga said, "The most important species is still disenfranchised homo sapiens." Had she gone overboard, bringing arms for the servants on the island? Such ingratitude, to foment insurrection of a gracious host. Wasn't the only *real* revolution... a person thinking for herself? Or was illness turning her into a navel-gazer like Marion?

"What do you mean?" Marion asked, her mind wandering. How did she get a stain on her skirt? "Giving fangs to disadvantaged women?"

"Yeah, and other delicate things like trees and flowers. Don't mind me, I'm babbling." Farraga exhaled, lungs pervaded with the scent of the bouquet at her bedside.

"You must try chanting. Repetition does wonders for centering. I can feel it relax the walls of my vagina. Chanting makes me feel at one." Marion intoned, "*Num mambi pramgo kyoto, num mambi pramgo... I* wish you'd been here for that workshop, 'How to be more Vaginal.' We can become a clear channel for male energy to pass through."

Ahem. "How are your grand kids?"

"Fine. Noah's still in Muddy Dog Charter School – a T-ball champ. And Mia's at Saint Francis. She's so cute. She's been studying Santeria. She said, 'If you throw your panties at a rock star, it gives him power over your second chakra.'"

How silly. "Do be sure to tell the kids that when there was a chance to save the last few remaining species, you were busy chanting." Farraga tried to sound facetious. "'Om' worked great for the monks in Tibet in 1959. It's as if you think chilling out is the cure for global warming. Of course, the environment isn't worth dying for; it's only worth your grandkids dying." She really felt disgusted. "What if the main food source when Noah and Mia grow up is cannibalism? Naming him Noah was prescient: does his school teach ark building?"

A stunned silence ensued. Then it was broken. "Honestly, Farraga. Who do you think you are?"

The invalid sat up, pushing back her pile of pillows. "If you don't constantly hear that question, you're wasting your life."

"I'm a Child of God." Marion was a little defensive, having dropped out of grad school. "Earth is just a classroom. Is antagonism all *you've* learned? You need a yoga class."

"The last yoga class I took was bootcamp for self-worshipping nihilists. Zen! *Ex nihilo, nihil fit.* They sucked you in with small truths then swallowed you into a big lie. Those antique religions developed in paternalistic societies. A citizen in a democracy is not so infantilized. Consciousness includes responsibility," she ranted. Farraga couldn't stop. *What was in that innocent herbal espresso?* "Free speech and an armed citizenry give you the moral imperative to oppose would-be tyrants and corporations that negate you. Instead, you've bought the epicurean line that you have to feel orgasmic to be spiritual. You're like an infant: one impulse after another."

"You live in fear and limitation. That's why you have cancer. If you had cleared your aura, think of what you could have achieved in this world, and the next."

The *next* world? Farraga contemplated running a charity in paradise: Heaven, for her, was to make use of her skills. "You're so 'clear' because you negate anything that doesn't make you feel Zen. You've become a solipsism."

Marion chanted under her breath for a moment, then sniffed, "Your ego makes you fear to be at One."

"Opinions are like belly buttons: everyone's an asshole." Oh, dear; that liver-flushing herbal medicine must have made the patient irritable. "Where did you get the idea apathy is enlightenment? You bought it. Consumerism of magic Kool-aid is still consumerism. Addiction to Zen is still addiction. If you can only be fully present in the moment by being slave to your senses and vanity, maybe you should look to the future of the world your kids inherit. Frolicking in Creation should include accountability. How can you pretend to be a strong woman when your decisions are morally decrepit? At the very least, it's rude to give birth to someone when there's the possibility their prom theme will be the Apocalypse, with ready-made decorations."

"Perceiving evil creates evil. Suspend judgment. Love what *is*. Love is all."

"Marion, it depends which herd you're in." Shouldn't liberals hold each other to higher intellectual standards, in honor of their namesake arts and education? "You're like a private jet: above it all. I'm just a *female, mundane like an earthquake's wishy-washy tsunami; volatile like a volcano; fickle like Mother Nature; sister to a twister; female like Mother Earth.*"

"You're an angry, bitter old woman."

"You're like a barnacle that thinks it's a ship."

The room was peaceful again after the abrupt end of the phone call. Farraga would have to call and apologize tomorrow, if there was a tomorrow; the weather report wasn't good. But for now, only a distant sea bird's cry was a reminder of the wide world. Plumping her pillow, the invalid felt thankful that she'd been given sufficient time on earth to get the Fanged Wilds and Women Program to the point where the protection of nature was no longer impossible. Human encroachment was contained almost indefinitely. On the eve of destruction, Eden would be saved, as it were, by atoms and Eves.

ASTURIAS PRINCIPALITY, SPAIN

Senoritas of the F.W.W.P. outpost in Villaviciosa started a write-in campaign to nominate Farraga Dentata for the *Premios Príncipe de Asturias* International Cooperation award. "Then maybe we can all meet the Prince," one fiery-eyed young woman exulted. Even though they all supported the Socialist Workers' Party and opposed royalty on principle, they still had a soft spot for the Prince of Asturias, who was a hunk.

But they were angry at his father King Juan Carlos for bear hunting. In Russia in 2006, he allegedly shot a drunken tame bear named Mitrofan. "The party sacrificed a good-humoured and jolly bear who had been kept at a farm in the village of Novlenskoye," wrote Sergey Starostin, Deputy Head of the Hunting Grounds Resources Department of Vologda. Mitrofan "was put into a cage and ... the party made him drunk with vodka mixed with honey and pushed him into the field. Quite naturally, the massive drunken animal became an easy target. His Highness Juan Carlos took Mitrofan out with one shot," Mr. Starostin said. Mr. Starostin was last seen being fed honey mixed with vodka.

In 2004, the King of Spain killed nine bears in central Romania. The names of those bears was unknown, at least to billions of humans.

CHAPTER FORTY-TWO

KHARUJAHO, INDIA

Tourists flocked there. Rediscovered in 1838 in a jungle close to Chharatpur, in Madhya Pradesh, dozens of temples, over a thousand years old, were famous for their high-relief friezes and statues of *Kama Sutra* S-E-X.

Despite that seemingly can't-lose attraction, many visitors' expectations were disappointed by their actual experience. What wasn't a let-down, in the internet-porn age? Eco-archeologists subsequently let the landscape revert from flowerbeds and lawns to more natural vegetation. And ethnopaleontologists oversaw the restoration of historical fauna: now tigers climbed on the monuments and lurked in the shade. As an attraction, beautifully devoted women had been trained by F.W.W.P. to protect tourists from the dangerous beasts. Guide books raved like it was 1839.

At dawn, Ganika, carrying a rifle, walked with Haadiya's brother Ashfaq. They passed an impressive depiction of a maiden captured for posterity in the act of offering herself to a lion. The statue looked like something out of a Greek myth, with a Tantric twist. Ganika shyly touched the hand of Ashfaq. He carried her parasol closed, under his arm. In a symbolic gesture – since he didn't share a language with her – he opened the parasol and held it over the brave young woman beside him. "Ganika," he pronounced her name.

Ganika attempted to communicate in English. "You are... man."

Ashfaq stopped. "Man," he confirmed, with a long, meaningful look at Ganika. In her almond eyes flickered passion and ambivalence. Ashfaq grew radiant with joy. They swayed in tandem as they paused. He bent down to kiss her lips. It is the first real kiss either had experienced: the meeting of equals. Their faces blurred, one for the other, as they wept with relief that life finally had meaning. They kissed again, deeply, *Kundalini* energy whirling up their bodies like a tornado. Time seemed to stop. But Ganika's training eventually prompted her to step back and register the location of the tigers. The carnivores scrutinized them from the highest steps. Ashfaq followed her gaze. He broke down and sobbed unashamedly, trembling as he placed the parasol in her tiny hands. Then, keeping his eyes on her – his head turning as if to mutiny from his body – he walked away from her, further along the broad path toward the monuments.

Ganika couldn't watch. Unable to bear what must ensue, Ganika turned and rejoined her village's F.W.W.P. team. These were women with whom she had grown up and worked. Loyally, they had made the journey to be at her side. They hadn't envisioned her kissing Ashfaq; like Ganika, shocked and amazed, they started clutching at their hearts and at each other. Faces contorted and shiny with tears, they were all overcome with romance and grief.

He had no choice. He was a man of honor, who had anguished, shamed and endangered his family. Ashfaq must martyr himself. May his blood fertilize the reawakening jungle around him. Tension rippling her muscles, a wide-eyed tiger leapt. Soon the mother shared food with her jubilant cubs.

LAKE COMO, ITALY

A polar bear swam toward the Alps. He'd survived the fashion industry, and was on his way home. He kept his head up, looking for an iceberg to ride.

YOSEMITE, CALIFORNIA, U.S.A.

Their camels loped at a clipped pace through Tuolomne Meadows. Sorraia and the real blonde prostitute rode towards the valley to deliver their load. Crotch sore, bouncing along in the leather saddle, Sorraia shouted, "Hetch Hetchy canyon deserves to get its virginity back." She didn't hear the response: something about

Camel Toes.

MOUNT RUSHMORE, SOUTH DAKOTA, U.S.A.

The secret underground facilities were back on line. Homeless women were abducted from city parks, abandoned financial-sector offices, and under bridges, then inseminated with Dick-Chainey clone product. The entire last batch of clones had gone bad and had to be thrown out. So, for "troop morale," the Queen Bee of another dynasty was summoned: a cloned Barbara Bush visited to encourage the laboratory technicians. The halls echoed as they marched to assemble in the observation chamber, where their white lab coats were brightly reflected in the mirrored glass. Her inspirational address warranted a toast, "To the hope of the future!"

The sensory deprivation of the surroundings called for extravagance, just as submarine commanders acknowledged that great food was no luxury. Here, Dom Perignon was served from buckets of ice. The popping of champagne corks disturbed some of the sleeping breeding-units. Groggy and disoriented, the women squirmed mutely against their restraints. Was that the return of an abandoning ex-husband, or a lost son? Sleepers hate to be awakened.

MANHATTAN, NEW YORK, U.S.A.

Diana stumbled over her slippers before she realized she wasn't asleep anymore. The alarm played "Manha de Carnaval." Morning illuminated the brick wall across from her window. On the bedside orange crate, her Tarot deck was open to the card for *Strength*: a maiden soothing a lion. Her suitcase lay open, clothes neatly folded and already redolent with the scent of herbal mosquito repellent: cinnamon, citronella, and eucalyptus. She had so much to do! What was she forgetting to pack? She had head netting, sun hat... She looked around at the studio apartment. It was messier than usual, as if, in spirit, she had already left. Books were scattered, half-read; atop one ambitious pile, *Ride the Tiger* lay splayed. She picked it up, closed it and put it back on the shelf. For months already, excitement short-circuited her attention span, so she couldn't focus on even the frothiest chick-lit, not even *Jane Eyre*. To think she had fantasized about writing a novel herself. "Write what you know" was the number-one rule. All she'd ever known was imprisonment, seemingly. But she wanted to write about freedom. Could she start to live her dreams? Nesting was her animal instinct, yet her home had begun to seem like an airless cocoon from which she was finally creeping out.

As she brushed her teeth, looing at her bed head, she thought of all the words she knew for "butterfly." *Mariposa, papillon, farfalla, borboleta... Schmetterling.* The jungle would be full of wings: toucans, macaws, harpies. Was it finally her time, too, for her spirit to fly? Could she even become an author? The #1 Rule was, "Write what you know." What did she know besides being cramped and caged?

Another primary axiom of writing was, "People dislike didacticism," which meant education. And the third #1 rule was, "Don't be preachy!" As if *she'd* ever be sanctimonious. Diana rinsed out her mouth and then brandished her toothbrush at her reflection, sermonizing, "Be bold! Species cry from their graves for your valor! What is the sound of one dodo squawking? Write what you *don't* know, wherein lies wilderness!" She exhorted to her own giggling, mussy-haired face, "How can ye know wilderness, if ye be not wild? Be wild!" She then mustered the temerity to pack the blank journal that Farraga had mailed to her as a going-away present. On its cover was pictured a fledging hawk. Diana did feel like an eagle-eyed raptor emerging from a cocoon. She took the notebook out of her luggage long enough to write on the first page, "I am setting out on a voyage south with my lover, Derek."

PEOPLE'S REPUBLIC OF CHINA

The city of Shanghai ("On the sea") was renamed Xiahai (Under the sea"). Thanks in part to the Three Gorges Dam, the People's Republic of China renamed itself: the People's Coal Corporation of Gobi Desert.

In the last stand of bamboo, it was said of a poorly punctuated panda as he waved his firearm, "He eats, shoots, and leaves." Bamboo was his only food. Fortunately bamboo now grew in Siberia.

CHAPTER FORTY-THREE

NANIRAUÁ, BRAZIL

Pristine jungle hosted a teak tugboat chugging along on a broad ribbon of brown water. From the stern of the tugboat, Diana watched a small F.W.W.P. motorboat in tow, its hull dancing languidly on the wake. She was joined by Derek, who had gone to change his sweaty shirt. He ran a quickly-melting ice-cube over her arms and neck. She moaned and shivered. He flicked off the drips, took her hand with his cold fingers, and proclaimed, "Now this is my idea of a delivery job."

Diana mimicked Farraga's words and inflexion. "You fly on the wings of your heart?"

Nodding, Derek glowed with adoration. He searched her eyes. "You sure you wouldn't rather be with that investment banker? *Glen?*"

"I was just being nice to him, because his mother was dying." She looked behind them at the steady spew of white froth. "But his boat *was* really fast." Diana winked sexily. The heat made her sultry. "It's okay, here in the slow lane. I hope we see dolphins." Limp, she added, looking away, "I have a confession: I know it's not politically correct, but I like dolphins better than sharks." She rationalized scientifically, "Dolphins won't eat me."

He regarded her. "Oh, they would eat you. Who wouldn't want to eat you?" Derek clutched and bit her neck, then spat out a mouthful of her hair. "You're *my* prisoner now. I'll make you confess everything. Admit! What did you tell the *al-Qarnas* under torture?"

"Promise you won't tell anyone?" Diana looked unexpectedly serious.

"Divulge it all! You know what I've always wondered: where did you guys – I mean, ladies – get the guns?"

"Wasn't that obvious? The way we pandered to the NRA? To its female constituency, at least...?" Making herself at home in his arms, Diana whispered, "Our supporters in the general public would pilfer one or two from their husbands' gun safes. What does America have plenty of? Weapons. And high-fructose corn syrup. We got the idea from Muslims who smuggle arms in vats of honey. We just mailed our ladies barrels of corn syrup."

"What did they do with the syrup?"

"Make barbeque sauce. Just add jerk powder: tamarind, chilis..."

"Some of those packages were as heavy as *lead*."

"We mailed some weapons in freeze-dried mushrooms. They weigh almost nothing. The fungi protect women and habitats from toxins. Did you know? Some fungi can eat asbestos and jet fuel, and actually thrive on dangerous ionizing radiation. Isn't that cool?" The long trip allowed plenty of time for chit-chat. "Without becoming radioactive themselves, certain fungi can utilize atomic energy, and biochemically transform contaminated dust into something more inert. That prevents the uptake of heavy metal by plants and microbes. Mycelium containment. Even stops water from leaching the toxins out of the soil."

"Soil? I love it when you talk dirty." Derek kissed her.

Diana added, pointing at the lush riverbanks, "Mycologists have recently identified hundreds of species of rainforest mushrooms previously unknown to science. These Amazon tribes here have sent us lots of valuable spore. The fungi are useful for detoxifying the new rainforests developing in Pennsylvania." She admitted, "You know how I sometimes let you have the impression I was off cavorting with another man? Now you know where I went on the weekends." Naughtily, she whispered, "You thought there was sperm, but it was spores."

Derek gave her denim shorts a spank. "Spore whore! Some of those mushrooms are very phallic. That's why you like them." He petted the area he'd spanked. Derek held his breath suddenly, pregnant with the air between them. "Okay, Diana, I have a confession, too." He spurted gleefully like a whale. "I am Mr. Sneckfrodpfeffer."

Diana was taken aback. "What? All those product suggestions? That was *you*?" She was incredulous. "You came up with the Tiger-Woody jockstrap?"

He giggled. "That wasn't my best. Hey. Isn't the jerk seasoning a good seller?"

"Why didn't you –" She gasped with frustration, trying to recall their conversations.

"You might have laughed at me," he explained shyly. "I had to think about *something* while I worked on deliveries. So I thought about you... and –" He shrugged. "The hard part was remembering my name. Sneckfrodpfeffer. Once I said it, I had to stick with it."

His girlfriend waxed playfully indignant. "You sounded like an old guy, dying of lung cancer!"

Derek said facetiously, "Farraga gave me some special mushrooms. They're cancer preventative."

"I can't believe I actually told her your jockstrap idea. Diana put her hands on hips. "I thought it was the old guy's dying wish. That was the *worst* idea!"

"See? I knew you'd laugh at me." The young man feigned moping. "Sneffrockfeffer's feelings hurt," he pouted.

Diana punched him. "Snodfeckpepper's got to toughen up! There isn't gonna be some cushy jockstrap protecting him! It's a jungle out there!" The querulous call of toucans and monkeys confirmed her statement.

"*Quase la!* Almost there!" the crew's mate called out.

Derek reached behind his neck. "Diana, before we get off, there's one thing I want to ask you." He released a Cougar Collar that opened above his head. Written on it in felt-tip pen was the immortal poetry: MARRY ME?

At that inopportune moment, Diana's phone rang. Diana was still gaping at Derek's display as she answered. "Hi Mama! Can you hear me? You'll never guess–" Derek held the Cougar Collar as if to help Diana read it better. Diana giggled and accidentally dropped her phone. It bounced off the banister, slid over the motorboat's bow, and disappeared into the silt-muddied water. "Oh no!" The couple leaned over the railing as if they could get the phone back by force of will, or, if only, go backwards in time just for a few seconds, erasing the accident with the power of hindsight, if only...

Then something else caught Diana's eye: "P- p- pink dolphins!" Two pink dolphins, their necks agile, dove and played in the wake, dodging the motorboat's erratic swings and thumps.

Glinting on the nose of one dolphin was an object. The dolphin dropped it, she nudged it back to the surface and, with a leap, tossed it toward her equally agile, nude companion. Diana and Derek recognized the phone. The second dolphin spun and batted it with his head so that it flew back on board the boat. Derek grabbed the device as it slipped past his feet. "Holy moly!" he spurted, and handed the dripping phone to Diana in disbelief. The dolphins swam away and dove out of sight.

Diana tentatively inquired of the phone, "Mama?" The wet instrument still seemed to be operating.

"Hi, darling. We broke up there for a minute," her mother said.

"Oh my god, Mama. I'd better wait to get home before I tell you what's going on. I can't possibly do it justice." She stared into Derek's face, and shouted over static. "I just have the feeling I'm with the man I'm *meant* to be with."

"Just be careful if you do that ayahuasca," her mother warned. "It can cloud your judgment if you have hallucinations or a *'folie à deux.'*"

"Sorry, Mama, I didn't get that. *Fois lit, adieu?"* Farewell, bed of liver? Not understanding a word, Derek was chuckling contagiously, as giggly as a pot head. Diana burst with the wonder of it all. "Don't say *'Adieu,'* Mama! Say, *'Au revoir!'* See you soon!"

Her mother's voice sounded resigned, no reassurance being strong enough once her little princess had set sail into the wide world. "Derek's a nice guy. He'll probably keep you safe. *Au revoir*, sweetheart. Cherio."

Diana let her arms drop as she clutched the now silent phone. "Oh my god, Derek. I can't believe that just happened."

"Were those albinos?" His eyes scanned the splashing water, from the boat wake to the river banks.

"No, they're called pink, um, *botos*. Those dolphins were almost hunted to extinction. I think medicine men used their penis as an aphrodisiac."

Derek gasped again. "They're an aphrodisiac, all right. I've never felt so completely in love with the entire world." A lock of his hair fell over his eye.

Derek and Diana burst into tears together. Groping, they locked into a kiss, with tears leaking down into the corners of their joined lips. It felt like the union of two tributaries flowing into the mighty Amazon, two familiar friends reuniting in an alien environment and making it home.

The faint sound of a motorboat alerted them to members of the Ribeirinho tribe approaching. Their boat was a growing dot on the wide, brown tide. "Now we find out if they have Brazilian wax jobs," Derek joked nervously. Diana swatted him. The Amazonians had their bodies painted ceremonially and looked pleased and at ease, as if their only mission was to greet the Americans. Alya, a tribe-woman in F.W.W.P. uniform, sat at the helm.

Rocking with the motion on the central plank seat sat the Shaman. Beside him, small but self-possessed, was his new protegee, the little Ribeirinho girl, Dilminha; she had impressed the medicine man with her empathy for jaguars as well as her national pride. The Ribeirinhos, faces festive with red tribal paint, got close enough to call out exuberant greetings to Diana and Derek. *"Bem vindo!"* Dilminha held up a staff twined with red vines and crowned with heliconias and other odd-shaped yellow and blue flowers. Their boat turned back to accompany the newcomers' boat to the village.

Bright in the afternoon sun, pink dolphins reappeared briefly and leaped in the wake of the caravan of boats, startling some river otters who cavorted toward shore. The tugboat, riding low in the water, followed the native inhabitants toward a thin, festively vine-bedecked pier that reached a short distance atop the broad river. The entire Ribeirinho tribe seemed to be trying to fit on the teetering dock. As the engine chugged more slowly, the first mate tossed a rope to Malicio Rego. Rego officiously backed the crowd away from the tallest piling; a naked child was pushed into the river, splashing and yelping. Rego tied the rope to the piling, and the captain cut the motor while a crew member dropped a small anchor. The pull of the river was enough to give the newly-sunk piling second thoughts; it had never been responsible for such a significant vessel.

Creaking heralded collapse. As the humans involved grew increasingly confused, and some hastened back on shore or jumped in the river, the wooden structure disintegrated and reverted to being independent logs and floating planks, interspersed with swimmers. Rego, who had built the pier, went down with his ship (so to speak) and clung to the buoyant piling, kicking vainly to direct it back toward the village. Derek and Diana tossed lifesavers into the thick of things; then Diana looked back to see the drunken captain wagging a stubby no-no finger at her, as if this sort of thing happened all the time and didn't warrant the possible loss of his valuable equipment. Rego let go of his log and grabbed an errant lifesaver while planks bobbed past his outraged face. Everyone else had got out of the water, except for a few laughing children who clung to planks. Resourceful, Alya gunned the F.W.W.P. motor boat so her passengers could lasso and retrieve as much wood as possible.

The tugboat's anchor held. When the commotion settled down, Diana and Derek talked to the insouciantly sauced captain about the original plan: how long would it take to build a new dock? They arranged to unload their heavy crates onto the natives' crafts and the two F.W.W.P. boats. Ropes would curtail further mishaps. The Ribeirinhos launched their dugout canoes, and the ordeal evolved into an organized routine: Derek, as commander of operations; Diana translating into

Portuguese; and Alya shouting in Nheengatu dialect.

As the sun set, all the small boats were beached. The smell of fire-roasted tapir became irresistible to all. Eventually the juice of it flavored the mounds of starch, zeolite, and cooked fruit that each salivating person received on a large leaf. After the satisfying dinner, Diana, full of meat, exhausted, and oppressed by the humidity, stood to explain the upcoming events. "Big day tomorrow. Very big. We're doing the right thing." Eyes surrounded her in the firelight. Her Portuguese jerked from her tongue. *"Uma media vida é melhor que nada.* Half a life is better than none." Alya's and other Ribeirinhos' translations rippled like echoes among the nodding heads and hundred brown ears. Derek, sitting behind her on the ground, got up and soon soundlessly returned. Diana felt something comforting: the giant tongs whose plush bear-claws Derek used to hug her waist. The tribe's laughter completed the evening, and, not long after, everyone fell asleep in their thatched huts.

"Good night, Mrs. Derek," Derek whispered, reaching through the mosquito netting to swing her hammock.

"Good night, Mister Diana," Diana mumbled, smiling.

The next day, unpacking a crate, Diana distributed "clean suits" to participating tribe members. Thus attired, Derek, Rego, Frank Mata, and a few other Ribeirinho men gazed apprehensively at the crate that still sat, lodged between seats, in the new F.W.W.P. boat that they'd pulled behind a bush. Freshly uniformed F.W.W.P. tribe-women handed them a crow bar and the four-foot long F.W.W.P. bear-tongs. The men braced and heaved the lid off. Inside the crate were metal ammo boxes marked with lime-green paint: "Fanged Wilds."

As the sun reached its zenith, noises approached from down river. Samba music swelled, with the purring of a cruise yacht, and women's sounds of jubilation: songs, taunts, impromptu off-tempo drumming, glasses toasting, amusement, and teasing remonstrances. Dilminha, the little girl, shouted in English, "They are here!"

The teak riverboat was identified on the side as "Fanged Wilds & Women's Paint-

Ball Adventures," underneath which someone had spray-painted in hot pink, "If it's full of animals, is it an Ark?" Aboard, vacationers caroused to celebrate approaching their final destination. Standing out among the less healthy female tourists, Igiri and other Brazilian fashion models towered over the crowd that surrounded Carylyn, Alice, and Ronelle.

The F.W.W.P. women issued paint-ball guns to the "civilians." Ronelle explained, "These were confiscated from an al-Qarnas training camp. In, like, Pakistan or somewhere. I met some actual Pakis when Tawona and I went to England," she announced dramatically, for the benefit of a model, Igiri's, video camera. The other fashion models posed with the guns, like Charlie's Angels, while Igiri caught their antics on film.

The yacht set anchor. On the forward deck, Gwen Bumppo, her sister-in-law Merrilee, and Amy Oakley demonstrated the guns. They didn't actually shoot any rounds; they focused instead on correcting each amateur's stance and grip. Some of the tourists were not athletic, and some were outright frail. But they were all having fun. Some older ladies even wept with delight. "I feel so rip-roaring... *powerful*," Abby trilled in her Scottish brogue.

Before the vacationers descended into smaller boats to be taken to shore, Tiara and Tawona handed each woman a "clean suit." The ferrying of small boats gave time for some of the new arrivals to tour the village, and to taste strips of tapir from the smokehouse. The Shaman and Ribeirinho Men were delighted to be surrounded with so many exotic women, particularly the ones who weren't too tall. The fashion models seemed grotesque to them, like deformed males.

After the models retired to the tour boat, everyone else got a pink tote bag containing a gas mask. The whole crowd helped one another put on their masks. Metal, lead-lined ammo boxes were marked "Paint-Balls – Biodegradable, Organic, All-Natural Dye, Color: PINK." From the boxes, Derek and Diana – unidentifiable in gear, except to each other's loving eyes – used tongs to distribute paint-balls to each woman on the beach. The balls were filled with cesium water from

Fukushima, and mushrooms from Chernobyl. "Who would deny their own mother radiation, if she's dying of cancer," Derek's muffled voice reached the international assembly of ladies. "People would get medicine for their own mother. Maybe even in America. Ha ha." He bellowed, "We must raze the village to save the village!" His declaration met blank stares behind glinting goggles. "You know – Eco-calypse Now!" Ladies nodded politely.

Later in the afternoon, when, decontaminated, Diana and Derek joined the fashion models and waved good-bye. "It looks like a steam-punk convention," Igiri said as the small boats reloaded with the tourists. Soon they launched, one by one. The fearless and dedicated F.W.W.P. women paddled noiselessly, heading to tributaries further up river, toward the thunder and snarl of logging. As the flotilla made its way, a pair of toucans beat the air above with a worried urgency and a raucous squawk. Looking up at the endangered birds, one of the tourists from Scotland, Abby, recited Isaiah: to the rhythm of the oars, her voice muffled by her mask, she chanted,

> *I have ascended the heights of the mountains, the utmost heights of Lebanon.*
> *I have cut down its tallest cedars, the choicest of its pines.*
> *I have reached its remotest parts, the finest of its forests.*
> *I have dug wells in foreign lands and drunk the water there.*
> *With the soles of my feet I have dried up all the streams of Egypt.*

Abby's lyricism came to a wheezing stop. Beside her on the dug-out canoe's plank seat, her Bible-literate neighbor Martha chimed in with Isaiah's conclusion: "*Your arrogance has come up to My ears, therefore I will put My hook in your nose, and My bridle in your lips, and I will turn you back.* Silly asses," Martha editorialized. Abby and her friend cackled behind their gas masks.

RICHARD BRIMSTON'S ISLAND, THE CARIBBEAN

Farraga was sorry not to be there. "But one woman can't do everything," she said to Sauli. Having arrived at the billionaire's island, her new boyfriend was rubbing her feet. "You're the first man who ever curled my toes," Farraga moaned. Sauli guided her most delicate digit with his tongue into his mouth. She squealed weakly. The couple had made a nest of a blanket and pillows on the white sand under a green market umbrella. The palm trees' shade was warm beside the rising Caribbean. Farraga wore a bias-cut, cropped pink muslin caftan with silk twine-and-satin ribbon gathered in a green bow under her bosom. Resisting pleasure, she muttered, "Maybe I can eventually get back to headquarters, to clean up for the next tenant. Diana's switching to field work. You know that. Oh, dear. You're fogging my mind with all this bliss."

Abandoning his massage of her feet, Sauli languorously crawled up to pet her hair, guiding her head from a white pillow onto his muscular, gold-velour thigh. "You, heal. Make ready for miracle. Dolphins heal from shark bites, spontaneous. You know? Rest, only," he insisted. "You done enough." A servant rattled the drink cart nearby, providing refreshments. After sips of a guava nectar and vanilla rum concoction, the two lovers settled again. Sauli caressed Farraga with one hand while his other shaded his eyes, watching the servant retreat. "That woman, she who give drinks; she does have a holster under shirt?"

Farraga shrugged innocently and set her drink aside in a filigree-and blown-glass goblet holder wedged in the sand. Then she stroked the blonde hairs on Sauli's arm and purred. "I was going to give up men, but a leopard can't change her spots. If only I had a tail to twitch. The best remedy in life must be the joy of stalking and pouncing." She wrapped her fingers around his free thumb and licked the salty pulse on his wrist. Scratching a grain of sand off her tongue, she observed, "Humans can be so much nicer than nature. Nature would have let me die, but you came to save me."

MANHATTAN, NEW YORK

Diana's office in Manhattan was dim, its shutters closed. Residual inventory lay in abandoned disarray on every surface of shelves, table and desk, with boxes piled in every corner. On its stand, the aquarium stood empty, its glass moldy. The building creaked, as if settling even deeper. In the gloom, the maps on the walls had green-ink locators that glowed like an old watch face. From somewhere crawled the sound of a clock's ticks.

THE END

ABOUT THE AUTHOR

V.C. Bestor is an activist living in a not-yet-clearcut forest in Oregon. Her first trip to Hawaii was to recover from writing this novel. There she met a cute mountaineer like the novel's character Sauli; the guy had also sailed his boat into NYC like our hero Derek. The mom of this sailor/mountaineer had a nickname for him: *el Tigre*.

When Tiger had just met V.C., he offered out of the blue to "come to Oregon to remodel your kitchen." That is exactly what the character Sauli said to Farraga on *their* first date!

(Yes, Tiger remodeled V.C.'s kitchen... and provided other renovations.)

Due 2014, V.C. Bestor's next book is Let Me Take a Stab at It, about health mishaps and miracles.

Fanged Wilds and Women Program

FangedWilds.org

www.ingramcontent.com/pod-product-compliance
Lightning Source LLC
Chambersburg PA
CBHW051418170626
46809CB00006B/2215